KEANE
LENNOX

The Mavericks, Books 9–10

Dale Mayer

THE MAVERICKS, BOOKS 9–10
Beverly Dale Mayer
Valley Publishing Ltd.

ISBN-13: 978-1-773364-53-7
Print Edition

Books in This Series:

Kerrick, Book 1

Griffin, Book 2

Jax, Book 3

Beau, Book 4

Asher, Book 5

Ryker, Book 6

Miles, Book 7

Nico, Book 8

Keane, Book 9

Lennox, Book 10

Gavin, Book 11

Shane, Book 12

Diesel, Book 13

Jerricho, Book 14

Killian, Book 15

Hatch, Book 16

Corbin, Book 17

Aiden, Book 18

The Mavericks, Books 1–2

The Mavericks, Books 3–4

The Mavericks, Books 5–6

The Mavericks, Books 7–8

The Mavericks, Books 9–10

The Mavericks, Books 11–12

About This Bundle

What happens when the very men—trained to make the hard decisions—come up against the rules and regulations that hold them back from doing what needs to be done? They either stay and work within the constraints given to them or they walk away. Only now, for a select few, they have another option:

The Mavericks. A covert black ops team that steps up and break all the rules ... but gets the job done.

Welcome to a new military romance series by *USA Today* best-selling author Dale Mayer. A series where you meet new friends in this raw and compelling look at the men who keep us safe every day from the darkness where they operate—and live—in the shadows ... until someone special helps them step into the light.

Keane

Heading out on a last-ditch rescue mission to Puget Sound one day after two women go overboard in a sailing accident isn't exactly what he'd expected ...

But Keane is nothing if not adaptable. He can only hope the two women are alive and doing everything they can to stay that way. Hearing from the local coast guard that more may be involved than just a rescue mission, he and his partner load up and head out to search the waters around the smaller islands off the coast. They have the GPS of the missing women's last-known location, but storms could have sent them anywhere ...

Lost, alone—except for her best friend, who's unconscious with a head wound—Sandrine wakes up in a small shelter to find they are locked in. When the door is finally opened, an armed stranger dressed in fatigues dumps a small amount of food and says they are on their own.

Finding the women was one thing, keeping them safe something else again. More is going on in this small island that any of them were expecting ... or had planned for ...

Lennox

Planning to meet his sister in Germany, but, when she's a no-show, Lennox has his first inkling that trouble has come home in a big way ...

When his sister and her best friend go missing, Lennox is determined to find and to keep his only family member safe ... and her best friend. They were both doctors, traveling the globe with the UN. Lennox was proud of his sister's accomplishments. He'd never tried to hide their relationship, thinking no one from Lennox's Navy SEALs past cared—or was still alive. Only now someone has decided to use Lennox's only family as a way to exact revenge.

Helena is caught up in a kidnapping of Lennox's sister, all designed to get back at Lennox—the most infuriating man she's ever met. And one she's cared for since forever. Now to know she was used as a trap to kidnap his sister and to take him out was the worst kind of punishment. But she *knew* this man. Knew him intimately—if only once—but also *knew* he was coming to rescue them, even if it meant losing his own life.

Lennox wasn't letting the only two women in his world be taken out without a fight, ... especially one who didn't even know how he felt ...

Sign up to be notified of all Dale's releases here!

https://geni.us/DaleNews

KEANE

The Mavericks, Book 9

Dale Mayer

CHAPTER 1

A WEEK LATER, Keane Lytton walked down Fisherman's Wharf in Seattle. The place was jam-packed with people, and he wondered what the hell he was doing here. Surely there was a better place for a meeting. Of course, if you want to get lost in a crowd, this was the place to be. It was overcast with a threat of rain. Still, he couldn't, for the life of him, imagine why he was here. But somebody with greater wisdom had decided this, and so a meetup was needed. He walked down the pier where he was expected, and, as he found the spot, he sat and turned his back on the crowd behind him.

Charlotte and Nico had holed up in Charlotte's house for the last few days, and Keane had been more than happy to take a break. He was eager to join the Mavericks with his own mission to head up and had listened to stories about many other ops from the others who had gone before him. He was okay with that. He was just waiting for it to happen.

When a hand landed on his shoulder, he turned in surprise and looked up to see Lennox staring at him. Keane's eyebrows shot up. "Man, am I glad to see you."

"Good," Lennox said. "Are you willing to work with me too?" He held up an envelope. "We've got orders."

Keane and Lennox sat on the side of the wharf, while the noise of the crowd around them completely faded away.

Keane said, "I was given very little information on it."

"That's because very little is to be had," Lennox admitted. "I've never been on a mission with less information."

"So, what do we know?"

"A group of people went out for a day of sailing. Two of them were washed overboard."

"And the coast guard didn't find them?" Keane asked, staring at Lennox in surprise. "Not terribly unusual, I suppose, given the size of the search area."

Lennox replied, "The coast guard and private yachts haven't seen any sign of them."

"The currents, depending on where they were at the time, could have taken the bodies to any number of places."

"Well, they went missing in Puget Sound," Lennox said.

"Seriously? Puget Sound is interconnected to multiple waterways and basins, not to mention the Pacific Ocean. The currents can change and can run really deep," Keane said. "A search like that involves any number of issues. They may never be found."

"Exactly," Lennox said. "In this case a special request has been made for us to look for them."

Keane gazed at the long lampposts that dotted the pier. "Are you serious?"

Lennox gave him half a grin. "Never more so."

"What? We're in the business of looking for bodies now?" he asked incredulously. "I was expecting to go up against a serial killer or work in the midst of a civil war in a dictator-ruled country or God-only-knows-what, but you're saying my mission is to look for two bodies?" Turning, Keane stared at the water. "Not only that, it's almost impossible to succeed at a job like this."

"Only a couple reasons explain why we're doing this,"

Lennox said, lowering his voice.

"Of course," Keane said. "It's got to be the daughter or niece or nephew to somebody pretty high up the line."

"An admiral," Lennox said. "His daughter and her friend."

"Has he been looking personally?"

"No. He's out on the Baltic Sea, but he's been calling in every favor he could."

"And so a special black-ops mission team of two is to go out into Puget Sound, and possibly beyond into the Pacific Ocean, and look for them?"

"Yes," Lennox replied.

Just then Keane's phone buzzed in his pocket, and he pulled it out to see Nico was calling. Keane lifted the phone to his ear. "Hope you have a better explanation as to why I'm supposed to look for two bodies," Keane snapped.

"So Lennox already told you about the admiral's daughter?"

"Absolutely, but what does this have to do with us? What's wrong with search and rescue, the coast guard or a private recovery company?"

"Because," he said, "they went missing from the same area where two other people went missing just one week ago. Both pairs somewhere in the same area. Plus, we received a distress call from one of those first two who went missing, saying they'd been captured."

CHAPTER 2

K EANE SLOWLY STRAIGHTENED. "Captured?"

"Yes," Nico said briskly. "Bodies showed up a few days later, both shot. So we don't know exactly what the hell we've got going on here."

"What islands are around their last-known locations? How about any permanent houseboats? Hell, what about speedboats passing through here? Just what the hell is going on?"

"We don't know," Nico said. "But once the admiral heard about his daughter, he asked for a team to be brought in."

"Of course he did," Keane said, staring at the water in front of them. "Puget Sound is full of islands. Most of them uninhabited. About 99 percent I would say," he said.

"That we know of," Nico corrected. "The fact of the matter is, we have narrowed it down to the closest four islands, where we know these latest two women were washed off the boat."

"Washed off in a storm or helped off?" Keane asked.

"Well, that's one of the questions. Two men were on the boat with them—they both survived," he said. They're not saying much though. Only that a really bad storm came, and the women were washed overboard."

"Life jackets?"

"Yes."

"And how long ago?"

"Yesterday morning."

"Well, if they're still in the water, they're dead," Keane snapped. "Hypothermia would have set in very quickly, and it doesn't matter what kind of life jacket they've got on. It won't keep them afloat for all that long, particularly if they're dead."

"We all know that, including the admiral. Especially the admiral. But, if the slightest chance remains that his daughter is alive out there, he wants to exhaust every avenue. The fact that we had a distress call after the prior incident, saying that first couple were captured, expands the potential scenarios."

"And makes no sense at all. It's not like we have pirates here," Keane said, interested in spite of himself. "I guess I could do a whole lot worse than spending a few days on a boat looking for someone."

"Less on a boat, more on the islands," Nico said. "Another thing I can tell you is that some research is going on in that area."

"What kind of research?" Keane asked, looking at Lennox, who was listening in on the call.

"Top secret," Nico replied.

"So, a top secret installation is on one of these freaking islands, near where two people disappeared a week ago and two more disappeared yesterday morning. Those most recent two are probably in the ocean, but, because of this installation and because of the distress call, you're afraid it may be something far more sinister."

"Exactly," Nico said. I can't give you too many details because we just don't have them. Apparently this research center involves a couple other countries, as well."

"Don't tell me—Russia, China, or both?"

"No, not necessarily. It's somehow in conjunction with Japan."

"Well, we are allies."

"They're not saying that the installation itself is in the wrong hands or that it's operating illegally," Nico continued. "Or that it even has anything to do with these missing people," he said. "The other thing is that this installation isn't manned all the time. It's a bunch of machines, run by computer mostly."

"What's it tracking?"

"Something to do with weather patterns," he said. "They are testing the technology. Technicians go to the island and check on it every once in a while."

"So, like seismologists and the earthquake points, they monitor up and down the coast? They pull up the data, copy over the readings and then reset it?"

"Yeah, something like that."

"So, does it deal with earthquakes too?"

"I think they're probably taking readings of everything, but I don't really know," Nico answered. "They're mostly concerned about tsunamis, I believe, so earthquakes are likely a big part of it."

"Well, Japan would be interested in that, I suppose. Are tsunamis a big issue around here?"

"These islands are on the outside of Puget Sound, so they'd be the first ones to get hit, so maybe. But again, no people are there. Just equipment."

"So you say," Keane said. "What we really don't know is if that island for the top secret research is used secretly for something else or if some crazies are out there, killing people.

Really, logic doesn't always apply to every situation."

"True enough," Nico said cheerfully. "But you'll have as much assistance as you want."

"Well, for a job like this, we can hardly use a huge team. We'll draw way too much attention as we search those islands."

"Exactly. We do have the coast guard. They'll take you out to the area where these two women recently disappeared and show you where the other two disappeared earlier."

"Do we have a location for that distress call?"

"We do, and it's not the same exact location where these four people disappeared from," Nico said. "I'll send you all the data we have."

"So, we're not up against anything other than Mother Nature potentially or some psycho?"

"We don't know what we're up against," Nico said. "So don't make any assumptions that would close off any possibility."

"Great," Keane said under his breath. He looked at Lennox. "Sounds like we're heading out today on a cruiser."

"The coast guard will meet you in two hours and twenty minutes at the GPS location where the women went overboard," Nico added.

"So we've got transport to get there on time?"

Lennox tapped Keane's shoulder and pointed. Not too far off the wharf was one of the large coast guard cruisers. "So we're going on the *Acadia*?"

"Yep, you sure are," Nico said, with a laugh. "Gear's already on board for both of you. A Zodiac awaits you at the end of the wharf. The driver will find you."

"Meaning, we've already been tagged, and they're just waiting for me to get off this call?" Keane asked.

"You got it. I don't need to tell you that somebody's daughter is out there."

"Two somebody's daughters, right?"

"Yes. Two women. Plus, remember the husband and wife from a week ago who are now dead."

"And who were they?"

"Electronic reports are coming your way."

Keane stood and looked at the end of one of the docks and saw a Zodiac watercraft with a seaman sitting in the front and staring at him. "I see our ride," he said.

"I'll send you more information when you're on board." And, with that, Nico hung up.

Keane pocketed his phone and motioned Lennox toward the wharf and asked, "You ready for a swim?"

Lennox gave him a big beefy grin. "I was born ready for swimming," he said. "Why do you think I joined the navy?"

"Well, for this job, it sounds like we maybe should have gone into the coast guard," Keane joked.

"Same diff," Lennox said. "But a little bizarre."

"The whole thing is bizarre," Keane said, "and hardly a black-ops mission."

"Disappointed?"

"Kinda, yeah," Keane admitted. "I get that some of these jobs are pretty wild and wonderful, but I was hoping for a little bit more than the usual for me."

"Who knows what this one could be?" Lennox said. "Besides, I'm just backup anyway."

Keane snorted at that. "As backup, you'll be right in the middle of it," he said.

"Good," Lennox said. "I hate being bored."

SANDRINE COULTER OPENED her eyes enough to realize she was still in whatever cell they'd been tossed into. Nearby, her best friend, Brenda Leigh, was barely conscious, her eyes fluttering as she struggled with a head injury. Sandrine rolled over and crawled to the side of her friend. "Hang in there," she whispered.

"I don't feel so good," Brenda whispered. "What the hell happened?"

"Well, I know we left the boat," Sandrine said, with an attempt to crack a joke. "But I think you were swept overboard, and, when I saw you in the ocean, I jumped in after you."

She kept another suspicion in the back of her mind because she had no valid reason for contemplating the idea that they may have been pushed. Except that she'd received a nudge as she went over. But that would call into question the actions of the two men they'd been sailing with. "We were on the sailboat," she said to Brenda. "Remember?"

"Yeah. What happened to Greg and Scott? Are they here with us?" Brenda's breathing was low and shallow.

"I don't see them," Sandrine said. "Apparently somebody saved us, and we're in some shelter that's keeping us out of the weather," she compromised. She was very concerned that their reality was much worse, but Brenda didn't need to know that, at least not yet. "Just rest," she said. "You've got a head wound. It stopped bleeding, but you've probably got a concussion."

Brenda gave her a lopsided smile. "Always giving orders," she whispered.

"Well, if you'd listened to the one about tying yourself to the sailboat," Sandrine said, "you wouldn't have washed overboard."

"Or I would have washed overboard," she said, "and been drowned while towed by the sailboat."

"Not likely," Sandrine said. "I'd been keeping an eye on you pretty steadily." She hated to remember the horror when the catamaran had run into trouble in the storm and that Brenda was missing. Then Sandrine caught sight of her best friend in the ocean, crying out for help.

The guys had turned around the sailboat and thrown her a lifebuoy, but, when she couldn't grab it, Sandrine contemplated going into the water after her, when suddenly she was in the water anyway. She had replayed the scene in her head over and over. Had she imagined feeling a literal nudge, or had she jumped in instinctively to help her friend? Going after someone in the open ocean in the midst of a storm was a recipe for two deaths.

Unfortunately she had no clue what happened after struggling to stay afloat as the catamaran was tossed farther and farther away from them.

The women were now in a room, almost like a root cellar, with a dirt floor and made of rock on three sides, but the double doors in front of her were interesting. She'd tried everything, but they didn't open, and that's where her fear began. She refused to even contemplate being a prisoner.

The immediate problem was that Brenda's head wound hadn't been treated. They had no bandages, and the wound hadn't even been cleaned. Her hair should be clipped away and stitches put in. She wasn't lying on a clean bed and was instead on the dirt, where they had been tossed. Exactly the same position Sandrine had found herself when she'd woken up the first time. She glanced at her friend. "Any idea who brought us here?"

"No," Brenda whispered. "I just woke up here."

"Me too," Sandrine said. She got to her feet and walked to the doors for the umpteenth time. "There's a double door," she said, "but I can't open it."

"Somebody's got to open it from the other side," Brenda said. "Lots of big doors are like that."

"Which is a stupid system," Sandrine said caustically, looking around again. "I mean, if you're inside, how do you get out? Another door should be here too."

"There could be," Brenda said. "I'd get up, but, every time I lift my head, the pain is excruciating."

"Stay still," Sandrine said, moving beside her friend once more and dropping beside her. "Definitely don't move. I'll see if there's any way out of here."

"Don't forget to look up or down," Brenda muttered, just as her eyes fluttered closed again.

Sandrine sat back on her heels, wishing she at least had blankets to cover Brenda. Her friend would catch a chill lying on the ground like this. It was a warm July day, but, after being in the water, their clothing was still wet, and, with that head injury, Brenda wasn't likely to handle the additional stressors on her body that well. It was getting light enough now that, with any luck, Sandrine could do a full search. She had tried earlier, but it had been pitch-black. Not much had changed with the lighting right now, but enough sunlight came through the cracks around the doors that she could see better.

She walked to the wall and very carefully moved along, looking and feeling the surface until she came all the way around to the doors again. The problem was, it was all rock. Wherever they were, it was like a rock cave, almost like a ravine with some man-made roof on top. She could see beams closing it off, but the beams rested on the rock walls, so somebody had taken a natural formation and had adapted their needs to the existing rocks. It wasn't that the ceiling was superhigh either, but Sandrine had nothing to stand on.

When on her tiptoes, Sandrine could reach up and feel the wood, but she couldn't apply much pressure to lift up a beam. And the wood was covered on top. She didn't know if it was topped by a mossy or a grassy slope by now or whether more wood or even roofing tiles were purposely laid down.

She returned to the double set of doors that should have opened from the center outward and checked the pins on the sides. The doors were made of wood, not steel, but some crossbar must have been on the other side because she couldn't see any latch between the two of them but did see a shadow, and she wondered if a two-by-four blocked the doors from opening. Which would make it very hard for her to get out. She didn't have anything small enough to fit in the crack between the two doors, and yet strong enough to lift the beam on the other side. Somebody had put her and Brenda in here and had secured the doors deliberately.

She hesitated calling out but knew that her friend needed help, plus Sandrine didn't want to stay locked in here another minute. Taking a deep breath, she placed her mouth close to the crack between the two doors and called out, "Hello? Hello? Can you open this door, please? My friend needs help!"

She wasn't sure what to expect, but, when no answer came, she returned to her friend and sat down. Brenda was unconscious again, her breathing shallow and low. And, just when Sandrine thought all was lost, she heard footsteps. She raced to the door and waited.

CHAPTER 3

A S SANDRINE WATCHED and waited in the shadows, a bar was removed from outside the wooden doors, confirming her suspicion of a two-by-four closure. Then both doors were opened. She stared in shock at the soldier standing slightly above her. She hopped to her feet and ran toward him, climbing out of the enclosure. "Oh, my gosh," she said. "Thank you for opening the door."

Then she stopped because the look on his face was anything but nice. "My friend needs help," she said, motioning toward Brenda. "I think she's got a concussion."

"She'll be fine," he said. "I have food for you though."

She brightened at that. "Any chance of blankets?" she asked hopefully. "We need to be dry."

He shrugged. "What do you expect when you come in out of the ocean?"

"I was hoping for a way to the mainland," she said, not exactly sure what was going on, but whoever this person was, she doubted he was a soldier, regardless of his attire. At least not one from her country. "Is there any way to get us back?"

He shook his head. "Not right away. And I don't have any blankets with me."

At that, her hopes plummeted. "Do you have any spare blankets you can bring later? Or a way to build a fire? We can't have one in there. Not enough ventilation." She looked at the ground, fairly sandy with little bits of rocks. "We could build one just outside the doors though," she said. "That would help."

He shrugged. "As long as you don't leave this area, that's fine," he said, "but you'll have to forage for your own wood. And I don't want you gone for very long."

She hesitated, not sure exactly what was going on. "That's fine," she said. "Do you have any paper or matches?"

He laughed. "If you want a fire, build it yourself," he said. He turned and picked up a plastic container with a big flat lid. Giving it to her, he said, "This is your food." Then he turned and walked away. At least he didn't lock the door. But then she was at the base of a long rock face. The shelter that they were in had a lot more rock above it, and they were nestled in a little sandy cove.

"Wait," she called, running behind him.

He spun around and glared at her, his hand going to his hip.

That's when she saw his gun. She swallowed hard. "I get that no wood is here, that I can't build a fire and that you're not very willing to help us," she said, "but I do appreciate what you've done so far."

His hand dropped slightly, and he stared at her, assessing her out in the light. "Well, make sure you stay grateful," he said. "I don't have to do this." With that, he turned and left.

She took several deep, calming breaths, trying to figure out exactly what was going on. She wasn't sure if they were prisoners or whether his words were a veiled threat that more would happen to them if they didn't behave. But, as she looked around, only sheer rock walls and sand were here. She saw no wood, nothing to burn at all. Only more sand. At least out here it was dry and a lot warmer. If she could get

Brenda out here, it would help. Sandrine put down the plastic container and walked back inside, but Brenda was sound asleep. Sandrine frowned at that but took off her shoes and her socks, then laid them outside to dry. If nothing else they needed to get some of these wet layers off.

It took a bit to get Brenda's T-shirt and pants off. Sandrine wasn't even sure it was the right thing to do, but wearing soaking wet clothing wouldn't help her friend either. Sandrine laid them out in the sun as well, then quickly stripped off the outer layer of her own clothing as well. She was hoping the guard wouldn't come back any time soon, since two women in just their underwear might put ideas into his head that she didn't want there. She wrung everything out carefully and spread them on the hot sand, hoping they would take no time to dry. Then she went back in and checked on Brenda. Now on the floor without her clothing, Brenda was bound to be that much colder.

Brenda woke up at that point and stared at Sandrine. "We're still here?"

"Unfortunately, yes. I need you to come outside into the sunlight," she said. "I don't know when we'll have our visitor back, but I want us to get dry and warmed up while we can."

With a great deal of effort, Sandrine helped Brenda to her feet, and they stumbled slowly out into the sunlight. They had not even a rock to lie on. She helped her friend lie down again and said, "Try to get warmed up, okay?"

"The sun feels really good," Brenda whispered.

"I know," Sandrine said. "But listen. At least one man is here, so we can't stay in just our underwear."

Brenda opened her eyes and stared at Sandrine in shock for a moment. Then she whispered, "I hear you. Let's get as dry as we can."

That was the best she could do for the moment, so Sandrine headed to the plastic container and lifted the lid. Inside was a cooked fish and a few biscuits. She swallowed hard because the man gave her no water. And, while she didn't know what was down in the little corner where the rocks opened up to the ocean, it wouldn't offer fresh water. She realized she'd come up against another issue, and it wouldn't be an easy one to remedy. They would need fresh water far more than food.

Sandrine slowly replaced the lid on the container and returned to sit beside Brenda. If nothing else, Sandrine would sit and guard her friend while the two of them warmed up and their clothes dried off. Beyond that Sandrine didn't know what else she was supposed to do.

THE COAST GUARD had laid out the marine maps for them. Keane and Lennox were already at the initial spot where the women had gone missing. Keane had the transcripts of the coast guard interview with the two men, Scott and Greg, and had heard the guardsmen's search stories as well. "Any reason to believe the men deep-sixed the women?" Keane asked the captain in a low tone.

The captain looked at him and shrugged. "We've seen people do worse."

"I know it's pretty easy to get rid of somebody out here, particularly in ugly weather."

From where they sat, watching the currents, and from the patterns on the map Keane had, it was hard to say where the two women would have ended up. "I understand several islands are around here where the women could have landed."

"Yes," the coast guard officer said. "We've taken our boats around all of them and found no obvious sign of the two women washed up on shore or even caught up in the shallows."

"Okay. We'll take the Zodiac and hit each one of these islands as well," Keane said.

"The Zodiac is yours to use," the captain said. "We'll stay out here for the next twenty-four hours, unless we get called away before that," he said. "I'm not sure how much longer after that we can wait nearby. Regardless, we will return here as often as possible over the next week. Send a signal for a pickup, and we'll be there."

"Good enough," Keane said. "That's another potential issue. Maybe another boat picked them up."

"They could have been taken to all kinds of places, though nobody has contacted the authorities."

"That's the best hope we have," Keane said. "We can certainly hope for something like that."

But, in his heart of hearts, he didn't hold out much hope. He studied the map a little bit longer. "I think we're ready to head out."

"Good," the captain said. "Keep in touch. We'll expect a check-in from you every six hours. If not, we'll send in the cavalry."

Keane nodded and headed to the lower deck. Lennox waited for them with scuba gear, in case needed, but asked, "What else do we need in the Zodiac?"

Keane said, "Rescue and tactical gear." Unbeknownst to the captain, Keane also had his duffel bag with additional firepower, in case they came up against something unexpected. Keane didn't like to be out in the middle of nowhere unarmed, plus the talk of that installation worried him. As did that distress call from a week earlier. The coast guard had no further light to shed on that phone call either, the officer said, but they had increased their search of the area, yet had never found anything to back it up in those initial days— until they found the couple dead thereafter.

With the gear secured in the Zodiac, Lennox hit the throttle, and he and Keane headed toward the first of many islands they needed to check, although one of the four largest were the estimated locations most likely to find the women. To start with, the men did a very slow pass around the first one, coming up along the shoreline as close as Lennox could, checking in the shallows and moving around each and every one.

As soon as they circled back to their beginning point on this island, Lennox put in at a small landing. It wasn't exactly a beach, but they could disembark and beach the Zodiac. Then the two of them crisscrossed the small island, looking for any sign of human inhabitants, but found no sign of anything, other than a few seagulls.

With the first island under their belt, they hopped back into the Zodiac and went on to the next one and did the same thing. They discounted the small islands first, and, when they came to the second largest, Lennox pulled onto a small beach with steep rock cliffs all around. After they landed and disembarked, pulling the Zodiac up onto the beach far enough that they wouldn't have to worry about it floating away with the tide, Keane and Lennox then stopped and searched the area.

"Interesting formations here," Keane murmured.

"I don't see any other way to search the top, except by air."

"And, if somebody is up there, how the hell did they get there?" he asked, studying what appeared to be really steep elevated sides to this island.

"I don't know," Lennox said, "but we have to check."

They had brought climbing gear with them and would need every bit of it, and they were both decent free-climbers too. They quickly scrambled their way up to the top and realized they only had to scale the first twenty or so feet, and then it was a much more gradual ascent. As they climbed, they widened the distance between them so they could keep an eye on the whole area around them. By the time they made it to the top, Keane noted a large plateau of a decent size. It made for a very unique island. They walked around at the top, searching along the perimeter, but found no signs of anybody.

"Looks like we're zero for three," Lennox said, "out of the four most likely islands."

"Unless they're dead or have been picked up by somebody else," Keane said.

Lennox just nodded. "I sure wish we had better intel."

"We have satellite images downloaded, but they don't show movement on any of these islands."

"Well, since we're here, let's take care of these little ones off to the right, and then we'll tackle the bigger one on our list," Lennox suggested.

"Good enough," Keane agreed. They were already well past midday and heading into early evening. "If we can get these little ones checked over today before sunset," he said, "I suggest we park for the night on the bigger island nearby."

"That makes sense. Otherwise, we can go back to the cruiser if need be."

Just then a crackle came on Keane's comm unit. He

tapped it to hear the captain saying they'd been pulled away to work a rescue mission. "We're fine," Keane responded, "at least for the moment. We've checked three islands of the four on our list, plus we've got four smaller ones to cover that we sighted nearby. Then we've got plans to park on the big one overnight."

"Good enough," the captain said. "Keep in touch, and we'll expect your next check-in at six hours from now."

"We'll let you know when we hit the big island."

With that, they boarded the Zodiac and kept working through their plan. The smaller islands were really small, but that didn't mean a body wasn't caught in the shallower waters between them. It was fairly slow and tedious work because they had to keep checking the ocean below as well, looking for anything out of the ordinary. It was almost dark when they finally made their way to the largest of the islands. They pulled the Zodiac up onto a small beach.

"What do you say we make camp right here?"

"I agree," Lennox said, and, hopping out, he stretched and rotated his shoulders. "You forget what looking over the edge of that boat does to the back of your neck and shoulders," he muttered.

"This island will take a whole lot longer to search too," Keane said, staring up at the various its layers. "It would be quite easy for somebody to get up the sides most anywhere here."

"We'll spend one day here, I imagine," Lennox said. "Look. It's almost dark. We may as well call it quits and start early in the morning."

"Sounds good."

The two of them built a small fire and laid out the bunk rolls they had brought with them. They didn't need much, since it was a summer day. Just to crash for a few hours so they could rest. Keane figured it would be daybreak by at least five, possibly four-thirty a.m. Once they had enough light to search the island, they'd be good to go.

Keane sat here under the stars, listening to the waves crashing on the beach around them. "It's pretty special out here," he said.

"It is," Lennox said. "But that's because we're both healthy, and our bellies are full, and we're not injured," he said. "Unlike these two women."

"And those first two people who disappeared, then were found dead. Out of all this, the damn distress call is worrisome."

"Right. That's a whole different story. Like you said earlier, we don't know of pirates in the area. So what gives?"

"Exactly. That's the part of this that makes me uneasy," Keane said. "The part that made me bring our duffel bag," he said, with half a smile.

"So far our search to date rules out any real chance for the women to be anywhere but this larger island—or another one of the other ones, farther out. And, of course, if this one's got decent camouflage, no way we'll find any research installation here."

"It's on this island though, isn't it?" Lennox asked, confirming.

"Yes, but, without the satellite imagery, I couldn't see anything. Could you?"

The two exchanged hard glances.

Keane shook his head. "I didn't," he said. "But that doesn't mean it's not here. How big is it anyway? Is it just something in the ground, tracking tremors, or is it something much worse, much bigger?"

"I did request that information," Keane said, "but Nico doesn't have any answers for us yet."

"Of course not. It's top secret need-to-know information that we obviously don't need to know," Lennox said, with a laugh.

"Well, is it a secret because they're killing people who have washed ashore or—?" Keane shook his head. "That's pretty far-fetched. It's not as if either of our two missing women washed ashore around here anyway. Their sailboat was quite a ways away, and they went overboard at least seven nautical miles from here."

"Way too far to allow for currents or even swimming to bring them here," Lennox said. "It doesn't make sense. Yet you and I both know that logic doesn't always enter these events."

"Agreed. So, if they were here, why would that be? How did they get here? And, of all places, why would somebody bring them here?"

"Unless someone was trying to help them but didn't want anybody to know because it would reveal where he is, maybe?"

"In which case we could be dealing not with an installation so much but maybe some loner."

"A prepper maybe?" Lennox asked, with a laugh.

"Out here?"

"Well, maybe not so much out here, but you never know, right? People choose places for their last stand all over the Earth."

"You'd think it would be more inland, where you could grow things and have animals for food," Keane said.

"Still, you have the ocean, which will give you pretty well everything you need anyway," Lennox replied sarcastically.

"Except for fresh water. The island sounds much dodgier either way," Keane said.

"True. I would think, if I went the prepper route, I would want to be on land. With fresh water around me, not the ocean. I would prefer lakes and streams, and lots of wilderness for the animals."

"Exactly. But a lot of crazy people are in the world, and a lot of people just want to be alone. This is a great place for people who want to be undisturbed."

"We're still guessing anyway." Lennox chuckled.

At that, Keane's phone buzzed. He checked it to see a text message from Nico.

Any news?

Quickly Keane tapped in a response. **Stopped for the night due to darkness. On the largest island, the last on our checklist for an immediate search. Nothing so far. Starting at first light.**

Good enough, Nico replied.

Any further word on the distress call?
Nothing.

"This whole thing is basically a waste of time," Lennox said, after Keane read the message out loud.

"It is, but, at the same time, although our mission is for a grim reason, it is nice to be out here again," he admitted. "After too many missions and too much training, you can kind of forget why you went into the navy in the first place."

"Because we love water? Because we love to be of service to our country? Because we're natural-born protectors?"

"Yeah, all that and more," he said. "Look at us. We're sitting here. We could easily be more sheltered backed up against the rocks, but we're down here close to the water, where I can watch the way the moonlight ripples across the waves. It looks like a storm is out there, and, if it crashes in on us, we'll be damned pissed off about it," Keane said with a laugh. "But, right now, this is pretty magical."

"I know," Lennox said. "I used to go camping with my dad all the time. We'd find a little island like this and just set up for the night. We'd stay, have breakfast and explore a little bit. Then we'd hop back into our boats and head to the next place."

"Most people, when they say *camping*, are really thinking *road trip*," Keane said with a chuckle.

"In our case it was boat trip," he said with a smile. "I was nearly born in a kayak for God's sake. They headed for land, and my mom gave birth to me, six weeks early," he said with a laugh. "They stayed for a couple days for her to recover and to adapt to having a newborn around. Then back in the kayaks they went and headed for home again."

"At least they went home," Keane said, laughing. "But that's very much the pioneer mind-set."

"Right. That was about all they had back then," he said with a smile.

"Well, we need to get some shut-eye so we can get an early start."

"I'll take the first watch," Lennox said.

Keane nodded, got up, taking his sleeping bag with him in case he got cold in the night, and walked farther up the shore to lay down in the warm sand. Using his bedroll for a pillow right now and crossing his arms over his abdomen, he closed his eyes. His last thought was that, if those two women were out here somewhere, he sure as hell hoped they were high and dry and a long way away from the latest storm threatening to break over the top of them.

Otherwise, their night would get much worse.

CHAPTER 4

T HE THUNDER WOKE her first. Sandrine opened her eyes to a black sky and the crashing of thunder somewhere a long way away. But, as she heard a thunder crash the second time, she confirmed the storm was getting closer. She bolted to her feet, noting the air had chilled. Although she was currently warm, she could see it wouldn't stay that way. And it wouldn't stay dry either. She walked to her clothes and found her T-shirt and jeans were dry and quickly got dressed. She pulled on her socks and her shoes, even though they were sandy. Not knowing what the night would bring, she wanted to be ready. She quickly went to Brenda, and, reaching down, she gently woke her friend.

Groggy, Brenda looked up at her. "What happened?" she asked.

"We're outside. I need you to get dressed and warm again. Our clothes are dry," Sandrine said with a smile.

Her friend's words sounded fuzzy and indistinct. Some of Brenda's words made no sense.

Sandrine gently helped her friend and slowly pulled the T-shirt on over her head and then got her into her jeans. She put on Brenda's shoes and socks, like for a child. When she finished, Sandrine got Brenda up again and helped her into the little shelter they had. She left the doors open but propped Brenda up against one of the rock walls. "We have a little bit of food," she said, "but we don't have any water."

As soon as she said that, Brenda, her voice dry and hoarse, rasped out, "I need a drink."

"I haven't seen our mysterious guy again," she said. "At the moment we don't have anything to drink." And she hadn't gone looking for any water source either, and she kicked herself for it now. Though she didn't want to leave Brenda alone either.

Clearly a storm was coming—and fast. She wanted to bury her head and cry but tried to say calm. Opening the bin with the food, she put it all onto the lid, and set it inside the shelter. Just in case there would be rain here, she wanted to put the empty container outside to catch fresh water for them. As she stepped outside, it started to rain. She quickly stepped back inside and watched for a moment to see if any particular area was better where water might pool. The rain hit the rocks and ran off at one particular spot, so she quickly placed the container underneath, hoping to get at least a little bit for drinking water.

When it began raining in earnest, it came down in a heavy deluge. The only good news was the fact that she was gathering some water. She quickly moved the biscuits and fish onto a rock inside their shelter and put the lid outside as well. They would need all the water they could possibly get. She held it up off to the side, using it almost like a slope to run water into the big container. She was just far enough under the shelter that only her arm got wet. She stood here for a long moment, watching Mother Nature completely obscure the world around her. Behind her, she heard Brenda call out.

"It's so beautiful."

Sandrine looked over, but her friend was smiling, as if

staring at something completely different than what Sandrine saw. "Just lie down, Brenda. You need to sleep." Sandrine was worried.

Brenda turned her face, still smiling. "I'm so happy to be here," she said.

Sandrine stared at her friend, overwhelmed with fear. The two of them had been friends for over a decade now. Whoever would have thought they would end up in this scenario? Sandrine had to hold it together and do anything she could to help her friend. Right now water was their most pressing issue, and Mother Nature was very kindly assisting them with that. If they could eat and drink a little, it would help.

Then Sandrine had to find that guy and see if there was a way off the island. If he had a boat, maybe she could pay him, although she couldn't give him the money until she made it back home again. But she had money at home, and Brenda's whole family was wealthy. They would definitely get her home, if they could. Maybe this guy had a cell phone or a radio. There had to be some way to contact people. He had a plastic container for Christ's sake—that had to come from somewhere. He came from civilization, and, if he came from civilization once, then surely he had a way to get them back again.

Just sitting here and waiting for Brenda to recover or die was killing Sandrine.

She stared out at the rain as it poured and poured, and then, just like that, it slowed to a trickle. She stepped out and picked up the bin. Walking along the edges where the rocks were still dripping, she collected as much of it as she could. The container was half full by the time she was done, and that was huge.

Bending underneath one of the rocks, she took several drinks as it filled her mouth and then took a long drink from the container itself. Walking back inside, she gently held a corner of the container to Brenda's mouth and helped Brenda get a drink as well. After several long sips, Brenda smiled and said, "That's great coffee."

"I wish," Sandrine said. "But here is a bit of fish and some biscuits, so let's eat."

She carefully broke off some of the cooked fish and fed bits and pieces to her friend. Sandrine split the fish as fairly as she could, and, since there were two biscuits, they each had one. And then with the water Sandrine had collected, the women managed to get it all down. Although it wasn't the best meal in the world, it tasted fantastic because she was desperately in need of nourishment.

With some food in her stomach, Brenda laid back down, mumbling and talking to herself.

Sandrine reached out and, lacing fingers with her friend, just sat at her side. "Rest," she whispered. "Try to sleep if you can."

And finally, after a deeply troubling conversation with herself, Brenda curled up in a ball and went to sleep again. Sandrine had napped outside in the sun, and the last thing she felt like right now was sleeping. She wanted to explore but was worried about leaving Brenda behind. But reality won out.

She could sit here and watch her friend die, or she could try to get her some help. The head injury didn't look that bad on the outside, but she wasn't so sure about what was happening on the inside. Like swelling on the brain? The worst thing would be for Brenda to die and for Sandrine to find out afterward that some simple medical care could have fixed it. She partially closed the shelter doors so that Brenda couldn't be seen from the outside. Then Sandrine stepped out. The sand had absorbed all the rain, but only the top was wet, and everything underneath was dry. She headed down to where she could see the beach and stood there, staring out over the vast ocean.

The storm had left behind clouds that blanketed any sign of other landmarks other than just a great big churning ocean. All she could see was a small bay that wasn't more than fifteen yards across with white sand and the rough ocean crashing up on the beach and pulling back again. No way to know where the man had gone to. Sandrine's worst thought was that he had taken off in his boat and had left them behind. But she had no reason to think that somebody would be so cruel. Yet, at the same time, they had been locked inside what amounted to a cave. Why were they stuck in a small shelter like that?

Of course she wasn't still a prisoner, but, with no other way to get off the island, the stranger hadn't needed to put a two-by-four across the doors. They were stuck here anyway. Hating the sinking feeling that they were completely isolated on this island, she decided that, rather than stand here and worry about it, she would check and make sure she wasn't missing something else.

With the sky darkening, she headed to the far side of the beach, looking steadily out over the ocean and then back up to the rocky cliffs. She couldn't see any side valleys or ways to get out other than what appeared to be some stairs cut into the rock.

She walked all the way around this little beach, all forty-five feet of it, past the opening that led to the tiny bay where Brenda still lay, and then came back to the stairs. With the rocks and the waves cutting her off elsewhere, at least without a boat, these stairs were the only way out. And they went up. Taking a deep breath, she moved slowly and carefully as the stairs were wet and had no railings or any handholds. She got halfway up and looked down, then caught her breath and leaned against the rock wall.

"Don't look down. Don't look down," she mumbled to herself. She kept going up because it was really her only option, other than the sea.

She was terrified of going back down again. As soon as she came around a little bit of a corner, it widened and became a much shallower incline. At this point she was quite comfortable climbing, as rock was on both sides. As she came through by the cliff's edge yet up to the top of the island, she could see more trees and foliage and still more rock, but no houses, no signs of human habitation. She frowned as she walked around the surface.

Where the hell were they? How had they arrived here? And who was the man who had brought them that bit of food?

As far as she could see out over the ocean, absolutely nothing was out there. Nothing was nearby. They were caught on an uninhabited island. Stuck somewhere in the middle of nowhere, with water on all sides. For the first time she began to realize just how truly isolated they were. Not only isolated but alone. She walked around on the topmost edge as best she could, but nothing more was to be found, no matter where she stood.

Behind her were more hills, more rocks and more trees. She walked a little bit farther but didn't want to go too far because of Brenda and the encroaching darkness. Deciding that she'd searched enough for the moment, Sandrine headed back to the stairs. Going down step by step and hanging on to the rock face, she made her way again to the sandy shore and stood, looking at the ocean for another long moment, feeling the vast uncertainty of her future. Something was so incredibly awe-inspiring about nature, but it could also make you feel like a tiny insignificant speck in the whole scope of things. They were stranded here, and nobody seemed to give a damn that they were here. Not quite true, considering that the one man had brought them food and had let them out of their cave prison cell.

He must have wanted them to survive, so surely he'd be back again. She'd been so certain that he had to be somewhere on the island. But what if he had left, and now they were here all alone? Shaking her head, she returned to the shelter as the darkness settled all around her. Hopefully in the morning things would look better. But, for the moment, the situation looked pretty dire.

As she got to where Brenda lay curled in a fetal position, Sandrine propped open one of the double doors with a two-by-four, like they had a floor-to-ceiling window. They needed to stay warm tonight, but she didn't want to be completely closed inside either. She was grateful that she could dry their clothes and that they had managed to warm up in the sun, but now it would be them against the elements.

Although they were winning at the moment, Sandrine wasn't too sure she could count on that continuing. It wouldn't be an easy night. But, if she could get Brenda through it, there was a much better chance of her being better tomorrow. With that thought in mind, Sandrine wrapped her arms around her friend to keep her warm and closed her eyes.

HE WOKE TO a storm crashing overhead.

Keane hopped to his feet to see Lennox with the boat flipped over and up higher on the sand. "We need shelter," he called out.

Lennox called back, "I've got a small pod tent here."

They quickly snapped it out of its casing and inflated it really fast. With both of them underneath, they were out of the worst of the rain.

"Where did that storm come from?" Keane asked.

"No clue," Lennox replied, "but it sure came up fast. Hopefully it'll disappear that way too."

The rain itself wasn't a problem, but hypothermia was. They were both seasoned travelers and outdoorsmen, so they would be fine, but Keane couldn't help but think of the two women and how they were faring. The storm carried on for a good forty-five minutes. Absolutely no way could the women stand up to these conditions with no resources. If they were alive, that is.

Luckily the storm finally moved on, yet it was still dark. "Any idea what time it is?"

"No, but it's got to be at least four in the morning," Lennox said.

"Well, I was planning on getting up soon anyway."

"Right, but we won't be going anywhere, until this dries up a bit, and we can see."

"We may as well eat then," Keane said.

"If you want to get the food out," Lennox said, "I'll pack this up, so we'll be ready to start exploring at first light."

And that's what they did. Just a few minutes later they were eating protein bars, an orange, some beef jerky, and they each had a hot cup of coffee, using a small single-burner cooktop. Instant coffee, of course, but it was something. And they would take *something* in these circumstances any day.

With one last look at the storm moving across the ocean, Keane said, "I sure hope they managed to miss out on that."

"Let's hope they're not even aware that a storm passed through," Lennox replied. "It could be a shitty deal for them, depending on their circumstances."

"I think the worst thing would be floating out in the ocean and waiting for somebody to pick you up."

"Especially without training or supplies or equipment," Lennox said.

After breakfast, everything was quickly cleaned up and packed away. Next, they took a serious look at where to start.

Soon, with ropes, grapples and a small safety kit, the two of them headed out together. They didn't want to split up at this point in time because too many unknown factors were here. It would have been a normal search-and-rescue scenario but for that distress call a week earlier, followed by two dead bodies. That changed the game completely.

The cliffs rose all along the white beach. One spot had a more accessible cliff, where the climbing was a little bit less onerous, and, as they climbed higher and higher, they realized that the island had multiple levels. It would take forever to search. They started off splitting the island into quadrants and checked out the first quadrant, going as slowly and as carefully as they could. They had to consider the chance that somebody made it onto the beach and then climbed but maybe had gotten pinned or had fallen. From all angles they studied and searched the first quadrant and found nothing.

With that, they headed to the second quadrant, another

part of the beach where they landed but off to the east. That search took a little less time as parts of it were sheer cliffs, and no way anybody would come up or down on any of that. They also looked for any sign of the installation or an earthquake-tracking system.

Keane had seen one before, during a previous mission, but it had been buried in the ground. He was looking for any telltale flags or poles to mark it, but, so far, he had found nothing man-made. Just as they headed to the third quadrant, he stopped and pointed—indeed, one of the poles he had expected to see. They took a look and could see a US-government-issued tag on the top. He quickly took several photos and sent it off to Nico. **Is this part of the tracking system?**

The answer came back almost immediately. **Yes. Should be three of those.**

Good to go, so they kept on walking. That meant humans had been here at one point in time, but were there still? And who was recording this information? He sent their questions off to Nico, asking for a schedule of who would have come, when they would have been here last, when they were next expected to visit this island and what kind of data they were collecting. And, perhaps most important, was anything else on the island besides these three locations for the research installation itself?

With the one site tagged on his GPS, they moved forward to the back section of this third quarter. They followed a big dip in the plateau here. It rose higher on the right-hand side in the back quarter, but the island itself was at least one mile across, and so it was taking forever. He sent back a note to Nico. **We may not finish today.**

When Nico's answer came back as a text with a single

question mark, Keane responded. **Island huge. Heavy vegetation. Somebody shipwrecked could have made it into some of these spots and collapsed.** After a moment of silence, he sent another text. **A dog would help.**

He got a reply right away. **Want one airlifted in?**

He thought about it for a moment, then shook his head. **Everything's soaking wet, and, while a dog would certainly make it easier, we've already come this far, so—** He looked at Lennox. "What do you think about bringing in a dog?"

Lennox's eyebrows shot up. "You know what? That's not a bad idea." Yet, as he looked around, he said, "But everything is so wet, it would really play with the dog's olfactory system. Plus, we don't have any scent of the women for a dog to search for. It'll mostly be a case of search and rescue, looking for signs of life."

"Or signs of death," Keane said. "A lot of the dogs are quite capable of finding cadavers as well."

Lennox said, "Let's give it today, and, if we don't have any luck, then maybe tomorrow consider the search dog issue."

"Good enough." Keane passed that message off to Nico and kept moving.

"I don't see any footprints," Lennox noted. "I don't see much of anything up here."

"But that heavy rain would have washed so much away."

"Sadly, that's very true. And the cliff edges are almost completely impassable," Lennox nodded, looking around. "I don't remember this island."

Keane looked at his partner curiously. "Do you know this area?"

"Part of the family camping trips. But I don't remember

this island."

"Lots of them are fairly impassable," Keane said. They kept walking, searching, but found absolutely nothing. They heard only wind and saw the odd bird. As they stood on the edge of what they had deemed the third quadrant, he said, "It feels empty."

"I know," Lennox said, "but that doesn't mean it is." He lifted his hands, cupping them around his mouth, and screamed, "Hello." A massive gust of wind seemed to carry his voice forever.

Just when they were about to turn to head in another direction, Keane thought he heard something. He reached out, grabbed Lennox's shoulder. "Do that again."

Lennox looked at him, clearly surprised, but he willingly cupped his hands around his mouth and called again. And this time what they heard a response a little clearer. "Is that a person?"

The two men stared at each other and then quickly raced toward the sound. It wasn't easy to decipher, and neither was it easy to find. They found nothing on this level, so they worked their way toward a lower plateau area.

Keane saw a large grassy spot and was hoping for their sake that the women had made it that far. It took the guys a good hour to make it down to the spot, and, when they arrived, he had Lennox call out again. This time the response was clearer but had an edge to it.

As he came over the top of the grassy area and looked down, he spotted a hollow, where the ocean had carved out a deep, circular area, completely surrounded by sheer cliffs.

Down in the center a woman stood, and, as soon as she saw him, she screamed and waved her arms.

He called out, "We'll come down."

She nodded and called back, "We need help. My friend is injured."

"Radio the coast guard," Keane said to Lennox. "We should be able to get her out of here."

"I'm wondering if I shouldn't go back to the Zodiac," Lennox said, studying the lay of the land, as Keane brought out his ropes and grappling hooks.

"That's not a bad idea," Keane said. "Leave me the first aid kit, and, if you want, head back, grab the Zodiac and come around to this bay. I'll make my way down and take a closer look. Then we'll decide if the water exit is best and easiest."

With that decision made, he hooked up his ropes, and slowly, while Lennox stood at the top, Keane made his way down the sharp cliff face. When he was almost down, Lennox called out that he was leaving. Keane gave his partner a thumbs-up signal and watched as his friend disappeared from the top of the cliff. Down below, maybe thirty more feet, he could see the woman still standing there, waiting for him to land. "I'm coming," he said.

"Good," she said. "I was afraid we'd been deserted again."

He heard the word *again* but would clarify that with her later. And it was hardly the time to ask. Some of the rocks were coming loose as he descended. He stared up where he'd come from, and he could see rocks crumbling down over his head. As several bounced off his helmet, he swore, then ducked against the cliff wall.

She cried out and quickly ran, backing away from the rocks.

What was going on up there above him? Unless Lennox's movement caused rocks to shift, Keane wasn't too happy about it either.

Keane clung to the cliff and waited until the rocks stopped moving. When it finally appeared to be safer, he let himself swing back out and quickly descended. As he got down within the last ten or fifteen feet, he felt his rope jerking. He looked up to see his rope cut loose. He fell the last few feet, rolling clear of the rocks. As soon as he could, he picked himself up and raced back against the cliff's edge. He motioned for her to run toward him.

She stared at him in shock but quickly joined him underneath a little dip where the rocks could continue to fall without hitting them. But the rockslide stopped.

"Who the hell is on this island with you?" he asked in a harsh voice. His mind raced with possibilities.

She shook her head. "I don't know. I don't know," she whispered. "A man dropped off a container with a fish and a couple biscuits, but he wouldn't give us any blankets or towels, and he wouldn't help us get off the island. He just left us."

Keane stared at her, shocked at the turn of events, but no doubt she was telling the truth. She had her arms wrapped around her chest and held her shoulder, which even now oozed blood. He leaned over to check it.

"I got hit by some of the falling rocks," she said and reached up to touch her head.

He checked out both injuries. "At least they're superficial. What I need to know is whether we're facing one man or a dozen."

"I don't know," she said, her teeth starting to chatter.

He wrapped his arm around her and tucked her up close. "Look. I'm sorry. I don't mean to scare you," he said, "but my rope was cut." He pointed at the rope that now lay like a coiled snake on the sand amid the rocks beside him.

Her hand clapped over her mouth as she stared at it; and she just burrowed in closer.

He waited for a long moment and then said, "I need you to get ahold of yourself."

She nodded. "I know. I know," she said. "It's been two very long days."

"Start at the beginning, and tell me what happened," he said, as he studied the area around him. "Tell me what you've seen. Like, where did you see this man?"

"He—well, we were locked inside that little space up there," she said, pointing. "A two-by-four closes the doors. When I called for help, I heard footsteps, and somebody came and took the bar off, opening those doors. He brought us food, but he didn't give us any water, and then he left. He walked down to the opening there to the ocean."

"Did you hear a boat? Did you hear him leave at all?"

She shook her head. "I did see stairs going to a flatter spot up there, but I don't know where else he could have gone. And he hasn't come back. I looked all around at the top of this plateau, but I didn't find anything."

"Do you need water?" he asked, unclipping a bottle from his belt.

"We collected rainwater," she said, "but, yes, if you don't mind."

He quickly popped the top and gave it to her and watched as she drank thirstily. He waited until she was done and then sagged back in place.

"My friend is hurt," she said. "She's got a head injury, and she's delirious. I don't know what to do for her."

"Not a whole lot we can do except get her to medical help," he said, looking around. "I want to make it to where your friend is, but, if somebody is watching us, we don't want him to know that we're alive. Especially me."

"You're hoping he'll think you died in the fall?"

He nodded. "Yes, but I don't know how long it'll take for him to come down and check on me."

"Oh, God. I don't know," she said. "We can walk around this corner, but, at one point, it's exposed. And, if he's watching us, we can't stop him from seeing you."

"So we'll stand here for a moment and make sure he's gone," he said. "He could be on his way down, and, if that's the case, I'll have to find a way to capture him before he tries to hurt us again."

"If it wasn't for the cut rope," she said slowly, staring at him, "I wouldn't think that he was trying to hurt us at all. He did bring us food."

"I get that," he said. "Can you tell me what happened? Like, who you are, and why you're here? Let me start, I'm Keane Lytton and I'm here on behalf of the coast guard."

She smiled. "My name is Sandrine Coulter," she said, "and I was out sailing with my friends. My girlfriend, Brenda, is hurt. We were out in her boyfriend's catamaran. We've gone sailing with them several times before but never this long or this far away."

"And what happened? How did you end up in the water and wind up here?"

"Brenda fell overboard," Sandrine explained, her voice gritty. "We caught up to her in the water, and I threw her a lifebuoy, but she seemed unable to grab it, so I jumped into the water after her."

He raised his eyebrows and stared at her.

She nodded. "I know, not exactly the smartest thing to do. But I couldn't do any less."

CHAPTER 5

"**H**ONESTLY, WE'VE BEEN friends since forever, and I wouldn't let her drown."

"Understood," he said. "What about the men on the sailboat with you?"

"It's all a bit fuzzy," she admitted. "I was screaming for help and trying to get Brenda to the buoy, so at least she'd have something to hang on to. But it got sent off in another direction, and the waves crashed over us," she said. "I remember keeping the two of us afloat, but I completely lost track of where the catamaran went. I don't even know if the guys are alive."

"They are. They got the boat back safely and contacted the coast guard, saying that you two were missing."

"Oh, thank God," she said. "I was so worried about them."

"And you ended up here, washed up on the beach or what?"

"I think so," she said, "but honestly that is where it gets very blurry. Because I woke up inside that little sheltered area. The thing is, we woke up behind the doors, and they were closed, locked, so we couldn't get out. Now a really cold wind can pass through the island, and maybe the man thought that we'd be delirious and get hurt or something. I don't know. Because, once the man opened the doors and brought the food, he left the doors open."

"As if he wasn't too worried that you could go any-where," he said sardonically.

"I hate to admit it, but the thought did cross my mind that he had no need to keep us locked up because we couldn't escape the island anyway."

"Which is possible," he said. "It is a fairly big island though, and I have searched three-fourths of it. Still don't know what's even here."

"It's not very easy to climb anyway," she said. "We've been sitting here, waiting for somebody to come, and nobody but that one man has."

"Well, I'm here now," he said, frowning as he studied her closely. "Brenda's father got me and my buddy in here to search all the islands. The coast guard hasn't given up, but, with the bad weather, they've gone off to rescue other people. They've searched the nearby islands from the coastlines and then walked the islands themselves and found nothing." He said, "We've searched seven islands nearby, before landing here."

"We've been here one night that I'm aware of," she said. "With the heavy rain, I managed to fill the food container he gave us with water, so we've been subsisting on that. But he hasn't come back."

"Well, I'd say he's back now," Keane said, pointing to the cut rope.

She nodded. "And that scares the crap out of me," she said, "because either he doesn't want us to be rescued or he doesn't know who you are and doesn't care, but he wanted you to join us down here."

"Or he was hoping I'd die on the way down," Keane said. "It wasn't exactly a friendly welcome."

"What about your friend?"

Keane's face turned grim. "Lennox is a hell of a fighter and a good man. I'll put my money on him that he makes it back to the boat."

"Boat?" She brightened at that.

"We have a Zodiac on the other side," he said.

She studied his face, then whispered, "Do you think it's safe to return to Brenda now? I don't like leaving her alone for long."

"She's probably better off alone over there than she is with us," he said, his voice harsh.

Sandrine winced at that. "How long before your friend gets here with the boat?"

At that, Keane's face narrowed. "I don't know," he said. "It depends. If it's a clean trip, he'll be at least two hours getting back to the boat. Another hour maybe coming around. If he's been injured or worse and can't get to the boat, it's a whole different story."

She stared at him in shock. "That sounds terrible."

"It's realistic," he said. "Either way, if he can get to us, Lennox will do it. He also has some communication gear with him, so he'll send out a message to the coast guard as soon as he can."

"Can messages get out from here?" she asked.

"Down here, not likely," Keane said. "But up top we should connect via satellite."

She breathed a deep and slow breath. "That all sounds so doable," she said. "I'm really, really glad that you're here."

He gave a clipped nod. "I am too. It sounds like you've been through the wringer already."

"You don't know the half of it," she said.

He looked at her curiously, as if she wasn't sure if she

should tell him something. He clearly read her face and gave her a hard look. "If you haven't told me everything, this would be a really good time to share. I need all the help I can get, figuring out what we're dealing with here."

"Look. I can't prove it," she said, "but, when I was screaming at Brenda to grab the lifebuoy, just before I went in, I'm almost sure I felt a push between my shoulder blades."

He stared at her, shocked for a moment. "Meaning, you didn't jump in after your friend? You were pushed?"

"I was planning on going in anyway," she said, "so I don't know if he made that decision for me or what. I just can't say. Such chaos was happening at the time."

"And which one of the men was it?"

"Scott," she said sadly. "My ex-boyfriend."

"And have the two of you had any problems lately?"

"We broke up a couple months ago," she said. "Before that, we had been fighting lots, and I found out he'd been with another woman, so I broke it off."

"And yet, you still went sailing with him?"

She winced. "It's a little hard to explain, but I had told Brenda about what happened. Except the part about me seeing him, she didn't believe it, and her partner swore that Scott hadn't been unfaithful. So the trip was a setup to try and get me back together with him."

"Without your permission?"

"Exactly," she said in a wry tone. "I admit I wasn't happy when I saw him there at the boat. They kept telling me that he hadn't cheated on me. But I saw Scott with that woman. I'd told him—and Brenda—that a friend of mine had seen him with her, had seen them going into our apartment in the middle of a workday, but it was me who saw them. I just didn't want to say it."

"Usually the truth works out better in these instances."

"There's no 'in these instances,'" she said. "How the hell does anybody know how to respond when something like that happens?"

"Good point," he said.

"It's not easy to deal with relationships. At least, not for me."

"No, it's not. And, in a case like this," he said, "there's absolutely no way to practice how you'll respond."

"Betrayal always sucks," she said.

"It does," he said, "but don't let it get you down."

"Well, if it wasn't for him, maybe we wouldn't be here."

"Do you think so?"

"I don't know," she said, "because, when you think about it, I wouldn't have been on that boat if I'd known he'd be there. And, if he hadn't been there, maybe we wouldn't have gone out quite so far. He's the one who urged us out into deeper waters. He wanted a *great sailing day.*"

"So are you thinking that maybe he wanted this to happen? Maybe planned it?"

"No, I can't say that," she said, "but I don't know." She rubbed her face with both hands, confused. "Don't worry about what I'm saying. I'm sure it's just the trauma of everything getting to me."

"Maybe. Maybe not," he said. "We'll keep it in the back of our minds anyway."

"Yeah," she said. "I'm sure he would deny it all."

"Yes, I'm sure he would too, so it depends on whether anybody else knows or saw him."

"That would mean Greg. And I highly doubt he would say anything about Scott because they've been best buddies forever."

"So, for now, maybe we should just deal with the problems we have at hand. It seems like we have enough of those already."

"I agree," she said. "Not the least of which is that Brenda really needs medical attention."

He glanced around and said, "Well, I need to take a look at her first."

"Sure," she said. "I can walk over there, but I don't know how to get you there without being seen."

"I'll risk it," he said, "because it has to happen sometime." He walked up along the edge of the cliff and around to the corner. Then, at the last bit, he ran around until he was at the center of the double doors. He stepped inside and crouched beside Brenda.

Sandrine was at his side instantly. "She's been like this since I woke up. Sometimes sleeping, sometimes delirious."

"Give me the symptoms," he said.

She gave him the little bit she knew and said, "I don't know how badly hurt she is."

"That sounds like a concussion, but the injury itself doesn't look too bad. She may sleep this off and wake up feeling pretty decent."

"I hope so," she said, "because this really sucks."

"I know," he said. "Let's just stay positive."

"Well, I was feeling positive until somebody cut your damn rope," she said. "After that, I didn't feel very positive anymore."

"I have complete faith in Lennox," he said. "It would take a lot for somebody to take him down."

"Not really," she said. "Bullets would do that just fine."

He looked at her, his gaze narrowed. "Did you see a gun

on that man?"

She looked up at him in surprise. "Didn't I say so?"

"No, you didn't."

"Oh, crap," she said. "He's dressed like a soldier and had a handgun on his hip."

"Shit," he said. Pulling out his phone, he sent Lennox a message, but, as he looked at the rock walls all around him, he knew his call or text wouldn't go through. "I wish I had known that before," he said.

"Yeah," she said. "I do too. I'm sorry. What about your friend? Will that be a problem?"

"No," he said. "It is what it is. It would take an awful lot to knock Lennox off his feet permanently."

She swore softly. "So we'll just sit here and wait?"

"Have you tried to get around at the edge of the beach?"

"No," she said. "I tried to go both ways down the beach but was cut off by the waves and rocks. Then I climbed some oddly natural-looking stairs in the cliff, but I didn't want to go too far and to leave Brenda for too long."

"Good point," he said. "Are you okay to stay here while I explore?"

She sucked in her breath but quickly realized they really had no options. "Fine," she said, "but please come back."

"I will," he said. "I promise."

She winced at that and asked, "What if that guy comes back here?"

"You stay right here beside your friend. If he asks if you saw anybody, just say that I fell and then got up, holding my head and ran."

"Ran where?"

He looked around, then pointed at the ocean and said, "Right into the water."

"He won't believe me."

"Maybe not, but he'll head in that direction."

She shrugged and said, "If you think so."

"Well, if you come up with a better idea," he said with a laugh, "you go for it."

She shook her head. "Yeah, that won't be so easy. Please, just be careful."

He gave her a quick smile and said, "Stay here. I'll be right back."

KEANE TOOK OFF toward the beach. He had tried not to let her see it, but he was definitely worried about Lennox. Whoever that asshole was who cut Keane's rope had never intended for Keane to get back up onto the top ledge. Now Keane had other gear with him, but it still wouldn't be easy to get back up to where he was. That's why the rope was cut in the first place.

As he made his way along the rocky edge down to the small beach, he took a look around. From where he stood, he saw absolutely nothing but the gray wet and drying stone rock face. It was a bizarre little inlet here, but perfect for the two women to be safe. The fact that this guy had delivered food meant that he hadn't wanted to kill them. At least not yet. And he had released them from their little prison.

Keane had taken a good look at the lock on it too, and it would have been hard for a woman to get out of there. A strong man probably could break apart the wood and gotten out that way, but the women were already weak from their ordeal and were small to begin with. Plus, with one injured, the other one was unlikely to leave. Sandrine probably wasn't thinking about shattering a wooden door either.

He, on the other hand, could feel his temper rising, and it would explode if he found out anybody had hurt Lennox. They'd been good buddies for a long time, but this was a very strange scenario. Lennox also had the equipment to get a message out, and that message was imperative at present. Keane checked if his phone had service now that he'd moved, but he had no bars. He had equipment back at the Zodiac to set up offshore communication to the coast guard, but he had to get there first.

When coming on a trip like this, he had to minimize the amount of gear he would carry because every pound would impact how far he could go each day. As it was right now, Keane and Lennox had made the decision to leave almost everything with the Zodiac. But, if this asshole got there first, he could completely demolish everything they had and leave them stranded too.

That wasn't a big concern for Keane, as several people already knew where he was, and, if he didn't report in, the coast guard would send out another team. His immediate concern was flushing this guy out, taking him down and finding Lennox.

Keane stood at the edge of the rock, but the waves lapped up along the sheer sides, giving him no break to walk around. He didn't give a shit about getting wet, but if it was sheer rock all the way on the other side too, then returning to where the Zodiac was beached would be a whole different story. He also would have to strip down and leave whatever gear he had here. Also not a good idea. He found the stairs that Sandrine had mentioned, and, as he crept his way up, he found it interesting that the stairs were mostly naturally hewn. Maybe somebody had come along with an ax and had chipped off a bit more to make it a little more stable, but these were natural for the most part.

When he came to where it widened, he slid along the side and stepped out to where he could see the lower platform. And it was completely empty. Was this where the asshole had been when he had cut Keane's rope? As Keane headed to the side, he realized this part didn't drop over to the edge; it just came up against more rock.

He searched the area but found nothing that worried him. He kept on moving toward the Zodiac, hoping to find a way to traverse the uneven cliffside to get where he needed to go. His only other option was to backtrack down the stairs, then strip down and swim around to the Zodiac. The problem with that was a storm was out there right now, with the potential for another to pop up at any time during the day. The waves bashing up against the cliff were strong and would have no problem picking him up and tossing him against the rocks over and over again. He could handle a few blows, but, at some point in time, his body would wear down, and the damage would be too severe. He needed to find another way around if he could.

This guy obviously knew his way around the island, so it would just take a little more time. Keane tapped the comm device he kept in his ear but got no answer from Lennox. Keane didn't let himself get too worried about that because the harsh rocky conditions made technical communication difficult in the best of times. He kept walking through the trees all along the edge of the cliff, looking for another way down, sure there must be another pathway. Ten minutes later he almost missed it.

He thought he caught a flash of light as he walked past. Stopping, he slowly backtracked, looking carefully, and saw just a cut into the rock. He had to shift sideways in order to make his way through. The flash of light he'd seen was from a bit of shiny black rock at just the right angle to make a reflection.

He crept around the corner to see the island opened up and another small plateau rose before him. Surprised and delighted, he searched the area first, then made his way up on top and over to the edge. From there he could see a series of slopes that led down toward where the Zodiac was. What bothered him was that he saw no sign of Lennox. While still up top, Keane tried calling Lennox, texting him and using the comm radio, but got nothing in response. Keane frowned and made his way slowly and carefully down to the Zodiac, watching the storm out on the ocean, hoping it stayed away for a little bit longer.

When he got to the Zodiac, he swore. The tubes had been completely deflated. Cut with a knife so they could never be repaired. He was as stuck as the women were, and that was a game-changer. Pissed, Keane checked his gear under the pontoons. Expecting to find it gone, he realized that whoever had damaged the Zodiac hadn't seen the large bag underneath. He pulled it out and quickly set up the offshore communication and contacted the coast guard.

Unfortunately, he couldn't get through because of the static. He tried several different methods and still got no connection.

Finally, he sent a Morse code message, repeating it several times before hoisting the bag on his back like a backpack, looking around for any sign that Lennox had been here. But there were no new tracks. Which meant he hadn't made it this far. Keane backtracked the way they had gone up in order to see if he could trace his buddy. Keane headed up the original pathway they had taken, grunting with the extra weight on his back, but not daring to lose it. He also had a handgun pocketed close enough that he could access it if needed.

When he got to the cliff where his rope had been secured earlier, he was tired, worn out and knew that hours had passed. Sandrine had to be completely terrified that he hadn't returned yet. He stood at the top of the cliff and stared down.

He could see the little shelter and the door partially open. His grapple hook was still where he'd left it but with no rope attached because, of course, it had dropped to the bottom when it was cut. He picked up the grapple hook and hung on to it. From here he followed Lennox's tracks back. No sign of him so far. It took another twenty minutes before Keane found his friend, unconscious and lying under some brush. Keane quickly checked Lennox's wound to see a bullet hole high in his shoulder.

Swearing, Keane unpacked his first aid kit, and, keeping his handgun close by, he quickly patched up his buddy. Then he found a head wound. Now he had two seriously injured people, both on separate levels geographically on the island, both in danger of more trauma from being moved. And no way to get immediate help. He checked out the head wound the best he could and tried to wake up Lennox. "Hey, buddy. Can you wake up?"

Lennox murmured.

"More than that please. I need you awake."

Lennox opened his eyes and stared at him. Then they narrowed, and he whispered, "Please tell me that you got that bastard."

"Not only did I not get him," he said, "I haven't seen

him. He cut my rope when I was climbing down, and he must have taken you out shortly thereafter."

Lennox looked confused, but then it seemed as if the tumblers clicked into place, and he whispered, "You survived the drop?"

"Yeah. Once I realized somebody was up there, I scrambled down as fast as I could," he said. "I still fell about ten or twelve feet, but I'm fine. He dropped a bunch of rocks down after me too."

"Bastard."

"It's been hours since you left me though," he said. "I found the two women. One's got a head wound, and so do you, by the way," he said.

Lennox reached up and touched his head, then shrugged and said, "I can't really feel much. Always been a bit of a hard head when it comes to this stuff."

"Doesn't change the fact that you're injured and that we've got a wild card on the loose up here."

"We need to get help," Lennox said.

"That's not happening," Keane said. "He killed the Zodiac tubes."

"Jesus," he said. "What a pain in the ass. Now what?"

"I want to get you down where the women are," he said. "I've got the bag of gear we had stowed under the Zodiac. He didn't find that."

"Good," he said. "That at least has the blankets, a few emergency rations and the sat phone gear."

"Exactly. Can you stand up?"

Immediately Lennox tried to sit up, but he put his weight on his bad shoulder and collapsed back down again. "Son of a bitch," he said. "What's wrong with my shoulder?"

"He shot you," Keane said briefly. "Through and

through. In the fatty part of your shoulder."

"You mean, the muscle in my shoulder," Lennox corrected.

"Dude, whatever," he said with a grin. "Use your other arm and see if you can get back up again." Moments later, with Lennox standing, albeit a little shakily, Keane studied the rest of his friend and told him to take a couple steps.

He took several shaky steps and moved his legs around a bit, saying, "I could use some food and water, but I'm not doing too bad."

Keane handed him a protein bar and said, "We don't have much, so rations are definitely at a premium."

Lennox nodded and ate the bar slowly. "The shoulder's a bitch though," he said. "Everything here we'll need ropes for."

"Yeah, the shoulder'll hurt, but it doesn't look like the bullet did any real damage."

"So he hit me over the head and shot me?"

"I think he probably shot you, then came over and smacked you one for good measure. You went down, and he left you there. Or maybe he hit you from behind, then shot you and left, thinking he'd killed you."

"Seems a funny place to go down, with the bushes and all."

"He may have dragged you out of sight, so I couldn't find you," Keane said.

"Makes sense. So is this little asshole still here on the island, do you think?"

"I don't know," Keane said. "I haven't found him yet."

"Well, that seems like the first order of business."

"The first order of business is to get you down with the women," Keane said. "I can't keep running back and forth between two places."

"Right, but I'm not that badly injured," Lenox said, flexing his muscles and rotating his shoulder gently.

"Good," Keane said cheerfully. "Because you know I can't nursemaid you."

Lennox snorted. "The day I need a nursemaid—"

"I know. I know," he said. "Let's get you down to where the other two are."

It took twice as long, since they had to go a little slower to baby his shoulder and head and because they were constantly looking for whoever had shot him. "Do you even know if the women are still okay?"

"No. Not yet," Keane said. "I hope they are though."

"This guy thinks he's just gonna pick us off, right?"

"It's hard to say," he said. "When you think about it, the whole thing is just weird." Keane had to lead Lennox back around the long and slow way that he had found. It took several hours, and it was late by the time they finally made their way to the beach. He stopped, waited for Lennox to catch up and then pointed out the double doors that were opened.

Lennox shook his head. "Who the hell would even build that?"

"And why?" Keane replied. "I didn't get a chance to take much of a look inside. But we'll do that now."

"And how do you know she's even there?"

"The only way to know," he said, "is to walk over there and hope the asshole isn't waiting inside for us."

CHAPTER 6

S ANDRINE HEARD VOICES and peered through the wooden slats of the door to the cavern, not even sure why she was hiding. But, when Keane didn't return, she'd slowly grown more and more terrified. Instead of sounding worse, Brenda seemed to be sleeping much deeper, but she wasn't responding to any verbal suggestions or reacting to any physical stimuli. And that worried Sandrine too. She watched, looking for anybody to go with the voices. She wanted to rush out and exclaim they were saved, but, at the same time, she was damn afraid it would be another container of fish from that soldier guy, who had no intention of helping her and Brenda leave this island.

Worse than that was if he didn't come with more fish.

She didn't know where Keane and his buddy were, but she hoped they were still alive.

Her hands started to sweat as she sat curled up in an awkward position, leaning so she could see through a small hole near the bottom of one of the doors. As she stared out, she could finally see two men coming toward the shelter, one moving a little slower than the other. *Keane.*

He carried a large bag on his back, which is why she hadn't recognized him as the same man she had seen earlier. But he was talking to somebody beside him, so she assumed it was his friend.

She stood, relief washing over her. She stepped out and called to him. He looked over and raised a hand in greeting. She raced toward him, and, not even giving herself a chance to think, she threw herself into his arms. She blubbered as she cried out, "You didn't come back. I was so worried about you."

His arms wrapped around her and held her close. "I came back," he said. "I ran into a few problems, but I'm here."

Keane's voice was so reassuring and his body so strong and solid that he made her feel so much better yet again. She wiped her eyes, feeling hot tears burning in the corner of her eyes. "I'm sorry," she said. "I'm not usually this much of a wreck."

"Hey, don't worry about it," he said. "It's a stressful time right now." He motioned to his friend. "This is Lennox."

She smiled up at him, until she saw the blood on his head and on his shoulder. "Oh, God, did you fall?"

"No," he said. "I was hit from behind and shot—or vice versa. I'm not quite sure."

It took her a moment to understand what he meant. "Oh, my God. Oh, my God. Oh, my God," she cried out. "He tried to kill you?"

"Maybe," Lennox said. "He didn't stick around and finish the job, for which I'm mighty thankful."

Keane motioned for the three of them to move into the small shelter. "That rain will break again," he said, "and we'll get another deluge."

She looked up at the sky and nodded. "I'll catch more rainwater, if so."

"Have you seen the same man at all?"

She shook her head. "I haven't seen anybody," she cried

out. "Absolutely no one. That's why I'm so grateful to see you."

"Hey, I said I'd come back," he said gently.

She tossed him a wry look. "So you did. But I expected you back hours and hours ago."

He nodded. "I know. I had some trouble, and I had to find Lennox too."

"Where's the boat?" she asked as they reached the shelter. "When the storm clears, do you think we can get off of this island?" She hated the urgency in her voice and the anxiety. But, between Brenda and herself and now Lennox, she just wanted to get away.

"Well, we would if we could," Keane said, but his voice was grim.

She turned slowly to look at him. "What does that mean?"

"It means," he said, "that's possible but not immediately. Whoever attacked Lennox also slit the pontoons on the Zodiac."

All her hope slid away. "Seriously? He destroyed our way off this island?"

"Which means he has another way off," Lennox said. "We'll just have to find it."

She stared at him in shock. "We can't even get around the corner with the way the ocean's splashing up on the rocks. How will we possibly find any other way off here?"

"If one guy's here," Keane said, "then he has a way to get on and off. This is too inhospitable a place to stay long-term, unless he's got helicopter drop-offs or something else."

She nodded slowly. "That makes sense," she said. "But I don't understand what kind of a boat he could have that we wouldn't have noticed."

"He could have any kind," Keane said. "Look at how narrow your view is from here. You have the whole ocean out there, but you see just a sliver of it."

"Did you see anything when you were up above though?" she challenged him.

He grinned at her, loving her feistiness. "No, I haven't had time yet."

She paced the small space under the shelter. "But it'll get dark again," she said, "and we can't see anything until tomorrow."

"Which is why I'm leaving you with Lennox to help stand guard while I go up there to take another look around."

Immediately she protested. "What happens when you can't come back because somebody shoots you and hits you over the head?"

"Not going to happen again now that we're all aware of someone on the island who's unhappy with us," he said cheerfully. "And Lennox has weapons and comm devices. So, as soon as it's possible, he'll contact the coast guard, who is waiting to hear from us. And at 2000 hours, eight p.m. tonight, if they haven't heard from us, they'll set up a rescue."

She stared at him hopefully. "But they still can't come in while there's a storm, right?"

"Right," he said. "We were sent here for a purpose. To find you and Brenda. So somebody will come after us."

She let out a long, slow breath. "Well, thank God for that," she said. "So why do you even want to look for this guy then?"

"Because he's already attacked us, Lennox in particular," he said. "So I don't want him coming along and causing trouble for the coast guard either. The last thing we need is for a crew to come in, trying to rescue us, only to have this guy shooting them."

"No," she said faintly. "We don't want that at all." She dropped down beside her friend.

He squatted alongside her and asked, "How's she doing?"

"I don't know," she whispered. "She seems to be sleeping easier, yet it's deeper, like she's not even asleep, but—I don't know," she said brokenly. "If you nudge her and try to wake her, she doesn't do anything."

"Well, at the moment, she needs to sleep as much as possible," Lennox said. "I do have some thermal blankets in our bag. They're made for these emergency scenarios." He motioned at the pack on Keane's back. "Let's get that off and get some of this stuff set up."

Keane dropped the large duffel bag and straightened, rolling his shoulder blades back and forth.

"Is it heavy?" she asked.

He looked at her, and a smile kicked up the corners of his mouth. "See if you can lift it."

She frowned and walked over. She considered herself very fit, but she didn't know what weight was when it came to carrying it on her back. She thought forty pounds was a lot. As she tried to lift the duffel bag, she realized she couldn't even get the damn thing off the ground. She stared at him as Lennox bent to open it. Everything from food rations and water were in there, plus some electronic gear.

With great joy she accepted an emergency blanket, which she immediately wrapped her friend in. "This will make a huge difference for her," she said. "Thank you."

"You may want to make up a bit of a pillow with the

sand," Keane said, showing her how to do it.

With her friend hopefully much more comfortable, Sandrine returned and stared at the food. "Any chance of a little bit of food?" she asked hopefully.

"Absolutely," Keane said. Then he gave her a protein bar to start with and said, "When I get back, I'll go fishing too."

"I can set up something once I get this done," Lennox said.

"Okay, thanks," Keane said. "Just make sure you don't overdo it."

He laughed. "I've been fishing since I was a tadpole," he said. "I can do it in my sleep."

"Good enough," Keane said, then faced Sandrine. "I don't have much time before I lose the sunlight, so I'll leave," he said. "I want to check another quadrant of this island, and I'll need a couple hours, so it'll probably be dark when I get back. Okay?"

She bit her lip and stared at him. "I really don't like the idea of you leaving."

"I don't like the idea either," he said with a smile. "But I don't want to get ambushed or have somebody come in here with a machine gun and shoot us all dead."

She took a huge deep breath and slowly let it out. "I really didn't need that image in my head."

"Neither did I," he said. "So let me make sure it doesn't happen."

Unable to help herself, she gave him a hug and said, "Please hurry back."

"Will do," he said, as he stroked his thumb across her cheek and whispered, "Give Lennox some help if you can."

She nodded. "We'll be fine," she said, but she knew she was trying to reassure herself as much as him.

"Listen. Lennox has an extra gun, so, if a situation arose where you needed to look after yourself, make sure you use it."

"Right," she said. "We'll be fine. Go so you can get back again."

"Right. I'm gone." With that, he turned and walked down to the beach.

Lennox stared up at her from the ground.

She frowned at him. "Is it safe for him to go alone?"

"As safe as it is for any of us right now," he said. "Come on. Help me unpack some of this stuff and set up the comm unit. Then I'll go to the beach and set up a fishing line."

"You'll have to ensure that asshole's not watching us," she said. "That's how he chopped the rope that Keane was on." She pointed to the rope and watched as Lennox's face became a little more drawn and serious as he studied the coiled-up rope on the ground amid the rocks that had fallen.

"Keane is lucky to be alive," he muttered. "We can't have assholes like this running around."

"Exactly," she said. "It's been a pretty trying day. But some food would help."

"The bar not doing much for you?"

"No," she said. "It seems pretty sucky to complain when I'm healthy otherwise, but maybe because I'm healthy is why I'm also hungry," she said with a smile. She watched as Lennox sorted through the materials he had on hand and then asked him, "What will you use to catch fish?"

"You'd be surprised," he said. He had a small amount of wire that he cut and formed into hooks, then tied onto some line. He smiled and said, "I'll go try my luck. Otherwise, I'll set out a line on a stick and see if we can find a place to set it securely amid the rocks. Not to mention find something to use as bait." And he laughed obviously looking forward to the challenge.

"Good luck with that," she said. "I kinda want to come with you because I don't want to be left behind, but, at the same time, I don't want to leave my friend."

"Your friend is fine," he said. "Come with me if you want, but let's get going while the fish are moving. Once that storm comes in, they'll be gone."

She nodded and smiled. "Okay, I'm sold," she said. "Can I carry anything or help somehow?"

He bent down and picked up a stick off the ground. "Let's see if we can find more of these. I can tie a bunch together, but, if any decent-size fish are out there, I'll need something stronger for a fishing pole."

She nodded, and, as they hit the beach, she almost wanted to smile at the churning waves. It was too dangerous to leave now, even if they had the Zodiac. No way they'd get over these swells. Mother Nature was cranky right now; however, she was tossing them some long sticks. Sandrine walked out into the waves a little bit and grabbed several.

Lennox nodded and tied his line with the hooks onto the end of the bundle of sticks and cast it out into a small shoal on the right-hand side. "If anything's around, we should find something here."

She shook her head and said, "Never thought I'd be doing this today."

His grin was bright and cheerful as he flashed it in her direction. "We must be open to all opportunities in order to change the way we live," he said. "Sometimes change is good."

"Not today," she said darkly. "Not today."

KEANE KNEW HE didn't have much time before sunset fell, and he didn't want to go over the same ground, but he had to retrace his steps to a certain point in order to return to the first of the plateaus. Instead of circling around, he headed straight across to the trees on the far side. He hadn't mentioned anything to the others, but he thought he saw something in the back of the trees. It would make that plateau the most sensible location for the installation because it was the closest to the sea, yet still had a huge grassy area for camouflage.

With the descent of darkness coming soon, he had maybe an hour of fading daylight left. As soon as he hit the trees, he immediately melded into the shadows. He stopped and waited, listening for the sounds of anyone approaching. He'd crossed that pasture deliberately, hoping that someone would see him and would be forced to make a move. He couldn't understand why they would be here. Earthquake monitoring stations alone didn't wash. No way any of the monitoring was done manually.

No, this was something entirely different.

It could just be some guy was all alone and wanted to stay that way, but it was definitely odd. Sandrine had said he wore military fatigues, but she didn't know what kind, what country or whether they were real military uniforms or just some of the commercial-made gear often sold as army surplus. Everything was available online these days. Much to his disgust. He could get the plans for making bombs and all the components from various vendors without a problem. Huge online companies would deliver it to your front doorstep so you didn't even leave your house. Talk about enabling the psychos of the world.

When no sounds came from the trees around him, he crept a little bit farther into the expanse of trees—a band that appeared to be a couple hundred yards deep and a good one-quarter-mile long. He was right smack in the middle of it, and, in order to search it, he would check both sides, and that would be so easy. He kept walking right through until he hit the cliff face on the other side.

But, just when he thought he was at a dead-end, he saw another one of those tiny rock-face fissures. He walked through it to the other side to find another meadow plateau a little bit higher up as it climbed all the way through the fissure. As soon as he got outside again, he thought he heard a voice. Stepping behind the rock formation a little bit, he realized the voices were coming closer. Shit.

He quickly ran back to the trees and found himself a hiding spot off to the right and in the middle of the thickest of the bushes. There he sat and waited. From the sounds of those voices, two men headed toward him.

"The girls should be okay still," the one man said.

"You shouldn't have given them any food," the other one said, his voice harsh and caustic.

"Well, until we decide what we're doing with them," he said, "no need for them to suffer."

"A bullet would stop the suffering."

"We said, *no killing*," the first one snapped.

"What did you expect when you cut that rope?"

At that, the man groaned. "What the hell are they even doing here?"

"You know what they're doing. They're looking for the women. If we let them find the women, they'll take them and leave. Now you've made this a big incident."

"We're not even supposed to be here."

"And we aren't staying," he said. "It was just shitty tim-ing."

"Well, what was I supposed to do? Just let them drown?"

"Hell, yes. Then we wouldn't be in the position of kill-ing them now," the second man snapped. "Just because we were out in the boat at the time, you didn't have to point them out, and we didn't have to find them," he said. "We smashed up on the rocks ourselves. Our boat is useless now. You do realize that, don't you?"

"Yeah, but I did find them. We did bring them in, and we did save them. It would feel wrong to kill them now."

Keane's eyebrows shot up as he listened. He had his phone on Record, ensuring he had an accurate accounting of whatever was said.

"Killing is not in my nature. You knew that at the be-ginning. We didn't come here to kill people. We're supposed to just be scoping out the island to see if it would work or not."

"Well, the answer is yes. It would have worked, but now it won't because too many people know about it."

"We haven't done anything though," the first man pro-tested. "We didn't get a chance to set up repeating stations or anything. Besides, who gives a crap about these islands? They are completely deserted."

"Sure, but, without a boat, you're stuck," he said. "I sug-gest we signal our ship and leave."

"And let them die?" the first man asked cautiously. "We could just as easily tie them up and take them back to the mainland and dump them somewhere."

"Like in the ocean," the second man argued. "If you think I'm letting them go once they've seen my face, you're dreaming. No way in hell."

"Well, they've already seen me," the first man said, "so I don't think it makes much difference."

"No," the second man said. "It means that you made the mistake. You're the one who picked them up. You're the one who let them see you, so you're the one who needs to pop them one."

"What about the guy you shot?" the first man said. "What about him? He won't live, you know."

"Maybe we should check to make sure he's still there," the other man said. "I didn't get off that good of a shot."

"We're just supposed to be checking out the system to see if we could pick up those satellites and bounce the signals as planned," the first guy said. "Just because we're trying to set up a communication system that will operate on the US satellites doesn't mean it's top secret or anything."

"But we don't exactly have permission to be here, and it's for our use, no one else's," the second man said. "The mission is compromised and at risk because we've been seen."

"But it's not worth killing someone," the first man said. "Just because they saw us shouldn't matter. Especially if we decide the island won't work anyway."

"It won't work now," the second man snapped. "Just remember. We took money for this contract, so we still need to find a place to set up a couple repeating stations."

"I don't get why it has to be out in the ocean," he said.

"It's for smugglers. Remember? It's not that hard to figure out."

"Maybe, but they've been doing fine without this communication system so far. What the hell difference does it make?"

"It's a warning system, they said. And I don't know if I believe that or not, but we were hired to set it up, and that's what we'll do."

"It's not our kind of gig," the first man protested. "Nobody said anything about killing."

"No, but they told us what would happen if anyone found out what we were doing."

"They didn't say we'd be killed," he said.

"No, but maybe I should have made sure it was spelled out a little more plainly for you," the second man said derisively. After that came an odd silence.

His voice turning snarly, the first guy said, "Don't you start in on me."

"Whatever," the second guy said, his tone off a little. "Let's go take care of those women."

"I still don't like it," the first guy said.

As they walked past Keane, he considered his options. The second guy would shoot the two women without a thought, whether his no-kill partner wanted to or not. But they didn't know Lennox was there with the women. Keane had no way to give Lennox any warning though. Keane was desperate to see what they had going on up in the back of this plateau and also where their ship was, but he couldn't let them fire on the women and Lennox.

Torn, Keane once again checked his phone and his comm system but got nothing. Just as he headed around to get in front of the gunmen, the two had stopped and stood there, arguing.

The first man raised his hands in frustration. "Look. We shouldn't leave all our stuff alone. I'll go talk to the woman," he said. "You go back and take care of the gear. I'd like to get on this ship and out of here overnight."

"Yeah, well, if you hadn't gone and cut up their Zodiac, we could have used that to get to our ship."

"I know," the first man said. "That was a bad decision. Much better if we had used it for ourselves and just left them here. We wouldn't have to kill them. They would have died on their own."

"Sure," the second guy said, laughing. "Perishing from lack of fresh water and food. That's a nice way to go."

"Whatever," he said. "Look. I'll go down, like I said. You head back."

"I'll head back, but I'll pack up first and make sure that the ship gets our signal."

"Right," the first man said, "but we should change our pickup spot to the new cove down where the women are."

"I don't think so. I don't want anything to go wrong with getting our ship in here."

"Well, they'll be pissed that we lost our boat as it is."

"Yeah, they will," the second guy said. "Just so you know, I'll blame you for that one too. We wouldn't have capsized if you hadn't been trying to pick up those women."

"Whatever," the first man said. "I told you that I couldn't just do nothing and watch them drown."

"Well, right now you don't have much choice," the second man said. "Go on, and I'll be down at the base soon enough. And take it easy. We can't afford any more accidents." And on that note, they parted.

Stuck, Keane decided to follow the second man, putting his trust in Lennox to handle the first man. These guys were watching and waiting for somebody to come their way. Keane didn't see a weapon on the first man, but he was probably the one Sandrine saw, and she had confirmed earlier that he was armed. Keane now knew the second one had been the guy who shot Lennox.

Clearly he was the more dangerous of the two, so it would be good if Keane could take him out. He waited until the second guy strode past, muttering all the while about imbeciles, fools and shitty-ass partners. After waiting a safe period of time, Keane crept up behind him through the same crevice walkway to see the guy with several boxes of supplies and his own gear.

He talked on a radio, signaling for the ship. "Change of location. Come in at the cove."

A voice crackled on the other end. "Storm coming in."

"Right. Come and get us first."

"Can't. Too much turbulence."

"We don't want to stay here overnight," the second man said.

"Can't come in. You can come out though. We'll come in as close as we can, and then we'll pick you up."

Dropping the microphone, the man swore. Now he had to tell the contact guy that they had lost their boat. Finally, as he sat here scratching his head, the radio crackled.

"Over and out."

"Boat isn't seaworthy."

Silence came first. Then *crackle, crackle, crackle.*

"I said the boat is no longer seaworthy. We can't get out to you. We need a pickup."

"Storm." *Crackle.* "No pickup."

The other guy swore and stomped around. "You fucking have to," he roared. "I don't want to stay out here another fucking night."

This time not even a crackle came from the radio.

Throwing the handset into the pile of gear, the second guy stormed around before stopping and glaring toward the ocean.

Following the direction of the man's gaze, Keane couldn't see any boat, but its location was obvious.

If his partner hadn't destroyed Keane's Zodiac, these two gunmen could have made their way out to their own ship and could have been picked up. If that ship couldn't get in due to the weather conditions, the coast guard probably couldn't come in close enough either. The coast guard cutters were something else, and they could run in the open sea in all kinds of weather. However, it would take a small boat to come to the island, so they could get on board and get back out again. And, with the waves coming in as strong as they were, Keane doubted anybody was going anywhere anytime soon.

Just then the guy spun around, as if he had felt Keane's gaze on him. Keane melted back a little bit farther into the rocks, desperately looking for a place to hide. He could climb up. A couple footholds and handholds were here, and a bit of a ledge was up above. Taking the chance that the scrambling noise he made as he climbed wouldn't be heard, he made his way up to the small ledge and stopped. The guy was halfway down the path with a handgun drawn as he searched his surroundings.

Keane stayed silent, studying what was in front of him. It looked like electronics and maybe a repeating station, with various parts and pieces. Some of that must have been airlifted in, since no way these two gunmen could have carried all that up the rock cliffs. But, as Keane studied it all again, much of it could be broken down, and, with four or five trips, these men could have done the delivery job easily enough.

Keane wondered if his own phone would work with that

station. He pulled out his phone and checked, but he wasn't getting any signal. He didn't have the other equipment with him either. He should have brought that too, damn it. Or maybe he could get access to the handset down below and contact the coast guard directly.

He knew the channel they were on. It was a marine radio, and that was the best thing for out here, an equal match to the one he had left with Lennox. If Keane could get his hands on that, it would help considerably. He hunkered lower and waited for the man to come closer. Best thing would be to take out this asshole and to remove him from the game completely. And, if Keane didn't kill him, the least Keane could do was knock him out and repay the favor for what he did to Lennox. And then the marine radio would be his.

He crouched and waited.

CHAPTER 7

"WHAT DO I hear?" Sandrine murmured from the cave's doorway, her gaze scaling the rocks. "I thought I heard footsteps."

Lennox shook his head. "I'm not hearing anything. But an odd stillness is in the air."

"What does that mean?"

"It means that something is stirring."

She thought about that and realized what an oxymoron it was. How could *stirring* mean something was *still?* She shook her head, about to say something, when he grabbed her hand in warning. She saw somebody coming around the corner down at the bottom. "Is it Keane?"

"No," Lennox said in a harsh whisper. "Get behind that door."

"What about you?"

"He can't see me yet."

But Lennox did shuffle enough that the guy couldn't see him until he came up to the doors. "I'll move a little bit too."

"Unless he followed the footprints," she said, suddenly pointing to the line of them.

"But it's also the tracks that Keane made," he said. "And the two of us."

She nodded, then looked at the four fish sitting off to

the side of her now. "I really wish we could cook them."

"Once we deal with this guy, we will," he said.

"And what about Keane?" She'd been asking that same question for the last hour or more. It was almost dark. "This guy coming now is not bringing us food."

"And he does have a handgun," Lennox said smoothly.

She studied the man approaching. "It's the same man from before."

"Good," he said. "It would sure be nice if he was the only one."

"It seems doubtful," she said, "but I don't know."

As the guy walked up, he took a look at the rock cliff, saw the rope coiled at the bottom and frowned, looking around, probably hoping to see Keane's body.

"Now he knows somebody else is loose," she murmured.

"Yeah. Now the question he'll have is whether Keane is here or if he left already."

At that moment, the guy seemed to realize he could be in danger. He pulled his handgun from his holster and held it against his leg, but his footsteps were loud as he approached. "Hello," he said.

She poked her head around before Lennox could stop her. "Hello," she said. "Did you bring a boat this time?"

He shook his head. "No, I didn't.

"Food?"

He shook his head again.

"Oh," she whispered. "I was really hoping we could get out of here."

"Not tonight," the gunman said. "What happened to the guy who fell?"

She looked where the rope was and shrugged. "Did you see him fall?" she asked.

He shrugged. "I saw him fall, yeah."

"He got up, and he held his head and moved funny," she said. "He headed toward the water, and I haven't seen him since."

He looked at her, surprised, and looked at the rope. "Seriously?"

"Yeah, some rocks came down on him," she said. "He looked pretty woozy."

She could feel the stillness from Lennox beside her and didn't know why he didn't just pop this guy one. She quickly surmised that, in these tight quarters, as long as the stranger had a handgun, it would be too dangerous. Oh, for a sharpshooter up in the hills to take him out. She didn't even know if the gunman was responsible for any of this hell that she was going through, but this guy had obviously cut that rope which tossed Keane to the ground below.

"When are you getting off the island?" she asked.

"Our boat's damaged," he said. "So it'll be a while."

At the term *our*, she could feel Lennox stiffening, almost like a caged animal ready to blow beside her. "You mean, you're not alone?" she asked.

As if realizing the slip of his tongue, he shrugged and said, "No. I got a buddy here with me."

"How come he hasn't come down here?" she asked, curious.

"He's not feeling too good," the guy said.

Hesitantly, as if offering an olive branch, she said, "My name is Sandrine."

"Nice to meet you, Sandrine," he said with a hint of a smile. "I plucked you out of the ocean," he said. "You nearly drowned, you know."

She brightened. "Was that you?"

"Yes," he said. "It was me. What about your friend. How is she?"

She looked down at her feet and said, "She's not great. I can't wake her up anymore."

Immediately he frowned. "I'm sorry. That's got to be tough."

"Well, if you had a boat, I could get her off the island," she said hopefully.

"Not happening," he said. "At least not while the storm is going on. Maybe tomorrow."

"So, another night here? It's pretty damn unpleasant," she whispered. "Especially with no food or fire."

"I told you to light a fire," he said, returning to the caustic tone he had used earlier.

"Remember that part about no matches and no dry wood?" she reminded him, even though she knew that they had stacks of sticks inside now, something Lennox had insisted on.

"I got a few matches here," he said, "but I don't have any paper for you." He took a pack of matches from this pocket, and, walking closer, he tossed it to her.

She stepped out and caught them. "Well, I guess I'll take what I can get," she said, "but it won't help much."

He shrugged and said, "If you've got a guy hidden in there," he said, "you need to tell him to come out gently with his hands up."

She looked at him in surprise. "What guy?"

"The guy who fell when I chopped off the rope," he said, his tone turning mean. "I really won't take it kindly if I have to come in there and shoot him."

She gasped in fear. "You cut his rope to kill him, didn't you?"

"We don't like intruders," he said. "Sometimes you just have to bite the bullet and do the hard things."

"And what hard things are you talking about now?" she asked.

He lifted the handgun and said, "My buddy doesn't think you should stay alive."

She cried out and immediately stepped back. "Why would you do that?" she whispered. "Obviously you saved our lives. Why would you not do everything you could to keep us alive now?"

"He says you're a problem and that you need to be taken care of."

"I promise I won't be a problem," she said.

"You already are, apparently," he said heavily. "I'm sorry. I should have just let you drown in the first place." When he lifted the handgun, as if to shoot her, she gasped and dashed under cover again, and one shot rang out. He'd hit the wood beside her face. She cried out and whispered, "Please don't," she said. "Even if you leave us here, we'll still die. You don't have to shoot us."

"I told him that," the guy said, "but he didn't seem to like the idea."

"Doesn't matter what he says though, does it?" she asked. "Aren't you the boss?"

He laughed. "I'd like to think so, but I don't see myself keeping that title."

"But it is your deal here, isn't it?"

"Well, I'm the one who made the deal," he said, "but somehow my buddy has gotten a little bit more assertive than I expected. There wasn't supposed to be any killing."

"Well, if you're planning on shooting me," she said, "can't you at least explain why?"

"It's got to do with smuggling," he said, "but that's about all I can tell you."

"Shit," she whispered under her breath. Her eyes grew hard as she imagined just how much could be smuggled through this area. From drugs to sex trafficking. "This is a deserted island. It doesn't make any sense that this has got anything to do with us."

"It doesn't have anything to do with you," he said. "It's literally a case of you being in the wrong place at the wrong time. But then so are we," he said. "I wasn't exactly planning on having to kill you."

"Please don't," she whispered. "We've already survived a pretty horrific ordeal. Can't you at least just let nature take its course?"

"I wouldn't mind that," he said. "But my buddy—"

She heard him coming closer and closer. She grabbed a chunk of Lennox's hair. He nodded ever-so-slightly. "Please," she said, "I'm begging you. Don't do this."

"It won't do any good," he said. "If I don't kill you, my buddy will," he said. Another shot rang out. "Come on back out."

"So you can shoot me?" she cried out.

"Well, I'll shoot you whether you come out or not."

"Then you'll have to come get me," she said. "You'll have to come in here and shoot a woman who's already dying. And you'll have to shoot me."

"Nah, I won't shoot her," he said. "You're right. She is already dying."

"Then leave me with her," she cried out passionately. Even though she knew Lennox was here, it was just all too real of a possibility that this guy would come in and shoot her between the eyes. "You know there's no way for us to get off the island, so we'll be dead soon enough anyway."

She could feel him hesitate. "Please," she said. She peered through the cracks and watched as he lowered the gun.

He took a few steps back and said, "If he finds out I didn't kill you—"

"I promise I won't say anything to him. I'll stay inside and make sure he doesn't see us," she said.

"I don't know if that'll work though," he said. "He's pretty tricky."

"I really don't want to die this way," she said.

"Okay, but you're not allowed to sit there and blame me," he said.

"No," she said. "Of course not." But she wasn't exactly sure what she wasn't supposed to blame him for. Of course this was ridiculous. He had been trying to kill her, but he agreed to back away. "Thank you," she cried out.

"Whatever," he said. Just when she thought he was done, he stopped, then turned around and fired into the wooden doors.

She cried out and moaned. Then all of a sudden she went silent. She looked down at Lennox, who had one shot lined up. He took a slow and deep breath and popped off one shot. As she watched through the slats of the wooden doors, the gunman stood still for a long moment, then slowly fell to the ground. She glanced at Lennox and whispered, "Is he dead?"

"Yeah," he said. "He's dead."

She curled up in a ball and burst into tears. "Thank God," she whispered.

"It's okay," he said, "but we have to move the body."

"I know," she said. "I know, but I'm too damn tired."

"I got it," he said and hopped up and headed out with his handgun still at the ready.

When he got to the body, she realized that she couldn't let him move it on his own. Not with his shoulder injury. He'd likely start bleeding again. Quickly she raced behind him. A pool of blood was under the guy, and the bullet hole in his forehead was unmistakable. She gasped when she saw that half his head had blown away.

"Don't look," Lennox said, as he reached down with one hand and grabbed the guy by the back of the collar, lifting and dragging him toward the shelter.

"Why are we taking him here? Why not over in the corner and just bury him?"

He stopped, and a look of realization crossed his face. "I guess if we're here for a while, we don't want this guy getting smelly beside us."

"No," she said. "We don't."

Looking around, he found a little bit of a depression, a short distance from the shelter. He dragged the dead man over there, dropped him in and then kicked sand over him. Sandrine followed suit, and, using the lid from the container as a little shovel, before long they had a mound over him. Then she went back to the cavern's doors, and, using the same lid, she swept away the drag marks and footprints. She wiped away all the footprints back to the water, and then, with Lennox standing and watching her, she slowly returned to him. "I don't know where Keane is," she said, "but he needs to come back. It's getting very dark out."

"He will," Lennox said. "He will."

KEANE'S JUMP WAS clean, but the other guy had that sixth sense and looked up just as Keane landed on him. The guy roared as Keane's weight hit him on the top of his head and crushed him into the ground. There was no room to fight, and they were both on top of each other in a very narrow space. The guy tried to back up, but Keane got one hand free and pounded him in the face. The guy shook his head, backing up a little bit from the blow.

"Who the fuck are you?" he roared.

Keane tried to get another fist punch in, but there was no room. The other guy backed up a little bit more, trying to get his handgun up, but Keane got a sideways kick in, sending the gun flying harmlessly behind him. The guy swore, then turned and tried to race toward the gun. Keane followed and jumped him, sending the guy flying to his gut down in the pathway. There Keane pounded the stranger's face into the rock underfoot, once, twice, three times. After the third punch, the guy didn't move again. Keane quickly pocketed the handgun, then grabbed the guy by his arms and dragged him onto the narrow pathway where he had more light.

There he stopped and took a look at him. He checked for ID and found his name was Wilson. Keane didn't know the name. He laid everything out and took several photographs of it, then put it all back in the guy's wallet. Wilson had a hefty stack of cash with him too. Keane checked his other pockets and found a little notebook filled with names and phone numbers.

All good. Keane put that into his pocket too and then, dragging the guy farther inside, tied him up with rope he found with the guy's gear. Keane waited, hoping the guy would wake up, but Wilson wasn't showing any signs of stirring. Keane went through everything in his stash, finding a lot of gear that would send out a signal—similar to a lighthouse. But once it was triggered by a boat close by, it looked like it could probably turn on a light. He thought about it and shrugged. "Looks like a smuggler's deal."

"Not quite," the other guy murmured.

Wilson was awake. "So, what is it?"

"We were hired by them to set up a repeating station. They wanted to use it for signals. Sometimes, with the storms that come out here, it's really hard to find these rocks."

"Did you crash into them?"

The guy stayed silent for a bit. Finally, he asked, "Who are you?"

"Well, I'm not involved with smugglers," he said. "I came looking for the two women."

"Ah, shit. Those damn women," he said.

"Yeah, those damn women. People care about them. All you had to do was help them," Keane added, "and nobody would have given a shit about what you were doing here."

"Maybe so, but we couldn't take the chance. The people we accepted the contract from are not exactly friendly."

"Well, if you hadn't killed our Zodiac," he said, "I'd have been out of here with the women already."

"That idiot, Adam," he said. "he wasn't supposed to do that."

"You guys could have taken it yourself."

"Exactly. Like I said, he's an idiot."

The last thing Keane wanted to do was take this Wilson guy back to where the others were, but Keane couldn't take the chance of Wilson escaping and coming up behind them and causing trouble. Keane really wanted answers, but some of the answers would be found in their gear. He studied what was here and went through their personal stuff. "We'll pool resources."

He wasn't exactly sure what he should take with him, but Keane would need that bag of food supplies for sure. He quickly assembled what he could into one bag and left several other bags tucked under the rock face, in case he needed to come back for them. And then, walking over to his tied-up prisoner, he said, "Get up."

"I can't go anywhere if you keep me tied up," he said. "This island is treacherous."

"Well, you were planning on killing those poor women," Keane said. "Why should I give a shit if you live or die?"

The man closed his eyes. "This has been a shit deal from the beginning."

"Why'd you take it then?" Keane asked. He kept glancing toward where his group was, knowing that time was running out and that it would be even more treacherous in the dark. "Come on. We need to join the others."

"What others?" he asked. "My buddy already went ahead and shot them. You missed him."

"Well, my guy that you shot is down there with the women, and he's armed, so I wouldn't count on it," Keane said brutally. When he saw the look in the man's eyes, Keane nodded and said, "So right about now your buddy is probably dead."

His prisoner swore and closed his eyes. "Adam always was an idiot. He should have gone in quietly, seeing the lay of the land, and then shot the guy first."

"Yeah. Well, maybe he did. But Lennox isn't exactly a fool when it comes to this stuff."

"The problem is, we don't have our boat and can't get a

ride out until morning," Wilson whined.

"Neither can we," Keane said. "So let's get everybody down in one place," he said. "You won't fare so well out in the elements here overnight."

"It's just rain," his prisoner growled. "No predators are on this island. It's fucking uninhabitable."

"Oh, there's plenty of them," Keane said. "They're just all on two legs."

With that, the guy groaned and stood. His hands were tied in front of him. He looked at his feet and said, "Unless you're carrying me," he said, "no fucking way I can go up and down these paths." Looking at the bag Keane carried over his shoulder, Wilson asked, "And you're taking our fucking gear too?"

"Remember that part about pooling our resources to get through the night?" Keane said. "You've got food. Those women need it."

"It's not much," he said. "I know that idiot Adam already delivered biscuits and fish."

"One meal for two women every second day is not enough."

"It's never enough," he said, yawning. He sagged back onto the rocks. "Just leave me here."

"And then what?" Keane said. "You want me to come back for you while you're sitting in your own shit in the morning?"

The prisoner's eyes snapped wide open, and he glared at him.

"You didn't have to order the women to be shot either," Keane said, completely unsympathetic. "Now let's go." He kicked him again to the ground, facedown.

The guy snorted. "What do you expect me to do like

this?"

But Keane was already carefully working at his ankles. He changed the ropes, and, by the time he stepped back, got Wilson to stand again, the guy had two feet of slack in the rope between his legs, which would allow him to maneuver. "Now walk."

The guy looked at the ropes, surprised. "Not bad, but it won't help when it comes to climbing though those rock pathways," he said, "but I can at least walk a bit." He took several small steps, then said, "This will take us fucking forever."

"Well, I don't have forever," he said, "so I'll leave you to work your way down there on your own." And he walked past the guy.

As soon as he disappeared from sight, the guy called out, "Wait for me!"

"Hurry up then."

Keane waited in the darkness for the other man to catch up. Wilson moved really slow. Keane could adjust the rope and give him an extra six inches, but the more room he gave him, the more dangerous it was too. Keane turned and kept on walking the pathway. When they finally got to the other side, he walked out into the trees and stepped to the side, so that he could walk beside his prisoner. "What the hell are you guys even doing here?" he asked.

"Just setting up a repeating station," the guy said in a noncommittal voice.

But Keane had already heard an awful lot before. "For the smugglers?"

The guy just shrugged.

"That really doesn't make any sense."

"They're around here all the time," he said. "This band

of islands is well known on the maps, but they've still had several crashes. They just thought it would help if they had a repeating station here. Plus they'd have better telecommunications, and it would give them a way to track the islands."

"I'm surprised no lighthouses are out here."

"I know. Lots of islands in this area are treacherous," he said.

"You ever come on these islands?"

"No," he said. "Never. I'm not a boat guy. We ended up crashing our boat into the rocks when Adam saved those women."

Keane looked at him with interest. "Well, it was nice of you to save them."

"We should have let them drown anyway. We would have had our boat, gotten our work done and been gone. Instead we've got the goddamn women to deal with, no boat, and we have to wait for a pickup. Not to mention you asshats."

"Will the smugglers be pissed about the boat?"

"With our luck, they'll probably take our damn paychecks for it."

"That's a possibility too," Keane said with a nod. "Presumably it wasn't very big if it capsized with the extra women."

"Capsized trying to get the women in," he said. "I was on the back end with the motor, but it wasn't very stable. Once he got the one halfway in, and he tried to help the second one, it completely unseated us. When I went over to help—"

"A bad wave hit you broadside, and the whole thing went over."

"Exactly," he said. "And then all Adam would talk about

was saving them."

"Which was the right thing to do."

"But they became a problem, and, without that boat, we couldn't get off here."

"Unless you'd been smart enough to take our boat," Keane said.

"That wasn't me. That was Adam again."

"Are you sure Adam didn't have ulterior motives, keeping you guys on the island?"

His buddy looked at him in shock. "No. Why would he?"

"Well, why would you intentionally sabotage a Zodiac with a big powerful motor on the back end, knowing that you needed a boat to get off this island yourself?" Keane asked, studying the other man's face.

"I don't know why he did that," Wilson said reluctantly. "He gets into these weird moods where he thinks he's like some Rambo guy. And, if he got into some mind-set like that, he would have taken that knife he has and just plunged it into the hilt."

"Exactly what he did," Keane said. "It just doesn't make any sense, considering you guys were stuck on the island yourselves."

"Well, I don't know what the hell sense that guy makes," he said. "He's the one who made the deal for this whole thing anyway."

"So he just hired you to come along?"

"More or less. I'm the one who does installations like this one all over the place. But I've never done one on an island like this."

"So, it's all different for you."

"Absolutely. I can't say I'm terribly impressed either."

"And you did check on all the little details with your buddy?"

"I don't know what you're trying to say," he said.

"I'm just wondering if the deal really is the way you said it was. That's all."

"Of course it is. Why wouldn't it be?"

"Who the hell knows?" Keane said. "I'm just making conversation." But he was also making his prisoner think. He didn't know what Adam was up to with any of this deal. "Does your ship out there know that you guys need a lift?"

"Yes," he said.

"Interesting," he said, "and what did they tell you?"

"Basically that—I hope you're not suggesting that Adam wanted us to stay here overnight," Wilson said slowly.

"I don't know what I'm suggesting," he said. "It just made no sense to damage the Zodiac."

"I know," Wilson said, but his voice was thoughtful.

They crossed the meadow as soon as they came out of the trees and headed to the steep stairs. As they got there, he said, "Let's see if you can walk down the stairs at all."

Wilson took a few hesitant steps and then hopped down one, using the wall to help. Moving slowly, they made it to the last two stairs, where he slipped and fell. He swore as he landed on the hard rock and sand below. "I didn't need that," he said, shuffling himself into a sitting position.

Keane reached down, picked him up and helped him to stand. "Maybe not," he said, "but we're down here now." They continued until they came around the cove edge to see the wooden structure. He pointed at it and said, "Did you guys make that?"

He shook his head. "No, it was already here."

That response added to the disquiet in Keane's consciousness. "Are you sure Adam cut up the Zodiac?"

"No, but he did mention it." Wilson looked at Keane and glared. "I gave him shit for it, and he didn't deny it or anything." Keane just nodded. "Why? What are you suggesting?"

"Another party may be here," he said. "Why the hell would anybody put up this shelter?"

"Maybe somebody else was stranded here too," Wilson said.

"If Adam had said he hadn't done in the Zodiac, would you have believed him?"

"I didn't know it was punctured," he said, "until I came and saw it myself." He stared around, worry creasing his face. "Besides, if another group's here," he said, "that's bad news."

"True enough," Keane said. "That's one of the reasons I'm asking."

"I don't know who it would be."

"I'm afraid it could be some of your own guys," he said. "What are the chances you two have become redundant?"

"Hell no," he said. "That's not possible."

"Why not?" Keane asked.

"Well, they would have taken us out before now, if that was the case."

"Maybe. Or maybe not. Maybe they couldn't find you. Maybe they only found one of you."

"Do you think Adam's dead?" His voice had turned harsh. "If he is, it's probably you guys who killed him."

"Well, if he came shooting at my buddy or those women, Adam would be dead," Keane said.

"He didn't want to get rid of them, but, once he makes a decision, it's like a switch goes off in his head, and he heads into this other zone."

"And he's not really a soldier, is he?"

"No," he said. "He just likes all that gear. He's a wanna-be soldier."

"I was afraid of that."

"Why?" Wilson asked.

"Because those are the worst kind."

"Whatever," he said. "It's not like you're a fucking soldier. What do you care?"

"I *am* a soldier," he said. "Navy. And I do care."

"Again, whatever. Doesn't make a damn bit of difference. He'll be up there with everybody else."

Keane didn't argue the point, but he'd already seen the small mound off to the side, and, as far as he was concerned, a body was likely there. He kept Wilson moving forward at a steady pace, and, when they got nearer, Keane called out, "Hey! You guys there?"

When no answer came, he frowned and pulled the handgun from his pocket.

"What's the matter?" Wilson asked. "Don't you think your friends will be there?"

"No. I don't know that they are," he said, feeling his gut twist. He looked at his prisoner, who was grinning. "What did your friend plan to do?"

"He was just supposed to take them out," he said. "How he did that, I don't know. He does have a decent imagination though."

As they made it to the front of the enclosure, he looked inside at the gun at the ready to see that it was empty. "Shit." *Where were they?* Then he heard a hoot. Turning, he hooted back. Moments later he saw Lennox and Sandrine coming around the far side, where they had just entered via the beach.

Sandrine raced toward them and threw herself into his arms. He wrapped her up close, loving this sense of welcome. With her crushed tight against him, he looked at his prisoner, staring at the floor. Keane watched as the emergency blanket moved. Keane whispered, "How is she?"

"I'm not sure," Sandrine replied, quickly moving to check her friend. She pulled the blanket down a bit to see Brenda staring up at her. She smiled. "Brenda! How are you?"

"I feel like shit," she said, "and I'm so tired. It also feels like, if I move, I'll be sorry."

Sandrine chuckled. "That is true. Head injuries always make you feel that way."

"But I'm okay, aren't I?" Brenda asked, her voice weak and anxious.

"Now that you're awake and talking and looking a little more normal, I would say yes," she replied. "I, for one, am very grateful to see you back in the land of the living."

Brenda smiled and looked up. "Who are these men?"

"Well, these two," she said, pointing at Keane and Lennox, "came to rescue us."

At that, Brenda smiled and said, "Good timing for me to wake up."

"Very good timing," Sandrine replied joyfully. This was a wonderful reunion.

"Who is the other man?" Brenda studied the prisoner, her gaze frowning at his hands. "And why is he tied up?"

Sandrine looked at Keane and whispered, "Who is he?"

"He's your buddy's partner," he said. "He's also the one who shot Lennox." Keane turned to study Lennox, worried about the confrontation that he assumed had occurred in his absence. But Lennox appeared none the worse for wear and had a relaxed look on his face, as if he had not a care in the world. "What were you guys doing around the corner?"

"Seeking a change of pace," Lennox said with a smile.

Then he held up his hand, and Keane noted several fish were on the line. "Good, so we get to eat tonight."

"Only if we find something to burn for a fire," Sandrine said. "I'm not eating them raw."

"We've got some emergency fuel and a small campfire stove," he said, "so we can cook those. No problem."

With his prisoner off to the side, Keane dropped the huge bag from his back and said, "Besides, we have their supplies now too."

"Good," Lennox said with a hard glance at the new arrival. "So you're the asshole who shot me, huh?"

Wilson stared up at him. "Jesus Christ! How can you be alive after I shot you and clubbed you over the head?"

"Good to confirm it was you," Lennox growled. "I'll be happy to return the favor."

"What else was I supposed to do? I didn't have a clue who you were."

"You always shoot strangers?"

"These men were here to rescue us," Sandrine said, outraged.

"Well, we didn't know that," Wilson said, "and we didn't care. We didn't want anybody poking around here."

"Oh, I hear you," she snapped. "But your buddy tried to kill us."

At that, Wilson stopped and stared. Then he said, "*Tried?*"

She nodded slowly. "He tried. He didn't succeed."

And, just like that, Wilson seemed to cave in on himself. "Are you saying Adam's dead?"

"Yes," Lennox said calmly. "When people fire at me, I have this thing about firing back."

"That kid didn't know how to shoot anything," he said. "The gun was more for show and to make him feel proud."

"Maybe," Lennox said, "but those bullets were real."

Wilson winced. "I hear you there. He prided himself on that."

"Well, he won't anymore."

"God damn it," he said. "The kid wasn't yet thirty years old."

"We've also got another problem," Keane said. "We need to figure out if we're alone on the island."

"You mean, more than our two separate groups?" Lennox asked, narrowing his gaze. "Why would you think that?"

"I'm not convinced that Adam destroyed the Zodiac."

"Did he say he did?"

"Well, he said something about it, yes. But it doesn't seem logical that he would have done it, since they needed that boat to get off the island themselves. They apparently wrecked their boat when they picked up the girls. If they'd taken our Zodiac and left us behind, I would understand. That's logical. But to slash our boat so that it was no more valuable than the piece of junk they crashed on the rocks makes no sense, and I'm thinking maybe some third party sabotaged it, so Wilson and Adam couldn't leave the island either."

"So somebody came in and cut up the Zodiac and then left again, hoping that Wilson and Adam died right along with us?" Lennox looked from Keane to Wilson. "That's pretty cold."

"Well," Keane added, "I'm not sure our third-party knew about us per se. But he knew about Wilson and Adam for sure."

"Regardless, all of it is ridiculous," Sandrine cried out. She walked closer to Keane, her hand instinctively reaching out.

He was surprised to see his hand reaching back, as if a bond had formed between the two of them. Plus, every time he arrived, she came to him like a homing pigeon.

"Why would anybody sabotage a boat on an island?" Wilson asked.

"You tell us," Keane said in a mild tone of voice. "Why would somebody sabotage a boat?"

CHAPTER 8

S ANDRINE TURNED TO Keane and frowned. "You're saying it was deliberately damaged so nobody could use it?"

"So nobody could leave." Keane nodded.

She stared at him. "Then wouldn't it have been better if it was the guy we shot? Adam, was it? The guy who brought us the fish in the plastic container?"

Wilson nodded. "That was Adam. And that was our dinner that he gave you, by the way."

"Well, I appreciated that, and we both certainly needed it. But I sure didn't appreciate him coming back and shooting the place up tonight."

"Yeah, that'd be him too. He went nuts at times. He was normal most of the time. Then sometimes he would just go off half-cocked."

"Yes, I saw both sides of him. He was a little bit scary."

"It's also why he had trouble finding work and why some of his friends were a little bit off as well."

"And maybe he was also somebody the bosses could afford to get rid of," Keane said. "Maybe even a liability."

"I don't like your theories," Wilson said, "but it's possible."

"But you did contact your ship, and they said they couldn't come in tonight, right?"

"Yes, and I told them that we'd already crashed our boat."

"Were they pissed?"

"There was so much static that I couldn't really tell."

"Right," Keane said, nodding. "I wouldn't be at all surprised if somebody else didn't come in and take out the Zodiac, then checked out the lay of the land to find you. Chances are good that *that* someone is still here."

"And then will come back and pick them up?" she asked. "I want to be close by when that hap—" She stopped, surprised when Keane's arm tightened around her.

He whispered, "No, you don't."

She looked at him in outrage. "I do so. I want to go home."

"These men are smugglers, who you want nothing to do with," he said. "And, if they think that you'll interfere in their plans in any way or could tell tales afterward, they'll drop you where you stand. And, unfortunately for you, they're likely to use you hard before that happens."

She stared at him as all the color drained from her cheeks. "Jesus Christ," she whispered. "What kind of mess have we gotten into here?"

"Well, for that, you can blame Wilson and his buddy Adam. They rescued you from drowning at sea and brought you to this island, but I think it was a case of going from the fat into the fire," he said.

Her gaze went from one to the other, and then she shook her head. "Well, now you guys have to get us off this island, some way or another," she said, "because I refuse to be a toy tossed around between men, and I've already fought long and hard to keep Brenda with me," Sandrine snapped. "So it's up to you guys to keep us alive. You can get us off here somehow, can't you?" She studied Keane, and, when he smiled with just a twitch of his lips, she nodded and said, "Right. You've already got that organized, haven't you?"

He shrugged and said, "Well, maybe."

She smiled and reached up and kissed him on the cheek. "That better be a definite yes, not just a maybe." But, in her heart of hearts, she already knew that she'd picked the right side. And this guy would help her get her injured friend back home again. As long as nothing else went wrong.

Even knowing something else was going on or that he had some plans was enough to make Sandrine feel a little better. Then she wasn't so sure again as she stepped back into the little shelter and said, "I guess we just hunker down and wait for morning."

"To a certain extent," he said. "We'll spread out a little though. Otherwise, it'll get very close in here."

"Well, I'd rather be outside anyway," Wilson snapped.

Keane looked around, nodded and said, "That's not a bad idea." Then he helped him move outside of the double doors. Leaving the doors wide open for a breeze to come through, he looked at Sandrine and said, "I'll sit out here too."

She nodded but quickly chose to go where Brenda was. Sandrine sat beside her friend and whispered, "How are you doing?"

"Well, against all odds," her friend whispered back, "I'm still on the planet."

At that, Lennox chuckled. "And a good way to have it," he said. "Packing your body out of here would be a bitch."

Brenda gurgled with laughter. "I imagine it would be. Though I must confess that, while I'm grateful to be alive, I would much rather be in a five-star hotel, holding a glass of red wine, staring out over the city lights … from the bathtub."

"Ooh," Sandrine said, "if we're dreaming, I'll take that steak and prawns now." She kept up the light banter with her friend as she studied how fatigued she was. She asked Lennox, "I know we said we would cook, but is that anytime soon?"

Lennox nodded and got up, then closed one side of the shelter doors and started up his little burner.

"Did you close that for the wind?"

"Yes, and no," he said. "Partly so the wind won't blow out our gas flame and also so that we don't fill the cave with smoke." With his flashlight on, he sorted through the additional food Keane had collected from Adam and Wilson.

Outside it was silent, with neither of the two men sitting there saying a word.

Sandrine slid closer to Lennox. "Is Keane out there to stand watch?"

"More or less," Lennox said, his tone as low as hers.

"But, if anyone else is here, they can see him."

"Can they?" he asked, a half smirk on his face.

She thought about that, and as she went to peer around the door, he grabbed her arm and said, "Don't show your white face." From where she sat, she could barely see Keane. He blended into the rock so well. "That's amazing," she whispered.

"He's good at what he does," Lennox said.

"And you? Are you also good at what you do?"

"Sure," he said. "We both do the same thing."

"Is it safe to light a fire?"

"It's a calculated risk. We have this small burner for emergencies, but, in this case, a small fire will cook the fish quickly. I doubt you'd eat it raw." He looked at her questioningly.

Immediately she scrunched up her face and shook her head.

"Hence the fire," he said gently.

As he started cooking the fish, she realized they desperately needed this food right now. "There's such comfort in a hot meal, isn't there?"

"There is, indeed," he said. "We don't have a ton to go with this, but there are some canned goods."

"I'm surprised they brought cans. They're heavy and hard to pack."

"We have army rations. Not sure you'll like that any better."

"Any chance of a coffee or a cup of tea?" she asked hopefully. But the single burner was currently busy frying fish. He'd cut the fillets off the bone to make them cook faster and planned to cook one fish at a time in the small pan. While he cooked the first one, he was busy filleting the others.

She whispered, "Do you want me to hold the flashlight?"

"No, I've got just about enough light to do this," he said.

She brought over the lid and, with a little bit of water, rinsed off the top. "This is all I can offer as a plate," she whispered.

"It'll work," he said, and he quickly flipped the two pieces of fish that he had cooked onto the lid, then refilled the skillet with more. She couldn't resist breaking off a few flakes of fresh fish and tasted it. She moaned. "God, that is really good."

"Nothing like fresh food when you're hungry," he said

cheerfully. "Take that to share with Brenda."

Sandrine didn't need any urging and made her way to her friend. As soon as Brenda smelled the fish, she said, "Well, I guess I'd really like to try eating."

"Let's see if we can get you up on your feet or at least sitting up again," Lennox said, moving their way. With help, he and Sandrine got Brenda sitting up, then slowly and gently propped her up against the rock wall, so she could sit as the two women slowly ate the fish.

"I guess there won't be any more, will there?" Sandrine asked Lennox.

"We have some other rations, and there are quite a few fish," he said. "I was hoping to save some for breakfast, but I'm not sure we can."

"Will it keep overnight?" Brenda asked, sounding curious.

Lennox grimaced. "If we can keep it cooler—like, if I could put it back in the ocean—that will stop it from going bad overnight, but we'll likely eat it all now." He went through the motions and cooked another six fish. By the time everybody had one for themselves, a couple were still left. She watched as he and Keane split one, then handed one to the two women. Wilson protested outside that he wasn't getting seconds.

"You're alive," Keane said, laughing. "At least we gave you something to eat. That's a lot more than you let these women have." Keane stepped inside and rummaged around in the bags. "I think we still have some fruit leather, beef jerky and granola bars in here." He handed those out, while they filled the pot with water. As soon as the water boiled, he pulled out a disc, which then elongated into a large glass. He dropped a tea bag inside and poured boiling water over it for the women. Sandrine stared in fascination as a cup of tea was presented to her.

"I hope you don't need cream or sugar with this though," Lennox said. "I can offer you this much, but that's it."

"We'll take it," she said gratefully. With her arms wrapped around Brenda, the two of them huddled over the hot cup of tea, waiting until it was cool enough to drink. "This is absolutely wonderful," she whispered. "Thank you so much."

Lennox shrugged, then Keane handed over a pack of fruit leather and said, "You can also split a granola bar if you need it. If you don't need it," he said, "then save it, since we don't know how long we'll be here."

"I think we'll probably be fine," Brenda said. "My stomach is quite full after the fish."

"I could eat more," Sandrine said slowly. "But you're right, we probably shouldn't."

"See how you feel after the tea," Lennox said. "Having a hot liquid will help fill some holes."

She nodded, and, as Lennox sat here, Keane went back out and resettled in the rocks. She saw Wilson sitting there, staring up at the sky. While his arms were tied in front of him and so were his legs, he appeared to be quite comfortable. "What will we do about him?" she murmured to Lennox.

"Not sure yet," he said, glancing at the prisoner. "That's tomorrow's issue."

She nodded and smiled. The two women finished their tea, and Sandrine helped Brenda to lie back down again. Instead of joining her, Sandrine sat propped up, her head back, and just let her eyes close. When she heard a weird *zing* in her world, she opened her eyes to see Lennox standing right in front of her, a finger at his lips, whispering, "Do not move."

She opened her mouth, but he placed a finger against it and said, "We have company."

Instantly her stomach twisted and churned in fear. She nodded slowly. "Is Keane okay?" she asked, letting the words slide out on a breath.

He nodded. "They shot Wilson."

Her eyes widened in shock, but then, just like that, Lennox was gone. She laid down beside Brenda and wrapped her arms around her friend. When Brenda murmured something, she whispered against her ear, "We have to be quiet. Company's out there. Somebody just shot Wilson."

Brenda stiffened in her arms, and Sandrine kept whispering to her friend calmly and quietly. "The other two men are fine. They're on the hunt. Right now just the two of us are inside, and we must stay calm."

"Great," Brenda said. "Will we ever get out of this nightmare?"

HIDDEN BEHIND THE rock, Keane stayed motionless. The first thing he heard had been a tiny scrape up above. He hadn't expected to see any four-legged predators tonight. He hadn't seen signs of any wildlife, only birds. Which ruled out any other larger animal. The only ones at issue now were two-legged predators. He studied the cliffs around him. He had already memorized their natural shape, in case anything hunkered down and tried to blend in.

As his gaze went across once and then came back again

even slower, he stopped and studied one little hill that wasn't there before. This newest intruder had sunglasses on, hiding the whites of his eyes, and the glasses had a tint that would stop any reflection. But he was still taking a chance.

When Keane caught a reflection, he realized that they really did have a visitor. The shot, when it came, was both a surprise, yet not unexpected. What he hadn't expected was the target. Wilson's body jerked once. He'd been half dozing against the rocks and had never seen it coming. He never felt a thing. The only change was the blossoming red spot in the center of his forehead.

And that told Keane a whole lot more. It wasn't that easy to shoot downward, and whoever was up there was good at his job. But he wouldn't have come alone, and that meant at least one more guy was out there. Keane heard Lennox nearby as he whispered, "Bull's-eye."

Keane nodded and gave a thumbs-up. The figure up above quickly disappeared backward again. But was he gone? Did he suspect that his target was the only person here? Did he not care? Had he come and done his job, or had he not even realized that Wilson wasn't alone? With the first two gunmen now dead, the question was, who were these other men, what were they up to, and why would they have taken out Wilson?

When it was safe, Keane slipped toward Lennox and they both snuck silently to the wooden doors. "I figured two," he said, "and they likely came in where our Zodiac is."

"One going low. One going high," Lennox said, already strapping weapons onto a hip holster and securing a knife at his ankle. "Yeah, we'll need to take a little bit more weaponry with us though."

They headed back inside to the two women. Keane

caught sight of the whites of both of their eyes. "We're going after the shooter and his partner," he said.

Both women gasped but didn't say a word.

"Stay inside, and don't make a sound," Keane said. "We don't know that they even realize you're here, so let's keep it that way. They've shot Wilson dead, and they could be looking for his buddy Adam. In which case they won't find him, or maybe they'll just take off."

"What will you do?" Sandrine whispered.

"We're going after them. They got here somehow. That means they have some way to leave."

She nodded slowly. "Or they were dropped off."

"Or they were dropped off and somebody is circling the island. I haven't heard any boat motor though," he said. "Have you?"

"No, but it wouldn't take very much for them to cross that little distance in front of us during the storm, and we wouldn't have heard anything."

"Quite right," he said. He reached down and stuffed a granola bar and some fruit leather into his pocket and grabbed a bottle of water, then leaned over, gently stroked her cheek and said, "You'll be fine."

"Will I?" she asked, her voice low.

He smiled and said, "I'll come back for you."

She nodded gently. "Make sure you look after yourself," she said. "That shot came out of nowhere."

"Not quite," he said. "I did see the guy first."

She stared at him, awestruck, her gaze widening. "Magical powers or what?"

He smiled and whispered, "Remember? This is what we do."

She let out a long slow and somewhat shaky breath. "I'll

keep that in mind." As he got up to leave, she grabbed his hand and pulled him back down again.

Thinking she needed to say something, he crouched low and whispered, "What?"

Pushing herself up on one elbow, she gently brushed her lips against his. "For good luck."

He chuckled. "Then I better come back for good luck lots of times." Then he stepped out as Lennox looked at him with a raised eyebrow. Keane shrugged. "What can I say?" he said. "Women like magic."

"Right," Lennox said, shaking his head.

They shared a silent laugh, then quickly raced along the cliff. They were out of sight from anybody above but knew that the danger would be as they came around the cove. It would be interesting to see what they came up against. With the two of them moving silently on the rocks, Keane led them up the narrow staircase to where it opened up in the meadow. As they stopped and studied the area, Keane whispered, "Across there through the trees is another very narrow pathway," he said. "I found Wilson up on the top, and still more of their gear is up there."

"We may grab that too," Lennox replied.

"Later," Keane whispered with a nod, his gaze studying the trees, looking for movement or for any sign of something that didn't belong. But it all looked innocent, and, of course, that was the last thing it was. The better these men were, the harder it would be to find them.

Keane heard a noise off to the right and melted back against the rocks. Sure enough, he saw two men. Both of them carrying rifles. As they crouched down, they quickly dismantled the weapons and put them in their cases. In other words, they didn't think they had any further threats and were packing up, ready to leave. Keane watched silently as the two men moved efficiently and quietly.

They both had swarthy complexions, with darker skin, suggesting Latino backgrounds. They were good enough that he knew they had spent considerable time on the other end of a weapon. These won't be the same caliber of men as Wilson and Adam. These gunmen were ones who had been sent to clean up the mess.

Guns packed up, the two men stood and looked out at the ocean, one lifting his hand to study the horizon. "They're still not around."

"We're early," the other one said. "It was a little too easy."

"Yeah, but we only got one."

"They're always together," he said. "So we only got one. The other one isn't there to get."

The logic was interesting. Clear-cut and simple.

"Well, Mother Nature will take out the other one, if something didn't already. We didn't even need to bother in this instance. We could have just abandoned the two of them, and they would have been fine."

"Fine, as in *dead*, you mean." The man laughed. "How many times have we had to go in and clean up this shit? I'm getting tired of it."

"Tired in what way?"

Something in his tone had Keane melting farther into the shadows.

"You know what I mean," he said. "The money is good, but, after a while, you realize you've got to live in order to enjoy it. We spend all this time killing and accruing money, but we never get a chance to spend it."

"You know what happens if you quit," his partner said.

"Oh, I know," he said. "There's no quitting. That's just a fact of life in this industry. We were born into the smuggling world. It's not like we've ever had a chance to get out. At least we're in the independent world, not back on the mainland, following orders."

"Don't let anyone ever hear you say any of that though. I mean, I understand discontent," he said. "We deal with that all the time. But the thought about retiring? Yeah, you'll get a bullet between your own eyes if that gets out."

"I know," the other man said, but there was an edge and a wariness to it. "Don't you ever wonder about getting out in that ocean and sailing across to some completely different country and away from this lifestyle? Where you can sit back on a beach and see what that is like?"

"We haven't sat on a beach and enjoyed ourselves since we were kids," his partner growled. "And I don't have to tell you, Carlos, just how damn dangerous this talk is."

"I'm only saying it to you, for Christ's sake," Carlos said with a yawn. "Come on. Let's go."

"Well, you know what'll happen if you get overheard."

"I know," Carlos said.

"And what about the money? It's not like you'd do without that."

"We've got millions in the bank," he said. "If they had any idea how much money we had, you know we'd be forced to give that up too."

"I wasn't planning on telling them. It's our own money," he said. "It's our bank account."

"Oh, I get you," he said, "but we do have the money. If we wanted to leave, you know we could."

"Well, what you're saying is, we could in theory, but it's not gonna happen."

"Maybe not, but it should," he said. "One day it should."

"Well, I'm not ready yet," he said. "I want to keep living."

"Yeah, I hear you."

They headed to the far side, but not in the direction that Keane expected. He watched as the one guy stood again at the top of the cliff and said, "Still, it's kind of sad."

"What is?" asked the other man impatiently.

As Keane watched, one man turned to face the other, and a shot rang out.

One man stood, staring, clutching his chest. "Seriously?" Then he fell to his knees and smashed onto the ground.

The remaining man walked over, his rifle still pointed at his buddy. "Yeah, seriously. The money is in our joint account, for fuck's sake. You were either coming with me or I was going alone." He looked around at the options for the body and then swore, stripped it of gear and weaponry, and pushed it over the cliff's edge.

Keane and Lennox exchanged hard glances as they heard the sounds of the soft body hitting rocks all the way down.

"That's shitty," Lennox whispered.

But the last guy just stood there, his face up to the sky, almost as if he'd been freed from something. And then he slowly made his way to the far side and disappeared from sight.

The question Keane and Lennox had to answer was whether they would take out this guy or see if he disappeared quietly into the night? It appeared to be a falling out among thieves, but Keane and Lennox had learned long ago that there were times to get in a fight and times when it wasn't theirs to get into.

If this guy had a boat, that was a different story. But, in theory, Keane and his companions were probably getting picked up tomorrow. It was just hard to know how this would play out right now.

As the guy made his way to the far side, he stopped, looked back toward where Keane and Lennox stood in the shadows and said, "Shit."

Keane tensed, fearing the guy had seen them as he walked toward them. Keane looked at Lennox and shrugged as they both stepped out of the shadows and leveled their weapons at him. "Were you going somewhere?"

The man stopped in front of them, all anger and ugliness as he lifted his rifle.

Keane shook his head. "I wouldn't do that if I were you. Nobody'll spend your millions if you get yourself killed."

"Who are you, and what are you doing here?" the man raged.

"We came after the two women."

The surprise in the guy's face was shocking. "What women?"

Keane laughed. "The two guys who came here to set up your transmitting station rescued two women who had washed overboard. In the process, they crashed their own boat, and all four of them washed overboard."

"You're kidding?" He shook his head. "Those two were just a mess-up from the beginning. I couldn't believe it when the boss hired them. They said they needed a ride, but we were here to give them a bullet instead."

"Well, you took care of that nicely," Keane said.

"Not quite. I only took care of one. I'm one of those people who likes to cross my *T*s and dot my *I*s. I was heading back to make sure the other one wasn't hanging around anywhere."

"Don't worry about him," Keane said quietly. "We took him out."

"And why was that?"

"Because he was trying to kill the women."

The man's face was a confused mixture as he sorted through what he'd been told. "*Now* he wanted to kill the women after saving them?"

"Yes. The one you shot told him that he needed to."

"Got it. Well, he shouldn't have rescued them in the first place." He shrugged and said, "But we all have sisters and mothers and daughters. It's hard to watch women suffer."

"Unless you're into smuggling. Do you smuggle women?"

He shook his head. "No. Drugs."

"Of course," Keane said. "So now we're at a stalemate."

"What do you want to do?" the smuggler asked.

"What are you trying to do?" Keane asked.

"I wanted to ensure the other guy was dead and then take off."

"And your buddy? You'll just let the birds eat him?"

"The ocean will probably take him out to deeper water," Carlos said with a shrug. "I gave him a chance. You heard me practically begging him to come with me. I did give him a chance."

"Right. And now the question is, what chance are you looking for?"

"To return to my boat, to leave this island and to head off in the opposite direction from the bosses."

"Won't they come after you?"

"I doubt it," he said. "That's one of the reasons for setting the stage for both of us being dead."

"And you think they'll just disappear and come back in six months and see if anybody's still alive?"

"If I don't report in," the smuggler said steadily, "it won't matter, because they won't come looking anyway."

"Is that the kind of job you do?"

"It's the kind of job I've always done," he said, with a world-weariness. "Cleaning up messes. I'm just so damn tired of it all."

"And how can we believe that you'll just take off and disappear?"

"You don't need to," Carlos said. "But, if my bosses find me, I'm dead anyway, so either shoot me or give me a chance at having a decent life. I was born into this bullshit, and I've not had two seconds to myself to call my own, let alone refuse an order," he said.

"I'm not terribly interested in your sob story," Keane said, "but I want to make sure you're not bringing any other people back onto this island. We have enough trouble as it is."

Carlos laughed. "Believe me. Nobody's coming here after us. We're the last stop to clean up the bullshit," he said. "A ship is out there, but it's a good fifteen miles away. They won't come any closer. We either make it back, or we don't."

"What kind of boat do you have?"

"I have one down below," he said. "It's hidden."

"Are you the one who took out our Zodiac?"

The man looked at him in surprise. "Was that yours? Sorry. I thought it belonged to the other two. I was trying to make sure they didn't leave the island."

"That makes more sense," Keane said. "Yeah, it was ours. Speaking of which, another couple people were shot in this area a week or so ago."

He nodded. "Yeah, that was us. Like I said, there's no getting away from this work. They were in the wrong place at the wrong time. We captured them. I fought to keep them alive, but it wasn't going down well, so they were taken out." He shrugged. "It's a shitty life." He studied the look on Keane's face. "I can see you don't like my answer. But it's the truth. Why the hell do you think I want out?"

"Understandable but will you get out is the question?"

"If you give me a window, I'll take it. Chances are you have somebody coming in for a pickup then, don't you?"

"We do," he said. "In the morning."

"Let me leave then," he said. "No guarantee I'll make it anywhere with my boat as it is. It's small, and the waves are big, but it's my only chance at a new life."

"Good point," he said. "So disappear."

They dropped a line of fire at his feet, and he disappeared around the rocks.

"He didn't protest too much."

Keane exchanged a glance with Lennox, who just shrugged and said, "You know the ocean will get him, or his bosses will."

"I know. But he didn't kill any of us." Walking to the edge of the cliff, Keane looked down. It was too early yet to see Carlos, but, before long, he came through a little hollow, and there on the side, he tugged his boat into the water just around the corner. Another Zodiac type of watercraft, with black pontoons and a big-ass motor on the back. Keane wondered at the seaworthiness of it out in a big storm, but that wasn't his problem.

Carlos hopped in and pushed out until he could turn and pull at the engine. As soon as it fired up, he headed around the island, away from their view.

"Something tells me that's the opposite direction of the smugglers."

"If he's smart, it is, but he'll have to go up the coast to get away from this squall. He won't head across the ocean in that thing." But he let his thoughts trail off, because he didn't really give a shit. As long as they were alone now, he was fine with it.

"We need to make sure the other guy's dead and that neither left anything behind."

"He should have left enough behind so that anybody landing and checking up on them would see that they were gone."

"And what are we supposed to do? Add Wilson's body to the mix?"

"If we could ever get some comm set up," he said, "we could report what happened and let the coast guard or whoever deal with it."

They followed his footsteps, carefully navigating to the bottom.

"Are you getting the feeling that we should have killed him?"

"Not really," he said. "This has been a bizarre mission right from the beginning."

"I know," he said, "not exactly the same as the other Mavericks ops."

"No, but it's all good," Keane said quietly. "We're still doing what's right. We're helping others."

They checked to make sure that Carlos's partner was dead. His body washing up against the rocks along the shore wouldn't take long for nature to deal with him. Lennox and Keane left the body where it was and took several photos. They checked where the other boat had been hidden and couldn't see any signs of it left. If they hadn't seen Carlos leave themselves, they'd never have known he was here.

The two looked at each other, and Lennox said, "Let's head back."

"Yeah," Keane replied. "When we hit the top again, let's try to communicate with the coast guard."

"Good idea."

CHAPTER 9

SANDRINE MUST HAVE dozed off because, as she woke up again, the sky around her was nowhere near as dark as it had been. As she lay quiet, Sandrine felt an almost rested and relaxed feeling, as if she'd gotten a couple hours of real sleep. She looked over to see her best friend resting peacefully. Sandrine's bladder was killing her though. She got up and shuffled outside, wincing at the sight of Wilson with the bullet hole still shining bright in his face.

"Poor guy," she whispered. With no place to hide to take care of her business, she headed off to the side, dug a small hole, quickly relieved herself and buried it. As she pulled her clothes back into position, she walked back to the cavern, remembering what Lennox had said about not being seen. But she hadn't even thought about it when she had bolted outside to go to the bathroom, and now such an odd sense to the air hung around her. She made her way slowly down to the cliff's edge and the water, wondering if the men were coming back or if something had happened to them up top.

And then she saw movement on the staircase around the corner. It was Lennox and Keane. She raced toward them, and Keane opened his arms.

"You should have stayed in the shelter," he said. "What if it wasn't us?"

She looked at Lennox, who was frowning at her. "I

know," she said. "I was supposed to remain inside and stay quiet, and then I fell asleep. When I woke up, I had to pee really badly. I didn't even think. I bolted outside, and then an eerie stillness took over. I knew I'd screwed up."

"Well, we found two other men," he said. "One killed the other and then took off in their boat."

"You didn't stop him?"

"It would have meant killing him," Keane said. "Something we don't do casually. He wasn't out to hurt us. It wasn't really worth taking him back if we could have kept him alive. Yes, he was an enforcer for a drug smuggling team. And, yes, I'm sure somebody gives a shit," he said, "but honestly that wasn't our priority just then."

"Neither was the boat obviously," she said with a smile.

"We have the coast guard coming to pick us up. Remember?"

She nodded. "I do remember, so that's good. What time is it anyway?"

"It's about four-forty," Lennox said.

She groaned. "So, not quite morning yet."

"Close enough, but we need to grab some shut-eye. It's likely to be a long day."

"Well, I can stand watch," she offered.

"You could," Keane said cheerfully. "At least you can with me. Lennox, you go down first. Your shoulder has got to be screaming."

He nodded, silently acknowledging Keane's observation, and they headed up toward the shelter. Lennox headed straight inside, and she watched as he dropped to his knees, laid down gently and rolled over onto his back.

"Just like that?"

"Just like that," Keane said with a smile. "We rest whenever we can, so we've learned to take advantage of the opportunities as we get them."

"Do you think we're safe now?"

"Well, we definitely still have some unknowns," he said, "but hopefully we are safe."

"And there won't be any trouble getting picked up, right?"

He smiled. "I doubt it." He motioned to the rocks where he had been sitting before, on the opposite side from where Wilson lay.

"Should we move him?" she asked worriedly.

He sighed. "We'll retrieve the bodies anyway," he said. "That'll be in the morning."

"You mean, in an hour or two," she said drily.

He smiled and nodded, then sat down, leaning against the rocks, and closed his eyes.

"Do you want to rest?" she asked. "I can certainly keep watch."

"I'm half awake right now," he said. "I do need to rest, but Lennox needs it more. We'll switch soon enough."

"Okay," she said and sat down beside him, a little bit of a distance between them, which she couldn't quite leave alone until she moved over closer.

He smiled when she snuggled up against him. "You're quite safe, you know?" he murmured.

"Maybe," she said, "but something about being alone for all those hours makes me appreciate the comfort of someone beside me."

"Being alone is both the best and the worst."

She thought about that and realized how very prophetic it was. "I've always loved alone time," she said, "but being alone with Brenda so very sick was just so devastating. I couldn't do anything. I didn't know what to do, and I didn't have the skills to deal with this outdoor living."

"Maybe not," he said, "but you've survived it really well." He rolled his head to the side so he could study her.

She smiled up at him. "What are you thinking?"

"Well, I was thinking about the push that sent you into the water."

She winced. "I keep trying to convince myself that I just imagined it."

"Any problems between the two of you?"

"No, I wouldn't have thought so," she said, "especially if he wanted to get back together. We were both up for the same job, so that caused a little bit of dissension," she said. "I got it, and he didn't. He ended up moving to a different location within the company—a different building actually. It made it less stressful to see him—or maybe for him to see me." She shrugged. "I thought it would be okay, but obviously it wasn't. He started to harass me when he saw me. On my way in and out from work. After we broke up, it was way worse."

"Surely that's not a reason to kill somebody though."

"No," she said. "I wouldn't like to think so ... but maybe in a rash moment of anger or something. I don't know."

"Well, what I was told was that he had a garbled statement about how the one went in and then the second one went in. Both men said they weren't good swimmers, and, beyond throwing you guys life preservers, they were stuck trying to keep the boat upright."

She thought about that and then agreed. "I don't know if they are good swimmers or not," she said, "but I can imagine the waves would have been trying to send them into the water too. I'm glad they're both safe."

"Maybe," he said, "but did you think about what happens if he did try to kill you and if you make it back to shore?"

She stared at him. "Well, he didn't come on shore and try to kill me, so I'm sure he would write it all off as my imagination."

Keane stayed quiet at that. "Tell me again about breaking up with him and how you got on the boat."

She frowned, not liking the way he was thinking.

"Come on."

"We were together for about a year when I found him with someone else," she said. "So I broke up with him. I told him that my friend had seen him with another woman, but really it was me."

"Okay, and the boat?"

"I was supposed to go sailing with Brenda and Greg, but, when I got there, I discovered Scott was there too."

"And yet, you still went out?"

"We were all friends once, and we still work together," she said. "I wasn't really happy about it, but Brenda did tell me it had been Greg's idea and not hers."

"But Brenda still went along with it."

"I never told her that I was the one who found Scott in bed with somebody else," she said calmly. "Scott and his new girlfriend were so involved in having sex that they never heard or saw me. So I ducked out of the apartment as fast as I could. When he denied it, Brenda had hoped it was all a mistake and that this outing might help. The whole job thing made it more confusing too."

"But it was more than that, right?"

"Well, I found out about getting the job on the same day I came home early to find him in bed with somebody else I knew," she said. "I quietly left, then later told him that my friend had seen him with her in the middle of a workday and entering the apartment I shared with Scott, stopping to kiss each other outside on the front steps. It was a pretty ugly scenario. I moved out of the apartment, took a few things, leaving him all the furniture. I found a studio apartment closer to work, so I didn't have to commute. I thought it was all a done deal, so I was nursing my broken heart, working my new job, and I wasn't even thinking about him beyond the inevitable occasional contact at work. And then Brenda and Greg contacted me to go sailing, which is something we used to do a lot of. When I got there, I found out Scott was going with us."

"Wasn't that awkward?"

"Awkward, yes. But not as awkward as it would have been if he'd been there with his new girlfriend."

At that, Keane snorted and laughed. "Good point," he said. "So what happened? Were they really trying to get you guys back together again?"

"Yes, apparently. But the weather was building, and I was keeping quite a distance between us. When Brenda sat down beside me, she apologized, saying she didn't realize things were as bad as they were. I told her then about finding him in bed with this other woman. It was somebody she didn't know, but I had talked about her before, having seen that woman and Scott together at a coffee shop a couple times. I had believed him when he told me that she was an old friend. I'm very much the trusting type," she said drily.

"Again, both good and bad," he said.

She laughed. "Definitely. Anyway, it was a terribly awkward sailing trip. Then the weather got ugly, and things got even uglier when we ended up in the water."

"It sounds like it was also uglier because you're worried that he may have tried to kill you."

"I don't think he tried to kill me," she said. "More a case of getting angry for a moment and seeing an opportunity."

"Right. An opportunity to *kill* you," Keane said drily. "And didn't you tell me that he was the one encouraging the other guy to go farther and farther out to sea?"

"Yes, but—"

"No buts," he said firmly.

"Yeah, I guess. Fine. It is possible that he took an opportunity to take advantage of an accident. But it's not like he would get anything out of the deal, except the satisfaction of knowing I wouldn't be there to bug him again. I mean, I walked away, so he got the furniture and everything else in the apartment. So what the hell difference does it make?"

"Unless he wanted you back?"

"Well, that wouldn't happen and hardly makes sense to kill me then, does it?" she said. "I hold very few things in life really dear, but loyalty, honesty and honor are three of them."

"A woman after my own heart," he said. "That makes us dinosaurs in this world. You know that, right?"

"It's not the first time I've heard that," she said sadly. "My mom taught me these ethics. When she died of breast cancer a good eight or nine years ago now, that was one of the things I wanted to maintain for myself in her memory because she did the job of raising me right. The rest of the world is a messed-up place."

"Amen to that," he said, but his voice was getting a little slurred.

She whispered, "Just sleep. I'll keep watch. I promise."

He stirred. "I know you will," he said, "and I don't think

there's any immediate danger, but I'm on duty so—"

"Good, so just doze then. That internal radar system you have seems to work rather well."

"Oh, it does," he said. "It's just that, every once in a while, you can't necessarily trust it."

"I think trust for you is hard."

"What about you?" he asked. "You're the one dealing with the aftereffects of a cheating boyfriend."

"At least you said *cheating* and not *murderous*," she quipped.

"I was hoping you wouldn't defend him again," he said, his voice light.

She curled up tighter against Keane, letting her head drop onto his shoulder. When he lay his head to rest on hers, she smiled and just held his arm close. Something was very soothing about being out here. She could see the whitecaps bouncing off the waves in the distance—only a couple hundred yards away—but they were protected in this alcove. That was a very strange thing to say, considering the fact that a sharpshooter had taken out Wilson. She stared at the dead man, feeling a sense of peace and unease at the same time. She was amazed at the human ability to cope under stress and to make the abnormal normal in order to deal with it.

She'd never seen a dead man before; yet here she was already dealing with Adam and Wilson. She'd never been almost drowned or had to deal with her best friend being critically injured out in the middle of nowhere like Brenda had been, but it was yet another sign of how Sandrine was coping. Maybe her connection, this bond she felt toward Keane, was the same thing, but she hoped not. She didn't want it to be a stress response or a coping mechanism.

Something was so very special about him. He was so

different from her last boyfriend, and that was a bonus in itself.

She had been the one who had told Keane about the push in the middle of her shoulder blades, and, as she lay here with her eyes closed, she relived that moment when she was panicked because Brenda was in the water. Sandrine threw that life preserver at her, seeing Brenda struggling to keep her head abovewater. Sandrine had just made the decision that she should go in after her when she felt that hand—a solid thumb, long fingers and a palm pressed up against her back—and it pushed. It wasn't a case of *Hold on. Don't jump* or *Careful or you'll fall in*. No, it was clearly a shove, and she realized that her ex-boyfriend really had tried to kill her.

As she lay here dry-eyed in the morning light, she had to wonder, *What would she do about it?*

She was pondering her options when Lennox came out of the shelter. He looked at Keane and quietly said, "Your turn to crash."

As awake as ever, Keane replied softly, "Okay." He looked down at Sandrine at his side and whispered, "I'll go crash. Are you okay here, or do you want to come with me?"

She grinned. "I'm coming with you." She slowly stood, groaning as her body unwound itself from her very uncomfortable position up against the rocks. She followed him into the shelter, checking on Brenda first, relieved that she slept normally. "Looks like Brenda'll be okay," she said, as she settled in the sand beside Keane.

He rolled over, wrapped himself around her, and she snuggled back, spoon style, and closed her eyes. She could feel his chest rise and fall in a deep rhythm behind her. It amazed her that he was so capable of dropping off like that.

A skill she should try to cultivate, so she yawned once, closed her eyes and fell asleep.

KEANE SLIPPED FROM the cozy position with Sandrine wrapped in his arms and stepped outside to relieve himself. He then walked to where Lennox sat near the water, pulling in a fish. "You're really good at that," he said.

"Practice," Lennox replied. "It might not be the ideal food, but it's good and fresh, at least."

"Any thoughts on the smuggler?" Keane asked.

Lennox shook his head. "No. I think Mother Nature will take care of him. At least I hope so."

"We need to contact the coast guard."

"I already did," Lennox said. "They're on their way. Apparently the two boyfriends are with them."

"What? Why?"

"They were trying to show everybody exactly where the women had gone missing because apparently they didn't trust that the coast guard would find them."

"We gave them coordinates."

"I guess the admiral, Brenda's father, approved it."

"Of course he did. Something you need to know," he said quietly. Then he told Lennox what Sandrine had said about her ex-boyfriend pushing her into the ocean.

Lennox sat back and stared at him. "Seriously?"

"She hinted at it earlier, unsure that she wasn't just overly upset. But I quizzed her about it, while you were sleeping. I don't like it. We'll talk to her more this morning, and we probably should talk to Brenda as well," he said.

"Wow, so we have a murderer on board?"

"Attempted murderer anyway," Keane said. "And I'm wondering if that isn't partly why he's trying to get onto the coast guard ship."

"Uh-oh," Lennox said.

"Right, so he can finish the job."

Lennox studied him to see if he was serious and then shook his head. "It's a pitiful world out there. But, if he does finish the job, he doesn't have to face her accusations that he tried to kill her, does he?"

"Nope. She has no proof either."

"And, given the circumstances and what she's been through, it would be easy to suggest she made it up."

"Particularly if he can use the breakup—or, hell, the fact she got the big promotion and he didn't—and say she's just after revenge."

"And he gets away with it," Lennox said.

"Exactly," he said. "Something I'm not a big fan of."

"And yet, you are a big fan of her," Lennox said, laughing.

Keane chuckled. "There's an awful lot to like."

"No argument there," Lennox said, "but we have to get off this island in order to move on with anything."

"Right. So do you think the drug smugglers will come back in again?"

Lennox thought for a moment. "Our guy didn't seem to think so, and, if they find the body of his partner floating in the ocean, then the answer is no." He lifted out four fish and said, "That's one for each of us. What do you think?"

"Looks to me like it's time to eat," Keane said, hopping to his feet. "And then we need to pack up and get to the shore and see about leaving this place."

"Yeah, to face the next stage of the mission," Lennox

said. "Sounds like we'll flush out an attempted murderer."

"Stop him from making a second attempt at least," Keane said. "That would not be cool at this point."

"No, because then he'll face you."

"Yeah. In a big way," Keane said, laughing. But inside he knew it was no laughing matter. Ever since Sandrine had mentioned it, something had been in the back of his mind. "When we were talking before, it really cemented the problem she would face heading back again. I hope she's wrong," he said.

"And how will we know?" Lennox asked.

"I'm not sure," he said. "I'm just wondering if maybe his buddy saw something."

"But would he tell? From what you're saying, it seems like they tried to bring the two back together, meaning this guy is a friend of her ex. So would he talk in a deal like this? Especially now, after all this time as buddies?"

"More than likely he'll say he doesn't know what he saw."

Lennox nodded, and they returned to the shelter, where the two women were sound asleep. He started up the little cookstove, while Keane went through the food and laid out what they had left.

"We've got plenty here," he said, "even if we stay another day."

"I hope you don't mean that," Sandrine said.

He chuckled. "So you're awake, are you?" he asked in a teasing voice.

"I am," she said, "but I woke up more chilled than when I went to sleep." Smelling the frying fish, she asked, "Time for breakfast?"

"You'll be sick of fish after this," Lennox said.

She smiled and shrugged. "I'm alive. I'm safe, and you're filling my stomach," she said. "I don't really care, and I'm particularly grateful that you're cooking it first."

At that, he laughed and said, "Well, you're first up."

And, using the same darn lid, she ate while he cooked the next fish. Brenda woke up next. As soon as she was up and settled back in after a trip outside, she sat beside Sandrine. Brenda had a smile on her face and said, "I know it's been a pretty shitty couple days for you guys, but I don't remember very much of it."

"Well, hopefully there won't be much more to remember," Sandrine said.

"Well, I am remembering a lot of it. The whole thing is pretty shocking with everything that happened," she said. "I can't thank you enough for saving my life."

Keane looked over to see her smiling at Sandrine.

"I couldn't do any less," she said.

"Now the question is, would you have done that on your own," Brenda said, "or was it only because Scott pushed you?"

CHAPTER 10

"**D**ID YOU SEE him?" Sandrine asked Brenda. "I wondered if I had imagined it," she said, "I was standing on the side, hanging on to the lines, and he pushed me in. But I was afraid it was my imagination."

"No," Brenda said. "Remember? I was behind you, so I could see the two of you clearly. I wasn't even sure what I was seeing. But he shoved you in and then stood there, with that look on his face."

"What kind of a look?" Keane asked.

"Anger, joy, fury, almost vengefulness. I don't know. It's hard to say, since I was struggling in the water and, at the same time, trying to comprehend what I'd just seen." She turned to Sandrine. "Can you ever forgive me?"

"For what?" Sandrine asked.

"For listening to Greg and trying to patch you two up again. Obviously Scott is not who we thought he was."

"No," she said. "He certainly is not. Besides, I told you on the boat why I broke up with him. I knew he and Greg were friends, and I didn't want to complicate things for you guys, so I didn't tell you the whole story earlier. I figured just saying that we broke it off and that I was moving on would be enough."

"Greg took that really badly. He thought you guys were perfect together," Brenda said.

"Yeah, except for the part about Scott being a lying cheater and apparently an attempted murderer," Sandrine said quietly.

"What will you do about that?" Lennox asked.

She looked at him in surprise. "What do you mean?"

"What will you do about the attempted murder part?" he asked again, looking serious.

"I don't know," she said. "Is there any point in doing anything?"

"You can't let him get away with it," Brenda said. "He could try it again on someone else."

Sandrine winced at that. "And yet, to go through pressing charges and maybe a trial, when it's just an accusation in the midst of a storm, seems difficult. It could be twisted around so much. I can already hear what the attorneys would do to me. And you, since you're a witness," she said.

The two men were suspiciously quiet.

She looked at them. "What do you guys think?"

Their gazes were steady and strong, but Keane said, "Remember what you said to me earlier? About the things that you value the most?"

She nodded. "And?"

"How would you feel if he killed another woman?"

She glared at him. "Not fair."

"No," he said, "it's not. But maybe you should think about it."

KEANE HADN'T WANTED to bring it up, but, at the same time, they would face it and soon. He was wondering about that as they packed their gear, then got them all to where the coast guard long-range interceptor boat would land to pick them and their gear up.

Lennox called out at the top of his lungs, "Ahoy."

Keane spun to see a boat approaching the small cove. He looked at the two women and said, "Stay here." He raced to the shore. When he recognized one of the coast guard boats farther away, he smiled and waved. It took another ten minutes for them to gain the beach, and, at that point in time, he turned to see the two women and Lennox were halfway to him. When the three uniformed men hopped out, a lot of shoulder slapping and handshaking followed, but they were all good guardsmen and nothing like what Keane had been dealing with so far. "Before we leave, we need a confab," he said.

One of them looked at him and said, "Oh?"

"Yeah. Plus, did you guys bring any body bags with you?"

The officer frowned. "No, I don't think so, although there might be one in the storage kits. Why?"

Keane waited until Lennox joined him, and then, with the women standing and listening, he gave as clear an accounting as he could of what had happened since they'd arrived. All three search-and-rescue men stared at him in shock.

"Seriously?"

Keane nodded. "So the one guy took off, heading around the island to our left," he said. "Presumably he'll go all the way around, then turn south, but I don't know that. His partner's body was dumped in the ocean around the corner, and we have two up here."

The guardsmen just stared at him.

Keane shrugged and said, "Come on. Let me take you

up." He looked at the other officers and said, "You might as well stay here, if you want."

They shook their heads. "No. We're with you all the way."

Sandrine asked Brenda if she wanted to wait alone here at the beach.

"I'll wait with Brenda," Lennox stated.

After getting a nod from Brenda, Sandrine said, "Then I'll come with you too, Keane."

The conversation continued as the men asked question after question. Keane answered as well as he could, and even Sandrine chimed in with any answers she had.

By the time they made it to the small shelter, where Wilson sat with a bullet in his head, everybody stood in a circle of silence around the body. Then Keane pointed to where they had buried Adam. "So we have two here," he said, "and they both need to be taken back."

"Well, crap," the one guy said.

"I know. It hasn't exactly been what we thought we were signing up for."

"And the Zodiac that you took to land?"

"It's around the beach, unusable," he said. "We'll take you there too. But, between here and there, we should find another body around the rocks."

"We can try to retrieve that one." One of the men stepped back and brought out his phone. "I'll walk back to the interceptor and call the cutter. We'll need a second boat out here and some body bags. We'll do a full recovery."

Keane nodded and watched as he walked away.

The other two guardsmen walked into the little shelter, then stepped back out again, studying the makeshift doors. "Somebody went to a lot of effort, yet I can't imagine how long this has been here."

"I don't know," Keane said. "The wood is old but must have been brought here. Those are two-by-fours and one-by-sixes."

The men nodded. "Looks like old barn boards."

"Maybe, but it was built deliberately. Smugglers?" Keane asked.

"It's hard to say. Maybe this was a good place for meetings. I don't know."

"Wow," another said, studying it. "We've seen some interesting islands, but this one takes the cake."

"I'd just as soon get off this one," Sandrine said, yawning. "I admit to feeling a little bit like the ocean waves out there. Kind of battered and blown against the rocks."

Understanding crossed the men's faces. "You've had quite the time of it."

"I have, indeed," she replied.

Keane wondered if he should mention what had happened to her or leave it for her to bring up, when one of the coast guard guys smiled at her and said, "That's okay. You'll feel better when you realize that your boyfriends are on the coast guard ship."

Sandrine stared at him in shock. "Both of them?"

"Yep, both of them."

She glanced toward the shore, where Brenda was. "I'll tell Brenda," she said, shooting Keane a worried look, then racing toward the beach.

"She looked happier for her friend than for herself."

"Yeah. A bit of a story comes with that," Keane said. "It's not really my story to tell, but the guy is her ex-boyfriend," he said. "They broke up a while ago, and the other couple was trying to get them back together on this trip."

The guy whistled. "Well, that didn't go as planned."

"Not even close," Keane said. "And there's more. She believes her ex pushed her off the boat in the first place." Both men stared at him. He nodded. "Again, not my story to tell and I don't know if she's willing to bring it up or to go any further with it, but let's keep an eye on the ex-boyfriend."

"Jesus," the one officer said. "Hasn't she gone through enough already?"

"That's partly why I hesitated to bring it up," he said. "The event was witnessed and independently corroborated by the other girl, by the way."

"Wow, that's crazy. He's been incredibly friendly and seemed worried about her," one man said.

"I hear you," Keane said.

"That doesn't mean a whole lot to me at the moment though," the other man replied.

"Right," Keane said. "But we don't know if it's because he wants to know if she remembers or if he's looking for a second chance to kill her."

"Well, *that* he doesn't get," one said.

"No way," said the other.

"I know. I'm giving you a heads-up, just in case."

"Appreciated," he said. "And you didn't shoot these guys, right?"

He shook his head. "Lennox shot the one buried over there, but that's because Adam was firing on them at the time." Keane pointed to the bullets still slammed into the wooden doors.

"I noticed those," the man said. "What the hell? It's bad enough they ended up in the water in the first place, but to get rescued only to end up on a deserted island like this and have the people who saved your life turn crazy and try to kill you is too much. Not to mention their smuggling buddies coming back and trying to kill you all too."

"It's been a hell of a couple days," Keane said. "They cut my rope when I was rappelling down, so I took a hell of a fall. Lennox got shot and slammed over the head." He studied the man in front of him and the little shelter. "I, for one, won't be sad to leave this place either, and I've been here a lot less time than the women."

"It's amazing, isn't it?"

"It is. Have you been on this island before?"

"Yeah, we've done a couple training expeditions here, but not on this side. We were on the south side."

"Right," Keane said. "It's pretty vast and has lots of different plateaus. Different levels and little pathways. Some man-made but some natural from what I can see."

"Right," the guy said. "We weren't exactly sure of some when we were here before, but, like I said, we weren't in this little cove."

The other coast guardsman added, "I remember riding past it, but I don't recall seeing any shelter up here."

"It's so far up that we wouldn't see it from shore," the first replied.

Just then the other group at the beach walked back toward them. Keane studied Sandrine's face, but she had her head bent toward Brenda, the two of them talking back and forth.

"So, the other one is Brenda, and she's the admiral's daughter?" one of the coast guardsmen asked.

"Yeah, and it's a damn good thing that we found them," Keane said. "Brenda has quite a head injury. She's doing better now, but she's still very weak."

"We can get her to the coast guard ship and give her a medical checkup there," he said. "She can go back with us first."

"Agreed," Keane said.

"Good enough for me," the coast guardsman said. "I guess what we should do is get the women back, and then we'll get the rest of this collected."

Keane nodded, his bags already packed. He said, "You want me to stay here and give you guys a hand?"

"I think, once we get everybody back on the boat," he said, "we'll take a run around to see if we can pinpoint where that body in the water is. There's a chance it's not even close to the island anymore," he said. "The turbulence and currents out here could have taken him anywhere."

"I could see him from up above, and, when I came down, he was already getting churned up, so I'm not sure where he is now," Keane said.

"Right. Let's go." Then he looked at the two women, smiled and said, "Are you good to go?"

"Absolutely," Brenda said. "I wouldn't mind sleeping on an actual bed for a bit."

"Well, we've got a doctor on board the main ship," the coast guard officer said. "He'll take a look at your head and make sure you're good to go. Then we'll definitely find a bunk with your name on it. Not the most comfortable, as beds go, but, compared to the floor of that shelter, you're gonna love it."

"That's the best news yet," she said. "And, as much as I love getting fed, fresh fish would never be my first choice."

"Hey, I thought I did a good job," Lennox said.

She looked at him with half a smile and whispered, "You

did an excellent job. I just happen to hate fish."

At that, he looked at her in shock, then laughed. "Well, you were a good sport about eating it anyway," he said.

"That's because I didn't have any choice," she said. "I knew I needed to eat something in order to keep up my strength. So thank you very much for what you did for us."

"Not a problem," he said. "It was fun."

"If you say so." She smiled and carried on, walking slowly toward the beach.

Keane watched as she went, only to realize that Sandrine stood beside him.

In a low voice, she whispered, "Did you tell them?"

He looked down at her. "I mentioned it. Yes."

She wrinkled her face up at him.

"We'll make sure that you stay safe on the ship," he said. "This guy won't get a second chance to hurt you."

Her shoulders sagged as she looked at the uniformed men. Then asked, "What if I'm wrong?"

"Come on. You heard what Brenda said."

Sandrine sighed and said, "I just wish you hadn't mentioned it."

"I'm sure you do, but remember? *Honesty*, right?"

"Okay, fine. He'll probably avoid me anyway."

"Well, we'll see," he said. "Are you planning on going back with them?"

She shot him a horrified look. "Are you kidding me?"

"Just asking," he said. "Maybe absence made the heart grow fonder."

"Not likely," she said. "Besides, *we* have a thing going."

"We do?" he asked cautiously. But the coast guard guys were ahead of them, making plans, out of earshot, and she had looped her arm through his, as they brought up the rear.

"Obviously," she said, as she raised her face to the sun. "Not exactly sure what this thing is. But it sure eclipses anything I had with Scott."

"Really?" Keane felt inane for not coming up with a better answer. Where was the suave can-do attitude now? But something about this woman always caught him sideways.

She squeezed his hand. "That's okay. Big strong silent types like you don't have to talk much."

"That's not exactly what I was thinking."

"Or am I crazy? Is this my imagination?" She stopped, stepped in front of him and frowned. "Am I?"

"Are you what?" He spoke cautiously, easily recognizing the pitiful yawning silence in front of him.

"Am I off my rocker? Am I crazy to think something is between us?"

He gave her a special smile and whispered, "No. You're not. But I don't even know where you live. I don't know anything about you."

"Yeah," she said. "What if we both don't think that love, honor and loyalty are important?" Her quirky smile meant she was teasing him.

At those words, something inside him settled. He nodded. "You're right. We could both think that lying cheating assholes were people we wanted to spend time with."

She twisted her face up and said, "Ow. Sure glad you're joking. That was a pretty painful experience."

"I'm sure it was," he said gently. "But listen. I'm not the cheating kind."

"Neither am I," she said, then kissed him gently on the cheek. "And see? We've got this thing between us." With that, she entwined her arm with his and walked toward the beach.

CHAPTER 11

THE TRIP TO the coast guard ship was simple and the transition easy. They were quickly ushered into a medical room, where a doctor waited for them. He gave Sandrine a quick cursory once-over and then sat down for a longer checkup on Brenda. Sandrine stayed with Brenda for support and for further information for the doctor, while they went through what had happened, her injuries and the reactions she had. Sandrine filled in the details of symptoms that occurred while Brenda was unconscious or sleeping.

Finally the doctor nodded. "Both of you had a pretty near miss," he said. "Any which way you look at it, you're lucky to be alive."

"I know," they both said, nearly in unison. And, with that, they were both led to a room with bunks inside. Brenda sagged on the bottom one and said, "I don't know about you, but I'm exhausted."

Still worried about the pale color on her friend's face, Sandrine helped her get under the covers. "Are you sure you don't want to strip off first?"

Brenda shook her head. "No, I'm not that comfortable yet. I just want to sleep." She patted Sandrine's cheek and said, "Thank you for watching over me."

"I'm just so grateful you weren't hurt even worse," she said. "It was pretty rough watching you with blood oozing out of your head and clearly delirious and talking crazy," she said. "But I'm so glad you pulled through." As soon as Brenda seemed comfortable and her eyes started to droop, Sandrine stepped out into the hallway in time to see Keane coming out of a nearby room.

"I wasn't sure if you guys would even stay on board," she said with a bright, welcoming smile.

"Just for a little while. I'm heading out again in a bit," he said. "I just got back from the second boat. We collected a couple bodies."

"A couple?"

His face sobered. "We couldn't find the one in the water."

She groaned. "That'll provide ugly thoughts for my nightmares to feed on."

"I know," he said. "Me too. I'm sorry about that." He looked down the galley. "Are you heading up?"

"I was hoping to," she said. "Honestly I haven't seen Scott and Greg yet."

"That's another issue," he said. "They're here, but I think they're in one of the lounges. They know that you're both on board, but I don't think they've been told anything else."

"The thing is, Brenda's asleep," she said. "She didn't even want to see her boyfriend first."

"Are things okay with them?"

"I'm not sure," she said. "This trip has definitely been a bit of an eye-opener. She buckled under pressure from Greg and agreed to bring Scott on our trip. But, when she heard all of it as to why I broke up with him to begin with, she was pretty angry. Then, after seeing him push me in, I think she's really confused."

"Understood," he said. "Come on. You can come with me," he said. "We'll go on up and see if we can get you a cup of coffee and maybe some real food. Although I'm not sure they carry that much on board."

"A kitchen or something should be here, right?"

"There will be," he reassured her. "At least coffee and maybe some sandwiches."

She smiled. "It's hard to believe it's still morning," she said. "A part of me says I should go crash, but I'm still too keyed up. I feel like I should wait a little bit longer and then have a nap." He motioned for her to walk down the aisle in front of them. She came to the first set of stairs and hesitated. She looked at him, and he smiled.

"Let's go on up."

As she did, she spotted a large lounge off to the side. Computers were available on both sides, and chairs were at one end. A couple men were there working. Not Scott and Greg thankfully. She walked inside the room with Keane at her side, studying the general layout. "This is pretty fascinating." She smiled at the two men.

"It is. We have living quarters on these big coast guard cutters," one man said. "The smaller ones are just for day trips, but these are meant to go out for a few days at a time."

A man in uniform stepped forward to join them. He reached out to shake her hand. "Captain Schmidt, at your service," he said in a gruff voice.

She smiled up at him. "Thank you so much for the rescue, Captain."

He gave a clipped nod in response. "Sounds like you had a difficult experience."

"Definitely. Quite the time of it," she said softly.

A voice came from behind the captain. "Sandrine?"

She looked at Keane. "That'll be Scott."

Suddenly Greg was right here too. He reached out and wrapped her in a gentle hug. "I'm so damn glad you two survived," he said.

Sandrine searched his face but couldn't see any sign of deception. She stepped out of Greg's embrace. "Brenda's sleeping. She's doing better but not feeling very strong yet. It's been an ordeal."

He wiped tears from the corner of his eyes and nodded. "After all she's been through, that's totally okay. Hopefully she'll feel good enough to come up. Otherwise, maybe I can go down." He looked at the captain.

"Maybe later when she's awake but not right now as long as she's sleeping. Rest is what she needs, I'm sure. And I'll speak to the doctor about her condition and check in with her. I'll report more to you later."

Just then Sandrine could see Scott.

He gave her an affable look and a big beaming smile. "I'm so glad you survived that terrible storm," he cried out. He stepped forward and gave her a hug, even though she was stiff and unwelcoming. As soon as he let her go, she stepped closer to Keane to stop Scott from trying another move like that again.

The coast guard captain looked at Sandrine and Scott and said, "Maybe you'd like to tell us all what happened."

"Do I have to?" she asked.

His quick nod convinced her that she might as well get it over with.

She sighed and said, "Yes, of course I do. Is there any chance of a cup of coffee?"

"Absolutely, and I understand Lennox made you some lovely fish for breakfast," the captain said with a grin, completely changing his expression, making him even more approachable.

"Absolutely," she said, "and I was grateful to have it, but, if any other food is here," she said with a smile, "I would appreciate it."

"We can probably find a few things," he said.

She was led over to an area with a comfortable chair and a love seat. She immediately sat in the love seat, and Keane sat beside her.

Scott looked at Keane and asked, "So, are you the guy who rescued her?"

Keane nodded but didn't reach out a hand. "I'm one of a two-man team sent looking for them, yes."

"How did you know where to find them?"

"Wasn't too hard with their last-known GPS location," he said. "We cleared the other islands, then searched that biggest one. We found them in the third quadrant."

"It's amazing they survived it all," Scott said.

"Particularly considering the odds against them," Keane said.

She looked at him. He just gave her a quick smile, but she could see the anger in the back of his gaze. She looked at Scott and Greg and asked, "You guys made it back okay?"

"We made it, but we were hours getting back home again," Greg said. "We made it back to shore and sent out the alarms. We told the coast guard what had happened and that started the circus."

"A circus with a good ending," she said. She sagged into the couch, absolutely loving the fact that she had comfort again. "You don't realize how much you take the simple things in life for granted until you do without them."

Just then a man walked toward her with a tray. A small

table was clicked open in front of her, and the tray placed beside her.

She looked at it and smiled. "Well, I see a lot of food here," she said, laughing.

"You eat whatever you like," the captain said. "We all know what it's like to be without a meal or two."

She nodded. "I really hope I never go through another scenario like that again."

"How bad was it?" Greg asked anxiously.

"Well, it was way worse," she said, "because I had terrible nightmares about the boat and how I ended up in the water," she said smoothly, without even looking at Scott, "plus, being afraid that I would never reach Brenda. ... In the end, I woke up on the island, locked inside this weird little fortress. Some guy turned up, giving me a little plastic container with some fish and some biscuits, telling me how he saved us from drowning and brought us to the island. But then he left, and it just went downhill from there."

"So bizarre," Greg said, shaking his head. "I mean, it's awesome that he saved you and that they put you on the island, but what happened after that? I mean, we only got bits and pieces of what happened."

"Well, I think a lot of it is also Brenda's story," she said. "So maybe we'll wait for a bunch of it until she's up to it, if you don't mind," she said. With that, she picked up the cup of coffee, looked at it and smiled. "Ah, real coffee." She glanced sideways at Keane. "Of course I still really appreciated the cup of tea."

He laughed. "Go ahead and eat," he said. "This is definitely what you've been waiting for."

She hugged the cup, took a sip and just closed her eyes, sagging gently into the corner of the love seat. "Nothing quite like a good cup of coffee." She drank half of it, just holding the cup and sipping. Finally she put it down and looked at the feast in front of her: a breakfast sandwich and several muffins, some pastries, fruit and even yogurt. She picked up the breakfast sandwich and said, "This I will take care of, no problem."

The men had an easy conversation around her as she ate, though she caught the edge in Keane's voice every time he spoke. A definite sense of unrest was in Scott's gaze as he studied her. The captain asked a few more questions, and she answered everything she could. For now. What she hadn't considered was the cost for this rescue. She hated to even bring it up and decided she wouldn't ask about it in the open like that. She would ask Keane about it privately. When she got to the end of the breakfast sandwich, she started in on the muffin, but, halfway through, she knew she couldn't finish it. Putting the muffin on the plate, she handed it to Keane. "Can you finish this for me?"

"Wow," he said, "I figured you'd get more down than that."

She shook her head. "No, and somehow the coffee's making me really tired."

As a matter of fact, with her feet curled up on the couch and a big pillow beside her, resting her body into the corner, she was almost too relaxed. "I probably should go back down and have a nap with Brenda," she said. "I don't really want her to wake up alone either."

"I could go down there," Greg said anxiously.

She looked at him, smiled and said, "Not until the captain says so."

He sagged in his chair and nodded. "I guess that's fair." But he wasn't terribly impressed with the idea.

She looked at Keane and said, "Otherwise, I'll fall asleep right here."

"No, we won't do that," he said. He helped her to her feet, smiled at the rest of the men and said, "If you'll excuse us, she's going below for a nap." Then he slowly led her to the stairs.

"How come I'm so tired now?" she asked. Going down the stairs was almost a chore. He led her back to her room and said, "Part of it is just the end of the adrenaline wearing off. Finally knowing that you're safe and that everything's okay."

"If you say so." She yawned.

He opened the door and checked on Brenda. "She's still asleep." He looked up at the top bunk, then smiled. "Will you get up there okay?"

She nodded. "I'll be fine." She stumbled to the ladder, completely shocked at how absolutely exhausted she was. "Don't let me sleep too late though, please," she said anxiously. "And please don't let Scott come in while I'm sleeping."

He looked at her in surprise. "Do you think he'll try?"

"I don't know, but he'll probably try to come down when Greg does, at least. I don't want either one of them in here while I'm sleeping," she said. "I won't sleep soundly if I'm afraid somebody will come in."

"Well, I can sit here and keep watch, if you want," he said. "I'm pretty sure you'll be fine, but—"

She looked at the small quarters and said, "There isn't any room for you to sit here and wait," she said, "so don't worry about it."

"If I sit in my bunk across the hall and keep the door open, I can see if anybody tries to come in or out of your place."

She looked at him for a long moment. "I hate to ask you—"

He shook his head firmly. "You're not asking," he said. "I just offered."

She smiled, then whispered, "If you wouldn't mind, I'd really appreciate it. I feel like we've been through so much already, and I'm seeing danger where there isn't any. But I don't know. I just felt very uneasy up there."

"Good enough for me," he said. "Now lie down," he ordered in a gentle voice.

She collapsed downward and tucked the pillow up under her head and whispered, "I'm so damn tired."

"So, for that reason, you'll sleep." He stretched up a little bit over the upper bunk to drop a kiss on her forehead. "Now be a good girl and sleep."

She smiled and whispered, "That's one order I'm happy to take." With that, she closed her eyes and dropped off into a deep sleep.

KEANE SAT ON the side of his cabin, without even a chair. In such a very small sleeping area, he was content to just sit in the corner on his phone as he went through the information he had. And that was damn little. He was more concerned about Sandrine's ex-boyfriend and the look on his face when he'd seen her. He had hugged her, and she had allowed it, but stiffly. Of course the fact that she'd snuggled up closer to Keane afterward had warmed his heart.

But he also understood that she was trying to get away from a predator. They'd be home in a few hours, and that was important, so she could get back to a normal life. But what would that mean for her? What would it mean for this boyfriend of hers? *Ex*-boyfriend, he corrected himself mentally. His phone rang just then, and he answered it to hear Lennox on the other end. "The body recoveries are done and stowed, so everybody is heading back to port now."

"Good enough. Do we have an ETA?"

"They're figuring two and a half hours."

"Okay. She's likely to sleep that long anyway."

"And then what?" Lennox asked curiously.

"I don't know," he said. "I guess drop her off at her apartment, a job well done. A weird job but, hey, I'll take it."

Lennox laughed. "So my job to head up next will be a search and rescue too?"

"Hell, they'll probably send you off into the bowels of Africa or some dang thing," he said, laughing.

"Hey, don't say that," he said. "It seems like this one was a bit of an anomaly."

"No, I don't think so. Nico's job was pretty wild too."

"So we're just out there to help whoever needs a hand?"

"Sounds like it," Keane said. "You know I'm okay with that."

"I'm not having a problem with that part of it," Lennox said. "It certainly beats the heavy military drilling. But we have to keep in shape too. We Mavericks don't have the same schedule for that."

"No, I think we'll set that up ourselves."

"Yeah, but one of the best things would be a gym with everybody," Lennox said. "It kept us all motivated and fit as SEALs."

"As Mavericks, we're scattered in a lot of locations," he said, "but, anytime you want to go, just let me know."

"Good to know," he said. "I'll hang up now and talk to a couple of the coast guard guys. They've still got a bunch of questions on the extra visitors we had. ... Hang on a minute," he said.

Keane waited, knowing from Lennox's voice that something was up.

"You there? They've spotted another boat up ahead."

"What kind of boat?" Keane asked, standing up.

"A small black Zodiac, but they said it appears to be struggling."

"Any passengers on board?"

"The guardsmen have gone up on deck to see," he said. "I'm standing at the pilot's station. The storm is picking up again."

Keane paced in his tiny space.

"Okay, somebody is on board, but they aren't sure if he's okay or not."

"You know who's coming to mind?"

"Of course. Carlos. The guy who killed his partner and supposedly made a run for a new life."

"Yeah. What are the chances that the smugglers realized he was going in the wrong direction?"

"I wouldn't doubt it," he said.

"I'll be right up," Keane said. Then he stopped. "I promised Sandrine I'd stay here."

"Stay where?" Lennox asked curiously.

"I'm in the room across from where the girls are sleeping," he said. "She said she wouldn't sleep, afraid Scott would sneak in."

Lennox was silent for a moment. "She's that worried?"

"Yeah. But I don't know if it's residual stress from the island or what. No way to tell really until she gets some rest."

"Interesting," he said.

"It is. I'm just not too sure what the end result will be here."

"Okay, well, I've got this. I'll keep you posted."

Just then Keane heard a knock on the door across the hall. Keane hung up the phone to see Greg.

Greg looked at him in surprise and said, "I was hoping to talk to Brenda."

"They're both sleeping," Keane said, motioning at the closed door, to Greg who was still knocking on the women's door. "Did you want something?"

Greg's face fell. "I've been waiting to see her," he said. "It breaks my heart to know that I can't touch her yet."

"I guess that depends on if you had anything to do with her going into the water in the first place."

Greg looked at him in shock. "I would never do that," he said. "I was planning on asking her to marry me."

"Are you still planning on it?" Keane asked.

"Yes. If she'll have me. I know she is quite perturbed with me at the moment. At least she was angry on the sailboat."

"And why is that?"

Greg hesitated, and then his shoulders deflated. "These last few days have been the worst days of my life," he said. "Trying to find out if she was alive or dead, and knowing that she had fallen from my sailboat. It was even worse because the last few hours we had together were so bad."

"How bad?" Keane asked.

"She was mad at me," he said simply, "and I guess I deserved it."

"Mad at you why?" Keane leaned against his door, studying the tall scholarly looking man in front of him.

He did look distraught. "She had gone along with me, trying to get Sandrine and Scott back together again."

"Even though they'd been broken up for two whole months?"

"Scott wanted another chance," Greg said simply. "He's been my buddy for a long time, and I didn't think there was anything wrong with giving them the opportunity to try to work things out."

"If he only needed an opportunity, he could have stopped by her place or called her."

"He tried calling her, but she wouldn't answer. She never seemed to be home whenever he went there, but he figured she wasn't answering the door because she knew it was him."

Keane shook his head, incredulous. "So, even though you knew she'd been avoiding contact with him, you thought it was a better idea to put them both on a boat out in the middle of the ocean where she'd have no choice?"

"I figured at least they'd talk and get it over with," Greg burst out. "I was just trying to help out a buddy."

"And Brenda didn't appreciate that?"

"No. I guess she hadn't known the full story behind why they broke up, so, when Sandrine told her, Brenda got pretty upset with me."

"But you knew?"

Greg shrugged.

"You knew the guy was a cheater and a loser, but you were totally okay trying to hook him back up with your girl's best friend?"

Greg looked at him strangely. "Well, when you say it like that, it's not very nice."

"What other way is there?" Keane asked. "None of this is

nice. She finds her boyfriend in bed with another woman and breaks it off, and, instead of supporting her, you support him, even though he's a cheater."

"He's a guy," Greg said.

At that, Keane just stared at him and then laughed. "Really? Yeah, I'm a guy too, but that doesn't mean I cheat on women."

"Okay. Whatever. He made a mistake," Greg said, trying to backtrack. "He's been a friend for a long time, and we all make mistakes. He wanted another chance, and I was okay with trying to help him get it. That's the end of the story."

"Except that, when Brenda found out, she was angry, upset and pissed off."

"Yeah, she was. She didn't like what I'd done and thought less of me for it. But I got angry too because I didn't like being judged about it. I don't like it now either," he said, clearly angry with Keane.

Keane said. "And did you see how she ended up in the water?"

"Brenda was trying to move closer toward me, and she was hanging on to one of the lines," he said, his face twisting with the memories. "Next thing I knew, a wave came up, and she was gone."

"Life jacket?"

"Oh, yeah," he said. "Everybody on my boat wears a life jacket."

"But you couldn't get back to her?"

"We threw her a life preserver, and I was trying to get the sailboat turned around so I could come back and pick her up," he said.

"And then what happened?"

"And, before I knew it, Sandrine's in the water, heading

toward Brenda. And that was pretty damn stupid."

"Stupid?"

"Well, it's tough enough to rescue one, but now I've got two to rescue."

"Any idea how she ended up in the water?"

"Well, she jumped, I'm sure," he said. "That's Sandrine. She jumps into trouble without thinking."

"You've known her for a long time?"

"A few years, yeah," he said. "Not as long as I've known Brenda though."

"Did it look like she could save Brenda?"

"At that point she might have been doing a better job than I was because I couldn't get back to them. The wind was trashing my sails, and the waves were washing over us, completely hampering our progress. I was tied in, and so was Scott, but we just couldn't seem to get back to them. Next thing I knew, they were gone. We stayed out for a long time while I searched, looking all over for them, but found no sign of either of them. As soon as the storm calmed down, I circled around that area, while we called for help. Then I came back to shore and found the coast guard, and we told them what happened."

"So you must have thought they were dead."

"Of course I did," he said. "What else was I to think?"

Keane shrugged. "They were picked up by two guys," he said, "then carried to shore and left on land."

"Thank God for that," he said. "I don't know how far they must have traveled, because no land was close to us."

"Sandrine hooked their life vests together, and those plus the one preserver was enough to keep them up."

"She would do that," he said, "but apparently Brenda hurt her head?"

"Yes. Which is one of the reasons you're not allowed in their room now," he said.

"She probably hit some rocks. I told you that storm was something else."

"Maybe she hit her head on the boat on the way over?" Keane asked.

"I don't think so," he said. "She was there, and, the next thing I know, she wasn't."

"Brenda or Sandrine?"

"Same thing. Sandrine was standing there, yelling at Brenda, and she's the one who threw the life preserver to get her up. The next thing I know, Sandrine was jumping off in Brenda's direction."

"What kind of a jump was it?"

Greg leaned back slightly and looked at Keane. "What do you mean, *what kind of a jump?*"

"Well, you saw her go in, right?"

"Yeah. I was yelling at her not to do it, yet she looked like she was getting ready. Then I turned to look at Brenda and to see her hand reaching for the life preserver, but she looked pretty weak. The next thing I know, Sandrine's in the water."

"Did she dive in? Did she cannonball? What did she do?"

He frowned and said, "I guess a wave must have hit her sideways or something. Hell, I don't know. Maybe she fell because she didn't go in gracefully. She went a little sideways, with her arms out."

"Almost like she was pushed, huh?"

Greg stared at him for a long moment, and then all his friendliness was withdrawn, and his anger rose up. "You better not be saying what I think you're saying."

"Oh, I'm not saying anything," Keane said, "but I know what these two women said."

Greg looked from Keane to the door hiding the two women and back again. "What the hell are they saying?"

"Where was Scott when Sandrine went in?"

"They were standing together," Greg said, but he shook his head. "No way he would have hurt her."

"No, of course not," Keane said, "because she was completely receptive to his attempts at making up, wasn't she?"

Greg frowned. "No. He was trying hard, and she wasn't having anything to do with it. I got quite angry at her."

"Angry *at her*?" Keane shut his eyes and scratched his head. "So you tricked her into going sailing with an ex she has been very clear about not wanting to be with. She doesn't accept his advances on the boat, for very legit reasons since he's an undisputed cheating, lying sack of shit, and you're mad at *her*? That's messed up."

Greg raised both hands in frustration. "I don't know about that. It just made for a very uncomfortable sailing trip."

"Ya think? And you couldn't see that coming? How is any of that her fault?"

Greg ran his hands over his face. "Look. I don't know what the hell happened. I don't know anything at the moment. I feel like you're putting me on the spot. I didn't do anything, okay? I was trying to help a friend, and maybe that wasn't the best way to do it. And, yes, I was getting angry because I wanted Sandrine to relax and to tell Scott that it was all okay."

"*All okay?*" Keane said, studying this very strange male in front of him. Greg was the opposite of the kind of guys who Keane hung out with. "So, if it's okay for *him* to cheat, does that mean it's okay for *you* to cheat too?"

"No, it's not okay for anybody to cheat," Greg said, "but it happens."

"It happens, and everybody's just supposed to forget about it?"

"Well, she could have been friendly, at least. No reason she couldn't have made an effort to be friendly."

Keane nodded as if it made sense, but, to him, it made no sense at all. "So what did Scott do when Sandrine went into the water?"

"Nothing," Greg said. "What was he supposed to do? No point in a third person going into the water after them."

"Well, why would he go? If she had jumped, surely she would have said something to him."

"Yeah, of course she did. She had a life jacket on, and she did head straight for Brenda," Greg said. "You should talk to Scott about it," he said eagerly.

"Yeah, that's a good idea. Where is he?"

"He's upstairs. You should go up and see him."

Keane crossed his arms, leaned against the doorway and said, "I'm not leaving these women."

Greg started to get angry once more. "It's almost like you think I'll hurt Brenda," he said. "I love her."

"Yeah? But it's okay for your friend to be a cheating, lying sack of shit. You think it's okay to cheat too on the woman you supposedly love, but you're here to make sure that you get a chance to see her."

"Just because he cheated doesn't mean I cheated," Greg said. "And I do happen to love Brenda."

"Ah, okay. So you didn't cheat because you love her, but the other guy cheated so, therefore, he didn't love her?"

Greg looked very confused. "Look. Somehow we got off

into a very strange conversation, and we need to get back on track. As long as Brenda's okay and she's healthy, I'll wait until I can see her."

"Good," Keane said. "Maybe you should send Scott down, so I can have a talk with him."

"Sure," Greg said. He took a few steps away, then turned back. "I just don't understand what capacity you are here in," he said. "You're acting like you're security or something."

"Or something," Keane said softly, very softly. His gaze narrowed as he looked at the tall man, Greg was suddenly looking for a way to retreat.

"And, if I find out that you haven't been faithful to Brenda in these last few years, I'll be having another talk with you too."

"What the fuck, man?" Greg said. "There's no law against having an affair."

"No," Keane said. "But there are morals and ethics, and, you know, honor. Reasons not to do such a thing. But I gather those don't really matter to you."

"It happened way early in our relationship. It's not an issue," he said. "She probably even knows about it."

"Then no reason to hide it, is there?" Keane asked.

"No. No, there isn't. I can talk to her about it later, if it's a big deal," he said, backing down the hallway.

"I guess it depends on if she knows about it or not, right? I mean, you're the one who said she knows."

"I'm sure she does," he said. "Like I said, it was a while ago."

"And what's the lady's name?"

The guy gave him a haunted look and said, "I don't have to tell you that."

"If it was a long time ago, and she already knows about it, what difference does it make?"

"Lily," he murmured as he bolted backward. "Her sister, Lily."

That's when Keane heard a voice behind him.

"What a lying sack of shit," Brenda roared at the open door. "My own sister?"

Keane turned and looked at her with interest and said, "Oh. I guess you didn't know about it, huh?"

CHAPTER 12

SANDRINE WOKE UP to the sound of Greg's voice. For some reason their door was slightly open letting them hear all that nastiness in clear audio. She lay here, listening to the conversation, almost giggling at Keane twisting Greg's words around and making Greg tell the truth. When she heard that he'd had an affair, it made her sick. But when he admitted it was with Brenda's sister, her heart broke for her friend.

No way in hell Brenda knew about that. She never would have accepted it. Her sister was one who would have never let it be known either. Lily was always the jealous type, always one to be taking toys away from Brenda when they were younger. And it continued when it came to boys. But Sandrine had thought Greg was different and had hoped they had something solid together. Then she heard Brenda below her. First yelling and screaming, then bursting into tears. Sandrine rolled over slowly, and, moving carefully, she hopped down to the bottom bunk, wrapping Brenda in her arms.

Sandrine looked at Keane, who winced at her and quietly mouthed, "I'm sorry."

She shook her head. "We're better off knowing," she said. And that started Brenda bawling her eyes out again.

Sandrine said, "Now that we're awake, you don't have to

stay on your post though."

He nodded and disappeared, closing the door behind him. She hugged Brenda, who was draped in her arms, hot tears rolling down her cheeks.

"How could he do that?" Brenda mumbled.

"It was early, he said," Sandrine muttered. "And you know what your sister can be like."

"And I warned him about that too," she said. "He just laughed and promised me that he didn't like her at all."

"Yeah, but men can be men," Sandrine said sadly. The two women just held each other close.

Finally Brenda sat up. Looking at Sandrine, she took a deep breath. "I don't even know what to do."

"You'll do nothing for a while," Sandrine said simply. "We've both been through a lot. It's been a stressful and traumatic couple of days. We need to go home and let things calm down for a little bit." Stroking Brenda's hair, she continued, "After that, you'll be in a better position to think about how you feel about Greg and what you want going forward. Then you can process all that and find out anything else you need to know."

Brenda nodded and sniffled. "No matter what, he's still a lying sack of shit. And I really do like that phrase."

Sandrine chuckled. "Yeah, it's definitely colorful and obviously hits the spot in some cases." Stretching, she said, "I think we'll be home soon."

"Good," Brenda said. "I'm exhausted."

"Exactly. So let's get you home, then into bed, and maybe, when we're both up for it, we'll do some shopping. Get us a little retail therapy," she said with a laugh. "It's good that you aren't living with him yet. I think you need a few days to yourself."

Brenda sat up, wiped her eyes and whispered, "God, what a shit trip this turned out to be. What a nightmare."

"Yep," Sandrine said. "But at least it's almost over."

In fact, the next couple hours passed quickly, as the two women talked quietly. Before they knew it, Keane was at the door, telling them they were coming into the docks. By the time they disembarked and headed to the parking lot, Keane was already waiting for them up ahead with Lennox. Sandrine looked at Keane and said, "I suppose I say goodbye now, huh?"

He shook his head. "We'll see you both home. Neither of you drove down here, did you?"

"No," Sandrine replied. "I caught a ride with them, and we came in Greg's truck," she said.

"I'm not going anywhere with him," Brenda said. She had steadfastly refused to even talk to Greg. Although he had tried several times, she had just held up a hand and said, "I have some things to think about, and I'm not talking to you until I've done that and until I'm ready."

He had such a crestfallen look on his face that Sandrine almost felt sorry for him. *Almost.* She looked at him and said, "You really shouldn't have had an affair with Lily."

He raised both hands, palms up. "I knew I should have told Brenda," he said, "but I didn't know how."

"You shouldn't have done it in the first place," Sandrine said. "A woman can forgive a lot of things, but something like that—I don't know how they can." With that, she turned and walked away.

Nico was there with a large SUV. He held open the rear passenger door and said, "Ladies, we'll be taking you home."

Sandrine smiled and waited for Brenda to get in, then crawled in behind her. "Have you made contact with

Brenda's father yet?"

"Yes. He's waiting for her at home."

Brenda cried out, "What? He's there?"

Lennox nodded as he got into the driver's side. "Yep. We'll drop you off first," he said. They drove through the traffic, everyone fairly quiet until they got to Brenda's apartment. When they made the turn, they could see her father standing outside her apartment, waiting to meet them. Brenda let out a broken cry as Lennox pulled up. Barely waiting for the vehicle to come to a stop, she opened the door and jumped into her father's arms before anybody could say anything.

Sandrine sat in the back of the vehicle, tears in her eyes. "Will you guys get out and say anything?"

Keane looked back at her and asked, "Are you getting out?"

Sandrine frowned, then shook her head. "No. Look at them." The two had their arms wrapped around each other as Brenda's father led her to the front door.

At that moment, Brenda realized she hadn't said anything and came racing back. "I wanted to say, *Thank you*," she explained.

Sandrine took the moment to hop out and hug her friend. "Get some rest. I'll call you."

Still sniffling, but with a smile on her face, Brenda waved at the two men. "Thank you so much for everything."

Her father lifted a hand, and that was it, and the two walked inside.

Sandrine jumped back in the SUV. "I'm surprised her father didn't thank you."

"He already has," Keane replied. "We spoke to him on the phone earlier."

"Wow." It seemed rather cold to her.

"He's an admiral," Keane said. "We did our job, and he knows it."

"I guess it doesn't matter if you're okay with it," she said. "Just seems like a handshake and a thank-you wouldn't have been out of order."

"But neither is necessary," Lennox said. "So shall we drop you off too?"

"If you must," she said. "I'm not looking forward to going home though."

"What? I thought you were," Keane replied.

She nodded but frowned. "I know. It's just the thought of being alone doesn't thrill me right now."

"Well, I can always drop off Keane too," Lennox said. "I've got to report in and do a couple other things," he said, "but Keane can spend some time, if that's what the two of you decide on."

Keane looked back at her and said, "I wasn't planning on leaving you alone tonight."

She looked at him, relief washing over her. Tears gathered in the corner of her eyes. "Thank you," she whispered. "I know I'll have to get over it soon, and that some would say I don't really have anything to get over," she said. "It's just—it was so goddamn lonely out there."

"Hey, let's get you back home and settled in your own space," he said. "You just need some time, and you'll be fine."

She smiled and nodded. Soon they pulled up in front of her apartment building. She hopped out and patted her pockets, where she had put her house key, so she didn't need a purse when going sailing. "I don't have my key anymore." She stared at the brick building. "It doesn't look like much, does it?"

"It doesn't matter," he said. "It's not about what you live in. It's about who lives there."

She loved that. "I'm glad to hear that. Most of the time people are all about what you own."

"But they haven't lived through something life-threatening. You have," he said. "And you already know that what you own has nothing to do with who you are."

She looped her arm through his and said, "And it's midafternoon, and I'm already exhausted."

"You probably need more food too," he said.

"Well, a solid meal would help," she said. "If I can convince you to stay at my place overnight, maybe we could order in something."

"Or we could go out for dinner," he said.

She looked up at him and whispered, "But that's almost like a date."

He laughed. "Almost," he agreed. "Would you be against that?"

"Hell, no," she said. "I certainly would not. I was hoping to see you again, naturally. After all, we have this thing between us. I just didn't know what the protocol was."

"No protocol," he said. "Just life as we choose to make it."

"It's hard to argue with that," she said.

"Let's get settled in and see how we do. You might just want to go to bed and stay there," he said.

"Maybe so."

At the door, she stared at the lock. "I don't have a key. I used to keep a key under the mat... then decided it wasn't a good idea considering my ass of an ex..."

"Good. And no key is no problem." He reached into his

back pocket and pulled out a small case, then a small tool. Within seconds the door was open. As soon as she got inside, she walked into the living room, looked around and said, "You know what? I really don't like this place."

He laughed. "It took you getting washed out to sea and abandoned on a not-so-deserted island to decide you don't like where you live?"

She turned to look at him. "I know it probably sounds foolish, but I think it's more a case of suddenly wanting to change things that may have bothered me before, but I wasn't willing to make the effort." She glanced around the apartment, shrugged and said, "I need a shower and a change of clothes."

"Do you have any coffee?"

"Oh, of course," she said. "Coffee." She headed into the kitchen, put on a pot, then turned to face him. "Did you bring a bag or anything?"

He pointed at the bag by the door. "I've got my laptop and stuff in there," he said. "I have some work to do."

She beamed. "So, are you okay if I have a shower?" she asked hesitantly.

His eyebrows shot up. "Why wouldn't I be?"

She shrugged irritably. "Never mind."

"Wait. Does it have something to do with Scott? No, don't answer. Just let me tell you something about me. This is your home. You can take a shower or do anything else any damn time you please. And the day I have a problem with it is the day you should throw my ass out." Taking her gently by the shoulders, he turned her and pointed her in the direction of the hallway. "Go get a shower. You'll feel better."

"That I will. Thank you." She headed down the hall and

into the bathroom. Turning on the water, she quickly got undressed.

When she stepped into the hot water, the whole sensation was such a shock to her system that she stood there shuddering, her body enjoying the hot water streaming over her. The last few days—exposed to the sun, sand, salt water and wind—had dried out her skin, and she still felt like she had sand everywhere. She was reminded of her early attempts to even relieve herself in that difficult environment. Not exactly her finest hour. Hopefully she wouldn't have any other chance to practice.

She quickly scrubbed herself down, washed her hair twice, scrubbed herself once more, and, when she finally felt clean again, she turned off the water and wrapped herself up in a big towel, grabbing another for her hair.

As she stood here in front of the mirror, she realized fatigue was once again draining her. But was it relief or fatigue or just the shock and adrenaline release now that she was home? Something had shifted, at least.

She made her way back into the bedroom and sagged onto the side of her bed. It was supposed to be just a nice day out on the boat with her friends. Just the three of them. But instead, it ended up being four of them, and even now she didn't know for sure what she wanted to do. The fact that Brenda had independently backed up what Sandrine had said was huge. But what did Greg say?

She dressed in some shorts and a T-shirt, then walked barefoot into the living room. Keane looked at her with a smile and said, "You look like you're eighteen."

"Well, you can add a decade to that," she said cheekily. "Thankfully I'm a few days older than I was when I went off that boat."

He nodded in understanding. "Nothing like a brush with death to make you rethink your life."

"Have you ever come close to dying?"

"Several times," he said. "I was a Navy SEAL for a long time, so I was in and out of dangerous situations often. I've never come close to drowning though. I did go parachuting and ended up with my chute not opening once," he said. "Thankfully it was a training session, and I survived. I've been shot several times and stabbed too."

She gasped, and her eyes were wide and round. "What?"

He shrugged. "Like I said, it makes you a little more aware of what's going on in your world, and a little happier to do the things you need to do. I find it makes me a little less tolerant of bullshit as well."

"Right," she said. "So what I'm feeling isn't all that odd?"

"Not at all," he said. "Expect it, and realize that it's a normal response to an abnormal situation. You will recover from this and will come away with a different perspective, which isn't a bad thing."

"I guess not," she affirmed. "I suppose I won't realize in what ways until a few days have gone by."

"Probably longer," he said. "You'll start to think about the things that are important in life. Things that you still want to do."

"I was thinking about that when I was on the beach, waiting to see if Brenda would survive or die," she said. "I thought of all the things I still wanted to do and what I would regret the most if I didn't get rescued. And I thought what I would change if I got a second chance."

"See? That's all really normal," he said. "Now that you have your second chance, what will you do with it?"

"That'll take some thinking."

"Well, you've already done something," he said. "You've broken things off with your boyfriend."

"But I did that before," she said with a smile. "That was a pretty easy decision."

"Nothing he said while you were sailing convinced you to consider going back with him? Greg said Scott got angry because you were being difficult."

"I was, in a way," she admitted. "I was really angry that they had finagled that whole scenario in the first place. Scott was pressuring me to come back and wanted me to say I forgave him and all the rest of it right there on the spot, and of course I couldn't do that," she said. "Finally I'd had enough. I started yelling and told him that I didn't want anything to do with him, that I'd have never gone on that trip if I'd known he'd be there and that he was the last person I wanted to spend time with."

"Fair enough," Keane said. "How did Greg react?"

"He snapped at me and said I shouldn't be so childish. He said that men had affairs. That's what they did, and I should forgive Scott and get on with it."

"Wow," Keane said. He tilted his head to the side and said, "Well, that pretty well lines up with what he told me in the hallway."

"Right? What I don't know is what Brenda will do now."

"Again, she needs time," he said. "It had to be really hard for her to hear that information, especially after all the trauma she'd been through already. And the trauma will put things in perspective."

"Right," she said. "I hope she ditches Greg."

He chuckled. "Why? Because he had an affair?"

"Because he had an affair and because he had it with her sister of all people and because he's lied about it all this time. And, if he did it once, he'll do it again," she said with a shrug. She walked to the coffeepot, grabbed cups from the cupboard and poured two cups, handing him one.

"Let's go sit outside on the small deck."

She led the way to a small deck off the living room. She sat in one of the two chairs and, with a huge sigh of relief, tilted her head back and lifted her feet so they rested on the railing. "That's it. I'm here for the night." She chuckled.

"Will you ever go sailing again?"

She had to stop and think about it. "I don't know. It was pretty traumatic."

"Have you done much sailing?"

"Yes, and no. I had gone out with them many times, but I've never been sailing on my own."

"So you might like it under the right circumstances?"

"Maybe in a bigger boat. A much bigger boat," she said. And he immediately started to laugh. She looked at him and grinned. "You're really easy to be with, you know?"

"GOOD," HE SAID. He reached out a hand immediately, and she reached back. They sat like that, quiet and comfortable for the longest time. He wondered what he was getting into. "So, are you over the breakup with Scott?"

"I was over the breakup the minute I realized what had happened, and even more so as I managed to get through the actual act of breaking up," she said. "That was more traumatizing than anything. It took a while to recover from the betrayal afterward, from a man who was closer to me than anyone else. But, once I realized he was a cheat, I was done with him emotionally."

"But do you regard all men like him?"

She rolled her head and looked at him and said, "Meaning, do I see you the same as Scott is? No."

"So, if we went out for dinner tonight, you might be okay with that? If you're feeling up to it, that is."

"I'd be totally okay with that," she said with a bright smile. She sat back, did a self-assessment and said, "Yeah. I think I'm strong enough to go out. And maybe that's a perfect plan. Go out for a nice dinner and then come back and finally get a good night's sleep."

"That's probably a good idea."

"The police, they won't need me for anything, will they?"

"Yes, they probably will," he said. "I'm not exactly sure to what extent, but it's quite possible."

"*Ugh*," she said. "I was hoping it would end with the coast guard."

"Maybe, at least if we're lucky. But otherwise it won't be that big of a deal."

"Well, there's no point in worrying about it now," she said. "I'll deal with it if I have to."

"That's the way to do it," he said, just as his stomach gurgled.

She looked at him and gasped. "Of course you're hungry," she said. "You haven't eaten, have you?"

"I have but not a whole lot."

"Where do you want to go for dinner?" He named a popular steak and seafood place close by. She nodded and said, "I'll get changed." She hopped up and walked back inside again.

"Don't change for my sake," he said.

She stopped, looked at him, frowned and said, "Really?"

He raised his eyebrows. "I can't change. I'm wearing the only clothes I brought with me," he said.

She smiled, walked back over and said, "Do you think the restaurant will let us in?"

"They'll let us in just fine."

She laughed and said, "Okay, prove it to me."

He grinned, then hopped up, grabbed his wallet and his phone, and sent a text message to Lennox to tell him what they were doing. Then he headed out the front door with her laughingly towed behind him. "Do you have a car?"

"I do," she said with a grin. "It's not fancy, but it does the job."

"That's fine," he said. "But we're close enough to walk. I thought maybe it would be good to get out for a bit."

"Walking is a great idea."

As they walked, she suddenly said, "I told the captain. About being pushed."

"I heard," he said comfortably.

"I'm afraid now that I shouldn't have."

"Why is that?"

"Because I'm sure it's gotten back to Scott."

"Won't matter as I told Greg the same thing. He was supposed to send Scott down to talk to me while we were still on the cutter, but that didn't happen."

"I don't really want to face him over it."

"Maybe not," he said, "but do you know if there is any chance that he overheard the fact that Brenda saw him?"

"I don't know," she said. "Maybe Brenda said something to Greg, but I'm not sure when that would have been."

"Or to her father."

"Right," she said. "I really didn't want to open that can of worms."

"The can of worms is open," he said. "The question is, what will you do about it?"

"I don't know," she said. "I guess I was hoping to avoid the whole thing."

He smiled and nodded. He worried about it though because he didn't know what Scott's basic character was. "Is Scott likely to be vindictive?"

"He certainly won't appreciate anybody accusing him of trying to knock me off the boat," she said. "I'm sure he'll try to spin it as a joke."

"Some joke."

"I know," she said.

"Well, how about we forget all about it for now," he said, as he led her across the street and into the restaurant. Inside, they were given a table and spent the next two hours thoroughly enjoying their meal and each other. He really liked who she was as a person. He didn't know that he'd ever pick her out of a lineup as being somebody that he'd enjoy spending time with, as he tended toward brunettes. She was a blonde. As he got to know her, her real beauty started to shine.

By the time they were ready to head back home again, he tucked her arm into his elbow and led her outside.

She yawned. "I'm sorry."

"Come on. Let's get you to bed."

She yawned once more and said, "I'm so damn tired."

"I know. That's understandable. You'll be fine. You just need a little time." They walked slowly all the way back, and she let him into the apartment.

Once inside, she turned and said, "I'm just too tired all

the time now."

He placed a finger against her lips and whispered, "I know. Go on."

She smiled, hooked her arms around his neck and gave him a big hug.

He held her close, surprised but delighted, loving the feel of her warm and sexy body in his arms, but knowing that nothing would happen right now. She was too exhausted and confused for anything right now.

She kissed him gently. "Thank you for a wonderful evening," she said, then slowly made her way to the bedroom and closed the door.

He pulled out his laptop and settled at the kitchen table. First he sent Lennox a text message, saying they were back and that she was safely locked inside again. When his phone rang, he pulled it out. "Lennox, what's up?"

"You clear?"

"Yeah, she went to bed."

"I got a phone call from the admiral," Lennox said. "He called me about ten minutes ago."

"What's up?"

"He was taking Brenda back to his place," he said, "over in the Hillcrest area. Anyway, they had just barely gotten out of the parking lot, and they were involved in a head-on collision."

"Oh, Jesus," he said, straightening. "Is Brenda okay?"

"Well, maybe *head-on* is not quite the right word," he said. "Basically a vehicle smashed into the passenger side, right where Brenda sat. She's been taken to the hospital, banged up but okay. The hospital's keeping her overnight because of her other injuries and all. The admiral has posted two security guards as well."

"Security guards?" Keane's voice hardened. "Are we thinking this was deliberate?"

"The admiral said the other vehicle, which was driving on his side of the road, suddenly came across the center line and targeted the passenger side."

"So somebody tried to kill her?"

"That's what he's afraid of. He's opening a full investigation and has already found out that the vehicle was stolen."

"From where?"

"The same apartment building where Brenda lives."

Keane sat back and thought about that. "God, she just gets back after a trauma like nearly drowning, then the bullshit afterward with Greg, and now gets attacked?"

"Yeah. So then came the question of why."

"Of course, the first off the top of my head is the smugglers," he said.

"Exactly. That guy we let loose in his Zodiac, by the way? The other rescue boat did locate it and our smuggler. Dead, with a bullet between the eyes."

"Wow," Keane said. "Talk about tying up loose ends."

"What are the chances somebody else was on that island?" Lennox asked.

"It's definitely possible," Keane said. "We knew that. Honestly, half a dozen people could have been there if they were familiar with the island and knew what they were doing. We could have been under watch the entire time."

"There's a disconcerting thought," Lennox said.

"I know, right? Now the question is, where and how do we find out who was after Brenda tonight? I doubt the smugglers followed us all the way back to her apartment." But then he stopped. "Shit. I mean, we could have been followed all the way back," he said.

"I didn't see anyone," Lennox said. "But, if they wanted to make sure she didn't survive that trip to the island, that's one hell of a way to do it."

"Nobody else survived," Keane said.

"The four of us did," Lennox said, "but that's it."

"Great. Obviously, if Brenda's in the hospital under guard, Sandrine is potentially in danger as well."

"Which is why I'm calling," Lennox said. "Brenda's dad couldn't identify the driver, but it was a lone male."

"Well, that's something, but that could be the smugglers, or it could even be her stupid ex-boyfriend, Greg."

"*Ex*-boyfriend?"

"Well, I don't know that Brenda broke up with him *yet*," Keane said. "If she was smart, she would. Sandrine thinks she should. But the two of them haven't had any time to talk. I've been with Sandrine the whole time, and Brenda's been with the admiral."

"But still, it's quite likely that's what she would have done. Especially if Greg kept trying to contact her when she made it clear she wanted some alone time."

"But that's not a reason to kill her."

"No," Lennox said. "I'm down at the hospital now, and I'm hoping to ask both her and her father some questions."

"Well, maybe you should come here afterward," Keane said. "I'll stand watch on Sandrine tonight. She's gone to bed now that we're back from dinner, but I wouldn't feel good about leaving her alone until we find out what's going on."

"Yeah, you definitely need to stay there. I'll be by in a couple hours to give you a break on watch."

"Well, check in with me when you're done at the hospital," he said. "I'll see what's happening here."

"Hopefully nothing," Lennox said.

"I hope so," he said, "but I'm not that confident at the moment."

"Later, man," Lennox said as the hung up.

Keane put away his phone, his mind spinning. He looked up to see Sandrine standing nearby.

"What was that?" she asked. She wore the tiniest of nighties with little spaghetti straps.

Not only did it not hide a damn thing, it seemed to highlight every damn thing that he wanted to see. He swallowed hard and closed his eyes for a moment. "Do you mind putting on a robe?" But she either didn't hear him or didn't understand.

"What was that? What's going on with Brenda?"

He groaned. "That was Lennox. He's calling from the hospital. At Brenda's bedside in fact."

"What's wrong with her?" Sandrine cried out, rushing forward. "Is she okay?"

"She's okay," he said, "but there's been an incident."

Sandrine stared at him in shock—her jaw literally dropping. "What kind of an incident?"

He motioned toward the table, and she sat across from him, her hands immediately reaching for his. Trying to avoid seeing her plump breasts right at the edge of the table, he swallowed and kept his gaze on her face. "She and her father were in a hit-and-run accident."

"What?"

He explained what Lennox had said, and she sank back in shock.

"She survives nearly drowning in the ocean, being injured and stranded on a deserted island, drug smugglers trying to kill her, and, after she finally makes it home, somebody tries to run her down a block from her apartment?"

"Not exactly. Sounds like both vehicles were driving on a small side street, but the admiral felt the driver seemed to accelerate and to target her position in the car when he rammed it."

"My God!" she said, huge tears welling up in her eyes. "What is going on?"

"Well, one of the first thoughts that Lennox and I were just discussing," he said, "is whether the drug smugglers knew anything about her, and we wondered if they had decided to cross off more loose ends."

She stared at him uncomprehendingly.

"After we got picked up off the island, as we were underway, we saw a boat floating out in the ocean," he said. "The second coast guard boat went to check it out and identified the one smuggler that we had seen earlier on the island."

"The one that left after shooting his partner?"

"Exactly."

"And was he alive?"

"No, he wasn't. He'd been shot between the eyes."

"But why though? So he couldn't say anything?"

"Yes, and probably as punishment for leaving the smuggling profession. Jobs like that are permanent. They probably assumed that he was trying to take off. Or maybe they had a conversation with him first. I don't know. But the end result is that he's dead."

"So they definitely were eliminating outstanding threats to their operation."

"Exactly. So the question is, did they know that you and Brenda were there, and are they trying to take down the rest of their loose ends?"

"Jesus," she said, staring at him in shock. "Does this ever end?"

He nodded. "It does. Just not as fast as we had hoped."

"Do you really think that's likely?" she asked, speaking slowly. "The only ones who saw our faces are dead now."

"The only ones who saw your faces *that you know of*," he said quietly. "Lennox and I were just discussing whether somebody else could have been on that island. Who maybe didn't know we were there or where we were at."

"But, if we didn't know they were there, and they didn't know about us," she said, "why would they care if we lived or died?"

"Because it could be a place they use on a regular basis," he said, "and maybe they want to make sure nobody'll keep sniffing around their operation."

CHAPTER 13

"**T**HAT IS JUST so bizarre," she whispered.

"I know," he said. "But it is what it is."

She shook her head. "I need to go to the hospital and see her."

"No," he said. "You need to stay here, safe and sound."

She jutted her jaw out at him.

He grinned. "Lennox has gone to the hospital to see what's going on. The admiral has hired two security guards to make sure Brenda stays safe there."

"None of this makes any sense," she said, feeling bewildered. "We just went sailing for one stupid day."

"And sometimes you cross paths with all the wrong people," he said.

"Exactly," she said. "And now what?"

"Now we wait," he said. "You go to bed and sleep until morning, when hopefully we'll have more answers. Lennox or I will be here all night. We also must consider the possibility that it could have just been an accident."

"Because we're all hypersensitive and think the boogeyman's turning up in every corner?" She liked that idea. But somehow she knew it wouldn't be that easy.

"Listen. I have to ask you this. Would Greg do anything like this?"

She stared at him in shock. "I don't know," she said.

"I'm clearly not the best judge. I wouldn't have thought he would sleep with Brenda's sister or go with the 'all men are cheaters' defense. Hell, I wouldn't have thought he'd set me up to ride on the 'happily ever after' sailing adventure."

"Got it. I understand," he admitted. "And why would he try to hurt Brenda now?"

"Only in rage," she said. "It doesn't make any sense any other way."

"Right," he said. "Okay. So I really suggest you go back to bed and see if you can get some rest. Lennox will call me after he's learned whatever he can at the hospital."

"Nobody could identify the driver? If it was Greg, Brenda should have seen him, right?"

"Apparently she was lying back a bit, with her eyes closed, when they were hit. By the time the admiral managed to get his wits about him, the driver was already long gone."

"And the vehicle?"

"Stolen from the same apartment complex she lives in."

As he watched, Sandrine shoulders sagged. "I don't want to believe it was Greg," she said, "but I just don't know anymore."

Keane stood. Tugging her to her feet, he wrapped her in his arms and said, "Go on back to bed."

"I can't sleep now," she said, staring up at him. "You can't possibly think that'll work?"

"I know, and I'm sorry," Keane said. "I was hoping you would sleep and find this out in the morning, after we knew more."

"I don't want to find this out any time of day," she said, but she did turn and head toward the bedroom. "God." Not getting far, she collapsed on the couch in the living room and said, "It makes no sense at all."

"I know," he said, "but look. You still need to try to sleep," he said.

She shook her head, yet she wandered back to the bedroom. "I just hate to think of Brenda and all she'd been through. I can't believe it's Greg," she said.

"So who else?" he asked, leaning against her doorway.

She loved the look of him here. She looked back at her bed, then at him and said, "I know one way to put this all out of my mind."

He shook his head. "Oh, no. I won't be an exercise to help you forget the things going on in your life," he scolded lightly.

She smiled. "Maybe not," she said, "but you know it's something that you and I both want. And right now, I sure as hell would appreciate something to take my mind off all this." With a shrug, she crawled into bed. "It's a pretty shitty world out there."

"You don't have to be part of it to that extent," he said.

"Bullshit," she said, surprising them both. "It's already on my plate, so what am I supposed to do about it now?"

He frowned.

She nodded. "Exactly." As she lay here, she looked up at him and said, "What if it was Scott?"

His mouth formed a tight grim line as he shook his head. "We can't try to cram somebody into the role," he said slowly, "just because we would like it to be him."

Well, he was right that she would like it to be Scott. She was so done with that man. "What if he heard that Brenda had seen him push me?" At his indrawn breath, she nodded. "I don't know how he would have heard that, or maybe he didn't know for sure," she said. "I'm grasping at straws. But, if he found out what she saw, maybe, by taking her out of the equation, it becomes my word against his."

"And if he tries to take you out again?" Keane asked.

She stared at him and swallowed hard. "Jesus, I don't like this theory." She sat up against the headboard, grabbed her covers and pulled them up to her chest. "So, if it is him, how do we find out?"

Keane had his phone out and was walking into the other room, probably talking to Lennox.

She groaned and dropped her head against the headboard. She really did want him in bed with her, but not just as a teddy bear for comfort for the night.

As she lay here, staring at the balcony, she remembered something else. She got up slowly and went to the glass doors. Opening them, she stepped out. She stood there for a long moment, and, reassured that nobody was here, she finally stepped back into her bedroom.

Keane stood there, staring at her. "What's the matter?"

She shrugged and then said, "I just remembered that one time we were locked out of the apartment. Scott managed to get in by climbing onto the balcony."

His eyebrows shot up, and he strode over to the balcony and looked down. "You're on the second floor, and those trees are too damn close."

"And," she said, "look. Dumpsters over there by the lower patio, and they have that long trellis there."

He looked at it and nodded. "Still a bit dodgy but, if it doesn't work, that's a short fall to recover from."

"But that would mean we were thinking that he might try to break in."

"Well, who knows at this point?" Keane said. "And why would he need to, if you'll leave him a key under a mat?" he said, raising his eyebrow and shaking his head. "Greg told me that Scott tried to call you multiple times and tried to come see you, and you didn't answer."

She frowned at him. "I didn't answer the phone calls, but I don't know anything about him ever coming here. I didn't know he even knew where I was living since we broke up two months ago."

"Have you noticed any trouble?"

She shook her head. "No, nothing. And, for the record, I just stuck that duplicate key there because I wasn't taking my purse or anything on the sailing trip."

"I don't know," he said. "Is everything still the way it's been? Any valuables missing?"

"Everything's the same. No, nothing's missing that I've noticed." She studied where his focus landed, places oddly inconsistent with his questions. She looked up at him. "Come on. Something is on your mind. What is it?"

"The reasons why a boyfriend who doesn't want to break up with somebody might come into her place."

"And you're thinking what?"

"Video cameras," he said bluntly.

The color drained from her face, and she felt her stomach sinking. She sagged down on the bad. "What for?" she asked faintly.

"To put on the internet for revenge is one thing," he said. "For his own personal voyeurism is another."

She buried her face in her hands as she thought about it. "I haven't noticed anything, but can you check?"

"I'll check now," he said. "But tomorrow morning, let's get these locks changed." As he looked at the balcony, he frowned and said, "On second thought, how about you just move? This place isn't very secure."

"Right," she said. "I really don't like this apartment anyway."

"You don't really need anything else to give yourself permission to move," he said; then he went through the apartment. When he came back, he shook his head. "I don't see anything."

"Oh, good, thank you," she said. "You hear such nightmares about an ex posting sex pictures to humiliate their partners and things like that."

"Did he ever take videos or pictures of you like that?"

She shook her head. "No, it's not my thing," she said slowly. "I've always been a little worried about that."

"Good thing," he said, "and we don't know for sure that he had ever done that before, in your former apartment or his, when you were together. Guys with bruised egos aren't always that truthful with their friends."

"Right," she said, giving her face a scrub. "You'll stay for the night, right?"

"Yes, and, should I need to leave, Lennox will come over," he said.

"And you'll call me if Brenda's condition worsens? Or if she needs me?"

"I promise," he said.

"Okay then, I'll try to sleep because it sounds like I'll have a lot to do tomorrow. First thing I'll do is give notice and find a new apartment."

"Let's get you through tonight first," he said.

"But seriously, I don't want to be here any longer than I have to." And, with that, she dropped her head onto her pillow and waved her hand.

"Does that mean *goodbye, get out of here* or what?" he asked with a smile.

"Well, I'd ask for a good-night kiss, but that would be

too dangerous."

"I wouldn't mind a good-night kiss," he said, his voice thickening. When he came over and dropped down beside her, he gave her a gentle kiss.

She wrapped her arms around his neck. "A real kiss would be better."

By the time he kissed her for real, and he finally lifted his head, they were both panting. "Jesus," he said, dropping his forehead to rest on hers.

"I know," she said, sliding her tongue along his mouth and just inside the edge of his lips. "So much damn heat is between us."

"It's not always like this," he said, gently kissing her on her cheeks and her chin. "And this doesn't change anything. I won't be just a fling to get you through the night."

"You're not a teddy bear to comfort me tonight," she said. "You're somebody I want to spend some time with. To figure out if what we have can go anywhere. And that's not a surprise to you."

"No," he said. "That definitely isn't, and neither is this." And, with that, he kissed her harder.

She wrapped her arms tighter and clung to him. Her body twisted as she realized one of Keane's hand had reached under the covers to come up and cup her breast. "You're playing with fire," she said. "I'm already so damn hot that, if you aren't coming to bed with me, you need to back up several paces."

He chuckled. "I don't think I can, Sandrine," he whispered.

When he slowly withdrew his hand, she grabbed it, then gently placed it back. "Please stay."

He took several long, slow breaths, and she knew he was

reaching for control.

She slid a hand down his chest, his abs, to the ridge just under the heavy denim fabric of his jeans and gently stroked him. "Why not?" she whispered.

"Because it's not the right thing to do."

"You think I'm traumatized and I'm not going into this with the right emotional balance or something?"

"Something like that," he said, arching when her fingers wrapped around his ridge. "But you're really shaking my resolve."

"It needs to be shaken," she said. "It needs to be shaken a lot."

He stared down at her, feeling torn. She didn't know how to convince him to stay.

"You know this is what we both want," she said. "And I don't want it just for tonight."

"We'll see," he said, leaning down and kissing the side of her neck, before nibbling his way up to her earlobe as he gently sucked on the end. She twisted her hand, sliding down to reach around his buttocks and squeezed. He swore as she laughed and pulled his T-shirt up above his belly and over his head. And, just like that, he stood, chucked his jeans, and he said, "If you're sorry in the morning—"

She threw the covers back and kneeled on the bed and said, "I'm just sorry we wasted the last three hours," she said. "You know we could have ordered takeout and had it delivered."

He laughed, but he stood in front of her, completely nude, proud, erect and so damn male that she almost panted with need.

She shook her head. "I don't think I've ever wanted somebody as much as I want you right now," she whispered.

"You're so damn gorgeous."

"Hell, no, I'm not," he said. "You're the one who is."

As he stepped forward, she wrapped one hand around his erection, and the other was already sliding up over his chest. "You are gorgeous," she whispered. "You can't lie about something like that." His muscles clenched under her touch. She leaned over and gently kissed the tip of his erection, hearing him groan as she let her tongue play at the top and then slide down ever-so-gently.

Suddenly she was picked up and tossed on the bed. "Playing with fire will get you burned," he whispered.

She groaned as he slowly lifted the nightie up past her hips, his gaze burning deep when her hips and belly were exposed up to her breasts.

Then he lowered his head and took one of her nipples into his mouth, sucking deep and sending a heavy pulse through her lower abdomen. And then his hand slid down to cup her most intimate parts, playing with the moisture already gathered there.

She pulled the nightie over her head and tugged him down to her. "I want more," she said. "I want it all."

"Greedy much?"

"Very." She used her hands, her tongue, as she stroked and kissed her way down, gently cupping his balls below his erection, stroking, tasting his body with her tongue, and wrapping herself over and around as she tried to explore every bit of him.

Finally he captured her traveling hands and tugged her up so she straddled him. "Easy," he said.

"I can't," she said. "There is no easy right now." She reached down and positioned his erection as she slowly lowered herself onto his shaft. He groaned but held himself still as she settled deeper and lower, adjusting to the size of him. She arched backward. "How do you feel about riding?"

"Go, baby," he said, "ride away."

She slowly lowered and raised herself a couple times, then leaned forward and placed her hands on his shoulders and started to ride. And, with a natural movement she didn't know she had, she rode them both to the cliff. And just when she thought she wouldn't make it, he grabbed her hips and ground himself higher up before exploding inside her. Tremors echoed all the way through her, setting off even more tremors as her own climax ripped from one end to the other.

She cried out in shock, and he held her firm, whispering to her to let it go. She tumbled into a massive chasm of exploding color in his arms. Gently weeping, she lay against his chest, amazed, delighted and overwhelmed. "That," she whispered, "was fantastic."

His chuckle rumbled through his chest, making her smile as she stroked the inside of his thighs and then the outside of his hips.

"You are a marvelous male machine," she whispered.

"Ditto," he whispered. "Very female, obviously."

She chuckled and shifted upward slightly, and he left her body. He pulled the blankets over them, settled her beside him, and whispered, "Now will you sleep?"

"If you'll be here when I wake up so we can go for round two, then, yes."

"I promise."

"I'm still stressed," she murmured, "but I feel so much better."

"Sleep," he grumbled, wrapping an arm around her.

She closed her eyes and immediately slept. She woke

several hours later, Keane's two fingers busy between her legs, and gradually came to consciousness.

"I couldn't wait," he whispered. As he slid inside her from the back, he took her on a long and slow rise to temperatures almost as hot and as fast as the first time, but the dropping-off-the-cliff was smoother, easier and so damn emotional. She had tears in her eyes when he was finally done, and her body lay trembling in his arms.

"Sleep," he ordered.

She closed her eyes for a second time and fell asleep.

KEANE OPENED HIS eyes, hearing something off. It took a moment to reorient and to determine where he was. But still hearing that inner voice, he grabbed his phone and sent Lennox a text, asking if everything was okay. The answer came back immediately.

Yeah. At the hospital, still standing guard. Didn't want to leave yet, Lennox explained.

So you're not headed here? Keane confirmed.

Not immediately. Why? Lennox replied.

It means, it's not you who I hear.

Slipping out of bed, Keane pulled on his boxers and jeans, checking outside the balcony's glass doors to find nothing. The bedroom door was open just a fraction. He had no weapon with him, as he hadn't had a chance to take the gear out of the vehicle Nico had dropped them off in.

Keane nudged the door open ever-so-slightly and slid down the hallway, where he could look at the living room. It was empty too. But then he heard the sound again. And, even as he watched from the corner, he could see the front door slowly open. He watched and waited as the man crept in and closed the door behind him.

He had ropes with him, which was not a good sign. He laid everything down on the kitchen counter and took off his jacket as if preparing to relax or at least to get to work. Then he slipped through the kitchen to the living room.

Not sure exactly what this guy thought he was doing, Keane then saw the handgun. He sucked his breath back because now a confrontation was out of the question. He backed up ever-so-slowly toward the bedroom. From the shadows he couldn't see the man's face either. As the intruder came around the corner, it was all Keane could do to duck back out of sight in the bedroom, but he was also on the far side, where he couldn't make it behind the bedroom door now. He crept to the closet as the man stepped into the bedroom. He had the ropes in his right hand. The mask he wore hid his face.

He was white and about five-ten and lean, maybe 180 pounds. That was all Keane could see. But he heard the voice.

"Wake up, you stupid bitch! Wake up!" He reached down and smacked Sandrine on her feet.

She woke up in shock, then looked at him and screamed.

He grabbed her ankle and gave it a hard slap. "Stop screaming," he said. "I've already got enough lessons I have to teach you. I don't want to sit here and shut your mouth up too. But, if you don't stop, I will."

She immediately stopped, grabbing deep, gulping breaths. "What do you want?" she cried out.

"What do you think I want, bitch?" he said. "I want you to fucking die."

She stared at him in shock.

Keane waited for his chance, but, from where he was, he didn't have a clear move. He didn't want her to get hurt, and he didn't want that damn gun to go off. But the guy was now pacing back and forth at the end of her bed. If he would just walk a little closer to the closet, Keane would have him.

"Why do you want me to die?" she asked. "I've never done anything to you."

"You were supposed to die in that goddamn boat," he snapped.

"What?" Slowly she pulled her legs up and kneeled with the blanket pulled up to her chest, since she didn't have any clothes on. She stared up at him in the dark. "Scott, is that you?"

He reached up and pulled the hood off his face. "God damn fucking right it's me," he spat. "Why couldn't you have just died in the fucking water?"

She shook her head. "It wasn't enough that you pushed me into the water and left us to drown?"

"That storm was a godsend," he said. "Any opportunity to knock you overboard would work for me."

"Why?" she asked. "I didn't do anything to you."

"You broke up with me," he said, "and made me a laughingstock."

"Because I broke off our relationship? Who gave a shit about that?"

He shrugged. "Nobody dumps me," he said. "I'm the one who decides when the relationship is over."

She stared at him in horror. "All of this because I broke up with you, after I found you in bed with another woman, and somehow that's *my* fault, so you're trying to kill me over it?"

Keane could hear the anger rising in her voice. He really

loved the spirit in this girl. She'd been through so much and right now was facing a killer head-on instead of backing down and becoming a victim. She was strong and standing firm.

Scott stopped at the end of the bed, but he was still too damn far away, and he was now holding out the handgun. "If you don't shut your fucking mouth," he said, "I'll shoot you right now."

Immediately she closed her mouth and glared at him. She looked around casually. "How did you get in here?"

When her gaze landed on the closet, she caught sight of Keane but drifted past and then came back to look at Scott again. She twisted toward the closet ever-so-slightly, and Scott immediately stepped into her line of vision. Keane realized she'd done that on purpose.

Changing her position caused Scott to move as well, giving Keane a little more opportunity to come out and attack. He really liked that she was staying calm and thinking things through, using her head and trying to help, without giving his position away.

"Nice of your landlord to give me a key," he said, "for the surprise party and all." He cackled at his own joke, sounding deranged.

"Well, I'm leaving this apartment anyway."

"Too bad you didn't leave already," he said.

"Well, if you had your way, I'd already be dead," she snapped. Suddenly she stared at him, slack-jawed. "Jesus. Did you try to kill Brenda too?"

"She saw me push you off the boat," he said.

"Do you know that she saw you, or are you just afraid she might have?"

"I was hoping that I'd have a better position where she

wouldn't see me. And I couldn't take a chance, so I figured she had to go anyway."

"Even if she didn't see you push me off? Even if, in the middle of a storm, it was so confusing that nobody knew anything for sure? No matter what, you decided she had to die?"

"Can't have loose ends. They have a habit of coming around and biting you in the ass," he said.

"You realized you failed, right?"

"She's in the hospital," he said. "She's not protected forever. I'll get another chance."

"So this is your second chance to kill me, and you've already tried to kill her once with the hit-and-run. Or did you push her off the damn boat too?"

He just grinned at her.

She stared, stunned. "Seriously?"

"What can I say?" he said. "She was fucking irritating. She was stopping Greg from doing all kinds of shit we used to do together."

"So she didn't fall accidentally?"

"She had a little help," he said. "And you had a little help. That should have been the end of it. Dumped in rough seas in the middle of nowhere with a fucking storm raging. It couldn't have been more perfect."

He shook his head, getting pissed all over again. "But not you. Trust you to end up getting rescued. What are the chances of those smugglers coming along and picking you out of the water and taking you to that island?" He shook his head. "You're always the one who comes up golden."

"Really? Brenda got a bad head injury, Scott. And now I know why. Because you probably hit her over the head when you knocked her over. Didn't you?"

He shrugged.

She took a slow and deep breath. "And, yeah, we got picked up by smugglers, or guys associated with smugglers anyway. We were dropped on a desolate island and locked away in a tiny shelter. Yeah, really lucky. And instead of getting rescued, we ended up in the middle of a drug-smuggling fight with people getting shot all around us. Yeah, so lucky," she murmured.

"Well, that's okay," he said, "because you won't remember any of it by the time I'm done with you."

"And this will be what?" she asked. "Just your average breaking and entering?"

"Why not?" he said. "They happen all the time. I'll make it look like some rapist went crazy, and I'll leave you to die in your little pathetic apartment."

"All because I broke up with you?"

"All because women are bitches," he said, his voice suddenly cheerful. "And because I can."

"So pushing us off the boat gave you a feeling of power. But then fear kicked in, and you realized you hadn't done a good enough job, so now you'll do it all over again. You can feel that power, and you like that feeling, don't you?"

"I sure do," he said. "I'm so damn tired of women taking over the world. Taking my job. Women pretending to be equal to men. Women not doing what they're told." He shook his head. "You should all just fucking die." As he went to lunge at her, Keane jumped from the closet, threw a chokehold around Scott's neck, and, using the same momentum Scott had used to push forward, pushed him to the ground. The gun skidded free and ended up spinning wildly under the bed.

Scott roared, "What the fuck?"

"Yeah, you see your mistake now?" Keane asked. "It was coming here and assuming she was alone."

As soon as he looked up, she had already thrown the nightgown over her head and raced into the kitchen. She came back with zip ties, which they quickly used on Scott's arms and then his legs, while Scott struggled enough that Keane felt perfectly inclined to give him a couple good hits to the head.

"That's for what you already did," he said, "and this one"—he hit him hard in the ribs—"is for what you were planning on doing. What I *could* do to you for what you've already done would leave you dead, so I'll avoid doing that," he said. "I'm sure jail will take care of you nicely and put you in your place when you become some big man's bitch."

Scott glared at him, and the hate spewing from his mouth had Sandrine racing off again, and she returned with a hand towel and shoved it into his mouth.

"Nobody wants to hear anything you've got to say," she snapped. "I hope they throw you into prison and leave you to rot. Thanks for supplying all the details, by the way." The red Record light on her phone shone brightly.

As she snatched up her phone, Keane looked at her and said, "Grab mine, will you, honey?"

She brought it over to him, and, while he literally sat on Scott's back, Keane dialed Lennox, who answered immediately, having been on alert since Keane's earlier text.

"No need for security at the hospital now," he said. "It was Scott. I've got him tied up here in Sandrine's apartment. And Sandrine got everything recorded. Scott tried to run Brenda down, thinking she had seen him try to kill Sandrine on the sailboat. He's also the one responsible for Brenda going off the boat in the first place. He hit her in the head, knocking her off the boat. That's where her head injury came from."

"What the hell?" Lennox said. "Are you serious?"

"Yeah. Brenda was cramping his style with his buddy Greg apparently."

Keane held the phone by Scott's head and said, "Say something to Lennox, Scott."

All Scott could do was scream his fury through the gag in his mouth.

Lennox laughed. "Okay. I'll be there in a few minutes, and I'll bring the cops with me."

"Yeah, you better. This guy's pissed, and I don't want him to get loose. By the way, he came with a gun too. He was prepared to make it look like a breaking and entering gone bad, a rapist into bondage. He planned to mess her up pretty badly, then walk away in the night. Clearly he hates women, and he's still pissed about that job thing she was telling us about. Remember? When she got the job, and he didn't."

"Wow," Lennox said. "Well, it's pretty easy to know who was the better candidate, right?"

"We sure do," Keane said. After the call, he pocketed his phone and spoke to Sandrine. "You'll probably want to get dressed. Lennox and the cops will be here soon."

She nodded. "It's really over now, isn't it?"

This time her voice was hopeful, but she waited for him to confirm it. He opened his arms, even though he was still sitting on Scott. She shook her head and gestured that he should stand up first. He nodded, and, rising, he walked over and wrapped her in his arms. He whispered, "It's over, and now you get your life back."

She reached up, kissed him and said, "I've got an idea.

Since you've already saved my life several times, how about just looking after it from here on out?"

"Instead of me looking after it," he said, "how about we share the responsibility together?"

"That works," she said. "I just want to spend as much time as possible with you."

"Ditto," he said as he leaned over and kissed her once more.

LENNOX

The Mavericks, Book 10

Dale Mayer

CHAPTER 1

LENNOX CUMMERBUND LANDED just outside of Munich, Germany. He was meeting his sister, Carolina, for a couple days, hoping to get that much time with her before he got called on a mission himself, having finished with Keane's assignment. As Lennox walked out of the airport, his duffel bag over his shoulder, he gazed around, looking to see if she had gotten in before him and was here to pick him up.

A couple days ago they'd made arrangements to fly into the same airport, roughly around the same time. He had her flight number on his phone but hadn't had a confirmation from her that she had managed to catch it. As he walked through one of the lengthy areas of the airport, he saw the computerized flight board above. He quickly checked her flight info. So she should have gotten in about ten minutes before him.

He sent a text her way, saying he would wait outside the front doors near her baggage pickup area. They could grab a cab and head to her apartment that she had here. She was a Red Cross doctor and traveled all over the globe. Breaks off together were hard to come by.

She was his only sibling, and they liked to touch base, if they could, at least once a year. When Lennox received no responding text, he frowned, wondering if Carolina was still stuck on the tarmac, but, even then, they were allowed to turn on their electronics again. He waited inside now, at the luggage pickup. Carousels rolled through for her particular flight. She should arrive here at any time, and, indeed, a crowd had showed up.

He scanned the faces but found no sight of his sister.

His frown deepened, wondering if she couldn't make it. He sent her yet another text; when that didn't work, he dialed her phone number, and his call immediately went to voicemail. Shrugging, he sat at the exit, watching as people came and went. Maybe she got in on an earlier flight, or possibly she was still stuck in whatever godforsaken part of the world she had been in last. He thought it was Somalia.

And given the connecting flights that she probably had to take, she could have been stranded anywhere. Usually she'd send him a message, if that were the case. He checked his email while he was here, but still he had no word from her. Now he was starting to worry.

"Lennox?"

His gaze shot up as he studied the tall dark-haired man in front of him. "Gavin?"

Gavin reached out a hand, and the two shrugged, shook hands, and half hugged in a typical bro manner.

"Damn, it's good to see you," Lennox said. "Odd place, but then, maybe not. I hardly recognized you. You're not in uniform, so you're not here on business?"

"Oh, I'm here on business," Gavin said. The smile fell off his face. "And I'm still in the military, just not the same unit."

"Ah. A lot of that going on. I'm here visiting my sister," Lennox said, holding up his phone. "At least I would be if I could find out what flight she's on or where she got stuck.

Her flight arrived, but she's not on it."

Gavin nodded, his expression turning serious. "That's why I'm here."

Lennox felt something inside him still. "Why?" He straightened his duffel bag at his feet as he glanced around. It seemed everybody suddenly moved slowly, as if only his world had sped up to the point where it all focused entirely on Gavin's face.

"We have reason to believe she's been kidnapped. Your sister, as far as I know, landed at this Munich airport and was snatched outside the terminal here. We waited until you landed to inform you and hoped we'd have more details by now. But we're still digging."

Lennox stared at Gavin in shock. "Seriously?"

Gavin nodded. "Come on," he said. "I've got wheels."

"Well, if Carolina's been kidnapped," he said, "we should take a look at this airport, where she was snatched."

"We're hoping to find her trail more effectively and more efficiently via the video feeds."

"*We?*"

"I'm part of the Mavericks team now."

Lennox nodded, then pointed at the airport behind them. "Then we should be heading inside to review their security feeds, awaiting intel before we book our next flight."

Gavin shot him a look. "We *are* securing a flight, but we're taking a military transport."

Lennox stared at him. "So I've been tagged for this mission to head up, or is this assignment just because it involves my sister?"

"Both," said Gavin. "In most military and even civilian cases, you wouldn't be allowed anywhere close to this op. But the Mavericks get to make the rules and have decided you're probably the best person to track her down."

"You're damn straight, I am!" Lennox said, swearing fluently. He threw the duffel bag over his shoulder and said, "Lead the way."

Within minutes they were in a nondescript car, heading out of the airport, moving through lanes and lanes of traffic as they navigated toward the main US base on the outskirts of Munich.

"Have you ever been on this base?" Gavin asked.

"Lots of times," Lennox said. "Most of the personnel probably still remember me."

"Right, you were stationed here for a while, weren't you?"

"Yes, and I was here for training several months at a time too."

"Good. Hopefully we've got some orders when we get there."

"I can do without the orders," Lennox said. His voice was hard. "I need intel."

"That's coming too."

"Who's running ground crew on this one?"

Gavin looked at him. "I have no clue. I'm not even sure I understand how all this system works, honestly. When they tagged me for this mission, basically because I was so nearby, I told them that they needed somebody with more Mavericks experience, and they just said, *This is how we roll.*"

Lennox thought about it, then nodded. "That's exactly how they roll," he said. "It wouldn't have anything to do with my Mavericks experience either. I just ran my first Mavericks mission with Keane," he said. "And I knew the next one was mine to head up, but I hadn't expected it to involve my own sister."

"I don't think the Mavericks expected this either," Gavin said.

"Do we know a reason why?"

"Not that I've been told."

"Nobody's seen her since then?"

"No, we're not sure who's behind this or why they were targeted."

"*They?*" Lennox pounced. "So it wasn't just Carolina?"

"Four on the same medical team," Gavin replied. "Your sister, another doctor, and two nurses."

"Which means Helena as well."

"I don't know Helena," he said. "Who's she?"

"My sister's best friend. They've been working as a medical team since forever," Lennox explained.

"Doctor or nurse?"

"Doctor."

"So three women and one man are confirmed on the team. The Red Cross is taking this very seriously."

"Of course they do," Lennox said. "They can't get doctors and nurses to work for them if they're being kidnapped randomly. Safety for them is paramount." Lennox paused for a moment. "How do we know they were kidnapped? Or are we just going on the basis that they didn't show up for their connecting flights?"

"We think your sister's medical team members were seen being marched into the back of a vehicle. No visual confirmation yet on the captives," Gavin responded. "The witness got scared when he saw the men were carrying weapons and decided not to report it for at least an hour."

"Did he describe the gunmen?"

"Four white men in military fatigues with machine guns."

Lennox swore at that. "Well, that doesn't help."

"No, the witness did wonder about the direction they were traveling, as the road led to another part of the airport. So it's possible they were flying the captives somewhere else."

"Which would be smart on the kidnappers' part," he said. "When you think about it, a lot of traffic occurs at a major international airport. That hinders our progress tracking them, as we have to delve through massive amounts of security tapes. Plus the kidnappers and their captives could easily have been flown elsewhere. But where? Why?"

"If only our witness had stopped and waited longer to see where they went, ... but you know what the airports are like. The traffic comes and goes quickly."

"Cameras?"

"Yep," Gavin said. "The vehicle headed to the section reserved for private planes, but it only shows them taking that turn."

"And do we know anything about those private planes on the ground at the time?"

"No, we don't," said Gavin. "Outside of the fact that the terminal exists. However, the hangers we've contacted so far are not willing to hand over any security cameras."

"So hack into them," Lennox said harshly.

"In progress as we speak," Gavin said.

"If we don't know where or why she's been taken or who took her, how do we know where we're supposed to go next?" Lennox blew out a frustrated breath. "By going to the US base, we could be going in the wrong direction," he snapped in frustration. "That's a complete waste of time, if so."

"It will be, indeed," Gavin said, "but we're waiting on intel regardless."

"So, on to the military base, then—hopefully by the time the next naval plane leaves—we can hijack it to our new destination."

"That's the plan."

"Better be," said Lennox, muttering to himself as he stared at his clenched fists. With just his sister and him left in the family, the two were close, very close. The thought of her suffering sent shudders down his spine.

"Is your sister still feisty?"

"You mean, arrogant, snappy, domineering, and sometimes aggressive? Yes."

Gavin laughed. "Sounds like she can hold her own."

"She's had to," he said. "She hasn't had the easiest time climbing the ranks. She's had several incredibly sexist bosses and coworkers, plus an abusive ex-husband. Now that she's single and traveling the world again, she's learned that showing she has a backbone of steel and honesty can do her some good but can also do her some harm."

"True enough. But is she likely to keep her head in a scenario like this?"

Lennox thought about all the circumstances in Carolina's life and what she'd been put through already. "Yes, I think so."

"Good. What about Helena?"

"She'd shoot you in the balls just as soon as talk to you," Lennox said, his voice harder than he expected. He could feel Gavin's searching gaze, but he refused to rise to the bait.

"How long have they been friends?"

"From grade school," Lennox answered. "They determined they would be doctors a hell of a long time ago," he said, admitting his surprise at that. "I didn't think they'd make it, figuring their dreams would change as they got older, but they are committed to being doctors."

"Both married?"

"Both married guys named Peter. Both divorced. Both were in abusive relationships."

"Jesus," Gavin said. "A little too much twinning for me."

"They've always been that way. They were apart for a while, both working in distant parts of the country, keeping in contact via social media and Skype and the like. When they both came home around the same time with their respective Peters, they both married quickly, then kinda led separate lives again, neither one copping to their abuse yet in touch all that time, until their divorces happened within about six months of each other too. That had them getting reacquainted again."

"Seriously?"

Lennox looked at him. "Yeah, seriously wrong. But it did happen."

"I can't imagine such a life, but still that sucks."

"Well, they had each other to recover," Lennox said. "They were always the best of friends, and that didn't weaken throughout the marriages or the divorces."

"I'm sorry for both of them. Any children?"

Lennox sucked in his breath and shook his head. "They were both pregnant. Both of them lost their baby."

"Jesus!" Gavin said and went silent.

Lennox settled into his seat, wishing that he could forget about the trauma his sister had gone through. Or the trauma that Helena had gone through. Both of them had been pregnant early on in their marriages but about a year apart. And neither had known about the other's loss until they'd come together after the breakups of their marriages.

They'd both taken a beating somewhere around the time

of the miscarriages. He looked down at his still-closed fists, reminding himself of the beat-downs he gave both Peters. To this day he wondered how he had held it together enough not to kill those two sorry excuses for humans. Lennox shook his head even now.

He couldn't believe that his sister, who was so feisty and stood toe-to-toe over every argument, had let some guy beat her up. When he had talked to her about it afterward, she'd stared at him with tears in her eyes and said, "I don't know how that works. I'll yell at anybody who's abusive in a hospital. I'll protect every patient," she said, "but somehow I let my husband hit me."

She'd gone through all kinds of self-defense training afterward, plus assertiveness courses, shrink sessions, and had done everything she could to pull herself back together again.

As for Helena, Lennox had no clue how she had dealt with her recovery—other than her close relationship with Carolina. But Helena had been in a very rough foster care system for all her earlier life, so she must have learned how to cope way back then. Afterward, she had gone to med school on full scholarships. She was a brainiac, supersmart. But maybe knowing that she was finally loved—supposedly by Peter—had allowed her to let her defenses down, even when her brain was screaming at her that she was making a horrible mistake.

Lennox knew a lifetime could be spent on studying such a field, and still no answers are guaranteed to come up. He didn't know if Helena had done the same kind of assertiveness training that his sister had done; he hoped so for Helena's sake. This kidnapping though, it would be a rough go for all of them.

"Still amazing that the two are so close and that so much

synchronicity existed in their lives."

"I think they would have been quite happy to have skipped out on a lot of it though."

Gavin laughed. "No doubt. At least they both got out of a bad situation."

"Do we know anything about the other two people in the party?"

"One's a male nurse by the name of John Steadman, and the other is a female nurse, called Sasha Kempton."

"Is there any reason to consider this personal, as an act against the Red Cross, or just a political statement?"

"We haven't heard anything yet. We are doing a full rundown on all four of the kidnap victims."

"Well, I doubt your information will be any more detailed than what I already know about two of them."

"Hence why you're perfect for this job," Gavin added. "You know what? If this were a regular military op, you wouldn't be anywhere close to this."

"Oh, I would be," he said, his voice low and deep. "They just wouldn't have liked the way I made it happen."

"Right, still the same old Lennox then."

"Absolutely," Lennox said. "I'd have quit the navy and gone in myself, if that were my only choice to inject myself into this investigation."

"Well, the good news is, it doesn't have to happen that way."

Just then they entered the security at the base. By the time they were cleared and moved forward, heading toward the offices, Lennox was already on his phone contacting the Mavericks. Keane was on the other end. "Have an update on where my sister has been taken to?"

"We lost sight of them at the airport. No flight plans

were filed on the private planes."

"Do we have a satellite on them?"

"We do, but we haven't located them yet though."

"How long until we do?"

"With any luck, another ten to fifteen minutes."

"Okay," he said. "We're just pulling into the military base."

As soon as they parked, he hopped out, his phone in his hand, and tried to call his sister once again. With no answer, he quickly sent a text to Keane with Carolina's phone number, email address, and a couple other personal details. **Find her**, he added.

Keane answered. **We've got this. I'll have an answer for you soon.**

HELENA OPENED HER eyes and stared around the small cargo plane. She and Carolina were tied up, as were the other two members of their group. Somehow they'd been taken from a departure lane outside the airport at gunpoint and moved into the back of a small truck, then driven to a private airstrip, on another airplane even now. She had no idea where they were being taken or why. What did bother her was the half-military, half-mercenary–looking mix of males on board. So far there had been no sexual connotation, and, as a doctor, she knew her skills were highly valued, but her entire medical team had been taken. Why?

She exchanged hard looks with Carolina, who stared at her. Helena had taken a blow to the side of her head and was dealing with quite the headache. Then so had Carolina. Helena raised her eyebrows ever-so-slightly, silently asking

Carolina if she was doing okay, and Carolina gave her best friend the slightest of nods back. They'd always been very good at reading each other's thoughts, keeping track of what each other were doing and how they were feeling, so Helena was pretty confident that, although her best friend had taken a blow to the head, Carolina would be okay.

Helena glanced at the other two; John was sleeping. The kidnappers hadn't hit him at all. He was small, wiry, very efficient at what he did and hadn't put up much of a fight, so maybe that's why their captors had gone easy on him. Sasha, the fourth member, stared down at her feet, as if wondering about the state she now found herself in.

At the time they'd been accosted at the airport, they were all talking about their days off. Helena was heading with Carolina to Germany. Carolina would spend time with her brother, whereas Helena, who had a hard time being around Lennox, planned on visiting some other friends nearby. She would stay at Carolina's apartment because it was convenient and easy. They'd been friends for so long that sharing a space was just second nature. And it had been Carolina's idea that Helena come stay at the apartment. "You won't see much of Lennox. I promise."

Helena had snorted at that. "Anything is too much."

"You'll have to get over that," Carolina said. "He's not a bad guy."

"He rubs me the wrong way."

"And I've told you why," her friend had said in exasperation. "The two of you are so damn perfect for each other that you have to get past that initial almost hate-driven type of relationship you've got."

"And how will that improve anything?" Helena asked. "He's hardly somebody I want to spend time with."

"And yet you're attracted to him. You can't fool me."

"He's a healthy sexy animal," Helena said. "What's not to like?"

"So what's the problem?"

"He's more than a penis," she'd said, laughing. "I can handle the physical, but I don't think I want to live with the rest."

"And I think that's just because you're so damn much alike," Carolina had said.

"No, we aren't." Helena had been determined to shoot her friend down on that point.

"Yeah? Well, every time I ask him what's wrong with you, I get the same answer. Gorgeous body, gorgeous face, but you know, *I'd still have to live with her.*"

The trouble was, Helena *was* attracted to Lennox. And it was way more than just the physical. But she also knew that Lennox went through women like crazy, and she wouldn't be just another one among the many.

She'd been very particular about the men she hung out with, up until she got married. Then she had made such a shitty decision with her husband that she knew she couldn't trust herself to choose the right one. She knew Lennox quite well, especially after the number of times they'd seen each other, but she'd also thought she knew her husband.

Her husband had been tall, slim, almost that gentry-type male; she'd never thought such a beast would be under that smooth surface. Lennox was the beast on the outside; she could hope that a gentle male resided underneath, but she couldn't be sure, and she couldn't take the chance.

Her ex had taken his fist to her jaw, to her ribs, to her stomach. She was pretty damn sure that's why she lost the baby she carried at the time.

To find out Carolina had been hiding the same damn secret about her husband had been hard. They both wished that the other hadn't had to suffer as they had.

They figured each had a fifty-fifty chance of having a decent marriage, so why had they both ended up on the negative end of the scale? Carolina had devoted herself to her work and had ignored men, whereas Helena was still searching the world of men around her because she did want a family. Yet every time she considered another intimate relationship, she found herself drawing back.

She couldn't even look at the strong aggressive alpha males because all she could remember were the fists that kept pounding her into the ground. And, of course, the problem with that was, her husband looked the exact opposite on the outside—a compliant beta male. So she felt she couldn't trust any males.

If she didn't want children so much, remaining single suited her just fine. Being a doctor, she knew all about IVF and figured that could be the answer for her. But then, so many horror stories kept coming up in the news about that too. It was enough to stop her from moving forward.

And now she might not get a chance to rethink that choice.

She studied the two guards at the other end of the cargo plane. They sat, talking among themselves, their weapons turned casually in their hostages' direction. Still it's not like her team was any threat to the gunmen. The four who made up her medical team were tied up but not gagged and not likely to give their armed guards any trouble.

Both Helena and Carolina had martial arts skills and kept up their training, trying out new and more advanced techniques, but Helena couldn't imagine doing a whole lot in this scenario. These men outweighed her easily by one hundred pounds each. Regardless, all the gunmen had to do was pull a trigger, and that would be the end of her and the others anyway.

Except ... guns fired on airplanes were not her forte. Would their guards even shoot their weapons on an airplane midflight? Taking out a window on an airplane sounded like a really bad idea—one that would probably kill them all from the sudden depressurization of the plane itself if not when crash-landing. Would the gunmen risk that? Can a bullet puncture the hull of an airplane? Does it matter the kind of bullet from the kind of gun?

Helena knew absolutely nothing about guns either. Her mission was saving people, not shooting them. But rifles? On an airplane? These weren't handguns. Or she guessed they could be machine guns, not rifles. Regardless, surely rifles and machine guns were more powerful than handguns and were capable of long-range shots, correct? To her, it seemed even riskier to shoot a rifle in an airplane in flight than to shoot a handgun. Shaking her head, she wished right now that she had access to Google.

Helena thought, if the gunmen were carrying those weapons more for show, then it would be the four of them against the two visible guards and any they couldn't see. Granted, John and Sasha might be worthless in this situation. So it would be Helena and Carolina against the guards. Given the abusive relationships she and her best friend had been through, and the emotional consequences, Helena would pit her anger-fueled adrenaline against either of those guys. She bet Carolina would too.

Then her head reminded her of her injury as a piercing slash of pain bounced around like an echo in her mind.

She leaned back, closed her eyes, breathing deeply through the agony, until she felt the intensity of Carolina's gaze. She opened her eyes to see Carolina nodding toward the men. Helena quickly twisted slightly so that she saw the two gunmen. Both had their rifles down and were showing each other papers or something as they exchanged various pieces back and forth. Was it their IDs?

Helena had no idea if their kidnappers had taken their luggage or if their baggage was still sat at the airport. The gunmen *had* taken the captives' wallets, purses, all their IDs, and their phones. So that could be the paperwork they were shuffling between themselves.

How much longer would this flight be? Her head throbbed once more, interrupting any more thoughts on her escape plans. Maybe it would be better to tackle her captors once they were on the ground.

Just as she thought that maybe this would be a flight that never ended, the pilot called back to the gunmen, and they started their descent. She glanced at Carolina to see the fear in her best friend's eyes. Helena gave her a reassuring smile. But how do you do that when your hopes were sinking along with the plane?

Helena closed her eyes again and prayed for help.

CHAPTER 2

WHEN THE PLANE finally landed, the gunmen snapped orders in English to their captives, lifting them roughly to their feet and ordering them to disembark. Helena slowly made her way down the stairs, their legs free and no gags. *We must be far from civilization*, Helena thought. *Or isolated among the kidnappers' people.* At the tarmac they were moved into a vehicle. She glanced around at the small airport and at the mostly flat geography around her, which meant that she could be anywhere in the world.

She sniffed the air, feeling a warmth that she hadn't expected. She turned toward Carolina, but her best friend shrugged, as if to say she had no clue where they were. Helena glanced at the other two members of their medical team and only received questioning glances in return.

As they drove off, Helena noted a couple street signs, but she didn't understand the language. That gave her a sinking feeling in the back of her throat. The language might have been something like Ukrainian. Maybe Polish? Maybe they were within a Soviet red block country? And, if so, why?

Although the laws were a lot more relaxed outside of the US, they could have traveled anywhere. So why here? They hadn't landed at an international airport. The kidnappers' options would have been unlimited if they had, but here, a small airport, fewer people watching. Fewer people to pay to not watch ... And were she and her team any better off here—wherever *here* was—than in Africa, where there was almost no law? Where everything was available for a price? Then the Ukraine was likely to be the same too.

Her team didn't have their phones, although Helena had seen the gunmen checking them out, so their phones were close by. As long as the gunmen didn't break them, she had hopes of getting them back.

The drive ended rather abruptly as they were taken down a long driveway into what appeared to be some farming community. The vehicle backed up to a long metal building, and they were quickly unloaded and left inside the building in a large metal cage—resembling something made of a chain-link fence. She stared at the place in shock. A barred twelve-by-twelve-foot cage. She didn't know if it had been used for this purpose before or had been used to hold animals in the past.

"Bathroom?" Helena asked one of the gunmen.

He froze, glanced from one to the other, shrugged, and said, "Yes, just a minute." And then he went over to talk to the other man.

The man nodded, and they were each led to a small room in the same building and given a few minutes in there. She used the facilities in private, then barely had time to wash her hands and face before the door was opened again, and she was yanked out. As soon as they'd all had their time alone in the bathroom, they were led back to the cage and locked up again.

"Why are you doing this?" Helena asked in what she hoped was a reasonable tone.

But the men ignored her.

"We could pay you," she said hesitantly. One gunman

shrugged. And she realized money wasn't the motivator. Or maybe the other guy was paying them enough that they wouldn't be bribed. "Who is behind this?"

He looked at her, smiled, and said, in perfectly good English, "You're just a casualty." He pointed at Carolina and said, "She's the real reason you're here." And, with that, he turned and walked out.

LENNOX CONTINUED TO pace outside the main headquarters of the base, while Gavin passively watched his partner. Lennox's skin crawled to get into action. This waiting was not good for his mental health. This being about his sister made all his adrenaline rush through his body. When he got his hands on the guys responsible for this, … Lennox wasn't sure he wouldn't kill them all. He called Keane. *Again.* "Still no answers?" Lennox asked.

"Some," Keane said. "We're just figuring out why."

"Where is she?"

"Poland."

Lennox froze. "Seriously?"

"Yes."

Lennox shifted the phone to his other ear. And then decided it would be better on Speaker, as he spoke to Gavin. "This is Keane."

Keane calmly said, "Hi, Gavin. Back to your sister. Last we picked her up was in Warsaw at another private airstrip on the side of the main international one. Where her flight landed. We're still getting camera feeds off the airport itself, but it looks like she was down on the ground. We're looking for confirmation that they disembarked."

"Do we know if it stopped somewhere else first, before reaching Poland?"

"Always checking for stops," he said. "You know that. But we're working on it."

"So I'm heading to Warsaw then. Correct?"

"Yes."

"On it," he said, turning to Gavin. "We need to get moving."

The two walked inside the main office on base and quickly made arrangements and were then informed that the next flight wouldn't leave for another two hours. Lennox swore at that. "Is there no other way?"

The personnel quickly went through all the schedules but found absolutely no way to get into the Eastern Bloc country faster.

"Fine," Lennox said, pissed at the delay.

"It's still fast. Keep in mind she didn't arrive very long ago," said Gavin. "What? Two hours maybe, tops?"

"And now, with the delay here, we'll be at least four to five hours behind her," he said, shaking his head, his lips in a taut grimace, his pacing resumed.

"Again, not very far behind. We should get more intel before we arrive."

"I'm working on that too," Lennox said. He sat down in the small room, brought his laptop out of his duffel bag, and logged on to the Maverick chat box. **Need satellite on the Munich and Warsaw airports. I want video feed of the flights coming in. And I want all traffic cameras watching planes leaving the airports, around the pickup and departure areas as well.**

Immediately links showed up. **Glad you're on your laptop now**, Keane typed. **We've got all hands on deck.**

Still not enough, Lennox typed back. **We can't get out of here for two hours.**

With any luck, we'll have a more precise location for you to head directly to by then.

Not luck, Lennox typed. **We need to make this happen.** He quickly minimized the full-screen chat window on his laptop so he could take a look at the links. A distant image showed the suspect plane coming in for a landing at Warsaw. But the cameras were just ever-so-slightly not centered as he watched the passengers disembark. He couldn't see his sister, but a small male appeared on-screen. Maybe the male nurse?

Lennox brought up the chat box and typed **I need a closer image on this one.** He quickly took a screenshot and sent it. **And an ID confirmation.**

Will come back to you in a minute.

Lennox knew that the Mavericks ground crew were now hacking into other cameras at the airport, trying to get a better visual.

Five minutes later, Keane came back. **We've got this image so far. One of the team, I hope.**

Lennox brought it up, and there was his sister's best friend. **That's Helena. Any sign of my sister?**

I can't see her disembarking, no. They were flying together though, correct? This is taken from Warsaw.

According to our plans, yes. He kept going through the camera feeds, looking for a picture of his sister to confirm that she was there. Just then the ID on the male he'd requested came back as the nurse John Steadman.

Good, Lennox typed. **Two confirmed.** He caught an image of a third female and got her name confirmed as well.

Sasha Kempton, nurse.

Okay. That established three out of four. **Now I need confirmation of my sister.**

Not until the transport vehicle had been captured on camera leaving the airport via one of the smaller airstrips did one of the security cameras pick up Carolina's face in the back seat of a truck. He immediately typed **Four confirmed.** And Lennox gave Keane the license plate and the picture with his sister in it. **Track that.** He sat back, looked at Gavin, and said, "That confirms all four were taken together."

"And Warsaw has been confirmed, so that's a good place to start," Gavin said, nodding at Lennox.

"It's a shit place to start," Lennox said. "Money buys you everything there."

"Good," said Gavin, "because we'll need weapons. The kidnappers had firepower. We'll need the same."

"Do you have a contact?"

"No," he said, "not in Warsaw. You?"

Lennox thought about it and shook his head. "No, so we need to find one." Lennox quickly texted Keane but didn't get an answer right away. Impatiently Lennox waited, and then Keane came back with a phone number for Lennox.

Weapons?

Anything you need but black market. No names, no countries, no affiliations, just money.

We'll need cash.

It'll be there in your vehicle when you arrive.

Good. I want to hit the ground running.

Make that running, not shooting. Remember the law in Poland as a little on the left too.

I don't care if it's left, right, or center, Lennox answered. **They've got my sister. You know I'll erase that country if they do anything to stop me from getting her**

back.

Hardly subtle, Keane responded. **Remember. Stealth in, stealth out.**

You remember that, Lennox typed. **You guys brought me in on this. I'm not exactly known to be subtle.**

You can be when you need to be, Keane typed. **And, right now, you need to be.**

Why is that?

Because we think it's a trap.

He sat back, but Keane didn't say anything else. Lennox looked at Gavin. "They think it's a trap."

Gavin replied immediately, "Now that's interesting."

"Isn't it?" Lennox said. "But what kind of a trap?"

"I love that chat box," Gavin said, "but we need more answers."

"The trouble with being fast to respond," he said, "is when we can't get enough answers to set us free to just do this damn op."

"True. But we're on it," Gavin said, and the chat came back.

Almost immediately more information flowed. The vehicle his sister rode in was a rental. The company that rented it was a shell company, which the Mavericks were trying to track down for more details.

Waste of more time, Lennox thought. He highly suspected that, given the level of professionalism behind this kidnapping, the shell company's ID had been stolen, or the shell company's credit cards had been hacked, and still there wouldn't be a direct tie between the shell company and the real mastermind behind this kidnapping. **Ransom note?**

None.

So they aren't after money. Sex? Revenge? Power? Intel?

Trap. **Have you tracked a direction?**

North, but that's all so far. We're still running through the videos.

Lennox checked the time. They would be leaving soon. He quickly tapped in, **We'll be in the air in twenty. Or at least boarded.**

When you land, we'll have more for you.

You better. And he quickly shut down his laptop. He looked at Gavin. "Are you ready for this?"

"Yeah, first stop is getting the vehicle, and then we need to get geared up."

"Vehicle is waiting on us already. So is the money, and now we have a contact for the weapons."

"That's good news," Gavin said. "So we need food, and we need rest."

"There won't be any food on this flight," Lennox said. "So we'll have to grab that as soon as we land."

"I guess what we need now then is to get some sleep."

"Not a whole lot we can do otherwise, so we'll sleep on the flight," Lennox said, but he probably couldn't sleep and knew just more sitting and waiting midflight would eat away at his insides. His sister was not the most patient person he knew. Obviously he wasn't either. It's one of the reasons she made such a great doctor. She was driven to help others.

At one point in time, she had considered Doctors Without Borders but had opted for the Red Cross because they headed out to some of the more dangerous areas where doctors were desperately needed. Lennox had been all about her getting a practice in suburbia, and she'd laughed her head off at him. "Me? No, not happening. That'd be like me telling you to go get a job as a bookkeeper at a retail store."

Something he knew he couldn't possibly do either. They

were both very similar in their adventuresome spirits and even more so in their protective natures.

He wanted to fix the world, and she wanted to fix the people. They were both fools for thinking they could do either.

CHAPTER 3

SITTING STILL FOR hours already—before in the gunmen's airplane, then in the truck, now in this cage—Helena tried hard for patience, but this whole situation was wearing on her.

By the time they'd spent a few hours in the cage, seemingly all alone, the team had opened up enough to talk a little bit.

"Anybody have any ideas why?" Carolina asked.

"No." Sasha's tone was terse.

So far they hadn't spoken much because they were all concerned about somebody coming in and telling them off, but they appeared to be alone now. They'd been offered no food, no water, and only the one trip to the bathroom. Nobody seemed nearby where the hostages could call out if they did want something.

Helena expected to see several of the men with machine guns hanging around, but they must feel that their prisoners were well secured here. She got up, paced their cage, before coming back to the gate on their cage and its simple lock. She studied it. "Anybody any good at picking locks?'

Carolina snorted. "Really? Us? Not likely. If Lennox were here, that'd be a different story."

"Well, it's Lennox we want to see," a man said, stepping through the entranceway of the long metal building. A man stood in front of them, tall, more Swedish looking than the others so far. Maybe German was a better description, considering where they were, but then it was hard to determine his accent. He had a big ugly scar across his cheek and some burn marks on his neck.

"Lennox?" Carolina asked with a frown. "What's this got to do with my brother?"

"Everything," he said. "You're the bait. The rest of these people are just here to keep you compliant. It's Lennox we want."

Carolina and Helena exchanged hard glances, and Carolina spoke up. "What do you want to see my brother for?"

"A little payback for his betrayal," the man said, his hand going up to his neck. "He owes me."

"Well, not that we want to get in between the two of you …" Helena said quietly, "but what are your plans for us?"

"Depends on whether Lennox behaves himself or not," he said. "You can all go free if I get Lennox," he said with a laugh. He waved his hand. "Sorry about the lack of hospitality. These certainly aren't the most comfortable cages, are they? Though Lennox knows all about cages too. He's done enough intensive mind warfare training to understand the psychological effects of being in a cage."

Carolina and Helena exchanged confused looks, followed by shrugs.

"I'm sorry. I don't know what you're talking about," Carolina said quietly. Her voice low, almost contemplative, she said, "I haven't heard much about his missions, so I'm not sure what happened between the two of you."

"He hurt me and mine …" the man said. "That'll never go down well in my book."

"Have you contacted Lennox to let him know we're here?"

He laughed. "Hell no. I can't make it too easy for him. He's on his way. I know that for sure. You guys were taken from a very public spot, so he's backtracking now to find you. We can't make it too complicated, and we can't make it too easy. But never forget that it's Lennox who we truly want, so, if you guys behave yourselves, then you'll be released unharmed."

Something Helena completely didn't believe. "Is there any chance of food?" she asked. "We traveled a lot getting here, and most of us didn't get to eat before we left."

He looked at her for a moment and then shrugged. "Sure," he said. "I'll get them to rustle up something for you." He turned and walked back out.

She looked over at the others.

John and Sasha stared at her. "You asked for food?" Sasha said. "How about letting us go?"

"That's not something he'll do," Helena said quietly. "So I looked for something he might be willing to give."

"Besides, we need food for energy," Carolina said. "No point in starving ourselves and being so weak we can't go anywhere if we do get the opportunity."

"And Lennox?" John asked.

"My brother," Carolina said. "He was a Navy SEAL, until he started some new job recently, only I don't know the details."

"And next you'll say that he doesn't betray others," Sasha said, her voice hesitant, and yet her tone held obvious contempt for Lennox.

Helena glanced at her. "Lennox is one of the most honorable men you'll ever meet," she said. "The only reason he'd have hurt this guy or someone close to him is if there was a damn good reason for it."

"But it sure explains why this guy's pissed."

"He can be as pissed as he wants," Helena said. "It won't change the fact that Lennox is pretty damn smart."

"And you're expecting him to come here and rescue you? Both of you?"

"All four of us, yes," Carolina said. "That was a guarantee as soon as we were grabbed."

"Which is, of course, why this guy grabbed us," Helena said. "Unfortunately this isn't good."

"Why?" Sasha asked. "Carolina's brother can just come in, and they'll grab him and release us."

Helena looked at Sasha. "Do you think it'll really be that easy?"

Sasha's face closed down. "The guy said he would."

"So he did." Helena walked over to where Carolina sat quietly on the floor and joined her. "But you know talk's cheap, Sasha. Let's see what these guys do when the time comes."

Just then the guard walked in, and he carried a tray.

Helena hopped to her feet and asked, "Is that food for us?"

He nodded. "There's lots of it, just not much variety."

"That's fine," she said. "Thank you. We also need liquids. Water would be good."

"I'll bring some water," he said.

As she watched intently, the guard held his rifle pointed at them, pushed open the gate to their cage, and said, "Everybody stand back."

As they all obediently moved to the opposite wall, the tray was placed on the floor, and then the gunman backed out. As soon as they were locked up again, the guard said, "Now you can eat."

Helena walked over to the tray and took a look. She counted at least two buns apiece and some sausages, plus a big bowl of potatoes. Only one fork. She looked at the others. "Anybody else hungry?"

"Doesn't matter if we are or not," Sasha said. "As Carolina said, we need food."

"Indeed." Helena reached for a bun, opened it, popped a sausage in, and started to eat. She then made another sandwich to-go. Helena walked to the back of the cage and sat down, handing Carolina one of the sandwiches, but she shook her head, then winced. "No," Helena said, "you need food."

Glaring at her, Carolina grabbed the sausage in a bun and said, "My head hurts. My stomach's queasy. And I'd rather have vegetables."

"We can't do anything about your head or your stomach here. Sorry. As for the food, it doesn't matter what you'd rather have," she said blandly. "This is what we have available, so you'll eat it."

With a heavy sigh, Carolina followed through, and Helena glanced around, all four of them sitting with one sausage and a bun in hand.

Two armed men—the same guard and the same scarred man—came back with four bottles of water, but they could pop them through the bars without opening up their cage again. Helena hopped up, popping the last of the first bun into her mouth, collecting the bottles. Then she handed them out to everybody. "Thanks," she said to the scarred man, who seemed to be the leader of this group.

He nodded, and both turned and walked out of the

building.

Helena eyed the massive bowl of potatoes on the tray and the one fork, then looked around to the others and asked, "Anybody want any?"

Carolina immediately shook her head, her hands going to her temples immediately. "I don't," she said. "Potatoes aren't my thing."

Helena looked at John; he nodded. "Go ahead and have some," he said. "There are lots." She picked up the bowl and ate until she was full, then passed the bowl and fork off to John.

She wasn't sure where her appetite had come from, but she also knew her blood sugar could drop, and she'd suffer then. She planned on getting along and playing nicely with their kidnappers and waiting for Lennox to arrive. She had no doubt he was on his way. One thing she knew for sure about Lennox. When you didn't want him, he was always around the corner. And, when you did want him, he was still around the corner.

Only he wasn't hers to want.

WITH THE VEHICLE rented—in Lennox's name, since this was an obvious setup, and he wanted to acknowledge that from the get-go—he and Gavin were back on the road. However, on all missions, the guys wore gloves, even now in a vehicle clearly rented for him. It was a SEALs rule that had carried on into the Mavericks. It was a good rule. Gave the SEALs and the Mavericks the ghostlike quality of slipping in and back out again that they desired.

Gavin drove, while Lennox found the briefcase under

the front passenger seat. He quickly went through it: one sheet with some addresses, lots of money, and two handguns. He looked at the guns, frowned, and said, "I wonder if we'll need those to get the rest of the weapons."

"I wouldn't be at all surprised," Gavin said. "Nothing's easy over here."

"I haven't done much in Poland. You?"

Gavin shook his head. "No. Russia, yes, but I haven't been here before."

"Well, we are where we are," he said. "So let's get to it. I need a full arsenal before I go in after my sister."

"Did anybody ever come up with any intel as to why?"

"No," Lennox said, "and that bothers me. There should at least be a ransom note, even if just as a diversion or to start the bargaining." He checked with Keane and asked again, but still there had been no communication from the kidnappers. "So why?" he asked Gavin.

"That's the question, isn't it? Why your sister? Was it random or directed?"

"I feel like it's very directed."

"I do too," Gavin said. "So how many enemies do you have?"

"You mean, how many enemies does my sister have?"

"Good point," he said. "That's possible too. Is she that argumentative?"

Lennox laughed. "No, but she's fiercely loyal," he said. "I'd say the ex-husband is probably her only real enemy."

"Would he do something like this?"

"I doubt it," Lennox said softly. "If he did, I seriously misjudged him. I was pretty damn sure I'd scared the shit out of him, and he would never even be in the same country as my sister."

"Sure, but maybe he's in Poland?"

"Last I heard he was working out of Quebec."

"But maybe that's changed?"

"Time to find out." He sent a message off to Keane, who came back with a reply five minutes later.

He's still in Quebec. Showed up for work this morning.

"Would he have arranged this from a distance?" Gavin asked Lennox.

"Not if he had any clue I would be involved," Lennox said. "And, if it involves Carolina, I'm involved. I made it very clear what I would do to him if he ever hurt my sister again."

"Then it's not likely him then," Gavin said with a note of satisfaction. "I'm surprised you left him alive."

"I am too," Lennox said. "Thought for sure I'd kill the bastard. He did time, and he's still facing other charges. But he's working hard to keep his nose clean now, last I heard."

"What about other women?"

"No confirmation on that, but, had I heard even a whiff of anything like that, I'm pretty sure he knows I'll come around snooping, so he'll keep it on the straight and narrow."

"I hope so, for his sake," Gavin said.

"I don't know about that. I hope the bastard crosses the line," Lennox said. "Then I can take him out. One less abusive male on the planet sounds good to me."

"What about you? Enemies? Personal? Work?"

"Same as you," Lennox said, leaning back, closing his eyes. "Probably at least half a dozen, if not twice that."

As he sat, reflecting, a couple missions came to mind. One had gone bad, where another SEAL had been compromised. Another one, where a soldier had died from friendly fire. The shooter had been doing a training exercise. He'd turned and hit a couple of his unit. Several of them had been injured, but one had died. The deceased's family had accused the rest of the team because they hadn't protected their son.

But they had, from external threats. Just no one had seen the internal threat coming.

There'd been missions where Lennox had had to turn in a team member because he had betrayed their country. Lennox wasn't proud of the fact that he had worked with these traitors, but Lennox sure as hell wouldn't let one go out on more missions and endanger more of his friends and teammates.

"There's always one or two unexpected wild cards, isn't there?" Gavin said.

"Always," he said. "You do your best but …"

"Right," he said. "So anything else? Anything personal? Any married husbands angry that you have been screwing their wives?"

"Not my style," Lennox said. "Single and available is the only direction I travel."

"Maybe," said Gavin, "but women don't always tell the truth."

"Isn't that too damn sad?" he said. "But, yes, agreed."

"Got it," Gavin said, "but we do know one thing for sure."

Lennox looked at him. "What?"

"Somebody did this. And that somebody is pretty damn serious."

"I know," Lennox said. "We'll find the bastard. You can count on that."

CHAPTER 4

HELENA'S SITUATION WAS getting old very quickly. Once they'd eaten, everybody more or less crashed in various corners of their prison for at least an hour or two.

Helena sat in her corner, her head against the back of the steel cage, wishing for a bed or a pillow. But she'd gotten food and wouldn't push their captors' hospitality. She could ask for so many other things in life. Carolina was nearby. As Helena looked at the others, the two had distanced themselves from her and Carolina. They would blame Carolina no matter what Helena said to defend her best friend. She didn't know very much about John and Sasha. They appeared to be trustworthy workers and decent people in hospital settings; that's all she'd cared about so far.

Of course now they were under stress, and their very survival had been threatened. That would change everything entirely. What Helena didn't know for sure was how long they'd hold up. She already knew what Carolina was made of. The same as Helena. Nobody goes through the abuse and the beatings that these two women had gone through without understanding a lot about who they were on the inside.

They'd taken more than they should have. They both knew that, but neither had reached a breaking point or turned around and killed their attackers. She often wondered if whether maybe she would have been better off if she had. In theory, it would have been a lot easier to move forward and to forget the nightmares. She always held on to that fear that her ex-husband would show up again, but so far he never had.

Carolina's ex had had a visit from Lennox. Helena had often wondered about asking Lennox to do the same with her ex, but that would mean crossing the line the two had drawn in the sand. *After one very heady kiss.* She almost smiled at that. Lennox had been pissed, and the kiss had been more about the ultimate punishment at that time, given their near-hatred of each other—or maybe more about competing with each other for Carolina's attention? Regardless, that kiss had just been a byproduct of his temper, but it had quickly flared into something way past that. So Helena already knew that they were both trying to avoid igniting that short fuse which was always present between them.

Besides, she didn't want anything to do with men at this point; Lennox was safe as long as she didn't get too close to him. She already knew that, if she did, the two of them would burn up the sheets come hell or high water, and everybody else would turn to ash if they tried to stop them.

Carolina's low voice interrupted Helena's thoughts. "Are you okay?"

Helena smiled down at her friend. "Sure am. We've been in worse scenarios."

"I feel like suddenly we have a room divider in here," Carolina added in a low voice, deliberately not looking where the other two had huddled together.

"Sure. We're to blame. Remember?"

"You mean, I am," said Carolina, never afraid of stating the truth.

"By association me too," Helena said. "Don't worry about it. It is what it is. We will get out of this."

"Only because of Lennox. Do you think he'll get taken?"

Helena knew that a flippant answer wouldn't help right here, right now. She thought about the man with the steely gray eyes and his linebacker build and the pantherlike movements that made him a deadly predator of the night. "It'll take a tank to bring him down," she said.

"No," Carolina said softly. "Bullets will do it too."

"We've seen a lot of men get up after being shot multiple times," she reminded Carolina.

"I know. It's not the kind of work I like to do anymore, but you and I have both seen our share of gunshot wounds. I know it can do a lot of damage, but I also know many men who survived."

"Lennox will know it's a trap. He won't come alone," Helena said. "He's too smart for that."

At least in her heart, she hoped he was. Yet, with his sister as one of the kidnap victims, how would Lennox react to that? He was as impatient as his sister. Plus he had quite the temper. Could he pull it together to let his mind overrule his emotions? Helena hoped so. Otherwise Lennox could be the ultimate victim here.

Well, one of them. Carolina had been through enough already. The last thing she needed was to lose her brother, her only family. She'd been talking of nothing but seeing him this week. It was essential to her that they continued to meet, not just for a meal but for several days on end, where they could relax and talk. Helena understood Lennox offered another perspective and helped keep Carolina grounded, and the bond between them was the strongest she'd seen between two siblings.

Anything that kept Carolina in good shape and moving forward with her life was enormous. Carolina's pregnancy had ended with that last fight with her ex. She had left him immediately. It had been the final straw. And, of course, she'd spun into depression after that. She'd always wanted a family. Carolina and Helena had both talked about wanting children at some point in their lives. Maybe they both had jumped into those relationships because they thought they were getting too old to have babies, and maybe life was running past them. They were in their early thirties now. And time was marching by, without either woman in any current relationship, so having kids looked like a long ways away from where Helena stood.

Helena had felt that time pressure to have children a little more than Carolina had. Yet it was still there, always just that piece missing from both friends' world that Helena knew would come, but later. Now it would be that much later.

"How long do you think before he shows?" Carolina asked, obsessing over Lennox as usual.

"Well, as far as staying in this very uncomfortable cage, I hope he will be here immediately," she said. "But who's to say?"

"I need to sleep," Carolina murmured.

Helena glanced down at her friend, worried she'd been sleeping a lot since she took that blow to the head. "You sure your head's okay?" she asked, leaning closer and brushing the hair off the wound.

"The head's nothing," she said. "You and I both know we've taken worse."

Helena glanced over at the other corners of their cage, where the two were lying down, their heads together, but each lay alongside the cage, far enough away from Helena and Carolina to not overhear their discussion. That pair didn't know anything about the two women's histories. "Maybe," she said, "but we shouldn't have to again."

"*Shouldn't have to* doesn't make a damn bit of difference when we're caught in the middle of this."

"I know." That brought her anger rising. Helena swore she'd never again get caught in a situation where she would be reduced to a punching bag. Instead here she was. ... And who knew what the gunmen had planned for them. Talk of letting them go was cheap. ... Their actions were what counted. No, she wouldn't think like that. Lennox was coming. He might not come for her, but he sure as hell would come for Carolina. Helena just had to hold on and wait.

LENNOX STOPPED AT the entranceway to the weapons storage unit, as the breath almost sucked out of his chest.

"Quite something, isn't it?" Gavin murmured. "And who gave us this guy?"

"Keane sent me the address," Lennox said; he pulled out his phone and quickly sent Keane a text, asking him where they found this place.

An acquaintance of Levi's.

"Well, everybody knew Levi or at least anybody who'd been a Navy SEAL knew of Levi. And Ice. It was hard not to. And, if they had a connection like this, well, makes sense to check it out."

A man stood waiting nearby, holding a clipboard. "I don't have all day," he said testily.

"Got it," and they reamed off their list. Lennox grabbed a flat cart and collected items off the shelves. By the time they were done and had paid the bill in cash, the briefcase had a significant dent in it. But it was all good. They loaded up the vehicle and left the parking lot, Gavin driving again.

Lennox shook his head. "Already have two tails on us. Which is damn obvious in this neck of the woods."

"What's it look like?" Gavin asked, glancing in the rear-view mirror.

"Well, it looks like our friendly arms dealer plays both sides. He'll take our money and promptly give us up to the locals within minutes." Lennox sighed. "He gets paid twice for each gun deal."

Gavin shot another look behind them. "But they're not advancing on us."

Lennox fired off a text to both Levi and the Mavericks central command. "Probably just reporting our current position to the kidnappers. I doubt they will engage."

"You let Levi know?" Gavin asked, with a head tilt to Lennox's phone.

Lennox nodded. "Levi will handle it in his own unique way. And now ... we have to ditch this vehicle soon," Lennox murmured.

"Already in progress," Gavin said. "We'll get to the next town and switch up the rentals."

"I'd suggest ditching the rentals and just buying something cheap on the side," Lennox said. "The kidnappers, courtesy of the locals, will already have our license plate, our faces, and they now know that we've got not only cash but a lot of weapons."

"Movement behind us. One vehicle jumped in front of the other. Not aggressively but way too obvious. Do you think these locals are coming after us? I count two in each truck."

Lennox turned to look out the back windshield. "Well, they'd be a fool to try. They know we're armed, and they must also realize we know how to use our weapons," he said. "But all that doesn't mean they don't have a secondary business going on right now, where they take out trouble-makers."

"Which, by the very nature of what we just did, counts us as troublemakers," Gavin said with a nod. "I got no problem ditching our ride," he said. "We're probably better off to change wheels every town anyway." They came into the rental lot, and the two following trucks drove right by.

"Well," Lennox said, Gavin by his side, watching their tails until they were out of sight, "this one road seems to be the only path from this town to the next. They'll be waiting for us there."

Gavin nodded, returned the vehicle, grabbed all their gear—including all the firepower now packed in an extra duffel bag—and headed out to rejoin Lennox, still in the parking lot. "Any more friends following us?"

Lennox shook his head. "Out here, a tail can be seen so quickly. And I doubt the locals have the money for drones or have hackers who can tap into satellites."

"Yeah, but," Gavin added, "the kidnappers might. The guy arranged for air transport of the victims. That couldn't have been cheap. ... Or he has friends in high places."

They shared a knowing look, and Lennox repeated, "Trap. Yeah. I know."

"Where do you want to go?"

"I'll head into that restaurant over there," Lennox said. "We need food, and we need wheels."

"You order the food," Gavin said. "I'll take care of the wheels." Then Gavin took off, leaving the duffel bags for Lennox to tote around for now.

Lennox didn't even ask questions; he walked in, the heavy duffel bags in his hands, found a booth at the back, dropped the duffels under the table, and sat down. As soon as the waitress arrived with menus, he awkwardly ordered coffee and studied the food options as well. The translation app on his phone was a godsend in these situations. When she delivered the coffee, he ordered the special of the day times two, thought about it a second longer, and got two big meals to-go. He chose meals that could be eaten cold, big sub sandwiches, and several other dishes along that line. Also a refill of his coffee and a second cup. The waitress looked surprised but quickly wrote everything down and disappeared.

He sat here with his phone, wishing he could pull out his laptop but didn't take the chance of attracting any more interest. He was an obvious foreigner in this rural area. Many people in the restaurant gave him a critical once-over before resuming their meals. Lennox could feel their gazes on him every once in a while thereafter.

So the laptop wasn't a good idea here. Then he realized it didn't really matter because they likely didn't have any internet here. Cell towers were few and far between out here in farm country. He checked in with Keane to let him know where they were. Then asked, **Got me a location pinpointed yet?**

Give us two more minutes.

Lennox snorted at that, hung up, and set his cell phone off to the side. But he had to admit, so far—with everything that he'd been involved in with that chat box, between

Keane's mission and now this op of Lennox's—the Mavericks chat window had been a gold mine as far as resources went. He didn't know how many Mavericks were working on the back end, but Lennox knew this command center position right now was filled with like the seventh or eighth man who had done prior missions, and these were the only ones Lennox knew about. So he figured the Mavericks could easily gather an eight-man team, ready to go at a moment's notice. He pulled the phone toward him again and typed,

Are Gavin and I the only ones on a mission currently?

No. Kerrick and Griffin are off in Africa.

Any connection to my case?

No came back the answer instantaneously.

Lennox pulled his coffee toward him and took a hesitant sip. And then smiled. It was thick, intense, black, and damn-near scorched his throat all the way down. *Perfect.*

He sat back with a sigh, rotating his shoulders and his neck to ease some of the tension there. They were fully equipped now, which helped on these overseas missions where air travel was involved, as that was always an issue, making sure that they had what they needed and without all the red tape involved with a by-the-books military op. Not that the Mavericks couldn't get some help from the US Navy or other branches of the military if and when needed. The Mavericks maintained a symbiotic relationship with their SEAL brothers for sure.

Now if only Lennox had a location on his sister.

His phone buzzed; he pulled it forward to see a link. He quickly clicked on it and saw the kidnapper's vehicle that had been at the Warsaw airport. It was driving through the town he was currently in. The time and date stamp said it was four and a half hours earlier. That wasn't bad. They were gaining a bit on them.

Stay on the same highway. You've got three more towns to go through to catch up to the latest surveillance we have reviewed to produce this bread crumb trail on the kidnapper's vehicle.

Time frame on locating their final destination with the captives?

We still don't have that intel, but we're damn close. So, when you're done eating, start driving.

Lennox stared as the waitress returned with large plates. He dug into his, even before she left. He knew the folly of not having enough fuel to run on. And that wouldn't happen today. More than that, he didn't know if his sister and the others in her group were struggling with a lack of food either. As soon as he ate half his fries, his phone went off again, and there was a map, and he saw the three towns marked with dots. **Those three are confirmed sightings?**

Yes, still working on the one after that.

They go off the grid?

Yes. Now we're searching via satellite.

Lennox kept eating, and, when he looked up, Gavin walked toward him with a smile on his face. Lennox motioned at the food.

Gavin sat down, surveyed the plate in front of him, and said, "Now this is what I call a meal." He picked up his knife and fork and dug in. Ten minutes later both had polished off their massive platefuls. When the waitress came back with the to-go bag, she stared at the empty plates in surprise.

Lennox looked at her, smiled, used his phone then said, "We were hungry."

They got up, and Gavin grabbed both duffel bags this time, while Lennox grabbed the takeout and walked up to the cash register. The woman never said a word, just rang up the order. When he saw the amount, he paid cash for it, smiled at her, and walked outside to meet up with his partner.

"I could have used a take-out coffee," Gavin said.

"If you want one, go back and get it," Lennox said.

"Nah, we've already got enough attention."

"Even the best of us," he said, "have to eat and drink."

"I know, but it still feels like everybody's staring."

"We're Americans. I'm sure they are."

"No way to be subtle out here in the wide open spaces, is there?"

"No, not at this stage, and we don't need to be. We've got three more towns to go through by the time we're done heading into the next district," he said. "The kidnappers have gone to ground. That's when we'll have to go incognito."

"Good enough," he said. Gavin led the way to a small pickup truck. They stowed the duffel bags in the back of the bed and hopped into the front seat. As Gavin started the engine, Lennox asked, "Did you pay cash for this one?"

"Well, I caught somebody trying to steal it," he said, "so I persuaded him that he didn't need to keep it."

Lennox laughed and laughed. "Well, we'll have to leave it somewhere on the side of the road. Be even nicer if the guy stealing it in the first place left his fingerprints here."

"We've both got gloves on, and the kid didn't."

Lennox chuckled. "Well that's a twist, isn't it?"

"I figured it would work. We'll have to switch it out soon anyway."

"Maybe not at every town now. I don't see any more tails."

They kept driving the truck for another forty minutes.

They'd already passed the next town and were in the middle of the second.

"Time to change vehicles."

Gavin shrugged.

"Maybe a double-cab truck this time, enough to handle six of us?"

Gavin nodded. "I'll see what I can find in the next few minutes."

Luckily, ten minutes later they were in their new wheels and back on the road.

"One more town to go." Lennox's phone buzzed again, with the one-word text, **Close?**

Not close enough, he typed. **We're coming into the third town.**

Got it. And the chat box disappeared. Lennox pocketed his phone and said, "They still haven't got a final location."

"How big is the area?"

"Last seen in a parcel about twenty square miles," he said. "Lots of farms, old homesteads," he said. "They could be anywhere."

"Twenty isn't bad though," Gavin said. "We've hunted with way less information and a much larger area."

"Isn't that the truth?" Lennox admitted. He and Gavin had done many missions together when they'd both been Navy SEALs. And both had come to the end of the road where they knew it was time for a change.

Lennox had never in his wildest days imagined even more black ops though. And this one was different in so many ways.

CHAPTER 5

HELENA GROANED AND shifted her position again. Part of the problem was the lack of a floor. The cage rested on the hard-packed dirt. Although it could be worse if there had been bars on the ground in this cage too. That would never be comfortable. How was the cage was secured to the ground? A quick check at the four corners and on both sides of the gate confirmed her fears. Steel rods inserted at each point were probably buried at least six feet into the ground. *So no lifting up one side of this cage*, she thought. Even if it could work, with twelve-foot-long sides, she'd have to get help from Sasha and John too, which was not likely.

Doubly frustrated now, she tried kicking up some of the earth to make a little bit of a pillow, but that didn't help. She rolled over on her back again and stared up at the ceiling. This building was a sizeable machine shop, one of probably a thousand of them around the countryside. How could anybody find them in this nightmare? But she knew better than to doubt Lennox.

What had Lennox done? Or rather, what did this guy think Lennox had done? The guy had an obvious tell; he brushed his scarred neck whenever he had talked about Lennox. But she knew, if it had been a mission that had gone bad, well, it would have been gone bad for Lennox too. Right? And he had no burn scars that she had ever seen. And

Carolina would have mentioned that, if he had had some serious injuries. Just because this guy had been burned in some event from the past, that didn't mean that Lennox was to blame for this guy getting hurt. ... That was a pretty strong causal accusation.

Lennox wasn't the kind of man to do shit like that without a good reason. And what did *betrayal* mean to this burn victim? If it meant that this guy was caught stealing, and then Lennox turned him over to the authorities? Well, so be it. Because, in that case, hell yeah, Lennox would do no less. But then she would as well. That's the way she rolled— straight up, straight forward. Everybody else and their little side trips into the gray areas of life weren't for her.

That's why Helena did well at her career. They went in, they did the job, and they got out. Unfortunately, it also reminded her that there was an awful lot of gray in life and it just brought all that shitty marriage stuff back again.

She glanced down at Carolina, seeing her eyes closed and her deep breathing. Helena shouldn't be worried about her friend, but there was something about her five-foot petite stature that made everybody look at Carolina as if she were a child. But Carolina had a steel core and a heart of gold.

Now Helena wasn't much taller at five-four, but those extra four inches seemed to make a lot of difference. In many ways, they wore the same clothes. Helena was a little bustier and of course a little longer, but that length was more in her legs, whereas Carolina had a longer torso. They often played around with each other's tops and sweaters and even some of their dresses and skirts, borrowing them when needed. Wouldn't it be nice if they were doing that right now? It sure beat sitting here as a prisoner.

Helena would need the bathroom again. She winced and

shifted her position to see if that would ease her bladder. But she was already lying flat. When she stood, it would get even worse. She sighed and then called out softly, hoping to not disturb the others. "What about a bathroom trip?"

A gunman immediately stepped in from the open door to the building, confirming her suspicion that they weren't ever alone. He nodded and asked, "Just you?"

"Yes," she said, gently getting to her feet. "The others are asleep."

"You can't sleep?"

She shrugged irritably. "No, I'm finding the ground a little too hard for my old bones."

He made a scoffing sound. But, in truth, she'd taken enough blows during her lovely abusive marriage that she found it hard to lie in certain positions now. Her guard led her to the bathroom. After relieving herself, she opened the door so he saw her; she turned on the water and washed her face and hands, then bent her head down and took a long drink.

"Are you out of water?"

She nodded. "Yes, the bottles all disappeared with the food."

"Of course, with potatoes and bread, you need water for those." He stepped aside, pointed behind him at a bucketful of ice water and bottles nearby, and said, "Grab another bottle."

She hesitated and asked, "May I take one for each of us?"

He nodded.

Helena pulled out four bottles from the bucket sitting there, and she walked back to the gate of their cage. The gunman unlocked it, let her in, and then locked it back up again. She sat down with the water, opened one, and had a long drink.

Sasha opened her eyes, saw the water, and asked, "Is there more?"

Helena tossed her a bottle and said, "One for each of us." She threw another one and said, "Give that one to John when he wakes up."

Carolina rolled over, groaned, and said, "Man, why aren't we in a five-star hotel?"

"We would be," Sasha said, in a hard voice, "if it wasn't for you."

"That'll hardly help the situation," Helena said, her voice in a carefully neutral tone. Sasha wasn't making friends with her accusations. "None of us knew this would happen. It could just as easily have been somebody you knew."

Sasha shrugged, took a drink, and then laid back down again. "But I don't know anybody who would be in a situation like this."

"Well, now you do," Helena snapped.

Sasha looked at her and frowned.

"You're already in a situation *like this*," Helena added, "so now everybody in your sphere knows somebody who's been in *situations like this*."

At that, Sasha shot her a disgusted look, closed her eyes, and rolled over.

Carolina laughed. "You don't need to defend me. You know that, right?" she asked.

"Maybe not," Helena said, "but nobody needs to be blaming anyone right now."

"But it makes people feel better," Carolina said.

Her best friend had taken a whole pile of psychology courses after her divorce to try to understand not only her husband's behavior—which both Carolina and Helena did more or less understand—but about Carolina's lack of responses, why she had taken the abuse. The two best friends had discussed that issue many, many times. This wasn't the time for another discussion now, but at least her education gave Carolina a chance to understand why Sasha was acting the way she was.

For Helena, she didn't give a shit; she just wanted Sasha to stop all these unproductive verbal attacks.

Carolina and Helena heard a commotion outside the building, and then two gunmen stepped inside, one of them the scarred man from before. They glared at the four prisoners, walked around their cage, checked to make sure that no loose bars were found and that nobody had come inside. "Did you see anybody?" the scarred man snapped at her in English.

Helena answered, "No, I haven't seen anybody but the one guard and you."

The scarred man glared at her, as if searching for the truth, then gave her a nod. "Better not. If you aid in your escape," he said, "we'll take that as a mark against you, and we will shoot you the next time."

She took a long, slow breath, trying to reach for some control, so she didn't snap at him. "We're trying to be cooperative," she said calmly.

"No point in *trying*," he said. "We have the upper hand. You are our prisoner, so you'll do what you are told."

She didn't say anything, just stared at him, her gaze flat.

He snickered. "You don't like that, do you?"

"I doubt anybody does," she said, once again reaching for some serene calmness as she searched for anything that might get them released. "Lennox should be here soon, I gather?"

"I hope so," he said. "I don't plan on feeding you for too long."

She winced at that. "We do eat a fair bit, don't we?"

"You do," he said, "but that's all right. We're okay for a few days. After that, if he's still not here, we'll shoot you." And he turned and walked out.

Beside her, Carolina whispered, "*Shoot* us?"

"Yeah, but whether that was a scare tactic or not, I'm not sure," Helena said. She looked over to see tears in Sasha's eyes. "Take heart," she said. "It won't get that bad." Sasha stared at her. Helena saw the vulnerability on the woman's face.

"I don't know this Lennox guy," Sasha said. "I don't even know for sure that he's coming."

"Well, we do know him," Helena said, nodding toward Carolina. "And he is coming. The problem is, these guys know it too, and they're waiting for him."

Sasha nodded, her long hair drifting in the dirt, but she didn't seem to care. It wasn't a high priority at the moment. "Is he the kind of person to make it past those armed guards out there?"

"Absolutely," Helena said, thinking about Lennox. "If anybody can help us, he can."

"I hope you're right," Sasha said, "because we won't survive if he doesn't." And she rolled over, away from the two women, and ignored them.

Carolina nodded beside her. "She's right. Our kidnappers don't have the tolerance to wait for a few days. If this isn't done with by tomorrow, you know what'll happen."

"Maybe not," she said.

"Count on it," Carolina whispered. "These guys don't have any intention of playing around. If I'm not a big-enough lure to bring in Lennox, they won't waste their time and resources with guarding and feeding prisoners. They'll shoot us one by one until we're all dead."

Helena had to agree, but she didn't want to even talk about it.

Still, the commotion got her hopes up that Lennox had arrived. But now, since no gunfire had immediately erupted or no bombs went off or no truck on fire broke through a weak spot in the walls of this shop—what she considered Lennox's style in her mind—she decided it was not Lennox-related at all. Probably some wildlife in the area. Or just jumpy gunmen outside, seeing every moving shadow as a two-legged threat.

She had to trust that Lennox was coming. She knew his relationship with his sister was something that Lennox would bend over backward to save. What Helena didn't know was whether anybody would get hurt in the process. There were four prisoners. And any number of armed guards. Plus Lennox wasn't stupid enough to come in here unarmed. With all that imagined firepower, Helena knew it would be just too damn easy for one of them to get shot accidentally. The last thing she needed was to have anyone here die because of their own rescue attempt.

"WE NEED INTEL," Lennox snapped into the phone.

"I know," Keane said. "We're still looking."

"They couldn't have completely disappeared off the face of the earth."

"No. They didn't. We found signs that the vehicle went toward a farmhouse, then drove across the neighboring land.

But some black zone is out there. Yet we picked up the truck on the other side, and it appears to still have all the same people in it."

"Anything like that's an anomaly," Lennox said. "Tell me where it disappeared in the first place."

"I'll send you the GPS coordinates," Keane said. "Remember though. It isn't necessarily the final destination."

"Maybe not, but we'll start there, and, while we do, you'll keep the Mavericks working hard to find out exactly where they've ended up."

"Yes." And they hung up.

Lennox explained what had happened to Gavin.

"That's odd. I wonder if a big repeating station is here or if some power plant is sending off weird energy that's causing a glitch in the satellite feeds."

"Possibly. Let's take a drive out there and see." The GPS coordinates were not very far up ahead. When they took the left-hand turn, they saw other tracks ahead of them. "Well, somebody's been through here recently."

"Exactly. But it's anyone's guess who."

When they got to the spot, the dot on Lennox's phone buzzed and beeped. "Okay, my phone doesn't like this location at all."

"No, but as you can see,"—Gavin pointed out a big transformer station off to the side—"we never really understand the effects from these big power plants," Gavin said, "but everybody knows there's a hole in some areas because of them."

"And having this here means what though?" Lennox studied the area, realized the tracks continued, and said, "We might as well keep driving and see if anything suspicious is here."

"Alternatively," Gavin said, pointing to a hill, "we can go up there and take a look at the bigger picture and see if we can see anything of interest below us."

"Let's do that first, then follow the tracks if need be," Lennox said. A few minutes later they crested the top of the hill, parked, and hopped out with binoculars to take a look around. "Lots of small farms, little villages dotting the countryside," Lennox said. "I'm not seeing anything indicative of our missing people."

"No, I'm not either. I think we're too far away."

"Where do the tracks go from here?"

Gavin pointed them out. "They're coming around this hill and going down again. A road of sorts cuts through there. I think the power plant skewed the videos."

Lennox nodded. "Enough buildings and outbuildings are along here for any number of prisoners to be kept." He motioned to the barns, machine sheds, garages, even small houses, and what looked like a couple warehouses. "We're not short on places to search, and we're wasting time, so we need to make sure that we narrow it down as much as we can." Lennox assessed the area in front of them and said, "Probably got a good ten-mile area here. That'll take time to search on foot."

"True enough but we can hit almost every one of those buildings within the next couple hours."

"Maybe, but we should have a shorter time frame than that. Once we're moving around and checking out places, we're not foolish enough to think we won't be seen, not considering how many places we have to hit. The kidnappers will get word, and they'll be waiting for us."

"Hell," Gavin said, "they're already waiting for us now."

Lennox nodded. "I know it," he said. "And, of course,

that's what this is all about. It's a trap."

"Which is why we have to be smart," Gavin said. "I get that you want to go tearing in there after your sister. But it's *you* who they want."

"*Me* they can have," Lennox said, his voice icy hard. "But they don't dare touch my sister."

Gavin smacked him lightly on the shoulder. "We'll find her," he said. "You know that."

And Lennox nodded. He knew that. But the ultimate question remained. Would they get there before these assholes hurt her or even killed her? It depended on whether they thought she was a sound bargaining chip because, if Lennox got there and found her dead, he'd make sure that not one of them walked again. Hell, he'd be happy if not one of them breathed again. But he'd have to see just what went down first. If the kidnappers fought, they gave him a perfect excuse to take them out. And, if he saw anybody in any way involved in the kidnapping, well, that was good enough for Lennox to retaliate in kind.

The two men made their way back to the truck and drove down the hill to the small village. Just as they reached the first property with a massive farm, a barn, and a tractor machine shed, Lennox saw half a dozen people moving big machinery around and stacking up hay inside the barn. "This doesn't look like a good option."

"Too noisy, too many people, no visible guns," Gavin agreed. His phone buzzed at that point. He checked out the message. "*Keep going one mile. You should come upon a right turn.* The Mavericks lost sight of them there."

"Why?"

"A blink in the satellites as they connect to the next one, and it didn't catch that signal. *Be careful.*" Very quickly they hit the spot. They got out, walked on foot, studying the area. "Well, here's fresh tracks," Gavin noted. "I suggest we drive ahead to that pullout and the couple little tourist signs for that river, and we head back on foot."

Lennox didn't want anybody to have any idea they were coming. But, of course, everybody was waiting for them. Parking the vehicle, they quickly disappeared into the tall grass and bushes. They came along the neighbor's side, keeping an eye on the property in question as well as the one beside it. By the time they made it to the far side of the properties, Lennox saw multiple buildings, but there was no sign of anyone. He frowned, hunkered down into the brush, made himself a small area where he could lay down and use his binoculars, and peered through them. "I'll scan the east side. You take the west."

"Got it," Gavin said as he backed up to Lennox, facing the opposite direction and protecting his partner as well.

"People," Lennox whispered.

"How many?" Gavin asked.

"I see four men."

"Armed?"

"No. Not a one of them."

"Well, what are they doing then?"

"Good point," Lennox said. "They're just standing around and talking, near the opened double doors, yet inside that machine shop."

"So, are any weapons anywhere near those guys?" Gavin brought his binoculars around to search the same area.

"Not that I can see." Lennox shifted his binoculars, studying the next closest building in the area, a temporary shed—one of those metal half-circle-looking things that were put up fast and easy and usually reasonably priced. And they would hold everything from hay to equipment, and some had even been converted to housing when needed. There were rarely any windows on them in the back, like this one, although there was a window in the small rear door. And a window would help, but it was a long way away for Lennox to make a run like that to check if anyone was there. When he found his sister and her team, he planned on getting them out immediately. No return trip needed.

"Ten o'clock," Gavin whispered.

Lennox shifted to the left, checking out his ten o'clock. One vehicle and one man. And what was different about this one was he had a rifle on the hood of the truck in front of him, while he lit a cigarette. Lennox studied the weapon. "Nice piece of weaponry there," he murmured.

"Expensive," Gavin said.

"Absolutely. And in good shape. Not a spot of rust anywhere." Meaning that guy looked after his weapons, which meant he used them a lot. Lennox watched as the gunman had a smoke, walked around, studying the sky, then the woods around him. He never looked once in their direction. He continued to explore the rest of the area. "He doesn't appear to be guarding anything," Lennox said, his gaze zipping back to where the other men stood inside the machine shop. No one appeared in or around the shed.

"No," Gavin whispered. "But if there's one gunman ..."

CHAPTER 6

"**S**O WHEN WILL your brother get here?" John asked. His tone held a sense of overwhelming despair, as if he didn't believe that Lennox would really come.

Helena looked at Carolina, who was lying with her arm across her eyes. Her knees were bent, relaxed, but Helena doubted her best friend was asleep. And she didn't bother answering John's question. So Helena glanced at John and shrugged. "We have no way of knowing if he even knows yet that she's missing."

He stared at her in surprise. "Well, didn't the kidnappers send a ransom note?"

"I don't know if they did or not," she said. "I don't know what they've done to alert Lennox to the problem."

John stared at her, frowning. "And here I was assuming the guy was already on the way," he said, turning around in the cage, his arms wide. "How long do they expect to keep us in here?" he cried out.

"As long as necessary," she said, her voice calm as she tried to get him to understand the situation wouldn't have an immediate resolution.

"This is not where I want to be," he said, getting more and more agitated. He pivoted and shook the bars. But the cage didn't even budge.

She saw his body jolt as he tried to force the cage to do

something. "John, calm down," she said cautiously. She hadn't seen him lose it before, and he was basically calm and even-tempered and had a ready smile for everyone. At least under hospital conditions.

He turned to look at her, and clearly their situation was tearing into him. "I can't stay calm!" he said. "I want to go home. I want to spend some time with my family," he cried out. "Why are they doing this to me? I didn't have anything to do with whatever her brother did."

"None of us did," Helena stated. "Including Carolina. It's about her brother, whether he did something or not. It's not about her."

"It's the same thing," he roared. He came over to stand beside them. Not sure what his intention was, Helena slowly stood protectively over Carolina. "She's already been hurt physically by the kidnappers," she urged John to caution. "Let's not add any more trauma to her stressed system."

"She's stressed?" he said, staring at Helena in disbelief. "What about me? What about Sasha? We didn't have anything to do with this. You two are always joined at the hip, so it's fine if the kidnappers keep you. This has nothing to do with us."

"I don't think the kidnappers particularly care who is here," she said coolly, as she stood here, feet planted apart, her hands ready to stop John from attacking Carolina, if that's what he thought he would do next. "They had a plan, and they didn't ask us for permission."

He stared at her for a long while, and then his shoulders sagged. "Look. I get that you're not responsible," he said in the most persuasive of voices. "But surely you can ask the guards to release us." And he motioned at Sasha, who was now looking at them hopefully and then at him. "Once they realize it's got nothing to do with us, I'm sure they'd let us go."

"I don't think they're gonna let anybody go right now. Not before they get what they ultimately want. After all, having four hostages is an advantage over having just two," Helena said, raising her palms in John's direction. "But you can always try asking them yourself, when they come back."

"When are they coming back?" he asked, running his hands up and down his face, pinking his skin with the effort. "I need to go to the bathroom."

"I don't know, John. Why don't you call out and ask one of the guards to come and take you to the restroom," she said in a reasonable tone, not quite trying to humor him but wanting to keep him a little more balanced than the upset man she saw struggling to get free. "When I called them earlier, they let me out to go to the bathroom."

He looked at her sideways. "But maybe you're special."

"I'm not special at all," she said, her fatigue obvious in her tone. "Just call out and tell them you need to go to the washroom."

He looked at her once and then walked up to the gate and called out, "Is anyone there? I need to go to the bath-room."

Almost immediately one of the guards stepped forward, took one look at John, and nodded. The gunman walked over without a sound, unlocked the door, let John out, keeping one of his guns pointed in his direction, and quickly relocked the door. He led John away to the bathroom.

As soon as they were out of sight, Helena sagged in place.

"You can't stop him forever," Carolina murmured.

"I know," she said, "but I'm hoping I can stop it for a

little bit longer."

"Stop what?" Sasha asked belligerently.

But Helena just stared at her. Because this was precisely what Carolina was talking about. It was a case of not having the others turn against them. And sometimes when people turned against each other, they got a whole lot more violent too.

"We just want everybody to get along, so we can get out of here peacefully," Helena explained.

"Well, we're not gonna get along," Sasha said. "Why would we? Just like John, I know that we don't belong here. You guys are to blame for this."

Helena could feel Carolina stiffen at that. "*To blame?*" Helena repeated curiously, trying to keep her tone still even and low. "Do you believe that?"

Sasha looked momentarily confused, and a whisper of sorrow appeared on her face for what she'd said, but then she immediately stiffened her shoulders and said, "Well, if anybody's to blame, it's you guys."

"We didn't have anything to do with this," Helena said. But she knew that her words would fall on deaf ears. Because Sasha wanted to hear absolutely nothing, except that they were being released.

"Maybe," Sasha said, "but John and I had nothing to do with this. We hardly even know you."

"I get that," Helena said. "And I'm sorry you're caught up in this. Hell, I'm sorry I'm caught up in this. And I know that Carolina is not very impressed either. I'm pretty sure her brother right now is pretty pissed off about the whole damn thing too."

"Well, good," Sasha said. "He should be. Whatever he did wrong, he should own up to it and take the punishment."

"Did *wrong*?" Helena asked, her hand immediately going out to stop Carolina. She could feel the vibrating tension in Carolina's frame. "Do you think that her brother did something wrong? And that's why we're here?"

"Of course!" Sasha snapped. "It's only when people do bad things that they get caught up in this shit."

"Like you and me and John and Carolina? Did we do something bad?"

"Of course not!" Sasha said. "Now you're twisting my words."

"Well, I'm not trying to," Helena said, "but Lennox deals in wars, as do these men. And there's no use in blaming anyone. We are on opposite sides here with the kidnappers. We want different things. There's no right or wrong answer when it comes to a war with men on opposite sides. It doesn't necessarily mean either one of them did something that caused harm to the other."

"Is that what you think this is about?" Sasha said with a disbelieving laugh. "He made it very clear that Lennox hurt him and someone else. And that Lennox will pay for the damage he did. And I, for one, agree with him. I think he *should* pay."

"Well then, since your mind is closed on the issue— without any supporting facts, I might add, just the word of a gunman who had us kidnapped—not a whole lot of point in talking to you anymore, is there?" Helena said coolly. "Maybe you can use all those arguments to talk to the kidnappers instead and get yourself out of here." She was getting tired of these two. And fast.

Sasha stared at her. "Do you think it would work?" she asked cautiously.

"Well, I know John wants to try a similar tactic," Helena said, shaking her head wearily. "So talk to him. You and John figure something out for yourselves."

Helena couldn't really blame the others for wanting to get the hell out of here; it was a tough situation. It was their damn whiny attitudes and blaming posturing that she found fault with. Yes, it was a stressful scene, more so than some of their surgical theaters, set up in war-torn countries, where a stray bomb or bullet could kill them all. Yet that was fate. This was premeditated. This time, if they died here, it was because one of the gunmen had pointed their rifles at them and pulled the trigger.

So, yes. This situation was amped up, even compared to the normal Red Cross scenarios that they found themselves in. Helena just wished that John and Sasha would grow a pair. Where were their humanitarian instincts right now? Obviously those were just for show to impress doctors and to get paid to do a job. Nothing more than that. Helena let out a long sigh.

Despite all she had seen in her life—both at home and on the work fronts—she was still surprised when she found the likes of these cowards, whether dressed up in scrubs or with a mild-manner demeanor. They were all con artists.

Helena wanted John and Sasha to focus on something a little more than themselves, like the bigger picture here. If just for one hour. But Helena knew that was too much to ask for from these wimps. Without a true backbone, people like them fold at the first high winds that blow through. That's just the way they were, inside, regardless of what their outsides looked like.

And Helena wondered. If she were given a choice, would she leave Carolina? She could certainly go and get help and bring people back, but leaving Carolina alone would be a challenging thing to do. She shook her head. No way she could leave Carolina here. Not with the likes of these two left to do … whatever to her best friend in retaliation.

In a different situation, where Carolina was hurt, maybe unconscious, without kidnappers and weak-willed ninnies about, yes. Helena would secure Carolina in the best hiding place she could find and would then race to find help. Something neither John nor Sasha would do for each other, much less for Carolina and Helena.

Just then, John was led back to the cage. He was arguing fiercely with the guard. "I can help you," he said. "I have money."

"It's not about money," the guard said, as he unlocked the door and gave John a hard shove.

"But we don't have anything to do with this!" John said in disbelief. "Why won't you listen?"

The guard stared at him, a hard look on his face. "I listened," he said, "but you said nothing that I care to hear." And he turned and walked away.

John called out, "You don't care that we didn't have anything to do with this?"

The guard shook his head.

"But why? That makes no sense. You say you're doing this because you want her brother? We have nothing to do with her brother or her. You're just creating another bad mess because now our families will be angry too."

The guard turned to look at him. "Do you have any family in the military?"

John frowned and then shook his head. "No."

"Then I don't need to worry," he said and turned and walked out.

Helena wanted to laugh at the look on John's face at the utter disbelief that somebody would be so unreasonable. He didn't get it. She understood there was no getting *it*. There was nothing here to understand. The gunmen didn't care one little bit about who was here and who wasn't here. Well, except for Lennox's absence.

As far as the kidnappers were concerned, it was all about themselves. They had a goal. *Get Lennox. Get payback from Lennox.* The gunmen didn't care who got hurt in the process. It didn't matter that it was a similar attitude to what Lennox would likely have felt when he did whatever *wrong* that they assumed he did. Maybe he'd been so focused on *his* goal that he didn't care about who else got hurt.

But that wasn't anything like the Lennox she knew.

However, John made a good point because the kidnappers *were* creating a new problem. Still none of the kidnappers would care. Because the originating event seemed military-related. So the scarred man had a family member who was hurt by Lennox, someone not in the military? Even with Lennox's secret SEALs ops, no way Lennox would harm a civilian. Of any country. Helena would stake her life on it.

In a way, she already had.

But that wasn't the way most people thought. It was the way of life too many times where nobody cared. And the sooner that John got a handle on that, the better. Helena had learned that lesson the hard way; so had Carolina. They understood that Lennox cared and that there were probably doctors who cared and nurses who cared, but, given the general state of things, nobody else gave a shit.

You were expected to look after your world, look after everything going on in your life, without involving others. And deal with whatever came at you. If you couldn't deal with it, well, shut the hell up and go away. Because nobody gave a shit—that was the bottom line.

Helena groaned slightly and sank back against the cage wall.

"This is your fault," John said, turning on her like a rabid animal.

She opened her eyes to see if he would lunge and attack because that would be a whole different story. "What did I do?" she asked calmly.

"You brought this on us!" he said.

"I'm not so sure about that," she said. "I can see you want to believe it, but that's not logical."

"It is," he swore. "It seriously is."

She shrugged. "Maybe, but this is what we have to deal with. The sooner you accept it, the better."

"There's no accepting this!" he said, shaking his head, almost vibrating in a fury.

"So what do you want to do about it?" she asked, slowly standing up, stepping closer to John. "You want to hit me? Is that what this is all about? Do you need to lash out at Carolina and me to make you feel better? It doesn't matter that we didn't have anything to do with this either. It doesn't matter *to you* that we don't know what's going on and that we have no involvement in whatever happened in the first place."

He looked at her. "How is it possible that you can't know?"

"Because Lennox was in the military—special ops, as a SEAL. Highly covert missions. We don't know anything about his life while he was in the military," she said. "You do realize the secrecy involved in the military, don't you?" She huffed, crossing her arms, a frown on her face.

Seeing John not putting up a fight when first taken by the kidnappers, to turning on her and Carolina so fast, Helena gathered that John had probably failed the physical exam—or the psych test—or maybe never wanted to be in the military in the first place. His ego and his brawn and his brains—more important, his manhood—were again being called into question here, under these adverse conditions.

She knew where he was coming from now. A frightened little boy, putting up the big bully front, hoping she would back down. Wow. Did he ever pick the wrong person for this particular manipulation.

As she continued to assess him, she realized that some of the rigidity had fallen from his back and spine and shoulders and that—maybe, just maybe—it was safe to relax a little bit. "I get that you're upset," she said. "Believe me. None of us are thrilled to be here. None of us *chose* to be here either. But this pseudo-threatening attitude of yours toward Carolina and me won't change anything a damn bit right now."

He snorted and walked to where Sasha was, sitting, staring up at him. He looked at Sasha and said, "Sorry, I tried."

She nodded. "I was trying to figure out what I could do to help. But it's not like the guards want to be reasonable."

"The guards are only focused on what they want," Carolina said. "It doesn't matter what we want."

"So how can we fix that?" Sasha asked. "How can we get them to focus on something else?"

"Well, a diversion would be nice," Helena said, "particularly at the same time when we somehow get the gate unlocked. Maybe then we could escape."

The two of them looked at her. "Do you think so?"

"I don't know for sure," she said. "It's a work in progress right now. Only a theory. What I do know is that, even if we got out of this cage, I'm sure more men with guns are not very far away," she said. "Probably eight of them or even more are right outside this building. So the chances of us breaking out of this place will be harder than we think. So we need to take all that into account as we devise any escape plan."

"I hadn't even figured a way to get out of this cage," Sasha said, slowly climbing to her feet. "So what are you thinking so far?"

"I can probably pick the lock," she said, "but what I don't know is after that."

"And how would you pick the lock?" John whispered, his gaze focused on the gate into the cage.

Helena pulled a bobby pin from her hair and held it up. The two of them frowned at it, looked at the lock, and back at her. She shrugged. "I've done it once or twice before, but I won't know if it'll work here until I try it. Even so, it won't do us any good after that."

"Are you serious?"

"If we try and get caught, it's gonna be worse for us afterward," she said. "Some of us could even get killed in the attempt."

"We have to be strategic," Carolina said. "We have to wait for an opportunity. Then we can get out of here *and* get free and clear. Not just free."

"What'll that take?" Sasha asked, crawling closer.

Helena looked at her. "The arrival of Lennox."

Understanding settled on the other two's faces, and they curled back up in their corner, yet looking a whole lot more relaxed. If nothing else, a rough draft of a plan was in motion. And just having that much gave them a glimmer of hope. Helena wasn't sure that Lennox was even on the way yet. But she did know that, one way or the other, he'd find Carolina. Come hell or high water, Lennox was coming. It was just a matter of when.

LENNOX SHIFTED POSITION. They'd been waiting for hours. His instincts said that something wasn't as it seemed. It was too simple; only one man with a rifle didn't make any sense. The fact that a man with a gun was here at least gave Lennox and Gavin some inclination that maybe they were in the right location, but Lennox couldn't confirm even that much. Which bothered him.

He turned to find his partner. Gavin crept along the fence. There was just enough half-light that their body shapes were merging with whatever was around them. It was a perfect time to skulk. But anybody who was expecting their company would know that too.

Were the prisoners sitting in that one shed? Could they have been locked up in the machine shop? There was a barn too. That was Lennox's first location to search. And the closest building. People often considered a barn only for animals but would keep people penned in there too. But generally farmers needed more accessible ways to get out of a barn than a single door. That observation alone seemed to rule out that his sister was here in Lennox's mind.

Still they had to check out this farm.

Lennox waited for a moment and then moved silently toward the barn. He crouched low along the creek, where lots of brush could camouflage him a bit longer. Then he had a spot of about twenty feet to cross, without any barrier to hide his presence. And, once across, he leaned up against the barn and listened. But he heard nothing, not a creak of old wood nor of an animal shifting.

Lennox spotted a large window close by. He slipped to the side of it and slowly peered inside. But it was impossible to see clearly. And it was not meant to open to let the air inside—or even a curious passerby. Nor was it made for gazing but for simply letting sunshine in. Plus it had dirt caked on it from both sides; not to mention bird poop and dead bugs clung to the outside of it. Even in full sunlight, there was no looking inside through this window.

The door at the end of the barn was half open. Lennox could see that by the way the waning sunlight filtered inside. So he crept softly around the two sides of the barn to get to the other side. Once there, he slid inside, his weapon at the ready, only to find the barn itself was one big empty building. There weren't even stalls in it. No loft. Just four walls and a lot of empty ground for a floor. He glanced around, realizing there was no place for anybody to hide and slid back out the way he'd come. He tapped his ear comm to let Gavin know that this first place on his list was empty.

Next was the shed, but that was technically on Gavin's list of buildings to inspect. And then the large machine shop as well. That was an excellent option in that it was the closest building to the gunman taking his smoke break. But that didn't mean that the shed wasn't a diversion.

Lennox watched Gavin approach the shed, which was big enough for a prison to hold four, and noted a window in the door on the side Lennox could see. Quickly Gavin looked in that window as Lennox watched, and then Gavin switched his position, going to the other side of the shed—and out of Lennox's sight—maybe to look through a window in another door from that side too? Almost immediately Lennox heard the tap on his comm, confirming the captives weren't there.

Damn, that meant the machine shop was their best bet. And was right where that group of four men still loitered inside, plus their smoking gunman right outside hadn't moved, yet had finished his cigarette.

Lennox searched the area, trying to mark a pathway to get closer without being seen by the five guys involved in his next target. No point in taking out the gunman if he didn't have their prisoners. Yet the guy could be one of those happy little target shooters, a jumpy gunman with a quick trigger finger. And, if the smoker engaged with Lennox, somebody would get hurt, and Lennox knew perfectly well it wouldn't be him. So, therefore, he wanted to confirm that the prisoners were here first before any shots were fired.

He wasn't too far from the back end of the machine shop. He waited to listen to the sounds of the world around him. A large truck was going down the road. Using the cover of that noise, Lennox quickly moved from one clump of brush to the other, blending into the background, his shadow merging with the other shadows to keep his presence unknown. He'd been lucky in that he hadn't flushed out any wildlife hiding under the bushes.

As he made his way to the side of the machine shop, he stopped, shifted, and listened. He could hear men on the inside of the building but didn't understand the language. He quickly taped it and ran the clip through a translation app on his cell, inserting an earbud into one ear to get the gist of it. *Farming.* With his phone on Silent, he pocketed it and shifted around the corner ever-so-slightly so that he could take a look. Two men were at forklifts, already holding large pallets. They were dressed in jeans and simple cotton shirts; one was smoking, which wasn't the smartest thing on a job like that, but, hey, people did stupid things all the time.

No sign of prisoners so far but Lennox couldn't see a whole section of the machine shop on the other side of that forklift yet. Somehow he would have to get past this open double door and the four guys inside and go around to the far side, so he could then take a look at what was on that side of the machine. He waited until the men shuffled their positions; then Lennox made his way across the open door and slid down the far wall on the outside. Just as he thought he had safely made it, he heard his comm tap and afterward came Gavin's whispered voice.

"Guard alerted."

"Shit," Lennox whispered under his breath. He couldn't see the guard from where Lennox was, but he could hear that gunman arriving, speaking English, asking if they saw anything. Voices were raised, and one of the other men called out, "Nothing. Nothing here."

The gunman's footsteps seemed to retrace to where he'd been standing before, beside his truck.

Lennox moved carefully, crept up to the window, and took a look at the other half of the machine shop. He found glass and ceramic jugs and what looked like some homemade still.

These guys were probably making moonshine. Without a license in a place like this, they would need somebody on guard. With a rifle.

Even worse, Lennox found no sign of the prisoners. What a huge waste of time.

Swearing, he moved back slightly, sending a message to Gavin that this building appeared to be empty. Or at least not housing his sister and her team. As Lennox walked around the back side of the shop, a man came out a side door and shouted at him. He turned and looked at him and said, "Sorry, in the wrong place."

The man looked at him in confusion, and Lennox realized he didn't understand English. Regardless Lennox's presence would startle the others. He walked up with a big smile on his face, and, when he got close enough, he struck the man hard in the throat, sufficient to disable him and to drop him to the ground.

Racing silently through the encroaching darkness, Lennox made his way back into the bush and then headed to the truck.

There he met Gavin.

"That was close," Gavin said. "They were running illegal whiskey, from what I saw."

"Agreed," Lennox said. "Unfortunately I met up with one guy. He wasn't thrilled, so I put him down."

"You killed him?"

"Hell no. He's down, but he'll remember somebody skulking around his place, and the others will be pissed off at the guard."

"With good reason," he said. "If that were one of our guys, you know that we would have fired him for what we were able to do."

"True enough," Lennox said. "Next target?"

"I'm wondering if that road leading to that farm didn't carry on farther past to another property up in the hills there."

"It's possible the driveway continues on, but it becomes a dirt road. Up on the hill, I was thinking it headed to pastures."

"Maybe, but I don't think we can take that chance. We

need to scope it out for ourselves."

"Shall we drive closer?"

"Could save us a few steps," Gavin added with a shrug.

Lennox had his phone out, GPS running, while he looked at the area maps. "I think we need to go back along this way. Not exactly as far as that, but we would only have a few hundred yards to cross."

That's what they did. Lennox quickly turned the truck around and headed back, following Gavin's instructions. At the new location they parked off to the side of a ditch and crossed over a fence to the designated search area, about seventy-five yards away that led to the other driveway. Passing that as quickly as possible, they realized that this driveway continued for probably half a mile.

They made their way along that road in complete darkness. No vehicles passed by; nothing came by, not even wildlife or a stray dog. When they got to the small rise, they stopped; they found a large settlement below, including a house off to the side of another large machine shed again and what looked like a double-size barn.

"Everybody has multiple outbuildings," Gavin noted.

"Exactly," Lennox said, "but how do we know this is our place? We keep wasting time ruling each one out."

Just then two men came out of the house, both of them strapping rifles over their shoulders.

"Well, that's promising," Lennox said.

One of them called out to another man, and he stood; his form had blended in entirely to the machine shed. But he also had a weapon over his shoulder and a handgun in his right hand.

"Well, that looks even more promising," Lennox said, studying the long machine shed. "That thing's got to be fifty feet long."

"If not more," Gavin said. "I'd say it's at least twenty feet wide. It's that corrugated metal material with likely no windows."

"Which means, only one way in, one way out."

"But likely a second door is in the back," Gavin said, "but it won't be as easy to open or to maneuver through."

"So not a bad prison," Lennox said with a nod. "Far enough away from anyone that, although any gunshots will echo in the hills, nobody will give a shit."

"I think everybody's keeping to themselves out here. They're probably all running something illegal, in one way or another, which keeps them all away from everybody else's business."

"Right," Lennox said. "So how many have we got here? Three in the front right now but how many others do you think are in the house?"

"We can go through the house first."

"Or can use a diversion to flush them out of the house," Lennox suggested.

Gavin considered that and nodded. "How about a fire?" he said, pointing to a large pile of deadwood. "It's small enough not to do too much damage, even if it does take off."

"And, if it takes off, it'll come toward the buildings, and that's what the gunmen will be concerned about."

"Exactly."

"You got a way to start that?"

Gavin grinned, his white teeth flashing in the darkness. "Just wait for it," he said. "You'll have your diversion in no time." And he got up and slipped into the darkness, leaving Lennox all alone.

CHAPTER 7

H ELENA MUST HAVE dozed off for a few hours because, when she woke, the building was in complete darkness. Wondering what had woken her—outside of her uncomfortable position, the strange circumstances, and the terror that she'd recently gone through—was something she almost laughed at because she had any number of reasons not to sleep deeply and contentedly. But, when exhaustion had claimed her, she had slept. Maybe not well but she'd take any rest that she could get right now.

Outside she heard footsteps racing and people swearing. She immediately woke Carolina. "Something's happening," she said urgently.

Carolina stared at her, looked around, and then bolted to her feet. "We have to be ready."

"Oh, I agree," Helena said. "Now if only we knew what that would mean."

John mumbled from the far side, "What's the matter?"

"Hear all the shouting and running outside?" she asked him.

He stared at her and slowly sat up. "Do you think it's Lennox?"

"I have no clue," she said.

A man's voice interrupted their conversation. "I hope it is," he said, "because then I'll be ready for him."

That was the scarred man talking. The man in charge. He seemed to leave the building. Another guard slunk out of the darkness. A man she hadn't yet seen before stared at her. "What's going on out there?" she asked.

"Looks like a brushfire."

"Fire?" she cried out, staring at him in shock. "We have to get out of here!"

"I don't give a fuck," he said and spat out what looked like the butt of a cigarette onto the ground.

"A fire will raze this place to the ground," Helena said, waving her arm around at the shed.

"It's metal," he said with a sneer. "It does not burn."

"Maybe not," she said, "but the stuff in it will."

"And how does the fire get in?" he asked, studying her as if she were an ignorant schoolgirl.

"The bales of hay stacked along the back wall would bring it in," she said.

He looked startled for a moment as he turned to study the back wall. He walked past her to the far end of the shed.

Carolina looked at her. "Do you have a plan with that?"

"Maybe," she whispered, "but he has to leave first."

"Why are they always listening to us?" John asked, crawling over to where they were. "It's creepy."

She stood, peering in the darkness, when the door at the far end of the machine shop opened. And the man they'd been speaking with called out something. She saw flames crackling at that end.

"Shit," she said, "that's too damn close." She pulled the bobby pin from her hair, stripped off the plastic coating at one end, and walked over to the lock on the gate. Standing casually, she grabbed the lock and tried to pop it free with the help of her bobby pin.

And, just as she managed it, a voice close to her ear whispered, "Good girl."

She froze, but Lennox took over, taking the lock from her hand, opening the cage, and pulling her free. John woke up Sasha, but Lennox already had Carolina up and out. Lennox led them to the corner of the front doorway and said to Helena, "Race up the hill at that angle," he said, pointing in the right direction. "You're going for that biggest tree as your landmark. Do not make a sound. Just run."

And he got her and Carolina moving as fast as they could. She turned to look behind her to see John and Sasha following. But she had her orders, and she knew one thing— Lennox expected his orders to be obeyed.

And there would be no forgiveness from the kidnappers if Helena and her team didn't get to where they needed to go. She hit the tree and kept on going, not sure where she was supposed to go now. But she saw a vehicle at the far end of a path. She caught sight of an unknown man, and her steps faltered. But he urged her to keep going. She raced up to the truck, eyeing this latest stranger, who whispered, "I'm Gavin. I'm with Lennox. Get in."

Helena hopped into the back seat of the double-cab truck and helped John inside beside her, while Gavin helped Carolina climb into the back seat on the other side of Helena.

As Helena turned to look behind, Lennox picked up Sasha, lagging behind, and carried her as he raced faster and faster. He damn-near tossed Sasha into the back seat of the truck, calling out to Gavin, "Go! Go! Go!"

Gavin hopped into the front of the truck, and, as Sasha was climbing into the back, smashing onto John, Lennox dove into the front seat. Gavin had the vehicle tearing down the road in no time.

Helena wasn't exactly sure where the hell they were going, and she didn't give a damn. She just smiled up at John, who stared at her in shock.

She nodded. "Yes, that's Lennox."

He shook his head, leaned forward, and asked Lennox, "How do you get past everybody?"

Lennox didn't respond.

"A diversion," Helena stated matter-of-factly. "And did you note that not one gunshot went off?" She smiled smugly at John. "That's not what Lennox does. *Unless* he's forced to."

"And how did *you* know?" he blustered, glaring at her, ignoring her barb pointed at him.

"*Diversion?*" she said. "It's simple."

He frowned.

She shrugged. "The only way we could be rescued was if Lennox and his partner had a way to get the gunmen away from us," she said. "So, they started the fire. Then, when our guards left us, that's when I knew it was time to pick the lock."

Lennox twisted to look at her. "Did I teach you that, or did you learn it on your own?"

"You showed me," she said, "and then I learned it on my own."

"Good," he said, "at least you learned something."

She frowned at him. "I've learned a lot."

"Yeah, from me?" He waggled his eyebrows.

She glared at him. "Have you got a plan at this point?"

"Yep, to get the hell away."

"Great," she said. "In other words, no?"

He laughed. "We got this far." Only then something

hard pinged the side of the truck. "Everyone down!"

"Shit!" Gavin growled, and he drove faster.

"I presume we're being followed," she said. She tried to stare out the back of the truck, but bullets shattered the back window.

Lennox immediately ordered them to lie as flat as they could.

And, with all four of them taking up as little space as possible and flush low in the back, they bounced over the rough ground before suddenly hitting a smoother road. The truck picked up speed as it jumped forward.

Helena looked at Carolina. "Well, it's a half-baked idea, but at least it's a plan."

More shots hit the truck but not anybody in the truck.

Carolina grinned. "Trust in Lennox. If anybody can get us out of here, it's him."

Helena didn't need to be told. She already knew that. The only issue was the fact that, right now, they were between a rock and a hard place. Somebody was still firing at them, and she doubted this truck had the gas to keep going the distance. She also didn't think this area was particularly friendly to foreigners.

Just then they hit another rough road and bounced and jostled as the truck tore across new ground. Helena wondered if it even was a road or if they were going across a farmer's field. Crouched down as she was, she couldn't see. She groaned as they hit a particularly rough spot.

"Sorry about the rough road," Lennox said. "We'll be changing vehicles in a few minutes, so get ready."

Immediately she tensed, awaiting his instructions. She hoped they would stop—as in completely—before they were expected to switch vehicles. And suddenly they pulled up somewhere, hit the brakes with great force, and Gavin was out of the truck, opening up one of the rear doors.

Lennox had opened up the other rear door. "Let's go now!" He moved them into an SUV parked at the side. It was older, had no license plates, but would seat six nicely inside. By the time they got into the back seats of the vehicle, it still hadn't started. But Gavin waited while Lennox popped the hood, then did something, and got it fired up. He stepped up into the front passenger seat with his two duffel bags, and they took off across the road again before Lennox got settled.

Helena had no clue where they were and didn't have any idea what direction they were traveling because it was pitch black outside, what with the cloud cover blocking what little moonlight was to be had. Sometimes in the night you saw enough of the shadows to see where you're going—but not tonight. She leaned forward. "How can you guys see where you're going?"

"Gavin is wearing night goggles," Lennox explained. She looked over, and, sure enough, Gavin had some weird glasses over his eyes. "Okay," she said, settling back. "Any idea how to get out of here?"

"We're working on it," he said. "We're in Poland, by the way."

That was a surprise to her. She glanced at the others, who stared back at her wordlessly.

"Anybody got connections in Poland?" Lennox asked.

Everybody shook their heads.

"Sorry, we're no help back here."

"Not an issue," he said. "We're trying to roust up some other means of travel."

"Good," she said. "A flight would be nice. It's the fastest

way out of here. But our IDs, wallets, phones, etc., these guys had it all. I'm not sure what happened to our luggage."

Lennox laughed and picked up his phone to make a call. She wanted to listen in but couldn't hear the conversation anyway. She looked at Carolina, who was huddled up in her seat, quiet, her eyes closed. "Carolina, are you okay?"

"I am," she said. "We're getting out of here. That's all that I care about."

"Well, yes," Helena said, "and no. We're not exactly free and clear yet."

"No," she said, "but my brother is doing what he can. And I have to admit that's usually a whole lot more than anybody else can."

"I get it," John said. "He's some sort of Secret Service spy guy. As long as he gets us out of there, I promise I'll never say a bad word against him again."

"We can't make any guarantees here, not yet," Helena said. "That's not how life works. But he's good, and, if anyone can get us out of this situation, Lennox will."

"I know," John said. "I'd just appreciate no longer being in this mess."

"Exactly," she said, "and hopefully that'll be a distant memory soon."

While they drove through the night, having finally lost their armed pursuers, they pulled into a small town, where they stopped to fuel up. She leaned forward to speak to Lennox, who stood outside her door. "We need food, and we need bathrooms."

"I'll take you," Lennox said. "Nobody is to go on their own."

He opened up the passenger door and let the three women hop out. After that, John hopped out and stood beside Gavin. Lennox led the women to the outdoor washroom with a locked door and that held one person at a time. Sasha went in first. When she came out, Lennox motioned at Helena. She just shook her head and said, "We'll go in together." She opened the door, and she and Carolina walked into the bathroom. They quickly used the facilities, washed, and stepped back out again.

"Coffee and food?" she asked hopefully.

Lennox looked at her in the half-light, studying her face, and then his sister's. "Are you two okay?"

Carolina smiled, nodded, and said, "We're fine. I took one hit. So did Helena."

He swore when he realized that his sister had been smacked. He studied her face in the light of the bathroom and asked, "How bad?"

She reached up, cupped his face on either side, and said, "I'm fine, Lennox."

"Good thing," he growled, and he hauled her into his arms and gave her a big hug.

Helena stood off to the side, jealous in a way because she'd been looking for that human contact, which she had yet to get. Although she had known Lennox over many, many years, still he didn't know a lot about her. Like her feelings for him. And the heat that flashed inside her every time she saw him. And yet he'd scared her back then, with that kiss, and she'd turned away from that confusion—that heat—and had promptly found someone the exact opposite of Lennox.

While she stood here, looking out at the SUV, an arm reached out and snagged her, as Lennox hauled her in for his hug with his sister. She burrowed her face tight against him, hating that trembling coming from inside her.

But, once again, Lennox had come through.

That's the one thing—Carolina could always count on her brother. Hell, Helena didn't remember anyone having her back. She'd been walking alone for all her life, whereas Carolina always had her brother there to help. He let her make the decisions and the choices in her life and let her fall when they were terrible choices, but he'd always been there to give her a hand when she needed it. Helena had Carolina, but she hadn't had Lennox. Helena wondered just how different that would have made her world?

Right now it was huge. She was damn grateful for the warm arms that held her close.

When he finally released them, he said, "Get back into the SUV. I'll see if any food's available to go with that coffee."

She nodded. "That would be good."

"Do you all drink coffee?"

Carolina flashed a smile at him. "Of course we do," she said, "but I think two of them take sugar."

"I'll get it," he said. They raced back to the SUV and hopped into the back seat. This vehicle had three rows of seats, and they were in the middle; John and Sasha sat in the back. John leaned forward and asked, "Is he getting something from inside?"

"Depends if there is anything to get," Helena said. "I said we could all use some coffee and food, if that was an option."

"Yes," Sasha said, "both of those would be lovely."

"Safety would be our priority though." They sat quietly in the vehicle, but her heart pounded as she studied to see if they were still being followed. She leaned forward and said, "Hi, Gavin. My name is Helena. I'm a friend of Carolina's."

Gavin tossed her a quick grin. "I've heard about you," he said. "Lennox doesn't talk much, but he has mentioned you."

"All good things I hope," she quipped, but she was pretty damn sure it wasn't.

He just shrugged and didn't say anything.

As she watched the store, Lennox walked out of the small gas station, carrying a tray with four coffees. He walked to the passenger side. She rolled down her window and accepted all four. "Are you getting any for yourself and Gavin?"

He nodded. "I'll be right back." And he headed back inside.

Helena handed out the coffees. She smiled at Gavin. "He will get you one too, won't he?"

"He will," Gavin said, and she realized that they must know each other pretty well. "Our kidnappers said it was a revenge for Lennox. That they wanted Lennox to pay for a betrayal."

Gavin spun in his seat and looked at her. "Can you explain what he said exactly?" And then he stopped her. "Hang on. Let's wait until Lennox gets back."

Just then the store's door opened again, Lennox pushing it with his shoulder and then his foot, as he stepped out carrying another tray of coffee and a large bag. He handed the tray through the open window to Gavin and then walked around the front to his side and hopped inside. Gavin removed the two coffees from the tray, placing them in cup holders, and said, "Helena has something to say."

She quickly explained what the scarred man had said about it being a betrayal.

Gavin just looked at Lennox, and Lennox looked back.

He shook his head. "Can you describe him?"

"He's got a bad scar on his cheek," Carolina said. "And it's deep. It would have involved some jaw surgery likely, and he's got a burn mark on his neck."

"The burn goes down the inside of his shirt," Helena added. "And I would have called it third-degree burns. We saw a lot of scar tissue, and it looks like layers of it."

"I agree with that too," Carolina stated. "His muscle damage was quite extensive around the neck, where his longer hair covers part of it but does not go up as high as the jaw."

"What about the rest of him?"

John supplied that info. "Six-foot, 205 pounds, light brown hair, short with a light wave. His eyes are dark, maybe brown. Fair skin as if maybe European descent."

"Dress?"

"Fatigues," Sasha added. "No hats among the kidnappers, no gloves among them, and I would have said military work boots."

"Combat boots?"

"Yes," Sasha said.

"Weapons?" Gavin started up the engine and put the SUV back on the road while they talked.

Nobody had any details on the weapons, outside of the fact that they were carrying rifles or machine guns, plus handguns. "Outside of the original kidnapping crew, once we landed in that cage in Poland, we saw three different men who stood guard on a rotating basis," Helena added.

"We saw six," Lennox added. "All six will be after us."

"It was very personal," John said from the back row. "We tried to explain that we had nothing to do with it, and he didn't care."

"Of course not," Lennox said. "You were just part of the bait. Once they started shooting prisoners, it ups the ante as to when they'd get around to shooting my sister."

John stared at him and then collapsed back. "I was afraid you were gonna say something like that."

"Sorry," Lennox said, "but you were caught at the wrong place at the wrong time."

"All four of us were in the wrong place at the wrong time." Helena continued, "We all caught the same lift to the airport, so we were dropped off at the same time. Two of us were heading to Munich, and the other two were heading somewhere else, but all were international destinations. It's almost as if the kidnappers were waiting for us. We were led to another vehicle and tossed into the back."

"They approached you at the airport?"

"Yes, we were quickly surrounded by four men in military fatigues, who had handguns," Helena supplied, as she dredged up the memory of when they were first picked up and moved into a vehicle. "They didn't say much. But they didn't need to. The weapons are a universal language." Then she settled back with her coffee.

Lennox opened the bag he'd brought with him and handed out sandwiches and pepperoni sticks and string cheese and bags of chips. She gratefully accepted everything coming her way, making sure that it was an even breakdown, but Lennox had bought everything times six. She ate her sandwich first, then both the cheese and the pepperoni. As she looked at Carolina, she was not eating her lunch. "You're not hungry?"

Carolina shook her head. "My stomach is still not so great."

"You need to eat," Lennox said.

"I know. *I need to keep up my energy just in case we need to run again*," she said in a comical voice. "But since my head injury, my stomach has been on the queasy side."

"Not a whole lot we can do about that here and now," Helena said. "I'm pretty sure you had a slight concussion."

"Most likely," she said. "And it doesn't matter now because I'm healing. That's what counts."

"True enough," she said. "It's all good."

Lennox shot Helena a questioning look, one eyebrow raised. She nodded. "She'll be fine."

He settled back.

"So you listen to Helena now, huh?" Carolina asked, her tone sharp. "Without listening to me?"

"Yes," Lennox said, "because you've been known to not tell me the whole truth every once in a while."

"Seriously?" she said in outrage.

"Yes," he said, "if it suits you."

"That's just being a sibling," Carolina said with a laugh. "And having you as an older brother wasn't easy either."

"I've been there every time you needed me."

"You've been there every time I've needed you and more," Carolina said guiltily. "I did tell you how much I love you, right?"

He let out a bark of laughter. "Many times and often as you were ready to hit me."

She grinned. "Again that's siblings."

The wrangling continued back and forth, and it helped to ease the atmosphere in the vehicle.

At a pause in the conversation, Sasha spoke suddenly from the back row of seats. "Do you think we're out of danger?"

Lennox turned to look at her and shook his head. "No,

we are not. Not until we can get you out of this country. Yet ... considering you were tracked from Africa, kidnapped in Germany, then taken to Poland, I'm not sure that that's even the correct answer here."

Sasha stared at him. Her eyes were a vast well of fear. "But John and I should be safe once we're back in the US, right?"

Lennox considered that, shrugged, and said, "*Potentially*, yes."

"*Potentially?*" she questioned him, her voice turning ominous. "What do you mean by that?"

He glanced at Gavin, and Gavin glanced back at him.

"What does that silent glance mean?" John interrupted.

"The problem is," Lennox said, "we have to put a stop to this."

"Sure, I get that," Sasha said, "but why is it that we won't be out of danger even if we're back home again?"

"You will be safe once we capture the guy behind this," he said, "but otherwise you are in danger of always being able to identify him."

The other two sat back slowly and stared. "And that'll be a problem?"

"Depends on how he feels about it," Lennox said. "I don't understand who this guy is, or why he feels he has a grudge against me, but, as long as he's holding that grudge, then obviously my sister and her best friend will be in more danger than the two of you. However, if he's considering his actions from a criminal level and the chances of being charged with a crime, then to not be identified will be important to him. Therefore, they'll want to keep you from identifying him."

"And that doesn't sound very good either," Sasha said

faintly, "because that sounds like he'd planned on killing us."

"I would suspect so," Helena said quietly. "The fact that he didn't hide his face right from the beginning is very indicative of his intentions."

"And that seriously sucks."

"Obviously but that doesn't change the facts right now," Lennox added.

"So, you'll go after this guy?" Sasha asked.

"Right?" John repeated.

Everybody looked at Lennox.

Without hesitation he gave a crisp nod and said, "Yes. I'm going after this guy because he went after my sister."

LENNOX KNEW THEY needed to hear that, but they wouldn't like knowing that it wouldn't be so cut-and-dried in reality. The mastermind behind the kidnapping had skills, money, freedom to move as he needed to, and he had the know-how to hunt down people who were close to Lennox. He looked at his sister. "It might be time for an extended holiday."

She wrinkled up her face. "Well, I was looking for a short one. I'm not sure about an extended one."

"*Extended*," Gavin said in a hard voice. "All of you should consider it."

"Well, I just handed in my notice," Sasha said. "That's exactly what I was planning."

Helena looked at her. "I didn't know that," she said. "Are you done, or did you just give your vacation notice?"

"I'm done," she said. "They owed me time off anyway. So I just took it as part of my leave."

"Wow," Helena said, sinking back in the seat, thinking

about that. "We did get several more doctors in, so, in theory, they could do without us for a while."

"They could," Carolina said, "but you know how we feel about that."

"Sure, but we can't get in the way of Lennox going after this guy."

"And how would going back to work put us in Lennox's way?" John asked.

"This guy is determined to make Lennox pay, and so the scarred guy will come after us, no matter where we are," Helena said. She tilted her head as she stared at Lennox and asked, "Why don't you use us as bait?"

John snorted. "That's the most reasonable suggestion I've heard yet. As long as you keep me out of it."

"Me too," Sasha snapped.

Helena shot them both a hard look. "That's just because you'd like to see us pay for you being involved. You blame us."

Lennox turned, his steady gaze on John.

John shifted uncomfortably. "Okay, so maybe we were a little harsh in our assessment of the scenario."

"Don't go blaming Carolina and Helena for this," Lennox said. "Sounds like this guy wants me to pay for something. Yet I don't know this guy. Yes, it's an ugly scenario, and it is what it is. But you can't go blaming each other. And we can't have you guys being the bait." Now Lennox stared down Helena.

"Not me," Sasha said. "They're the ones who count. John and I want to go home."

Lennox nodded slowly. "I get that, and we're doing our best to get you home. As for my sister and Helena, well, if he went to this much effort, I can't imagine that he's gonna walk away at this point."

"No, he probably isn't," Sasha agreed. "So we need to get the hell out of here."

"We'll be on our way back to Warsaw pretty quickly," Gavin said.

"And how close is *pretty quickly*?" John asked.

Just then Gavin pulled into a supermarket parking lot, but everything was closed for the night. Big streetlamps were on the side, but a massive green space was in the center, and he pulled off under the lights, turned toward the back seats, and waited. "Finish your coffees," he said.

Helena looked at her coffee, tossed back the rest of it, and returned all the garbage to Lennox, who was collecting everything. He made one trip to a trash can sitting off to the side, came back, removed his duffel bags, looked at Carolina, and asked, "Are you ready?"

She groaned. "I might as well be," she said, "because, with you, it's now or never."

In the distance, they heard a helicopter. He smiled at them and said, "Our ride is here."

"Oh, awesome," Sasha said. They hopped out and walked over to him. "Can it take us wherever we need to go?"

"No, it's taking us into Warsaw," he said. "We'll catch flights out later tomorrow."

"Any chance of a shower and a real nap first?" John asked. "We've been traveling forever."

"At the hotel, yes. We can't get flights out before noon tomorrow anyway."

With the helicopter coming in and sending dust and dirt flying everywhere, he quickly led them to the chopper and helped them up into the back seats. With the duffel bags stowed in the helo, the vehicle was left behind, and they were lifted into the air. Lennox glanced around to make sure everybody was buckled in place. He caught Helena's eye.

She smiled at him. "Thank you."

When he looked at her, that same damn jolt hit him in the heart every time. He gave a clipped nod. "You're welcome."

"Well, you don't have to make it sound like the only reason I'm being rescued is that I'm with Carolina," she said.

He winced inside; they always bounced off each other, both of them trying to ignore their feelings, but, at the same time, making any communication harsher as they tried to avoid saying what needed to be said.

"It isn't that," he said. "Let's get to Warsaw, and we can get something arranged to get you guys out of there."

She nodded. "But it's not like the helicopter ride is a big secret."

"I'm counting on it," he said quietly. Helena looked at him in surprise, but he gave her a half smile. "Much better to bring them to us than to play in their backyard."

"Oh," she said in surprise.

Lennox shrugged. "Remember? It's what we do."

CHAPTER 8

T HE HELICOPTER LANDED on a hotel roof. They were quickly led down to their assigned rooms. Two suites. Helena thought that the women would be in one and that the men would be in the other. Instead Gavin was with John and Sasha in one, and Lennox was with her and Carolina in another. That made just as much sense when she thought about it because, in no way, would Lennox leave his sister alone.

As they walked in, Helena saw two bedrooms and a small sitting room. "We didn't need anything so fancy," she said.

"We have a connecting door regardless," he said, as he walked over and rapped hard.

The door opened immediately, and there was Gavin.

Lennox said, "Let's leave the door open."

"Got it," Gavin said.

In the background, Helena could hear the other two, discussing rooms, and then John saying that he would shower first. Helena looked at Carolina. "What about you?"

Carolina gave her half a stare. "What about me?"

"Bed or shower?"

She looked at the bathroom and then at the bed and said, "Tough to call. Maybe I'll have a quick shower, if you don't mind."

"Sure. Go have yours now," Helena said. She walked to the couch in the sitting area, plunked herself down, and said, "Was there any food left?"

"Here," Carolina said, and she turned and tossed the sandwich she still held in her hand.

"Aren't you gonna need it later?"

"We're in town now. We can get more food," Lennox said. "If you're hungry, eat."

"Thanks." She quickly opened up the sandwich and ate it slowly, as she waited for Carolina to get out of the shower. She watched as Lennox dug in one of his duffel bags, brought out a laptop, set it up on the small table here, and started sending messages. "Are those emails?"

He shook his head. "No, it's my team."

"Oh," she brightened at that. "Glad to know you have a team."

He looked at her with a puzzled look on his face.

Self-consciously, she shrugged. "Well, it's better than having to work alone."

"Well, there's always Gavin," he said, pointing out the obvious.

"I know," she said. "Just ignore me."

He shot her another strange look and went back to his laptop.

She always felt uncomfortable and awkward around him. There was just so much possibility between them, and yet so much that was wrong. Such was her life.

She finished the sandwich and hopped up, walked over to the kitchenette, and popped the wrapper in the garbage. There she grabbed some water from the tap. She had no idea if it was good to drink or not. She tasted it hesitantly, and, although it had an odd taste, it probably wouldn't kill her, so she had a bigger drink. She leaned back against the sink, just thankful to be here.

Carolina opened the bathroom door and said, "I'm done, and I'll be in bed." She walked out with a towel on her head and a robe on, heading to the bedroom she'd chosen. She entered and closed the door.

Although their suite had two bedrooms, it didn't leave one for Lennox. "Are you gonna sleep?" Helena asked him.

"Part of the time," he said. "I'll be doing shifts with Gavin. That's why we're keeping the connecting door open, so we can hear from both sides."

"Where are you gonna sleep?" she asked, staring at him. She chewed on her bottom lip. He deserved a good night's sleep more than she did. He'd gone through all the problems of tracking them down. She felt guilty as hell taking the only other bed. "I can sleep with your sister."

"Don't worry about it," he said. "I'm fine on the couch."

She looked at the couch, then looked at him. "It might be long enough," she said, "but no way that couch will hold your girth."

At her worry, he looked at her in surprise. "You're saying I'm fat?"

"Like hell," she said, "but you're big."

He shrugged. "I'll be fine. Don't worry about it. Go and grab a shower."

Helena sighed. "Okay, but remember I offered."

"Point taken," he said with a clipped nod. "Now go have your damn shower, please."

She walked into the bathroom, slammed the door with a little more force than necessary, and stripped down. Only now, as she stood here completely nude, did she realize she had no other clothes. What had happened to their luggage?

She'd had only the one carry-on bag and her purse. Was her carry-on back where they'd been kept prisoner? She wanted it, but there was no going back now. ... Could Lennox get it somehow?

Swearing, she hopped under the hot shower and shampooed her hair and scrubbed herself from top to bottom. All the time, her mind raced, figuring out just what she was supposed to do. She remembered getting out of the airport shuttle when they had arrived at the Munich airport, and a porter having taken their luggage. Was there any chance it was still sitting at the airport? Maybe the kidnappers only had their purses, phones, and wallets?

She quickly dried off, wrapped up in a towel, realizing that Carolina had grabbed a robe, but no more were here. Maybe another was in the second bedroom, but, of course, Helena hadn't looked for one there.

First, she scooped up her clothing—dirty, dusty, and not what she wanted to put back on again—and realized she would have to put on her underwear regardless. Quickly redressed in panties and a bra, then wrapped back up again with the towel, she grabbed the rest of her dirty clothes, walked out to her bedroom, where she looked for a robe, but there wasn't one. Of course not. She dropped her clothes on the bedroom floor and headed out to ask Lennox, "What happened to our luggage?"

He looked up at her. "It was picked up at the airport. The porter took it inside, but, when you guys didn't reappear, he contacted security."

"Any chance of getting it?"

"It's on its way to the airport, now that we have a location for you," he said. "With any luck, we should get it here in the morning."

"Fresh clothing would be nice," she said. "We all need our passports too, but the kidnappers had them."

He didn't even look up and nodded. "We're working on it."

"Thank you," she said, and then, as she walked back to the bedroom door, she added, "Have a good night."

And again he didn't look up.

Pissed for some reason, more because he looked like he was ignoring her, she said, "That's if you're even listening to me."

Exasperated, he gave a heavy sigh, turned, looked at her, and said, "Good night." And then he spun back around again.

She walked into her room and closed the door and threw herself on the bed. She had no reason to be upset at him. But it was so very typical of every time they'd met. At least since they had kissed. Now everything sounded harsh and just bounced off each other. But she was tired, worn out, and didn't want to wear a bra to bed. She took it off, dropped it to the floor in her pile of clothing, and crawled into the bed, in just her panties. Realizing that she was safe, and they were back in the city, and chances were that she'd be home again pretty damn soon, she rolled over and fell asleep.

IT'S ALMOST AS if Lennox could hear the moment that Helena had relaxed enough to fall asleep. He knew what was wrong between them, but no way was she ready to deal with the issue. Yet it had always been there between them. He'd struggled to not turn around and to see her rosy from a shower, wrapped in a towel. His blood pressure always rose whenever he was around her. Still she'd finally gotten the message and gone to her room. He needed a couple days with her to figure out if this was something they wanted to pursue or if they could walk away from it. But that needed time together, and that was something they avoided at all costs. Which was too damn bad.

Maybe now they'd be forced to address the issue, one way or the other.

Gavin walked through the adjoining rooms and asked, "You okay to stay up for the first watch?"

Lennox nodded. "You did most of the driving. Go rest," he said. "I'll see you in four hours."

With that, Gavin turned and headed back into his suite. Lennox was waiting for Keane to come back on the chat box. When he did, Lennox asked him, **Any news on the search of the identifying marks? How about pictures to match my enemy list?**

I'm sending a series of photos, he typed, **posting them via this link.**

When the link came up, Lennox studied the faces and saw the first man with deep facial scars and neck burns. He recognized a couple guys with similar wounds, but Lennox didn't have any reason to think those guys were after him. Hearing an odd sound, he turned to see his sister, standing at the doorway to her bedroom, her robe back on.

She looked at him. "I was coming for water," she said, as she padded quietly toward him. "You're trying to find the kidnapper?"

Lennox took the opportunity to pull out a chair for her and said, "If you've got a moment, do you want to take a look through these photos?"

She scrolled through the faces, one after each other.

"How come so many men have disfiguring marks like this?" she asked in amazement.

"War is a bitch," Lennox said, "and the injuries are very unforgiving."

She kept going and said, "I don't recognize anybody here." She clicked through three more and then a fourth and a fifth and stopped. Lennox looked at the one she'd stopped at, but she clicked back, and she said, "That's him. ... At least I think it's him," She hesitated, then pulled back slightly to view the face from an angle.

"What makes you think it is him?"

"The scar in that cheek," she said, "it was profound. As in deep into the actual cheek itself."

He studied the scar and nodded. "And some marks are on his neck, but they are hard to identify." He asked her, "What about the nose, the hair?"

"Well, his hair is long now," she said, "compared to the buzz cut in that photo." She looked at it and nodded. "Confirm with Helena," she said, "but I would say that's him."

"Did you recognize any other kidnappers in here?"

"No," she said. "I would recognize the guy who looked after us most of the time," she said, "but this scarred one was the guy who wanted you, and he is also just so very identifiable because of his scars."

"Right," he said. "Now get your water and go back to bed."

She beamed, reached up, kissed him on the cheek, and said, "You really should just go to her. You know that, right?" She walked over and grabbed her water, leaving him gaping at her, his mouth open.

"You didn't just say that," he said.

She stood at the kitchenette, drank her water, put the glass on the counter, turned to look at him, and smiled. "If you guys are staying apart because of me," she said, "that's the worst reason yet."

He shoved his hands in his pockets and leaned back into his chair. "More because of Helena's last relationship."

"That would make more sense," she said with a nod. "But still no reason to avoid a relationship because of that."

"She went through what you went through."

"She did," Carolina acknowledged. "That doesn't mean she's broken."

"Are you broken?" He zeroed in on that one statement.

She sighed. "No, I'm not. I'm just now very wary."

"And she isn't?"

"She is, true," Carolina said quietly. "But you were before that marriage, and you are after that marriage. You're constant. She's not afraid of you."

He frowned at that. "It's still a bad idea," he announced.

"Maybe," she said with a chuckle. "But it should be fun while you guys are at it. Besides, it would be a lot easier on the rest of us if you guys got it out of your system."

"That's just sex you are talking about there," he said.

"Glad you recognize that," she said but smiled, walking toward him. "And, if that's what she wants, then go for it. But the thing is, it's *not* what you want. Otherwise, you would have engaged a long time ago with Helena in a one-night stand or whatever *or* would have just moved on. Yet it hasn't left you alone. *She* hasn't left you alone in all these years because it's got nothing to do with sex. Sure, sex is a great enhancer. It's bonding. It's a great way to come together and to enjoy each other," she said, "but there's so much more between you."

"No," he said, his voice harsh. "There can't be."

That wording—and his stark tone—stopped Carolina in her tracks. "And why is that?"

He struggled to come up with an answer but couldn't seem to formulate one.

"Like I said," Carolina said in a warning voice, "I'm not just your little sister anymore. I still need help at times," she said, "but nobody could have foreseen this scenario. And so, if you're thinking that you're avoiding her because of me, because you don't want to disrupt her relationship with me or the relationship between the two of us as brother and sister," she said, "that's just wrong."

"Maybe," he said. "But what if something goes wrong? I don't want to do anything to upset you."

"I don't think that'll happen," she said. "We've weathered some pretty rough times."

"And I'm not sure she's ready."

"You mean, you're not sure *you* are ready?" she said.

"It's dangerous," he admitted. "Look what happened to you—and Helena—with the kidnapping, and that's just because you're my sister."

"Not necessarily," she said. "This is, like I said, a bizarre scenario."

"True." He nodded. "But it happened. So we don't want it to keep happening. I don't want to get close to Helena and then have people coming after her because she's important to me."

"Really?" Carolina asked with a smile. "How are you gonna stop that?"

He frowned and stared off in the distance.

"Because you realize it's *already* happened. Sure they came after me because I'm your sister. But I'm pretty darn sure that the kidnappers know how close you two are already."

"They can't know," he said, "because I don't even know what I am to Helena."

"Maybe not," she said. "However, you already know how important she is to you. You just hope nobody else does."

"*Does* anybody else?" His voice sounded harsh to him as well.

She smiled. "You mean, does *she* know?"

He hesitated and then gave a nod.

Carolina smiled again, bigger this time, shook her head, and said, "No, I don't think so."

Immediately he let out a sigh of relief.

"But I don't think that's a good thing," Carolina said. "Something's between the two of you, and I think you're cheating yourselves if you don't acknowledge it and at least see what is there."

"*Cheating ourselves?*" he said with a smile. "I'm not so sure about that."

"You won't know unless you try," she said, "and, as we have found out yet again, life is fleeting. It can end in a heartbeat, usually when you least expect it."

"Are you ever gonna have another relationship?" he asked her.

"I will," she said, "when I find a man who doesn't scare the crap out of me."

Instantly his face thinned with anger.

Carolina shook her head. "No," she said. "That's the wrong wording. I'm not afraid of men. I'm afraid of my judgment. And I can tell you that that's a big part of Helena's problem too. We thought we knew what we were doing. We thought we trusted the men we had chosen, but the fact of the matter remains that we made crappy decisions. That's what's stopping her. That's what's stopping me. What we don't want is for that to stop you too."

CHAPTER 9

HELENA HEARD PART of the conversation as she lay curled up in bed. The voices woke her from an uneasy sleep. She'd hoped for a deeply relaxing and rejuvenating sleep instead of the sounds of her best friend's conversation with her brother drifting toward her. It was interesting to hear Carolina's take on Helena's own abuse experience and Lennox's replies. Helena realized just how screwed up they all would be when going into future relationships.

With their backgrounds as victims of abuse, the worst that any relationship could offer, both women were hesitant to move forward. Helena knew that Lennox had absolutely none of the same qualities of her ex-husband; maybe that's why he'd been her ex? Lennox was also a very fit and powerful man, and, if he ever did turn ugly, Helena wouldn't have a hope in hell. It was hard to take a chance, hard to take that step forward. In her heart she trusted him, but did her mind? ... Moody, she lay in bed, wondering what her options were.

First off, they had to get home safe and sound, and next, well, she'd look at that when the time came. She let herself drift off to sleep again, waking several more times throughout the night, tossing and turning. When she finally did wake up in the morning, Carolina walked in with a smile on her face.

Helena yawned and asked, "What time is it?"

"It's ten a.m.," she said. "You slept late."

"No," she said, "I just finally got to sleep around four. It was terrible before that, and I'm still so tired."

"I'm sorry you didn't sleep well," Carolina said. "I'm only waking you up," she said, "because food has been ordered. It will be here soon."

"Perfect," Helena said, around a second yawn. "Did our luggage arrive?" She sat up in bed, looking around for her carry-on bag.

"They're due in the next five to ten minutes. Not sure about our purses."

She frowned. "Well, I don't want to go out there not dressed, and I don't want to redress in my dirty clothes if I have fresh ones coming," she said, "so how about I just stay here?"

"Coffee is out there though," Carolina said with a coaxing smile.

"Any chance of a room delivery?" Helena asked hopefully.

Carolina laughed. "I'll see." She disappeared from the room.

Helena smiled. That was the thing about good friends. You could ask them to go the distance, and one little step farther, if it was something you wanted. When the door opened again though, Lennox stepped in. He held a cup of coffee in his hand. "The luggage just arrived downstairs," he said. "We'll have it up here for you in a few minutes."

She beamed. "Thank you. I love the prompt service with our clothes. Any news on our purses and IDs?"

"Yep. We've got them too. Two of our men came in behind us and cleaned out any sign you were ever there."

"Perfect." She felt such a relief to know they could go home now with their proper identification in hand. She held up her cup. "Thanks for the coffee."

"Well, you won't get room delivery all the time," he said with a grin. His gaze lingered, and Helena realized that, since she'd gone to bed with just panties on, an awful lot of skin probably showed. She tugged the sheet a little bit higher and gave him a good frown.

"What's that look for?" he asked.

"Because of the one on your face."

"I like what I see," he said. "You can hardly blame a guy for that."

"I don't blame you," she said. "I just know that we're in this silent truce to stay physically away from each other."

"Maybe that's the wrong thing," he said, standing there with his hands on his hips as he studied her.

"And what brought that on?" she asked, straightening in surprise, trying to mask the shock to her system. As his words mirrored her own internal conversation, she didn't know what to say. *This was about his conversation with Carolina last night.* "It's been what, five years?"

"Right," he said, "five years, and we're both five years older."

"Maybe," she said, "but maybe I'm not any wiser."

"I don't know about that," he said. "I think you've been through enough that you've probably learned a lot."

"I have," she said, as she shuffled up against the headboard, uncomfortably keeping her sheet up high. She waved him toward the door. "It's not a good idea."

"Well, maybe I've changed my mind," he said in a challenging voice, his fingers spreading on his hips as he rocked on his heels slightly. "I've had five years to think about it."

"So have I," she said, hating the bitterness in her voice. "I'm not the same person anymore."

"You can't hide away forever."

She narrowed her gaze at him. "I don't plan on it," she said. "I'm not carrying a grudge against men, if that's what you're thinking—or afraid of them. I got myself into a shitty situation. But that doesn't mean I want to get into another relationship right now."

"I admire the fact that you did get yourself out of that one," he said. "I can't imagine that the two of you were very comfortable in your marriages."

"No," she said, "I wasn't, and, therefore, I won't be too eager to jump back into something like that."

"Well, you shouldn't jump back into *anything* like that," he said, "but you also know that I'm not like that."

She frowned up at him again. "Where is this coming from?"

He shrugged. "Maybe I've been thinking."

Her eyebrows rose. "About me?" She wasn't sure what to think about that. They had had one hell of a fiery kiss and, by mutual agreement, had backed off, deciding it was not smart to move forward. As a way to forget him, she'd gone in the opposite direction. Only it didn't work. She'd always cared. So why was she still arguing, when it's what she wanted? "Nothing has changed. Your sister is still between us."

"Yeah, and I wonder why we put her there?" he said quietly. "You and I both love her. That won't change whether we're together or not."

"Well, considering we're not together," she said, "we don't know that."

"I'm not explaining this very well," he said, his gaze first on her, then her coffee. "We'll pick it up later. Drink your coffee. The luggage should be here soon." And he pivoted and walked out.

She sat here, stunned, sipping her coffee, realizing that the conversation last night between sister and brother had potentially gone a lot deeper than the tidbits she'd heard. She would have to ask Carolina about that.

Just then Carolina walked in with her purse and Helena's purse. "We got them," she said. She dropped Helena's on her lap and then sat down at the end of the bed and said, "Mine appears to be intact. I've got my money, my passport, all my cards even."

"Wouldn't that be lovely?" Helena exclaimed. She checked out her purse and nodded. "It looks like everything's here." At the bottom of her purse was a large-tooth comb; she snatched it and grinned. "How I missed the simple things in life." She quickly combed her hair, plaited it in the back, and curled the braid around her shoulder.

"You look about twelve years old now," Carolina said.

"You're the one who looks twelve," she said teasingly. "I'm at least fourteen."

The two women laughed, both of them welcoming the lighter atmosphere and the chance to release some of the stress from the last few days.

"Oh, our suitcases are here too." Carolina hopped up. "I'll go grab yours." And she dashed out again.

Helena smiled, overjoyed to have her belongings back. There was just such a sense of loss, panic almost, when she didn't have her IDs or a credit card or any cash on hand. It was one thing to be at an airport, where there were assistants and phones and bank machines. And people to contact for help. But, when you were caught in the middle of nowhere,

where you didn't even know the language, … it made you vulnerable.

Carolina returned with Helena's single carry-on bag. "Lennox said we can't use our phones yet, in case the kidnappers are tracking us that way. He'll let us know when it's okay later. I'll go get changed," she said.

She dropped Helena's luggage on the floor for her and disappeared again, closing the door behind her. Helena finished her coffee, put it down, then stood and brought her bag onto the bed and opened it. There she took out leggings and a T-shirt and clean underwear. Dressed and feeling a whole lot better, she rolled up her dirty clothes, put them in a travel-size laundry bag, and stuffed them into the back of her carry-on. She hoped she'd be home pretty soon, but, if it wasn't to be, then she could always rinse these out some-where. And, with that, she picked up the empty coffee cup and headed out to the main room.

With perfect timing, the doorbell rang. She looked over to see Gavin already at the door, opening up for a trolley, followed by a second one.

"Wow, you ordered some serious food," she said with a happy cry.

"Some serious appetites are here," Lennox said. "Not to worry. You won't starve."

"Didn't expect to," she said with a grin. And, sure enough, as she looked at her options, she found a stack of pancakes, toast, scrambled eggs, some fruit, and little individual yogurts for each of them. She sat down with the rest of the crew and reached for a small yogurt and a spoon first.

"Make sure you eat more than that," Lennox said.

"I will," she promised. But she sat back with the yogurt

and ate it slowly, enjoying the slide of the tangy, creamy texture down her throat. With that gone and everybody else digging into the pancakes, she got her plate and filled it.

Carolina, seated at her side, had already eaten through her pancakes and eggs and was now working on toast. Helena looked at her best friend and said, "You must be feeling better. And starving."

"I am, on both accounts," Carolina said. "You don't know when the next meal will pop up."

"I hope there'll be regular meals from now on," Sasha said bluntly, "because I don't ever want to go through this again."

"I hear you," John said, "but it is a lesson. I find myself on Carolina's train of thought that we need to eat because we can."

"There will be more food," Gavin reassured them.

"Promise?" Helena asked. "Because, otherwise, you know not a scrap of food will be left here."

"Good," Lennox said. "No need for any to remain. Because we paid for it, we might as well eat it. And we can't take it with us."

"Good point," Helena said and took another bite. By the time she was done though, she was overdone. She should have stopped halfway through, but her eyes have been much more concerned about making sure she ate. She wondered how long it took being a captive before that mind-set became permanent. She would already have to watch this urge to eat everything in sight; otherwise she'd end up gaining a ton of weight. And it wasn't necessary. Not for feeding her body.

It was a security thing, an internal panic that she would starve. But she knew she was a long way from that. When she finally put down her fork and pushed back her plate, she groaned and said, "Outside of a cup of coffee, I'm stuffed."

"We'll get another pot of coffee," Gavin said. "We'll just empty these trolleys and take them back out again."

Everybody got up to organize the dishes on the trolleys. Helena went in the opposite direction to grab her coffee cup to keep it with her and returned to the couch, where she curled up into a corner. Her laptop had been in her carry-on bag and was still there, for which she was also damn grateful. She grabbed it and sat down again.

"What are you doing with that?" Lennox asked.

"I wanted to send a couple messages."

He looked up, frowned, and then shook his head. "No," he said, "no communication."

She glared at him. "Seriously?"

"Yes, seriously," he said. "We don't want the kidnapper to have any way to track you."

"Good Lord." *Was he serious? He looked like it.* She slowly closed her laptop. "So, when are we going someplace where I can send a few messages?"

"We're leaving on a commercial flight at noon today."

Feeling better, she set aside her laptop. "Right. Thank heavens for that."

"Maybe," he said cautiously. "You might not like what happens after that. We'll see how it goes."

She frowned at him. But he gave a small motion of his head, and she took that to mean, *Don't ask.* She groaned and said, "Whatever. How long until we leave?"

"We're not leaving for another hour," he said, "so, once you have more coffee, then we'll pack up and leave."

She nodded and pointed to her laptop. "Okay if I browse the internet?"

He nodded.

And she buried herself into catching up on the world news. But inside she couldn't help but wonder what was going on that Lennox wouldn't share with her yet. Still she was smart enough not to say anything.

LENNOX WAS GLAD that Helena had followed his cue and hadn't pushed for answers. He had a lot of discussions about flights going on right now. They needed to do a couple transfers to get back stateside. And that was a bit of an issue as well. The initial flights were booked and would take them to Holland. Lennox just wasn't sure where they were going from there. The next hour went very quickly.

Soon they had everybody packed up in a vehicle and heading to the airport. He already had extra alerts out. As they pulled into the airport, his phone buzzed. He took a look. And then swore and hit Dial. When Keane answered, Lennox said, "What the hell does that mean?"

"We've got two more boarding the same plane," he said, "both confirmed to have been part of that kidnapping scenario."

"Confirmed how?" Lennox asked, his temper thinning.

"Interpol had these two listed as known associates of the guy Carolina confirmed with the scars. We picked up their trail on a satellite. They've booked the same flight."

"Which means, we're not going on that flight."

"Exactly. That's changed. Now I need you to get out of the way and to keep out of sight."

"Are we still leaving from this airport?"

"Not anymore. Get back in the vehicle and follow the directions on the GPS." And he hung up.

Lennox took a look at the GPS, then turned to face the group. "Everyone, get back in the vehicle," and his tone brooked no resistance.

John immediately stepped back inside and said, "Why? I want to catch my flight!"

"We can't take the risk," Lennox snapped. "Our plan had been compromised."

"*Your* plan has been compromised?" Sasha said with a sneer. "What do I care? We don't have to go anywhere with you." She grabbed up her bag and marched toward the airport. John quickly followed her.

Lennox called out to them, "Two of the men who were part of your kidnapping have booked flights on the same flight as you will be on."

John frowned, looked at him, and asked, "So?"

"I highly suggest you don't share an airplane ride with them," Lennox said.

John shook his head as he followed Sasha. "You know what? We've been carted and packed and stuffed into various places for the last couple of days," he said, "and we just want to go home." As he held the entrance door open for Sasha, she waved at them with a big smile and cried out, "Good luck with whatever games you're playing." And they turned and both walked inside.

Carolina stepped up beside Lennox. "I guess we can't stop them, can we?"

He swore softly and steadily under his breath, barely even realizing what he was doing. "No, probably not," he said. "The trouble is, they're just two more pawns to be put into use. If somebody grabs them and tries to use them as hostages, what would you want me to do?"

"Well …" And then she stopped. "I would still try to do

everything to keep them alive," she said slowly. "But what are we supposed to do if they don't want to listen, much less to cooperate? Believe me. Sharing that cage with them was no fun, what with all the complaining, whining, blaming."

"Exactly. It also means that, if Sasha and John are taken, we can't allow them to be used against us."

"Right. ... Of course. ... So, do *we* have another way to get back home again?" Helena asked, as she stared back at the airport, where the two were already walking toward the security checkpoint.

"We weren't expecting a change of plans right now."

"Yes, you were," she said. "You were at least expecting the possibility of it."

"Yes," he admitted. "Because nothing is set until it's actually done."

"Of course," Helena said.

"So, now what?" Carolina asked.

"Get back in the vehicle," he said. "We'll go to a different airport."

Without a word, the two women hopped back in.

With Helena's furtive glance at the airport and then at Gavin, he shrugged.

"We can't force them," he said, "and they might be just fine."

"And if they aren't?" Helena asked, looking back yet one more time.

Gavin's face turned grim. "And, if they aren't," he said, "it's not something we can do anything about now. This is not your fault. We've given them the best advice we could. It's ultimately their decision. They don't want to listen. It's pretty shitty, but it's also a lot easier on us if we're only looking after the two of you. And you both listen to us."

"I know that too, in theory," Lennox said, "but we had room for all six of us in our new plans."

"They don't seem to think that our plans matter," Gavin said calmly, "so we do what we have to do. Now let's go, before we don't make our own flights."

With a nod and an angry look at the airport, Lennox hopped in, and they drove off.

CHAPTER 10

"WHAT KIND OF plans do we have?" Helena asked.

"It'll be a bit of a hopscotch trip," he said, "but, once we realized that the kidnappers' associates had booked seats on the same flight, we knew we had to get you a long way away."

"I don't have a problem with that," she said, "but where are we flying to?"

"To England before we jump the pond," he said. "We were supposed to fly to Amsterdam first, but now we're flying to England, and then we'll see how we're getting across the ocean."

"Hopefully by plane," she said. "That's the fastest."

"It is," he said, "but it's not always the safest." And then, at that, he sat back and went quiet.

But she saw him always working on his phone, probably setting up the rest of their arrangements. She looked over at Carolina, one eyebrow up.

Carolina shrugged. "Trust in him. He's kept us safe so far."

And that was the part that bothered her. Why the hell had the other two not listened? It's not that she really expected the kidnappers to do anything, once they realized John and Sasha had split from Lennox. So there was a good chance that John and Sasha would both be fine, now that they weren't physically with Lennox, who was the kidnapper's ultimate target. But why would you take that chance alone, unarmed, and unskilled to handle those people? Helena shook her head.

Still, before long, they pulled up into a smaller airport and hopped into a private plane. She smiled as she saw it. "Now this is nice."

"It is," Lennox said. "We'll have to stop for refueling, and we'll probably do that in France."

"We could take another flight from France back the US," she said.

"Maybe. Let's keep to the schedule and see." He quickly loaded their duffel bags.

They boarded the flight and took off almost immediately. One good thing about private airplanes, like this one, was how much more comfortable boarding the planes were—simple, nothing involved. The conversation on the flight was pretty light as everybody avoided the topic of John and Sasha. And even of where they were going, although Gavin did ask Carolina what her future plans were, now that she had been kidnapped. Like, if she was leaving the doctor's program or if she would continue to work with the Red Cross.

"I'm not sure," Carolina said. "I was contemplating doing more traveling, but now I'm not certain I want to." She slid a glance at Gavin, and he nodded. "Particularly with Lennox's issue right now."

Gavin looked at Helena. "What about you?"

"I was looking at making a change too," Helena said quietly. "Carolina and I weren't traveling while we were married. And then, after our divorces, we both resumed traveling around the world again, more to escape than to start again. Now I'm almost ready to put down some roots."

"We've already talked about it a couple times," Carolina said, nodding at Helena. "It's just a matter of where and what's next for us."

"But the whole world is ahead of us," Helena said, comfortably rolling her head back, her eyelids heavy. "And I think I'm about ready to nod off and have a little bit of a nap. How long till we land?" Helena let her eyes close.

"We're not too far away from Paris now," Lennox said. "It won't be a long stop there either."

"Okay," she said. She looked at Carolina and asked, "Did you recognize any of the men that he showed you?"

"Yes," she said; then she frowned. "Did you hear us last night?"

Helena shrugged. "A little bit. Something about a bunch of faces."

"I could identify one kidnapper. The main guy in charge. With all the scars."

Helena looked at Lennox. "Did you know him?"

"No," he said, his tone terse.

Helena studied his face as he worked on a laptop. "You hadn't seen him *ever*?"

He lifted his gaze from the laptop, studied her for a long moment, then shook his head. "Not that I remember, no. And we're trained to remember faces, even when disguised. Even faces that have undergone cosmetic surgery. Because some things can't be changed."

"Like what?" Helena asked, intrigued.

"The distance between the eyes for one thing."

"Okay. ... So why the hell would he be after ..."

"I'm trying to figure that out," he said. "I'm backtracking his history to see where we might have met—or at least had crossed paths."

"Or," Carolina said brightly, "what if somebody else used your name?"

Instantly silence settled in the plane. "What do you mean?" Gavin asked.

Helena got it though. "What if," she said to Lennox, "somebody hated you. And then did something terrible and let everybody believe that he was you."

"Well, that would be a shitty thing to do," Gavin said.

"But we already know that this whole deal is a really shitty deal," Carolina said.

"Does somebody hate your guts enough to do something like this?" Helena asked. "This is pretty nasty to consider. But also, if you wanted to get somebody who you hated in big trouble, this was not a bad way to do it."

"I don't know," Lennox said, confusion in his gaze. "Let me think about it. You guys got off on a different angle, so leave me alone to find the connections."

Helena looked over at Carolina with a raised eyebrow.

Carolina shrugged and said, "Naptime." She stretched out in the airline seat and let her head drop against the window and closed her eyes.

"Not a bad idea," Helena said and curled up in the opposite seat, using her window as well as the sweater that she had brought with her, and fell asleep.

It wasn't very long before Lennox woke her up. She stared up at him in confusion, glanced around, and realized where she was again. "Are we here?"

"Yes," he said. "We're in Paris fueling up."

"Are we getting off?"

He shook his head. "No."

She glared at him. "Did you have a reason for waking

me then?"

He grinned. "Maybe to get up and walk around, shake your legs out a little bit."

"Or maybe just go back to sleep," she muttered and curled back up. She closed her eyes, and the next time she woke up, *again* she saw Lennox. She glared at him. "Seriously?"

His eyebrows shot up. "Now what?" he asked.

"Aren't we still in Paris?"

"No," he said, his smile kicking up the corners of his mouth. "We're in London now, not that it was much of an extra flight, but we needed the fuel."

"Fine," she replied, and then she realized what he said. "So we're here? Now we can go home? Can we get off?"

"We are getting off, but we're taking another flight across to the Maritimes."

"Why Canada?" she asked, running a finger through her hair.

"So we can connect to the coast."

She shrugged. "We can go the other way and go straight across to California."

"We could, but it'll take a long time."

"All of these hops are taking time." But she closed her mouth and just endured.

They did get off the plane and had about two hours before they hooked onto a commercial flight and ended up in Halifax, where they grabbed yet another flight that took them to Chicago. By the time they arrived in San Diego, she was tired, frustrated, and fed up. She looked at Carolina. "You know it would have been much nicer if we'd just gone to Munich."

She nodded. "It was supposed to be that way. This time

it'll be both of us at *your* apartment."

Helena shrugged listlessly. "It doesn't matter. We're here together now, I guess."

"Yeah, but I don't want to fly anymore for a while," Carolina groaned. "Oh, for a nice bed!"

"Well, we had one," she said. "Apparently staying in it wasn't to be."

They stood outside this final airport in the wee hours of the morning—something like two a.m. by the time they finally cleared customs, got their luggage, and everybody had gathered outside. She tried to shrug the cobwebs off her mind. And then realized Gavin was missing. She looked at Lennox. "Now what?"

"Well, it depends if you think it's safe enough to go to your apartment."

Her eyebrows shot up. "Why wouldn't it be?"

He shrugged. "Because it's still associated with you, and you're still associated with me."

"Well, how about your apartment?" she asked.

"That would be the worst place," he said.

Just then Gavin drove up. They all stared at the lime-green Jeep. "Hardly a very unassuming rental," Helena said, as she got in the back.

Gavin laughed. "This one is my own," he said. "I left it at the airport."

"That could have been a big bill," Lennox said, "depending how much longer we were detained overseas."

Gavin shrugged. "It's a huge boon having wheels available," he said. "You do what you have to do at the time." Gavin pulled away from the side strip and headed back onto the main freeway to leave the airport and to get out of the traffic. Even though it was the wee hours of the morning, still plenty of vehicles moved about.

"Where are we going?" Helena asked him.

"To a safe house," Gavin said.

"So not my place?"

Gavin shook his head. "No, we figured it was better to avoid all known places."

"And for how long?" she asked.

Lennox answered, "Until I can find out what's going on."

And she sat back and shared a hard look with Carolina. "That doesn't sound very promising."

"Do you want to live to see tomorrow?" Lennox turned around in the front seat to level a heavy stare at her.

She didn't have to answer that because, of course, she wanted to. But she didn't want to be in a cage either. She didn't know exactly what was going on, but, for the first time, she realized how John and Sasha felt. This was *his* problem, not their problem. She wouldn't throw him to the wolves, but, at the same time, this felt like something he needed to handle and fast. "Okay," she said, "you have three days."

At that, Gavin snorted, raised his gaze to the rearview mirror, and Lennox spun around again and glared at her. "What?"

"You've got three days," she announced, staring at him. "Three days to get this over with."

"Or then what?"

"Then I'm going back to my apartment," she said. "We're okay to hang out because we need a couple days just to chill anyway," she said. "But we have to move on. We can't just sit here and be sitting ducks."

"And how do you figure, by going back to your place,

that you *aren't* a sitting duck?"

"I don't know," she said, "but that's the time limit."

He shook his head and said, "It'll take as long as it takes." Lennox checked his phone and told Gavin, "Take the next left."

Gavin nodded and promptly pulled into the lane farthest away from any exit.

"And that will be *three days*," she said, her tone inflexible. Of course she couldn't force something like that to happen, but, if he didn't think there would be real consequences, then Lennox wouldn't move heaven and earth to fix this. And then she thought about that and shrugged. It was Lennox, of course, so he would move heaven and earth to fix it regardless. "And, if you need us, you have to speak up."

"And I would need you *why?*"

"Well, to start with," she said, "I'd like to see the face of this person who hates you so much. Because maybe, if we know him—or at least know what he looks like—that might let us tell you if we see him involved from here on out."

Lennox looked at her, startled for a moment, then brought up his phone and flicked through the recent images. And then he held up his phone, reached over the front seat to give it to her. "This is the guy I had problems with."

She looked at the man's image with one eyebrow shot up. She held it for Carolina to see it too, and they exchanged glances. Helena said, "Definitely not the kidnapper, but... well, we do know him. Can't say we like him either."

He looked at her in shock. "What do you mean, *you know him?*"

"He tried to date both of us," Helena said. "It was about two years ago maybe." She frowned, looking over at Carolina for confirmation, who just shrugged. Helena continued, "It was after we were both separated, but before we headed off, traveling with the Red Cross."

Gavin again changed lanes.

"Seriously?" Lennox glared at her. And then he spun to look at his sister.

She shrugged. "I didn't place him. I still don't remember him."

Lennox now faced Helena. "How often did you see him, and how pushy was he?" Lennox asked Helena.

"He was looking for information," Helena said, "but he seemed quite frustrated that we weren't cooperating."

"Interesting," Gavin said. "It's possible." He made the next left, as Lennox had instructed.

"It's bullshit is what it is!" Lennox said in disgust. "Just because he hates me doesn't mean that he would do something like this."

"No, but then, I hate to say it, why would he want to date me?" Carolina said. "Not that there's anything wrong with me, but I'm still your sister."

"But then maybe he didn't know that," Lennox said, grasping for straws.

"No," Helena said. "Rob knew because he's the one who said he was a friend of yours."

"Shit," Lennox said, looking out his passenger's side window. "The one thing he is *not* is a friend. And for him to have even said that is very suspicious right off the bat."

"Exactly," she said, "so I suggest that you check him out."

"What do you think I've been doing?" Lennox asked in exasperation.

"Aha," she said with a smile. "Like I said—*three days.*"

LENNOX WASN'T SURE how serious Helena was or whether she was just being snarky. He couldn't even imagine what he would have done if he'd found out Rob and Carolina—or Helena—were dating. He would have lost it big-time. "You've met him before," he said to Carolina, his arm slung across the front seat of Gavin's Jeep as he spoke to his sister.

Carolina looked at him and shook her head. "No, I haven't."

"You have," he said. "When I was on leave one day. Remember the guy who came to my door when you were over for dinner? And he tried to force his way in, and we had this big argument?"

She froze, looked at him, and said, "Yes, I do remember that. Not a lot. I didn't get a good look at him though."

"Well, that was him," he said shortly.

"Why does he hate you so much?"

"He raped a young girl over in Thailand, and I turned him in."

Silence.

"Okay then," Helena said softly. "Well, I guess he deserved that."

"If that's the case," Carolina said, "why the hell was he trying to date us a couple years ago?"

"He was drummed out of the military and jailed in Thailand," Lennox said. "I don't know what happened afterward. I lost track of him."

"That's all bullshit," Helena said. "Why the hell would he be allowed back on the streets?"

"He shouldn't be out of jail. Which is why I find it interesting that he tried to date both of you," he said, twisting to look at Helena. "Why would he try to date you too?"

She glared at him. "I don't know why."

Her tone was just caustic enough that he realized how his question came off. He rolled his eyes. "It's not like he would know there was anything between the two of us."

"Some people think there's more here than there is."

"Right," he said. He caught Gavin's questioning expression, and Lennox shrugged, shook his head. "No, we didn't have a thing. Just keep your eye on the road, please."

Carolina piped up. "They should have had a thing. It would have made them both easier to live with."

With that, Gavin started to chuckle. And then he laughed and laughed. "Okay," he said, "now I understand all the undercurrents."

"You do not," Helena muttered.

"No," Lennox said, under his breath. "You don't."

"Maybe not," Gavin said, still chuckling, "but I can guess. You really should go to a hotel and take care of business."

"Is that what having sex is to you?" Helena asked in an outraged voice. "*Taking care of business?*"

"Well, if it'll stop all this crackling resentment around us, then, yes," Gavin said. "You guys should have had a thing five years ago, and maybe you, Helena, wouldn't have gotten married, and you, Lennox, wouldn't have been lost for all these five years."

"How lost was he?" Carolina asked with interest.

Lennox smacked Gavin on the shoulder. "I was not lost," he announced. "Gavin is just being an ass."

"If you say so," he said and started to whistle. Unfortunately it was the wedding march. When he caught Lennox's gaze, Gavin roared with laughter.

"Glad you're having fun," Lennox muttered.

"Best I've had yet." He quickly changed lanes, moving into another.

"Why all the sudden lane changes?" Helena asked suspiciously.

"I just want to make sure we're not being followed," he said. "And—before you ask—no, we're not."

"God, I just want this over with."

"And it will be," Lennox said, "soon."

"Three days," she said darkly. "*Three days* or else …"

CHAPTER 11

H ELENA WOKE THE next morning and froze, not recognizing the room. Her heart pounded, slamming against her chest, until she heard voices outside and recognized Lennox's. She groaned and sagged into the mattress, remembering that they were in a safe house. It was a rancher with lots of small bedrooms. They each had a bedroom; they each had a bed. Everybody was safe, and they weren't all that far away from her own apartment. Maybe twenty minutes if she drove and maybe an hour if she walked.

She got up, slowly walked into the bathroom, yawning. She only had her clothes in her travel bag, so at least enough for a week's holiday. But this was a long way away from a holiday. She closed the bathroom door, hopped into the shower, and, when she felt more refreshed, she stepped out, dried off, and dressed. She pulled out her dirty clothes, wondering if a washing machine was here.

With all her clothes laid out on the bed, she looked at the dresser and decided that, since she was here for almost three days, she might as well unpack. With everything removed, her dirty laundry to the side, she put her empty carry-on bag into the closet and then walked into the kitchen. "I guess this layout makes sense if it's a safe house," she said, "but, if it were my place, I would want my bedroom twice as big."

"I think they took the bedrooms and cut them in half just for that reason, so they could pack in more people," Gavin said without looking up. He motioned at the coffee-maker and said, "That's the second pot. You may want to get a cup now."

"Wow," she said, "have you already drunk a whole pot yourself?"

"Nope," he said, "Lennox has been helping me."

"Is Carolina up?"

"Yep, you're the last one, sleepyhead."

She chuckled. "I finally slept though. I feel one hundred times better."

"Good," he said, "so you'll have some patience when Lennox doesn't finish this job in three days."

"Nope," she said, as she sat down and reached for a section of the newspaper. "He's got three days. Now he's got half a day less."

Gavin let out a bark of laughter. "Well, you're nothing if not a hard-ass."

"If you want to get shit done," she said, "you have to have deadlines and discipline, and you got to make your goals."

"And so is your goal his goal?"

She stopped, frowned at him. "What does that mean?"

Gavin shook his head. "You make your goals," he said, "but that doesn't mean they're Lennox's goals too."

"Maybe not," she said, "but obviously we've been on his enemy's target list for a while."

"And I wanted to ask you more details about that," Lennox said, as he walked in to join them.

Carolina walked in beside him, came over, and hugged Helena. "You look much better."

"What kind of details?" Helena asked.

Carolina pulled up a chair beside Helena, the two women close as always. They both looked at Lennox with quizzical glances.

"How did he find you?"

"I remember him now. We were at a coffee shop," Carolina said promptly. "He walked up, introduced himself as one of your friends, and said that he happened to be around and recognized me."

"And how did you know that he was telling the truth?"

"Because he knew something about your place," she said. "Mentioned that you guys had done a couple missions together and also mentioned a couple other friends that you have in common who I also knew."

"Right, so confidence-building, letting you know that he really does belong in my world. So why didn't you guys go out with him?"

"You mean, besides the fact that we were both not going out with men at all then?" Carolina asked.

Lennox nodded.

"I can answer that," Helena said. "I didn't like something about him. I don't want to say that I saw a 'violent edge' to him, but something was in his gaze. It was just wrong."

"*Wrong?*" Gavin said slowly, as he put down the newspaper and looked at her. "Wrong, how?"

"Cold. Dead. As if something was going on in there that was completely disconnected from the world around us."

"Interesting assessment," Lennox said. "Gavin, you know him too, don't you?"

"I do," Gavin said. "And she's right. There's a coldness in him."

"Then our instincts were a whole lot better that time," she added, with a knowing look at Carolina. "I haven't seen him since though."

"Is that the only time he approached you?"

"No, we saw him several times throughout that week," she said. She frowned and looked at Carolina. "I think it's because of him that we switched coffee shops, wasn't it?"

Carolina looked thoughtful, as if casting her mind back. "You know what? I think it was. We went there every morning at nine a.m. to catch up," she said slowly to the men. "We needed that. Even though we probably spoke for four hours every evening, it was that physical contact that we needed with each other to get through the day back then. But Rob was disturbing," she admitted.

"I think we went to a coffee shop around the corner and then saw him again, and so we stopped our coffee shop ritual. Instead we ended up picking up coffee somewhere else and walking down on the beach."

"Right," Carolina said. "The more we distanced from him, the angrier he seemed to be, which then made us distance even more."

"Exactly." Helena agreed with a solemn nod.

"Did he ever follow you home?" Lennox asked.

"How would we know?" Helena asked. "We left soon afterward with the Red Cross."

"So, if Rob had any plans," Carolina said, "we probably ruined them right away."

"And it might have taken time for him to figure out just where and what you two were up to."

"Exactly. But when scar-man found us, apparently Rob had found us in a big way," Helena said. "Do you think he would have done something to this guy using your name?"

"It's possible," Lennox said. "I can't tell you what other people have done. I can tell you that I don't know who this guy with the scar is. As far as I know, I've never met or done anything to him."

"And this guy—Rob, your friend or not—what was his real name?"

"Just call him Rob," he said. "I think his real name is Robert McMillan or something."

"And did you find very many places where you crossed paths with Rob?"

"None that matter," he said. "They were all before he was charged."

"What about this scarred guy?"

"No way to know. But he was, as far as I can tell, in Thailand for a long time. So our time there could have overlapped."

"Do you think he would know the girl who Rob raped?" Helena asked.

Both men looked at her with added respect.

She shrugged. "I'm just looking for a link. The other problem is, if Rob did this once, what are the chances he did it again?"

"So you think that, maybe instead of something this Rob guy did directly to the man with the scar, Rob might have done something to somebody close to the man with the scar?" Gavin asked Helena.

"I don't know," she said tiredly. "You're making my brain hurt."

"You're the med school student with the 99.9% ranking, which probably will never be usurped," Lennox said, scoffing. "Your brain only hurts when it doesn't have a million things to work on."

She shot him a look. "My brain always intimidated you," she announced. "That's probably why you didn't want to go out with me."

Silence fell at the table. And then once again, Gavin chuckled. "As I said," he said, "you two need to spend some time together."

"Nope," she said. "We already spent some time together."

"Didn't go so well, huh?" Gavin asked.

Lennox glared at her. "Go ahead. Why don't you just air all our dirty laundry?"

"I would, but there isn't any to air," she said blithely, as she waved a hand in his direction. "That's the problem with nonstarters."

He gave her a loud snort. "Nothing happened."

"Nope," she said, "one crazy-wild kiss, and both of us backed off, deciding that it wasn't what we wanted at the time."

"And all because of me too," Carolina said. "Right?" The two of them exchanged looks, looked at her, and Carolina nodded. "I knew that's what you were doing. I kept telling you both it was okay."

"But it's not okay," Helena said, "because I wasn't prepared to jeopardize our relationship."

Carolina grabbed her best friend's fingers and said, "Why would you think a relationship with my brother, even if you two broke up, would jeopardize us?"

"Because it happens," she said, "and you're too important to me."

"You were just scared," Carolina said. "Admit it. You were afraid that Lennox was too good to be true."

At that, Helena laughed. "Well, he isn't, so it all worked

out."

Just then, his phone rang. Lennox pulled it out, checked the number, and answered it. "Keane, what's up?"

She looked over at Gavin. "Who's Keane?"

"One of our team who runs the communication center."

"Cool," she said, studying Gavin's face. Then she looked over at Lennox and said, "Or not cool."

Gavin nodded. "It looks like *not cool* to me as well."

"HE ARRIVED IN the US? San Diego? Walked right through security?"

"Apparently," Keane said. "He wasn't supposed to be let in without questioning."

"He was involved in the kidnapping and a hostage scenario. How the hell was he allowed to enter the country?"

"We're still investigating all that," Keane said. "The whole point of this call is to tell you to watch your back." And he hung up.

"So our scarred man is Stefano Hartland, both on his birth certificate and on his current IDs," Lennox said to the three staring at him in shock. "And he arrived two hours ago in the US. He's already cleared customs, and they're just now getting around to telling us."

"Wow," Helena said. "I thought we were all on the same team."

"The teams are variable obviously," he said. He glared at his phone. "So I want to get into the security in your apartment building to see if he's figured out where you are, and then there's my sister." He looked at her. "You don't have a place here any longer, do you?"

She shook her head. "No, just the one in Munich."

"So, if you were to come here, where would you stay?"

"If not with you, with Helena of course," she said.

"So we're back to Helena." Lennox worked away on his laptop, checking for cameras and security systems. "You have a high-end security system at your place."

"Well, as good as I could get," she said. "It's a new apartment for me, after I divorced."

He looked up and realized why she'd have extra security on her place, and he approved. But he hated the reason behind it. "I'll need permission from you and the building's owner to get into the system."

"Or you don't get permission," she said. "You can get in there anyway."

He immediately opened the chat window and asked for access to the building's security feeds. It took at least three minutes, and then a link popped up.

"And I'm in," he said, with a note of satisfaction. He really loved this Mavericks system. He worked his way back to this morning's video, checking to make sure that nobody suspicious had come or gone. "Nobody's been there so far today."

"That you know of," Helena said. "What if your other idiot, Rob, set up something beforehand?"

Lennox sat back, looked at her, and asked, "What are you thinking?"

"I don't know," she said, staring at him, and he saw the fear lurking in the back of her eyes. "But just to think that this guy even knows where I live won't help me sleep at night."

"Which is why," he said, "we have to find him."

"I get that," she said, "but this isn't exactly helping

now."

"It is if we can figure out if he's found your place or not."

"Why don't you go back a couple days?" Carolina asked. "See if Rob showed up early."

"No reason for him to," Gavin said, shaking his head, "but this whole thing has been one messed-up illogical incident." He had his laptop out too. The two of them worked away, checking on the various camera feeds.

And then Lennox froze. He tapped Gavin and said, "See if you can get a better picture of this guy." And he gave him the time and date.

With the second laptop, Gavin opened up angles from the other cameras. "Well, look at that," he said. "Rob." And he pointed out the stranger with a baseball cap and sunglasses.

"And how do you know it's Rob?" Helena asked, hopping up and running around to see him. Carolina followed.

Lennox pointed to the scar and the slightly distorted tattoo on the back of his hand. "Rob was injured with several bullets and some shrapnel in one of the missions, and it buggered up that tattoo."

"So this was what? Four days ago?" Helena asked.

Lennox and Gavin both nodded.

"So why is he in my apartment building back then?" As they all watched the replay, Rob headed toward an apartment on the main floor and, with keys, let himself in. "That son of a bitch has an apartment in the same building?" she cried out in outrage.

"Appears to be true," Lennox said quietly. "So now the question is, *Why?*"

"Well, it's too much of a coincidence to think that he

didn't have a long-term plan for this," Gavin said. "So he's there because she's there."

"I don't understand why it's me though," Helena stated, staring from Lennox to Gavin and back.

"Because, like I said, that's the only place I would go," Carolina said. "Although we *were* going to Munich."

"Except," Helena said, as she sat back down again, "we were originally going home to San Diego," she said, "and then we changed our plans."

"So who would know your original plans and then wouldn't have realized when you made a change of plans?" Lennox asked Helena and his sister.

"I don't know," Helena said, staring at him in shock. "We talked about it while we were at work all the time. Any number of people could have heard us."

"But who would care?" Lennox asked, pressing the women. "That's the real question."

Both women shrugged. "I have no idea," Helena stated.

"I wonder if he's still there," Gavin said thoughtfully. "Maybe he's living there."

Lennox shot him a hard look. "I suggest we go find out."

Immediately Helena jumped to her feet. "I want to go too."

"Well, that's not happening," Lennox said, with a glare in her direction.

She glared right back. "It's my apartment!"

"No," he said, "it's his apartment."

"So what does that mean though?" she asked. "Why would he be watching me?"

"To find me," Carolina said. "And, therefore, ultimately to find Lennox."

"So what about this other guy who landed at the airport?

Stefano?" Helena asked the guys.

"For all we know, he's part of whatever this angle Rob is working," Lennox said.

"Maybe they're working together on both ends. The kidnapping first and now Rob's part. Maybe Rob was lying to you," Gavin said to the women. "People lie all the time, particularly when it diverts attention away from them."

Lennox frowned. "Anything's possible." He hopped up and said, "Gavin, stay here with the women?"

"Absolutely. What about weapons?"

"Right, we had to leave the others behind." He stopped and looked around.

"Exactly, so now we're stuck."

"Or not," Lennox said, his mind buzzing. He sent a message to Keane, almost laughing when he got an immediate response to check out the back of the master closet. He loved this team.

Before Lennox took off, Helena stopped him with a look. "Wait. Talk to me."

Lennox sat down, knowing he had an arsenal at his disposal just feet away from him, so he had some time to spare.

"What does any of that have to do with my apartment?"

"Maybe nothing," Lennox said. He looked at Gavin, his fingers spinning his pen back and forth, back and forth again. "We need to pull in some information on what Rob has been doing since his incarceration, how he got out so fast. And see if this other guy with the scars has any connection with Coronado."

"Different country," Gavin said. "Digging won't be easy."

"I know," Lennox said. "But something else is going on here, unless it's just as simple as grabbing Carolina again—or maybe both of them—because where else would my sister and Helena go at this point?"

"*Anything* is possible at this point," Gavin said with a sigh. "We know more but not near enough. Yet."

"I know," Lennox said. Frowning, he looked at the women and said, "I need you guys to disappear."

"We're in a safe house already. They should be fine," Gavin noted.

Lennox looked at Gavin, shaking his head, and said, "This Stefano guy got into the States easily enough. Not one border crossing question made. He bypassed US Navy orders. What do you think the chances are that Stefano knows about this safe house?"

"If he has access to satellite, like we do, Stefano—or Rob—could have tracked my vehicle," Gavin admitted. "It's in the garage right now, but that doesn't mean they didn't see it earlier."

"Exactly." And Lennox's instincts rode him hard. "I don't like it," Lennox said. "Pack up and be ready to leave in fifteen."

He bolted to his feet and raced to the bedroom.

CHAPTER 12

H ELENA LOOKED AT Gavin. "Is he serious?"

But he was already nodding. "Move," he said, "now." There was a definite bite to his tone. The two women got up, and Helena muttered as she headed to her bedroom, "I just unpacked."

"Well, something set both of them off, but I don't know what," Carolina said.

"At this point, probably just gut instincts," Helena said, as she grabbed all her clothing from the dresser and picked up her dirty laundry. "I was going to ask if they had washing machines here so I could do a little laundry."

"Me too," Carolina said.

Quickly both women had everything packed up. Helena used the washroom for good measure and then stepped out into the kitchen with her carry-on bag and asked, "Where are we going?"

The look she got from Gavin was *Keep an open mind.*

"If you say so," she said. And the two of them headed out to the Jeep in the garage.

Very quickly they were back on the road—Lennox looking behind them often, while Gavin changed lanes more times than needed—but they headed into the Coronado base.

She frowned. "You think we'll be safer on the base? This

Stefano guy just waltzed into our country."

But, instead of stopping there, they moved to the pier and out to a wharf. At the end was a small boat where they were putting in their bags.

"Isn't this taking things a little far?" Helena whispered to Carolina, as they all headed out to a naval ship. Not a big one but a small one. "What is this?"

"A safe place for you to stay while we go to town on these two guys," Lennox said, and, sure enough, the women were lifted to the bottom rung, handed up, and, once on top of the deck, were moved off to an officer. He saluted to both Gavin and Lennox, still in the transport boat, before the women were escorted inside.

Lennox and Gavin took the skiff right back to shore.

Once inside, Helena looked around and said, "I'm sorry to be such a bother."

The officer smiled at her. "And I'm quite happy to have the company. Most of the men are on shore leave," he said, "so we have a skeleton crew. But you're more than welcome to stay." He led them to a small room with a top and bottom bunk and said, "This is yours, for the moment."

"I don't suppose the guys gave you any idea how long we would be here, did they?"

"For the day, possibly overnight," he said, "so make yourself at home."

Helena nodded and said, "And I hate to be a pain, but we didn't get a chance to eat. Is there a possibility of a coffee at least?"

His face broke into a big smile. "And that will make the cooks happy," he said. "So, if you're ready to drop your bags, we'll take you down and get you some breakfast."

And that's what they did. The whole time she looked

around with interest. She didn't imagine too many civilians were treated to a first-hand look at the inside of one of these cruisers. She kept peppering the officer with questions about how many men it took to run the ship and how far they could go on the fuel tanks, all kinds of stuff, because her mind just wouldn't let up on it.

Finally he stopped, looked at her, and asked, "Are you writing a book or something?"

Carolina laughed and said, "You have to understand that my friend's mind doesn't stop. She's constantly barraging all of us for more information. She reads tour books and encyclopedias."

The officer looked at her in surprise.

Helena shrugged. "I have an unending thirst for knowledge, particularly all sorts of minutia," she said with a grin.

He led them into a large open room and up to a large counter. He called out and said, "We have two special visitors for the next twenty-four hours, and they're hungry."

A massive guy on the backside with an apron wrapped around his waist gave the women a meaty grin and said, "Perfect! I hope you guys can eat."

"I can eat," Helena said. "Hard to get full actually."

"Watch what you say," the officer said. "Fill them up, Miko."

And they were led to a large selection of food, where they got to order exactly what they wanted. With trays laden down, everything from sausages and eggs and hash browns to fried tomatoes and half of a muffin filled with cheese on the side, topped off with a full cup of fresh coffee. The officer led them to a lovely table by the window and said, "Here's a seaside view for you."

As she sat down, Helena exclaimed over the view. "Oh, wow," she said, "this is beautiful."

He asked, "Do you mind if I join you?"

They looked at him in surprise, and both said, "No, of course not. Please do."

When he returned with his coffee, then Helena remembered her manners. "I'm sorry," she said. "I didn't introduce myself. I'm Helena."

"And I'm Carolina, Lennox's sister," Carolina piped up.

He smiled, shook both their hands, and said, "And I'm Ben," he said. "It's nice to have you two aboard. It can get annoyingly boring here at times."

"I imagine it can when you're just sitting around, filling the time," she said with a smile. "But I'm also sure there's never enough downtime so it's a welcome relief."

"Absolutely," he said.

The next hour passed in the beautiful daze of socializing and visiting as Helena plowed through a ton of food. Carolina's plate was half the size. But then Carolina was much smaller. Helena looked at her friend and said, "We ended up in sunshine and roses after all."

"We deserve it," Carolina said complacently.

Ben asked, "What do you two do?"

Helena looked at him and smiled and said, "We're doctors," she said. "We've just come back from a Red Cross trip." When she glanced at Carolina, silently asking for permission, Helena shrugged and added, "We were kidnapped. We just landed in San Diego, and our friends were looking for a safe place to stash us as they hunt down the kidnappers."

At that, the officer said, "I didn't get any intel on why," he said, "but that makes perfect sense. Are both of you doctors?"

Carolina launched into a tale about how they've been best friends since grade school and how they'd made a pact to become doctors and to help the world.

"Wow," he said. By then a couple other officers joined them. Everybody sat at the table, enjoying the discussion about how Carolina's and Helena's lives had gone from grade school to med school to being kidnapped. Helena smiled. "I don't even know that we're supposed to talk about it, but Lennox didn't tell me not to. Although he doesn't say very much."

"Lennox is like that," another man said as he approached the table.

She looked up, realized it was the captain. And she stood and shook his hand. "Thank you very much for keeping us for the day," she said in a formal note.

He smiled and said, "It's nice to have some fresh faces aboard."

And that set the tone for the rest of the day. They got a full tour of the cruiser, and later they ended up back at their room, with access to their laptops and internet. It was a lovely day. When Helena's phone rang, she looked down and didn't recognize the number. "Hello?"

"It's me," Lennox said.

"Did you catch him?" Helena asked instantly, putting the laptop off to the side of her bunk. Carolina immediately joined her, and Helena put her phone on Speaker. "Carolina is here with me too."

"Your kidnapper, Stefano, was seen at your apartment," he said. "We just missed him." His voice was frustrated and angry.

"And Rob?"

"His apartment is empty and had been cleaned out."

"Go check mine," she said.

"Are you okay with that?" he asked. "I need to take a look to see if he's been in your place at all."

"Do it," she said. "I didn't give you the key though."

"Don't worry about that," he said quickly. "I can get in without it."

"Fine," she said, "but then you'll get back to me and let me know what you find."

"Will do," he said, and he hung up.

She looked at Carolina. "Maybe this is progress."

LENNOX GLARED AT Gavin. "How could we have missed him?"

"I'm not even sure we did," Gavin said, studying the outside of the apartment building. "Do we know for sure he traveled alone?"

"No, not necessarily. We have a lot of videos still to go through. The Mavericks in command central are working on it now."

"You think Stefano's visit was a decoy of some kind? So we're watching him when Rob is up to something?"

Lennox nodded, his mouth a grimace. "We never see Stefano and Rob together on the tapes."

"Not so far," Gavin agreed.

"I think the bottom line is, we need to get into her apartment."

"Do you really think Stefano or Rob have gone in there?"

"Why wouldn't they have?" Lennox said.

"Aren't they looking for you? And, if we go in there, we're playing into their hands."

"Right," he said, "that's possible."

"I know," Gavin said, "and yet I guess this is our best chance to find either of them."

They made their way inside up to the second floor, where Helena's apartment was. They walked down the hallway to see eight doors on each side. It wasn't a big building, relatively small for the area, and security was pretty high-end. Once you got inside, cameras were on both ends of both floors. It didn't mean a whole lot though.

Lennox walked up to Helena's apartment, took out his pick, and quickly unlocked the door. They stepped inside, and immediately Lennox held up a finger. Gavin nodded. Lennox slipped out of his shoes, closed the door quietly, and stepped through to the living room.

Instantly he was faced with her kidnapper; anger surged through him. He glared at the intruder. "What are you doing here?"

With a handgun in one hand and what looked like a set of handcuffs in the other, the kidnapper's intention was pretty obvious. Stefano just grinned at Lennox and said, "I'm looking for someone. But you're not that someone."

"How do you know I'm not?" Lennox challenged.

"I'm looking for Lennox," Stefano said. "You're not him."

And that's when Lennox realized this *was* a case of mistaken identity. "Actually I *am* Lennox," he said slowly, "but I suspect the person you are looking for is Rob."

The man's face twisted with rage. "You can't tell me what I know and what I don't know!" he said. "Where are the women?"

"What women?"

The kidnapper made a broader arm sweep. "The one who lives here."

"Ah, Helena?" At the man's nod, Lennox said, "She is safe. Along with Carolina."

Stefano frowned. "Yes, his sister."

"Yes," Lennox said. "*My* sister."

"You are not him," Stefano said, his voice harsh, his fist tightening on the handgun.

"Well, how did you know that she was my sister?"

"I have informants," he said.

"You didn't confirm it yourself?"

The man slowly shook his head. "No," he said, "my information has always been excellent."

"Well, I'm Lennox," he said, "but I don't know you at all."

The man's gaze narrowed at him.

"I'm going to take my phone out of my pocket," Lennox said. "Okay?"

With the handgun still pointed in his direction, Stefano nodded.

Lennox pulled out his phone quickly, pulled up a picture of Rob, and said, "I presume you know what the guy you're looking for looks like?"

Again the intruder nodded.

"Is this him? I call him Rob." And he held up Rob's photo.

The man glared at it and said, "Yes, but that's not Rob. That's Lennox."

"No, it is not," he said again. "I'm Lennox, and this is Rob."

Stefano shook his head.

Just then Gavin stepped around the side of Lennox, and Stefano turned his gun on him too. But Gavin stood close and said, "You're wrong. This is Lennox. And I can prove it."

Stefano glared at him. "How will you prove it?"

Gavin pulled out his phone and said, "Take a look at this picture." It was a photo of Lennox, still in his Navy SEAL uniform, being handed an award.

Stefano looked at Lennox and frowned. "This can't be Lennox." But his voice was confused, his face twisted with fury, as if fearing a trick. But, instead of accepting it, he looked angrier. "This is not true!" he said. "I was told it was you."

"*Told?*" Lennox pounced. "Told what? By whom?"

But Stefano reached up and once again touched the burn mark on his neck, the same tell as Helena had described.

Lennox held his hands out. "I get that you've got something against someone," he said, "but I think you have it against the wrong person."

Instead of listening to Lennox, the intruder shook his head, waving the gun around. "That can't be true!"

"Why not?"

"Because the one is a friend," he said. "And you are not him."

"I don't understand," Lennox said.

"I got the information from a friend," he reiterated. And then he took several steps back, heading toward the patio.

"Look. My sister is Carolina," Lennox said. "I don't have a birth certificate here with me, but I have a family tree. I have all kinds of proof that I am Lennox," he said. "So, if it's me you're looking for, then tell me what your beef is?" he asked. "Otherwise, somebody is using my name and blaming me for something I didn't do."

The guy gave him a haunted look and was suddenly gone through the double patio doors.

Lennox raced after Stefano to find the guy already gone. Lennox stood here, studying the layout, and looked back at Gavin, but he had gone out the front door.

It made no sense. Well, it was starting to make some sense. Somebody—Rob—had chosen to blame Lennox and had given this Stefano guy a target for whatever rage and revenge fantasy he had in his mind.

But they needed Stefano to understand it wasn't Lennox who was to blame. As he turned to walk back inside, he came face-to-face with Rob.

He leaned against the open front door, one foot in Helena's apartment, the other in the hallway, and said, "Wow, you're still alive. I'm surprised."

"No thanks to you," Lennox snapped. "Are you the one behind all this madness?"

"Behind all what?" he asked innocently, yet sported a big grin on his face. "What are you doing here with her?"

"Who is *her*?" Lennox asked.

"Helena, of course. I moved close so I could get to know her. I can't say I'm too thrilled if you are hanging around, hooking up with her."

Lennox stared at him in shock and confusion. "What the hell are you talking about?"

But Rob appeared to be stuck in his fantasy world. "Helena asked me to move closer," he said, "so that we could spend more time together."

"What?"

"Or is she stringing both of us along?" Rob said. "Ask her."

"You ask her," Lennox said, frowning at Rob. He didn't know what the hell was going on, but Stefano and now Rob were not acting normal or sanely.

"She is going out with me," Rob said slowly. "So I'm assuming you're here on a visit because of her best friend, Carolina, your sister. How is that going? I just want to make sure that it's platonic because I won't take kindly to her having an affair with you."

"She's not having an affair with you," Lennox said, feeling something twist inside him. What was going on? "She can't stand the sight of you." And he shouldn't have said that because rage lit up Rob's eyes. "What is this all really about? And what did you have to do with that guy who just was in here?"

"I don't know what you're talking about," Rob said, and he turned to shut the door and walked away. Immediately Lennox stepped out in the hallway to see Rob disappearing down the stairs to his floor. Lennox followed him. "Rob, what's going on?"

"Nothing," he said, "except that you need to be out of the picture, and I plan on moving into Helena's place."

"Why would you be moving into Helena's place?"

Rob turned to look at him and said, "Because we're meant to be together."

"When did you see her last?" Lennox asked curiously, trying to understand what was going on in Rob's psyche.

"Well, I stop in whenever I can," he said, "but it hasn't been enough. It's been years since we've spent much time together," he said. "But she's left the Red Cross, so we can spend a lot more time together."

Wow. He thinks she would leave the Red Cross because of the kidnapping? Or was this just his mind stuck in a fantasy world? "But you had to get rid of me first, is that it?" Lennox asked cautiously.

"Well, I was planning on getting rid of you anyway," he said, "but this is a good way to do it."

"If we were talking about Carolina, then that would make sense. But why Helena?"

"What do you mean, *why Helena?*" Rob asked. "She's my girlfriend."

"Since when?" Lennox asked, quietly feeling as if his whole world had dropped out of focus. He didn't understand what the hell was going on, but too many different stories overlapped and yet conflicted, and nothing about this was normal. Rob was calm, acting natural, but the words coming out of his mouth were anything but.

"Since you walked away and didn't want her," Rob said. "Thank you for that."

He stared and frowned at Rob. "When did you last see her and me together?"

"Must have been about five years by now," Rob said. "You know we were pretty good friends, and I was pretty sure that I could show her the light, but then you turned out to be an asshole and got me into all kinds of trouble."

"You raped a young girl," Lennox said, his fists clenched as he remembered that nightmare time. "Did you actually see Helena and me together?"

"Sure," he said. "That was one hell of a kiss, dude."

He realized that kiss had been somewhat public. It's one of the reasons why they had distanced themselves afterward because that had been just too hot, too fiery, and had also gotten out of control too fast. "So you were at that party?"

"Of course. We went everywhere together back then, until you turned around and betrayed me." Rob gave a harsh laugh. "You got amnesia? Sounds like you don't remember anything. Too bad your memory wasn't as shitty back then. I'd have been fine."

"So you were behind the kidnapping?"

"More or less," he said, "but I didn't want the women hurt. I'd never do anything to hurt Helena."

"But somebody must be feeding you information."

"Sure," he said, "and, if you haven't figured that out yet, that's pretty damn sad too. You used to be smarter."

"I haven't figured anything out," Lennox said quietly, as he studied the obviously unbalanced man in front of him. "What happened to you?"

"Well, I was in jail in Thailand," he said. "After the military court-martialed me, they turned me over to the Thai police, as they considered it their crime, and I was there until I bought my way out."

"How the hell did you buy your way out?" Lennox stared at him in disbelief. That's not what he'd hoped to hear.

"We can buy anything over there. The guy who's after you is the one who paid for my release."

"What the hell?" Lennox said in shock. "Why would he do that?"

Rob shot him a cocky grin and said, "Jesus, you're even stupider than I thought," he said. "You're just not getting it." Then he laughed and said, "Don't worry about it."

Just then a crowd of people moved into the apartments. And Rob took that opportunity to duck into his apartment.

The crowd quickly swept past Lennox when he tried to get through them to get into Rob's place. When he finally turned the knob, the door was locked. He pulled his pick out and entered as soon as he could and ran inside, but he found no sign of Rob.

The glass doors to the ground floor patio were open, and he was gone.

CHAPTER 13

THE WOMEN WERE back in their bunks, alone in their assigned room, when a hard knock came at the door.

"Hello?" Helena asked, as she hopped from the bottom bunk.

"It's me," Lennox said.

She opened the door in surprise, and he looked to see his sister sound asleep. "I've got a room across the hall here. Come over and let's talk, so we don't wake her."

Helena shrugged and said, "Fine." Dressed in a camisole and shorts, still she was decently covered, only it felt more intimate than it should. As she headed to his room, she realized he had a place all to himself. "This is dangerous," she murmured, closing the door behind her.

"No," he said, "not really." Lennox sagged on the floor and said, "A lot of really crazy shit is going on."

She wrapped up in the blanket on top of his bunk and said, "Tell me."

"I've already shared it with Gavin, and he's gone to rest. To let his brain shut down," he said, "because we can't figure out what's going on."

"Well, talk to me as well," she said, "although it might be better if Carolina was here too."

"Well, it seems like this wasn't about Carolina as much as it was about you."

Her jaw dropped. "Who the hell cares about me?"

"Rob," Lennox said quietly. And he slowly explained what had gone down at her apartment.

She shook her head. "So not only my kidnapper was there but Rob is still living in the same building? And he came up while you were there?"

"Yes," he said.

"But I thought his apartment was empty. ... You know that makes no sense, right?"

"I hear you," he said, "but honestly, at this point, nothing makes sense." He continued with the rest of the story.

"What are you talking about, that I have a relationship with him? And was he there at the party? Back then?"

"Apparently," he said. "Although I don't remember too much about the circumstances."

"Well, a lot of military personnel and doctors were there," she said. "You brought the military, and I brought a lot of the medical staff."

"I remember that much," he said. "I guess it's possible Rob was there and that Rob did see the kiss."

"So he arranges to get you out of my life so he can have me?" She shook her head. "That doesn't compute. I get a vote as to whether I date someone or not. What does this asshole have to do with the kidnapping?"

"The kidnapping was to get me out of your life, courtesy of Stefano, so Rob could have you, as well as payback for Rob being court-martialed and then in jail."

"But Rob's the one who raped that girl."

"He says it was consensual. But, yes, she was younger, and she was beaten up pretty bad."

"And he says that you're to blame?"

"Well, if I had turned a blind eye to it," he said, "Rob

would still have his military career."

"Instead he was court-martialed and turned over to the Thai police to stand trial, is that correct?"

"According to what he said, yes, and there he somehow managed to get a connection to the kidnapper, who bought his release."

"Well, for whatever reason, the kidnapper needed a target, and Rob gave it to him."

"That's what I'm thinking, but, whether they were in jail together or whether somebody who knew Stefano was in jail with Rob, I don't know."

And, indeed, Lennox looked completely pissed and angry.

"The minute you suggested that somebody else was putting me forth as the bad guy, Rob is the one who came up in my mind."

"That guy is just an asshole and crazy to boot," she said. "He'd be a natural suspect for anybody's enemy."

Lennox laughed. "He was back then, and he still is."

"So I guess we're staying here then," she said, looking around the ship.

"Unless you don't want to. I can't force you to stay here. Plus the longest we can hide you here is another day and a half before the ship leaves the port."

"I can't even believe that Rob's saying all this. What a liar." That Rob would make up such lies, especially to Lennox, irritated her. Thankfully she and Carolina had already explained their feelings about Rob to Lennox. "You didn't believe him, did you?"

"No, of course not, but he did look ..." Lennox hesitated.

"What?"

"He did look unsettled, as in potentially not quite all there right now. I don't know what to say. He didn't look like I expected him to look."

"You were friends for a long time, correct?"

"Not good friends but friends, yes. After all, we were both in the navy," Lennox said. "He seems to think we hung out all the time together." Lennox shook his head. "It's unfortunate to see what's happening to him right now."

"I think it comes back to the simplest of things," she said. "Whether it involves me or not, he's all about getting back at you. If he takes you out, then he thinks that'll leave me free and clear, and, if I matter to you, having me to himself makes him that much happier too."

"I don't understand that," he said, "because it was just a kiss."

"For you and me it was just a kiss. We allowed ourselves to block it out and to believe it was just a kiss. But apparently, to everybody else around us, it wasn't just a kiss."

"Right," he said. He stopped, looked at her quietly. "And so, for you, was it just a kiss?"

She laughed. "That's what we agreed it would be."

"And I think we also discussed the fact that neither of us was necessarily prepared to leave that decision in the past where it belongs."

"No," she said, "but this is hardly the time to reopen that discussion."

"Well, I've got an idea," he said suddenly, as he stood up.

"Oh?" she said, looking up at him from the bunk. "What's that?"

"Why don't we try it again?"

"No," she said, "that's not cool."

"Afraid?"

"Of course I'm afraid," she said. "You know what I've been through these last few days. Hell, these last few years."

He stopped, appeared to think about it, then nodded. "So maybe a kiss for comfort?"

"Hell, no," she said, but she could feel the fear inside her. Not of him but of what could happen if they came together again.

"Would it be that bad?"

"This is ridiculous," she groaned, blowing the hair back out of her face, trying to keep him on track. "So Rob what? He sees our kiss and thinks that maybe it would be like that with him and me?"

"Maybe," he said. "Unfortunately it was right before he raped that girl. It might have pushed him into that direction."

"When you were in Thailand? It was then?" She didn't understand the undercurrents.

Lennox nodded. "Maybe you don't remember the exact timing of the party," he said, "but I was leaving the next day."

"Oh, shit!" she said. "Now I do remember." She thought about it and remembered how desperately she'd wanted him. To spend that night together. But it wasn't to be. "What would have happened?" she asked. "When you suggested we leave and go find a quiet place?"

"For a long time," he said quietly, "I thought of nothing else. But, like you, this isn't how I thought of our second chance."

Heat flushed through her at his words. Deliberately trying to keep the conversation focused, she said, "I still don't understand what that one man who kidnapped us is all about."

"And that's why a part of me says you need to stay here to be safe, but another part of me says I need you to come back with me, where we can set this up properly and hopefully bring this all to a head."

"Use me as bait?"

He winced, gave a one-arm shrug.

She nodded. "It makes sense. I can't say I like it much. But it makes sense."

"None of this makes sense," he said. "It's so damn stupid."

"Until it does make sense," she said with a smile. "That's the best answer."

"I'll have to set it up," he said, staring at her, watching her expression.

She rose with a nod.

Now that he had her permission, he could get moving on this. "I'll get some extra men and more intel. I've requested more information regarding Rob's time in Thailand, as well as his military record, to see just what's going on. I'm on it," he said, waggling his phone. "Are you sure? No kiss?"

She smiled, leaned up, kissed him gently on the cheek, and said, "Not until it's over."

"Why is that?" he whispered as she drifted past.

"Because, when we start," she said, staring him directly in the face, "this time we won't quit." And she turned and headed for the door.

"OR YOU COULD stay the night," Lennox said, his voice

husky and deep. He watched as she froze at the doorway. He wasn't sure if she was considering it or was just shocked.

Slowly, ever-so-slowly, she turned to face him. "Seriously?"

Uncomfortable, awkward, and certainly not the way he expected this to go down, he refused to lie. "Yes," he whispered. "Why not?"

"*Why not?*" she asked, her tone cutting.

He winced. "That's not what I meant. But I don't want to wait," he said. And that was a shit response too. Women liked to be wooed, and that's the last thing he was doing here.

She looked at him carefully. "It might distract you from all this." And she waved her hand, as if he was supposed to understand what *this* was.

"Or it'll laser-focus me on keeping you safe," he said. Then he smiled and whispered, "You know we're heading there." He shut the door behind her, locking it too.

"Yes, I know we're heading here," she murmured, "but I was thinking we'd take more time. Have more romance. A bed where we could relax and spend some time and have coffee in the next morning type of a thing."

"So next time," he said.

He saw her thinking it over and almost immediately discarding it. He reached out, lifted her chin, and said, "I want you," he whispered, and he kissed her gently. "But more than that, I've wanted you these five years that we've been apart." And he kissed her again.

When she could, she whispered, "Me too, but that doesn't mean this is the best time or place."

"I think it does," he said in all seriousness, slowly pulling her toward him until she was flush against him, from hip to chest. "Just think about it," he said. "You won't have to worry about this, our first time together, in the future. You won't have to anticipate or wonder or be scared or wake up with nightmares or anything along that line."

She started to frown, but he lowered his head and kissed the curve of her lips. "No objections?"

Her eyes popped open at that. And she glared at him. He smiled, lowered his head again, and kissed her deeply. She murmured when he lifted his lips. "You can't drug me into this."

"*Drug you?*"

The corner of her lips tilted up. "Seduce me."

"Actually," he said, "I think you were the one doing the seducing." He slid his hands over her shoulders up the back of her neck to sweep across her scalp, his fingers sliding through her hair.

She tried to shake her head gently. But she couldn't move for his hands.

He smiled and whispered, "Yes, you were inciting the flames. You know that," he said, dropping a kiss at the corner of her mouth and then again on the other side. "And you're right. Once we start, we'll never stop."

"So how will that work in our favor tonight?" she asked thickly.

"Maybe it won't," he whispered. "But maybe, just maybe, getting you a little bit out of my head will help me to focus." And he smiled down into that passion-clouded gaze of hers and whispered, "You're all I think about," he said. "That kiss. It was …"

And she whispered her answer at the same time. "… some kiss."

"I know," he whispered, his breath mingling with hers as

he slid his tongue inside, stroking, mimicking the act to follow. His hand slid down her back to her buttocks to cup and to pull her tight against his hips so that she could feel his erection. He shuttered his eyes closed, as it seemed she softened and wrapped even more around him. "You know we want this," he said.

"That doesn't mean we should do this."

"Is it just *this*, you mean?" he asked, but he didn't get an answer. He could feel her waiting. He smiled, his lips kicking up in the corners again. "Do you think I've forgotten you because that kiss we shared was just a moment of lust? You're the first person I think of when I wake up in the morning. You're the last person I think of before I go to sleep at night." He stared down at her, cuddling her close. "You know perfectly well how I feel."

Her eyes widened, and he reached up to place a finger against her lips as she started her protest.

"No. Stop. Remember who walked away on your wedding?" he asked. "Remember who was there when you got to the divorce court? When you were screaming for joy that it was over? Remember who was there to help you out when you got into trouble?"

"That was Carolina," she argued.

"Well, Carolina was there too," he whispered, his heated breath draping over her cheeks and her eyes and her ears. "Because I was. I was there for you."

CHAPTER 14

HELENA COULDN'T BELIEVE what he was saying, but it's what she had so badly wanted to hear. Had dreamed and fantasized about it, and to think that they were here now? Still that niggling sensation said it wasn't the right time. That they should push it off, and then she thought about the five years they'd already pushed off, and she slid her arms up his chest and around his neck and whispered, "Maybe you should"—then she kissed him on the chin, dropping a little tiny trail down his neck—"show me."

And suddenly she was lifted into the air, cradled against his chest, as he walked a few steps to the bunk. He gently lowered her on the mattress. She opened her arms. He shrugged and shook his head. "Too many clothes."

Her heart skimmed against her chest, constricting her breath even further, as he pulled the T-shirt over his head and quickly unbuckled his jeans, kicking off his boots and socks, and stepping out of his pants along with his briefs in the same motion. He was truly gorgeous. A well-built male in his prime and completely unselfconscious about it. She gave a happy sigh. Her body rippled with heat as she noted that his heavily muscled and otherwise incredible male form in truth matched up to the dreams that she'd had of him.

She tried to swing off the bunk, but he wouldn't let her. He sat down beside her, completely unconcerned about being naked, and pulled off her camisole. Next he slid her boy shorts underneath her butt and down, taking her panties with them. When the thin strip of hair showed up, he stopped, his breath catching in the back of his throat as a shudder wrapped itself around and down so visibly she could feel it herself.

When his hands slid under her plump breasts, he whispered, "My God, you're so beautiful."

She smiled, shook her head, and said, "No," she said, "not really. I'm fit. I'm slim, but I'm average."

His gaze heated up as he did one long, full, slow sweep of her body and said, "Sweetheart, I hate to tell you, but, for all that brainpower up there"—and he gently tapped her temple—"you have no clue just how devastating you are."

He lay down beside her, as if afraid to touch her, and just feasted his eyes. Embarrassed, she went to cover her breasts, and he immediately reached out to stop her. He leaned over a nipple, gently laving it with his tongue before taking it into his mouth and sucking deeply.

She moaned as her belly pulsed in response. She just knew Lennox would be slow and thorough. No way this would be a fast coupling. And, sure enough, he moved to thoroughly kiss the entire breast and to slide to the valley between them and to repeat his ministrations on the second one. She was already mindless jelly by the time he worked his way up to her collarbone, and then to her shoulders and under her neck, on to her chin, but he kept avoiding giving her the passionate kisses that she was so desperate to have. She tried to tug him toward her, but he resisted.

"We have all night," he whispered, "and I've waited too long to make this a rush job."

"Well, you can make it a rush job the first time," she

protested with a tiny smile. "The second time, we could take it slow."

"We'll take it slow the second time as well," he vowed.

And she groaned as his hands slid down her arms to gently stroke her fingers, her palms, and then back up the underside to glide along her rib cage as he plumped her breasts once again for feasting.

And then he slowly moved down her body.

She groaned and cried out, twisting as he gave her navel the same amount of care and intention as her breasts and then down to one hip bone, where he took tiny little nibbles.

She groaned. "I can't hold off."

"And why would you?" he asked, as he shifted enough to stroke the outside of her thigh to her feet where he picked up one foot and gently kissed her big toe before taking it in his mouth and suckled.

She groaned and then laughed and then groaned again as her body rippled in need, overwhelmed with awareness of every move he made. Every nerve ending was on fire. When he moved his hands up the inside of her thigh, she shifted her legs wide to give him access.

He gently stroked her curls and then slid one finger deep inside.

She gasped, her hips rising off the bed as he lowered his hand to find the tiny nub.

Without any warning, fireworks exploded in her belly, shooting outward. She cried out, shuddering in his hands.

He dropped kisses up her belly to her ribs and up under her chin before he shifted over her, holding his weight on his elbows as he lowered his head and finally kissed her full on the lips with mind-drugging passion.

She shifted her hips ever-so-slightly, sliding her heels up

the back of his calves and behind his knees, to wrap tightly around his hips. "More, I want more," she whispered. "Show me how you care."

And, with those words, he slipped inside her body.

She arched slowly up against him, pressing her breasts up against his muscular chest, as he seated himself deep within her.

She moaned, as her body stretched, easing at his complete possession.

He lowered his head and groaned, whispering, "I love you," he said ever-so-gently. "I think I always have."

And he ground his hips tight against hers and then slowly withdrew, only to drive in again. Shocked by his words, overwhelmed by her emotions, she could feel yet another orgasm rippling through her by his words alone. He wrapped her tight and drove both of them toward the cliff yet again.

Her heart was so damn full. Yet she realized she hadn't shared anything with him. She slid her arms up as he drove harder, deeper, faster. His eyes closed as he headed for his release. She reached up, snagged him by the ears, and whispered, "Look at me."

He stared down at her, not missing a stroke. His hot gaze focused on her. She realized the love in the gaze she recognized so damn well but had always thought it was something else. But, no, every time he looked at her, it had been with the same intensity.

She smiled. Her finger stroked across his lips as she whispered, "And I, I love you too."

He cried out as his body exploded with his climax.

And, just like that, his enjoyment sent her rolling back off the cliff yet again too. After that, she closed her eyes and dozed off. With she woke again, she was wrapped up in his arms.

He whispered, "Sleep."

She rolled over again, tucking up close, her legs entwined with his, and slept again. When she woke for the third time, he was coming out of the bathroom to join her. She looked up at him. "What time is it?"

"It's five," he whispered. "Go back to sleep."

And she was just too tired to argue. When she woke up the next time, she was alone. She sat up, looked around, winced from the unaccustomed soreness from her night of heavy lovemaking, slipped out of bed, and quickly put on her clothing. As she opened the door, she peered down the hallway, but she saw no signs of anyone. Grateful for that, she slipped across to her room and crawled into her bunk.

"If you think you can hide from me," Carolina said, with a chuckle in her voice, "you're wrong."

"Oh, God!" Helena said. "I was hoping you were still asleep."

"No, woke up in the night anyway," she said, "and I knew where you were."

"Are you mad?"

"If you were with anybody but my brother," she said, "I might be a little miffed, but I could never be mad at you."

"Well, I was with your brother," she said with a happy sigh, as she curled atop the covers and rolled over to face the wall. She didn't want to join the world. She just wanted to exist in her happy glow for a while longer.

"So why did you leave so fast?"

"Because he left," she said. "I didn't want to wake up and have somebody else come in."

"Ah," Carolina said. "Well, you might want to grab your shower now."

"Is that an option?"

"It sure is."

With that, Helena hopped up and headed into the bathroom, where she quickly stripped down and had a shower. She redressed in her same clothes from yesterday and brushed her hair, now freshly shampooed and towel dried as much as she could and then put it in a braid. "Well," Helena said. "Hopefully, this is okay." She stepped out of the bathroom.

Carolina asked, "Why wouldn't it be?"

"I don't know," she said. "I told him to use me as bait." And she explained some of what had happened with Lennox and first Stefano, then later with Rob, all at her apartment. "This Stefano guy seems to think that Lennox is the one who raped the girl in Thailand."

"And, of course, it was Rob."

"But, of course, Rob said that he was innocent. Somehow gave whatever proof that Stefano needed to seem to believe it was Lennox. Setting up Lennox at the same time. And I wonder if his whole thing about setting Lennox up wasn't to get to us," Helena said.

"Yeah, what's this about being completely smitten with you?"

"I don't see it," she said. "I think he just said that to throw Lennox off the trail. Likely drove him nuts at the same time."

"And maybe that's true," Carolina said, "but why?"

"All I think it is, is because he wanted me and possibly you at the same time back then," Helena said. "But I think it became more about destroying Lennox. To have him worry about what this known rapist would do to us."

"And, of course, the worst thought would be that he

brutalizes and rapes us and has our history repeating itself, but with the added edge of a rapist known to Lennox being in control of us, the two most important women in Lennox's life."

"Exactly. When you think about it, Rob's already sicced somebody very dangerous on Lennox. That Stefano guy. That's a lot of hate."

"Or Rob's just lost in that crazy mind of his, and he does think you're his girlfriend."

"I don't think so," Helena said. "I think, once we get to the truth of it, it'll be all about Stefano, the guy who's trying to take out Lennox. Just way too much about his revenge is at work here. I don't see this as a fatal attraction at all."

"That's because you don't see yourself," Carolina said. "You've always referred to me as gorgeous and beautiful, a China doll, and how stunning I was. And yet, for all the beauty and the brains that you have, you've never really understood just how gorgeous you are." Carolina's words were a reminder of what Lennox had said during the night.

Helena had to stop and wonder. "I don't feel beautiful," she said, "and, therefore, in my mind, I'm not beautiful."

"I understand that," she said, "but we can't let our exes make us into what they wanted us to be. Which were sluts in bed and ugly slaves the rest of the time."

"Isn't that the truth?" Helena said sadly. "I still don't see that I have any kind of beauty that would cause this kind of attraction."

"Well, you keep your theory, and I'll keep my mind open," she said. "But I still don't like the idea of you being bait."

"I don't know how it can work out any other way," Helena said. "While we're safe, the guys are chasing around after

Stefano and Rob in the city but getting nowhere. Sure, we know about facial-recognition software, traffic cameras, *blah, blah, blah*, but the bad guys are always a couple steps ahead of our good guys. I'm sure by now, our guys have tracked down the history of Rob's apartment in my building. They'll find out he never lived there, that he deliberately placed himself in those cameras. Misdirection or a decoy or whatever the reason. The apartment probably isn't even his. Maybe he just subleased it off some guy. Or he's living there without anyone knowing."

"Just to set the scene that you're dating him?"

"Yes," Helena said. "What bothers me more is this other guy, Stefano. How has he tracked us, and how is he so in the know as to what's going on with us? Then again, it's possible he had access to military intel himself. All these guys have connections," She sighed. "That was one of the things that worried Lennox."

"I would think so," Carolina said. "So, how well do you know Sasha and John?"

Helena walked toward Carolina with a frown and sat on the bottom bunk. "Are you serious?"

Carolina rolled over and propped herself up on one elbow. "Well, think about it. They've been with us for the last couple years that we've been doing Red Cross trips. And they happened to be on the same flight to Munich, letting everybody know where we were."

"They went home. We went a different way."

"But we still said we were going home, not necessarily where *home* was but back to the US."

She thought about it and nodded. "I guess it's possible," Helena said. She looked down at Carolina and her phone in her bag. "And I never even thought about it, but what are the chances that we're being tracked even now?"

"I don't know why they would have gone to the apartment, if that were the case. They would have tracked us to the safe house and then here, right?"

"True," Helena said. "I don't know. It's too damn confusing."

Just then a knock came on the door.

As Helena was closer, she walked over and opened it. Lennox stepped in, wrapped her up in a hug without giving her a chance to stop him, and kissed her thoroughly. As Carolina chuckled behind them, he finally lifted his head and said to Helena, "Good morning."

"Good morning," Helena said when she could finally speak. "Did you have to do that?"

Gavin stood behind Lennox, grinning.

"Absolutely," Lennox said. "This way, nobody is under any illusions about our relationship."

"And I didn't mean that," she said drily. "I meant, did you have to scramble my brains so early in the morning?"

And, at that, the rest of the room broke out laughing.

He grinned at her, leaned down, gave her another gentle kiss, and said, "How about the coffee?" he said. "As I recall, you're grumpy without enough coffee in you."

"Is she ever," Carolina said, hopping off the top bunk. "Come on. Let's get food too and set up a game plan. I really don't like the idea of you using her as bait."

"But I do," Helena said. "It's the only answer that makes any sense."

"It does make sense," Gavin said, "but I'm not a big fan of it either."

"And I also think," Helena continued, "that whole relationship spiel by Rob is BS. I think it's to throw you off your game. If he grabs me and potentially Carolina, it's to make us suffer as the Thai girl suffered. Just to get back at you."

At that, Lennox stopped and stared down at her.

She nodded. "Because he knows that, when you find out, you'll hit the red zone really fast and go after him."

"You're right," Lennox said in a suspiciously quiet voice. "I'm going to kill him."

And, at that, he turned and walked away.

LENNOX DIDN'T WANT to leave her to wake up alone, but he had had no choice. When he was called upstairs by Gavin, they had a lot of information coming in, and the biggest and most important was that both Stefano and Rob were still hanging around Helena's apartment area. They were quickly managing to stay ahead of cameras but had been spotted by a couple police cruisers. That chase had led them nowhere but was enough confirmation for Lennox to know that the two bad guys were in that area.

Now, as the group was seated at the table in the ship, and ended up with coffee and then food, Lennox smiled his thanks to the men who had delivered it all and said, "We'll be out of your hair soon."

"Too bad," one of the men said. "Helena and Carolina have been great to have on board."

"Good," he said. "I'm glad we're not putting you guys out."

The men just smiled and then walked away.

Lennox looked over at Helena. "More conquests?"

"Hardly," she said with a laugh.

"We'll see," he said. Lennox had a rough plan in his

mind, but he still needed to flesh it out. His phone buzzed. It was Keane. He handed over his phone to Gavin to read the text message.

He skimmed it and nodded.

"And what's that mean?" Helena asked.

"It's set up," Lennox said. "We're heading back to your apartment."

"I'm coming too," Carolina said.

He frowned at her, already shaking his head with veto power.

"No way I'm letting you take her into danger if I'm not there."

"Why? So you can be in danger too?" he said in exasperation. "You can stay here where you're safe."

"Ha!" Carolina said. "If she's going, I'm going."

"Not happening," Lennox said, his voice inflexible, at least he hoped so. "I have to look after too many things," he said. "My attention will be divided, and that'll put Helena and you and me and Gavin in danger."

She just glared at him. "What is it that you expect me to do then? Sit here and wait?"

"Well, that'd be nice if you would," he said, his voice serious as he stared at his sister intently.

"There are times to stick up for your sister," Carolina said.

"And there are times when you'll be in the way," Lennox parried.

At that, Helena grabbed Carolina's hand and said, "It's all right. I'll be fine. I'm sure Lennox and Gavin have backup lined up to be there too. Right?" Her gaze went from Gavin to Lennox.

"We have city police, and another unit from Coronado

will be there," Lennox said.

"Perfect!" She looked at Carolina. "Sit here and entertain these men while I'm gone," she joked. "It was on me last time. It'll be you this time."

Carolina looked at her, rolled her eyes, and said, "That's hardly fair. I get to be the entertainment while you get to be the main course."

Helena wrinkled her face up at that phrase. "That's not really a nice way to look at this."

Unfortunately, as far as Lennox was concerned, that was a little bit too real. As soon as they were done eating, he said, "We need to go."

She immediately stood and said, "I'm ready. So, is Carolina just sitting here with our gear?"

Lennox nodded. "We thought about taking her onshore, but we just can't take any chances of somebody snagging her too. She's safe here."

"Fine," Carolina said in a dark tone. "But you owe me."

He chuckled and hugged her, kissing his sister on the cheek. "Stay safe."

And, with that, he led the way down, where they disembarked on a small Zodiac that would take them to shore. Once they got back on the dock, they walked along the pier.

As they headed to the main parking lot, she asked, "Do you guys have wheels? And don't tell me that we're traveling in that neon-green Jeep."

"The Jeep is what we want right now," Gavin said. "We want to be seen."

She stayed quiet at that. "Okay," she said, "and I did eat, and I did have coffee, so I guess let's go and get this started."

Lennox looked at her, smiled, and kissed her gently. "It will be fine. I'll make sure nothing happens to you."

She rolled her eyes at him. "I have to trust that, if you came halfway across the world to save us, you'd keep me safe on home ground."

"Absolutely," he said. "Besides, now I've got an awful lot more reasons to keep you safe."

She flushed bright red as his laughter rolled through the Jeep. She shook her head and muttered, "Men." She stared out at the city around them.

He grinned. Life was pretty damn good right now. And it needed to stay damn good. Then the smile fell off his face. He would be pretty damn pissed if either of those men took away what he had waited five years for.

No way in hell he would let that happen.

CHAPTER 15

WITH LENNOX BESIDE her, she hopped out of the Jeep and looked up at her apartment. "You know something? For a long time," she said, "it looked like I would never come back here."

"I'm surprised you didn't rent it out," Lennox said.

"I didn't need the money," she said. "I always wanted to have it available, even for our breaks, even when we were going to Munich."

"That's what I mean. I thought you would have rented it," he said.

She shrugged. "I'm thinking about selling it."

"And buying something else or just not having a home base?"

"That was the problem. I did have a home base," she said, "but I never returned to it. The last two years I've only been here not even a handful of times."

"Well, you've been pretty busy traveling around the world."

"Yep," she said, yawning, "but that's coming to an end now too. So maybe I will be back here more often."

"More often or all the time?" he asked. He wrapped an arm around her shoulder and walked her toward the apartment building. She looked around but saw no sign of Gavin. She glanced up at Lennox sideways. "I presume eyes are on us?"

"Lots of them."

"It's a little too obvious, isn't it?"

"Isn't what too obvious?" he asked.

"Well, surely Rob and Stefano will be expecting surveillance."

"Yep, they will," he said, "which is why we have to be a little tricky."

She entered the security code, walked into the building as the door opened, and looked around. It felt foreign, yet familiar. "It doesn't feel like home anymore," she said abruptly.

"Particularly after all this mess," he said.

They took the stairs up to her second-floor apartment. As she walked down the hallway, she looked around and said, "I don't know any of the neighbors. I don't know anybody who even lives in the building."

"You haven't been here enough to make friends," he said. "You have to actually live in a place to meet your neighbors."

"Right." At her door, she looked at it and said, "I may not have my key with me." But she went through her purse, pulled out her wallet, and found her key. She popped it in and unlocked the door, and, as soon as it was open, Lennox stepped forward and entered first. With her following close behind, he walked in.

Helena put her purse down on the table and stared around that room. It was the refuge she'd built for herself after she had left her husband. For a retreat, nothing was friendly or cozy about it. Then she hadn't lived here enough to make it hers either. She needed a place stay, and this had been it. But, because the apartment wasn't home, she'd been more than happy to leave it behind. She shook her head at the vagaries of human nature and walked into her bedroom. As she opened up the closets, she found clothes that she'd forgotten about. She smiled as she pulled out several outfits and laid them on the bed.

"What are you doing?" Lennox asked.

She stopped, frowned, and then shrugged. "I guess I was picking up more clothes."

"Interesting," he said, but his voice turned to almost a growl, and he crossed his arms over his chest.

She looked up at him and frowned. "Why not? It doesn't feel like home," she said with a shrug. "I think I'd rather go to a hotel."

"Interesting," he said again, "because of Rob and Stefano both being in here?"

"Maybe," she said, "but you know what? The furniture I bought at a secondhand store, so it's not even what I wanted. I just needed a base after the divorce."

"Do you associate this place with the divorce?"

"I don't think so," she said slowly. "I don't know."

"But neither do you want to stay here, considering you're already packing up more clothes?"

She couldn't help herself from agreeing with that, as she walked back to her closet and pulled out a large suitcase. "I feel like I'm packing to leave," she said, "and I know I haven't really decided that, but it's what I feel like I need to do."

And she opened up the large suitcase, found a smaller one inside, and opened it up too. She proceeded to go through the clothing in her closet. Almost nothing was here. She'd taken a significant amount with her but, over time, had gotten rid of the excess and had only kept a few outfits because she wore scrubs most of the time. She packed up what there was, then went to the dresser, and sorted all that. And it still just barely filled the one suitcase. She looked around and said, "The place looks so sterile."

"Again because you haven't lived here."

"True," she said. "I don't want to live here either."

"And where do you want to live?" he asked, his tone curious, as if he wondered what she was doing.

She turned, looked at him, planted her hands on her hips, and asked, "Honestly?"

He nodded. "Yes, that's why I asked."

"With you." There, she'd said it. He had opened his heart up to her last night, and she hadn't had a chance to do very much in return. But, right now, in this cold empty apartment, it's how she felt.

He looked at her in surprise.

She raised both hands, then planted her fists on her hips. "And yet you don't say anything."

"Well, I'm a little stunned," he said slowly, as he walked toward her. His hands stretched out, reaching for hers.

"Well, you shouldn't be," she said crossly. "It's one of the reasons why I wanted to wait until this nightmare scenario was over."

"And I didn't want to wait," he said, tugging her into his arms. "And you're right. We've been heading for this moment for a long time, and there's no need for us to live apart."

She tilted her head back. "But I don't think we're ready for a commitment, like moving in together."

"I don't know about you," he said calmly, "but I am. And obviously you're not committed to staying here."

She looked around and said, "I feel like I've already removed the little bit that was me."

"I think so too. What about the bathroom? Do you have more in there? Because, when we leave today, we can leave permanently. We can get a company in to move all your furniture out. If you don't want any of it, maybe it can go to charity, or you can sell it."

"Not a bad idea," she said, brightening. "But," she said, turning to look back at him, "is it okay to move in with you? Do you live on base? Have you got a place of your own? What's going on in your life?"

And he laughed. "It's a good time to ask," he said, smiling at her. "I am in a new job, as you know," he stated. "I am still with the government, but it's black ops, so you won't ever hear too much information about the type of work I do. Sometimes I'll be home. Sometimes I'll be gone, but I have a home here."

"Good, I'll likely be gone too," she said. "A house or a townhome or what?"

He smiled, leaned over to kiss her nose, and said, "You'll find out."

She shrugged. "I'm good with that. I prefer a house over an apartment any day though." In the bathroom was a bottle of shampoo and conditioner and a couple creams, her toothpaste, and a pack of unopened toothbrushes. "Like I said, sterile." And she quickly packed up the little bits and pieces with the one suitcase still not quite full and the second one empty. She walked into the kitchen. "Maybe there's a coffeemaker," she said. "I think I have all that kind of stuff here."

He went ahead and opened up a few cupboards. "I see a few canned goods and a couple appliances," he said, "but not a whole lot else."

"And they're almost brand-new," she said. "Honestly I think some are still in the closet."

"What are?"

"The boxes that came with the appliances," she said. She walked over to the front closet. And she pulled it open, and there was the coffeemaker box and a toaster box and a coffee grinder box. He just laughed, grabbed them, and said, "Well, let's pack the appliances up in these too," he said. "You never know when you'll need a spare."

"Maybe we should make some coffee first," she said, and she quickly put on a pot. As she looked at him, she said, "How long do we wait?"

"We're here until ..." he said, and he didn't finish his sentence.

"Fine," she said. "That works." She had to avoid thinking about it. "We'll need lunch though."

He opened the fridge, but it was 100 percent empty, except for a box of baking soda. "There's not even ketchup or mustard packets here."

She shrugged. "Not exactly my thing."

"We can always order in."

"Or maybe we can walk down and pick up something too. After all, somebody has to have an opportunity to come in and grab me."

He just raised an eyebrow and shrugged.

She realized he already had plans but wasn't sharing them. She went through the kitchen cupboards and found a set of pots and some cutlery, but 90 percent of the cabinets were empty. This packing up activity pushed up bits and pieces in her memory. "I remember the last time I was here, about eight months ago," she said. "I was thinking how my home kitchen was like a hotel kitchenette. The basics but nothing personal."

"Did you walk away from your marriage with nothing?"

She shot him a shuttered look. "Mostly," she said. "I wanted nothing as a reminder. He wanted it all."

"I hope you got your fair share."

"I did," she said, "after the lawyers wrangled about it."

"He should have gone to jail."

"And I just wanted to walk away," she said. "Yes, he could have gone to jail, and we could have had a big trial and all the whole nasty mess of it," she said. "But he ended up with the house and all the contents, and I took the bank accounts. I was good with that."

"And then came a stern warning," Lennox said.

She stopped, slowly turned, looked at him, and said, "What stern warning?"

He just looked at her steadily.

"You?"

He shrugged. "How do you think I felt, finding out what he'd done to you for all those years? Years that I had wanted to be with you, and instead you were with him, with an asshole who used to take his temper out on you."

"Carolina's husband was worse than mine," she said slowly. "But I did learn what fear was, and that's something new in my life now."

"I'm so sorry," he said.

"I am too. It took me long enough to realize what was happening, with the verbal abuse—the bullying, the manipulation, the attack on my mind—but, once he really beat me up," she said, "I never went back. Up until then, it was just lots of threats and the odd smack and a grip that was a little too hard and a shove that was a bit too forceful. But, once he lost it, well, believe me, we were done."

"Good," he said. "He won't be beating up any other fe-male either."

"Did you scare him that badly?"

Again he just stared at her.

"Good," she said, her heart light, her voice cheerful. "I hope you punched him a good one for me."

"More than one. Pretty sure I identically bruised his body and inflicted the same damage on him that he inflicted on you."

She thought about that for a long moment, then smiled. "Thank you."

He gave a self-conscious shrug.

"No," she said, walking across the floor, stroking his cheek, before stretching up on her tiptoes to kiss him gently. "I mean, *thank you*. You did what I couldn't do."

He nodded. "Somebody needed to, and, if you wouldn't take him to court, he needed to know that his behavior wasn't acceptable and that he couldn't go around beating up women."

"He's one of those scaredy-cats. So, if you scared him right, he'll never touch another woman again," she said with a big grin.

Crack!

LENNOX THREW HELENA to the floor, her head coming down hard, only to land in his hand. She looked up at him in shock.

"Stay down," he said hoarsely. He raced to the living room window. Glass had shattered into the apartment. Standing where he was, he peered through the curtains, his phone out as he contacted Gavin. "Sniper's in the apartment building across from us," he said.

"We've got two cops over there," Gavin said.

"Well, somebody may have taken them out." He watched and saw a glint of light and said, "He's at the corner apartment."

"Yeah, that's not where the cops are," Gavin said. "I'll contact them to make sure they are okay. Are either of you hurt?"

"No," Lennox said. "Now the question is, *Who's the shooter? Rob or this Stefano guy?*" He turned to check on Helena. She curled around the kitchen counter, staring at him. "The shooter was on the apartment balcony across the street."

She nodded. "My first guess is Stefano. But then I doubt he'd miss. So maybe Rob?" She shrugged. "So, now what?"

"Well, it's a good thing you didn't want to stay here," he said. "Make sure you keep your shoes on."

"Is it safe to clean up the glass?"

"Not until we get the word that nobody is out there looking to take a second shot."

"And do you think they'll come here and check to see if they succeeded?"

"Somebody should," he said. "Why don't you take a cup of coffee and maybe just stay in your bedroom?"

"I can do that," she said. She walked over to the coffee-maker, quickly poured herself a cup of coffee, and headed back into the bedroom. She finished packing, even securing the smaller folding suitcase inside the larger one. She put it close to her bedroom door. That would go with her. She sat on her bed, intent on getting anything she really wanted during this trip. This visit would be her last one here. There was the bedding to pack up too.

She remembered she had a few moving boxes in the storage room too. She could use those to pack up the rest of her kitchen.

As she sat here, she realized that, if necessary, in an hour she could be completely packed up, and everything moved out. Such a bizarre feeling. She'd put a lot of time and effort into setting up her first marital home. That had been a complete wash by the end of two years of marriage. But she was okay with the mistake she'd made. She just didn't plan on making more like it. As she waited for Lennox to join her, a shadow fell across her bedroom doorway, and she still jolted.

"It's just me," he said in a calming tone.

"Of course it is," she said, taking a deep breath. She sat, frozen on the bed, and looked up at him. "It's just so weird."

"I know," he said, "but somebody has made a move, and that means people are jumping on it and trying to track him down."

"But is it the kidnapper or Rob?"

"I don't know," he said. "I'm expecting both to be here."

She smiled, nodded, and said, "I have empty boxes in my storage room downstairs. If we could get a few of those, we can have the entire kitchen and whatever else I've forgotten about all packed up and moved out right away. *Today.* A company can come in and move the few pieces of big furniture." As she looked around, she said, "I only have a dresser, a night table, and a bed in here. A couch and a chair in the living room, and that little kitchen table is folding."

"We can arrange for that later," he said.

"I guess that sniper shot means we can't get to the storage room and get those boxes, huh?"

He frowned, thought about it, and said, "You know that's a bad idea. Still, we can possibly meet our sniper head-on. Leave your suitcase here, grab your purse, and let's go down and take a look."

She frowned. "What are you expecting?"

"I'm not *expecting* anything," he said, "but we need to do something to shake them up."

"As long as you can protect me, I'm good with it," she said.

"Believe it or not, a half-dozen guys are here."

"I believe it," she said. "But I also know what these assholes are like. And I don't think they'll particularly care where they take me out, as long as they do."

"No," he said quietly. "It's not you they're after."

She stopped, frowned, looked at him, and whispered, "That bullet was for you, wasn't it?"

He nodded.

"Well then, I can go down to the storage locker, and you stay here." He just shot her a look, and she shrugged. "Otherwise we wait. Because it's you they're after. They're looking for an opportunity to take you out, and that is something I don't want to happen."

"Doesn't mean you've got a choice in it," he said.

She frowned. "But I should have a choice."

His phone buzzed then. He pulled it out, checked it, and said, "Gavin had one of the Coronado guys check the sniper's location and another to check on the cops in that building. No shooter was found in the apartment building on the far side of the street. The two cops are fine. They didn't see anyone."

"So this guy got into the apartments on the other side of the road, and the cops never saw him?"

"Exactly."

"Okay, so that's not good."

He shrugged.

When a knock came at her front door, she frowned and looked at him.

He said, "Don't answer it."

"But we need to," she said. The knock came again. And she hesitated. "What if I let him in?"

Lennox pulled a handgun from his back waistband and said, "Let me answer it." He walked up to the door and said, "Hello?"

"It's Gavin. Let me in."

Lennox opened the door and stepped back, and Gavin walked in with a couple bags of food.

"Believe it or not, I was just picking up lunch," he said, "when the shooting happened."

"Oh, good," she said. "I was hungry. There's glass everywhere though, so watch where you walk."

Gavin took a look at the glass doors, nodded, carried the bags to the kitchen table, and then looked around. "Are you guys okay? What's going on here?"

"We're packing me up," she announced. "I need the boxes from the storage room though."

He nodded. "I can go down and take a look. Where are they? Where's your storage locker?" Helena gave him instructions and the combination to the lock. "I'll be back in five," Gavin said, and he left again.

She looked at Lennox. "What's that look on your face for?"

He shrugged and walked over to the table.

She loved the smell of noodles. She quickly pulled out the containers, laughing because Gavin brought so much.

"Did he expect to feed the whole apartment building? Only three of us are here."

"Actually," Gavin said, "I thought you'd be hungry."

He was back awfully quick, and he had an odd tone to his voice. Lennox turned and swore. Because Stefano held a gun to Gavin's head.

"Move back," Stefano said, and he stepped in and closed the door behind him.

Lennox stood and stared at him. "So you took that pot shot at me through the living room window just now?"

Stefano nodded.

"I already told you that I had nothing to do with your sister."

Stefano nodded. "So you say. But I want proof."

"What kind of proof?" Lennox asked, swearing at the sudden turn of events.

"You need to tell me what happened to my sister."

At that, the tumblers clicked into place. "I can tell you," Lennox said, "but you won't like it." And he told him how he'd caught Rob with the girl in a hotel room. Lennox and Rob had been in town at the hotel's bar. Lennox rarely drank to the excess, but Rob had been on a weird bender lately, and he wanted to go out and get completely smashed. But halfway through the evening, he disappeared, taking an elevator up into the hotel itself. When Lennox had noticed, he'd gone looking for him, asking the hotel employees for any disturbance reports from the other guests in the hotel, and finally found Rob in a hotel room with a young girl. And he had already beaten her up badly. Lennox stopped him going any further.

"I spoke to my sister," Stefano said. "She says she doesn't know what he looked like, as he had a mask on."

"And it was dark, wasn't it?"

He nodded. "But now," he said, "now I can't tell whether it's you or Rob. Rob is one who told me it was you, and now you tell me it's Rob. I wanted to kill you earlier with my sniper round, but then realized I couldn't without knowing the answers."

"Of course Rob told you it was me," Lennox said, hearing the confirmation from Stefano. "Rob hates me and would do anything to punish me."

"So I have an answer to this problem," the kidnapper answered.

"I'm scared to ask, but what is your answer?"

The kidnapper grinned. "I will kill both of you. Immediately."

CHAPTER 16

H ELENA COULDN'T WRAP her mind around the
kidnapper's words. "How could you possibly think
that Lennox would have anything to do with a rape?" she
cried out.

Lennox tried to keep her back and out of the way, but
the kidnapper looked at her almost dispassionately. "He hurt
my sister," he said. "How can you think I wouldn't want
revenge?"

She opened her mouth and then slammed it shut because she knew precisely what Lennox had done to the two
men who had beaten up her and his sister. "I understand
that," she said quietly, "but what if you have the wrong
man?"

He just glared at her, then shrugged. "That's why I must
kill them both."

"And did you talk to your sister? Did you ask her for
details?"

"How can I possibly do that?" he cried out in frustration. "It's not like I'll have her dredge all that up again. It
hurts her."

"Of course it does, and I would hate to even imagine
what that would be like," she said. "But I do understand
what it's like to be beaten up, and I do understand what it's
like to be afraid of a man. What about his voice? Could she

say anything about that? Why was she in the hotel?"

His glare grew.

"Was she just traveling? Was she a tourist? What was she doing?"

"She was visiting my brother, who was teaching English there. She woke up to Lennox here in the room with her."

"And how do you know it was Lennox?"

"She said it was Lennox."

"Meaning, the guy *said* his name was Lennox?"

Stefano nodded.

"So a rapist went into a young woman's room, used her badly, left her beaten, and then told her what his name was?"

He stopped, shaking his head. "I don't know how it came out," he said, "but she found out that was his name."

"That's the name he *used*," she said. "That doesn't mean it was his name."

He glared at her silently.

"She didn't say anything about his hair, about the size of his hands, his scars?"

"I didn't ask," he said. "She was adamant. It was Lennox who had beaten her up."

"Okay," she said, "you got your sister's number on your phone?"

"I'm not calling her," he said calmly. "I'll just take them both out, and then I'll know for sure I got the right one."

"And how would your sister feel if you killed a completely innocent man?"

"She won't know."

"Maybe not," Helena said. "Maybe I'll contact her after this and let her know what you did."

Immediately the gun turned in her direction.

"So it's not about revenge," she said. "It's just about being another one of the assholes responsible for getting your sister raped."

Fury lit his face.

She nodded. "You're not here because of what somebody did to your sister. You're here because you couldn't protect your sister."

The shock from her verbal blow was a direct hit.

She nodded again. "I get that," she said, "but, if you were protecting your sister back then, you wouldn't now be looking to face down the man who physically hurt her," she said quietly. "This is not that man."

"So, because you love him, you defend him."

"Of course I love him. And, yes, I defend him," she said. "But I can tell you that he's not the rapist. I spent two years at the hands of a man who beat me up. I know the difference."

And, for the first time, she saw Stefano waver.

"I understand the feeling of violation," she said. "I understand the feeling of betrayal. But I don't understand why you would think it was Lennox, just because the man who raped her says it was Lennox." She nodded, motioning at Stefano's neck. "What do all the scars on your face have to do with this?"

"That's why I know it was Lennox," he said, but his voice lacked conviction.

"What are you talking about?" she asked.

"I was there too, and she called me, screaming, and I chased him down. This is from a bullet," he said, reaching for his cheek. "And the burns are from when he brought a shed down on top of me."

"And what about him? Did he get any injuries from all that?"

He nodded. "I shot him." And he glanced at Lennox.

"Where did you shoot him?" Helena asked quietly, having seen all of Lennox in his beautiful naked glory the night before.

"In his side," he said.

"So then, if I show you Lennox's side, and you see no bullet wound, will you believe that it's not him?"

Again the gun wavered.

She walked over to Lennox and said, "Sorry, sweetie," as she lifted his T-shirt to the middle of his chest. Then she showed Stefano. "No bullet wound. On either side of Lennox."

The man stared at Lennox, stared all along his waist, and then back up at his face. But obviously Stefano was confused. "You're a different shape," he said, but everyone in the room could tell that Stefano was still trying to fit what he wanted to believe into his hypothesis.

"It wasn't Lennox," she said. "And I understand that you're angry and that you're upset and that you desperately want to take down the man who hurt your sister, but it wasn't Lennox."

Stefano gave a harsh sigh and slowly lowered his gun and gave Gavin a hard shove, pushing him farther into the apartment. "Then who was it? Rob?"

"Yes," Lennox said. "Rob raped your sister. I'm the one who turned him into the military police. He went to jail because of me. And now we're after him because he's after my girlfriend," Lennox said quietly.

The kidnapper looked at Helena.

She nodded. "Thanks to you, three others and I were kidnapped and carted off to Poland," she snapped. "Held in a damn cage for a couple days. Terrorized and, at the same time, found out that Rob was the one behind all of it, and he's still trying to kill Lennox to get his hands on me. All as payback to Lennox."

Stefano frowned.

"You've been used," she said. "What I'm trying to say is that, Rob is trying to get you to take out Lennox so that it leaves the field clear for Rob to get me."

"Why would he want that?"

She gave a half laugh. "That's what I keep telling people. I don't know why. I'm not some femme fatale."

Stefano just waved it off. "But why would he want somebody else to do his killing?"

"Because he's not a killer," Lennox said. "When the circumstances demanded that, while we both were in the navy, he would step up to the plate and do it, but he's not a cold-blooded killer, and we were friends once," he said. "We were friends until I took him to court over what he did to your sister."

The man's eyes widened in shock. "You're the one who had him punished? You're the one who sent him to jail?"

He nodded. "Yes, that's why he hates me. That's why he told you and somehow convinced you that I'm the one who hurt your sister. And how did you hear that?"

"In jail," he said. "Our younger brother was there. With him—with Rob, who was unfairly accused. But I never saw Rob's face."

"No, he wasn't *unfairly* accused," Helena said calmly. "He was justly accused."

"And that's why you also said it wasn't me in this apartment earlier," Lennox said, as if finally understanding. "Because you already had a battle with Rob, and you knew his body and where your shot hit him, but you still didn't know his face, but then you couldn't fit my body type in with your memories."

Slowly Stefano nodded. "I don't like being used."

"Do you think your brother had anything to do with it?"

He frowned. "There's a reason my brother was in jail."

"Right," she said, "because he's not trustworthy."

Lennox added, "Maybe he had something to do with this. Maybe Rob paid him?"

Stefano frowned, took a step back, and said, "I must think about this."

"You do that," Lennox said. "And maybe don't point that gun at me or mine again, much less shoot at me. I've given you a couple passes for waving that gun around. But after that shot across the road into this apartment, I won't give you another one."

The two men gazed at each other; their expressions were hard and determined.

Stefano made one clipped nod and disappeared into the hallway. They could hear his footsteps running.

Gavin and Lennox looked at each other. It's almost as if they made a silent joint decision to not go after Stefano.

Helena spun around and said, "He still kidnapped me. Doesn't that count?"

Lennox grabbed her, tucked her up close, and said, "Yes, it counts. And how do you feel about punishing him, now that you have more details?"

And she realized what he was saying because it wasn't just about punishing Stefano for what he was doing. It was about his motivation behind his actions. He had simply wanted justice for his sister.

And that's precisely what Lennox would have done for both his sister and for Helena. And so, in his mind, he was already saying this Stefano guy did not need to be punished. If she didn't agree, he needed to know now because it would be part of the elements that built their ongoing relationship. She sagged against him and said, "Well, he's just damn lucky he didn't hurt any of us."

"I know," he murmured against her hair, holding her close. "What we need to do is find his brother."

"He is, hopefully, still in jail."

"Also," Gavin said, "I managed to get a tracker on Stefano."

Lennox grinned at him. "Perfect audio?"

Gavin held up his phone, which even now crackled as it began to receive. "We've got audio."

"Any chance we can eat now?" Helena asked. They walked to the table, and she could feel exhaustion hitting her. "How do you deal with all this adrenaline?" she asked, as she served herself up food. Just then a voice came over Gavin's phone. She didn't understand the language, but Lennox immediately brought his phone out and recorded it. As soon as the call was finished, he sent the file to somebody. "Are you getting that translated?"

"I am," he said. "An awful lot of yelling and shouting went on there."

"Yeah," she said. "I suspect my kidnapper contacted his brother for clarification."

"Yes," Lennox said. "That would be my take on it too."

She reached for a fork and dug into a large bowl of noodles. "At least we've got food." She beamed at Gavin.

Gavin smiled and said, "You keep your head remarkably well in these situations."

"So do you," she said. "I'm not the one who had a gun at my head."

"Maybe not," he said. "But it was pretty intense. How do you get that kind of experience?"

"Sometimes our circumstances when we're operating overseas are pretty intense too," she said. "I'm a surgeon, and I do very well under pressure."

Gavin studied her for a long moment, then nodded. "You're a good person to have around then."

"Glad to hear it. What's next?" She forked up noodles and chewed as she listened to the men.

"Maybe," he said, "the bottom line is, we make sure that we find Rob. Because, if this Stefano guy finally understands how he's been taken, he'll go after Rob too."

"I'm not against that," Lennox said. "Saves me from doing the job."

"In a way, it's the best of both worlds," Helena said. "Stefano gets his revenge. Rob gets what's due to him. And we get off scot-free."

Lennox looked at her and smiled and said, "You really do have that fairy-tale thing going on, don't you?"

"Absolutely," she said. "Just think about it. The fairy tales are coming true in so many other ways. Why not this one too?"

GAVIN ROLLED HIS eyes.

Lennox chuckled. "Poor Gavin. You'll find yours."

"My what?" he asked. "Revenge?"

"Partner," she said.

"Well, I hope I don't have to wait five years to make a move on her," he said in disgust.

At that, she burst out laughing. "Good point." She

reached for one of the other cartons and said, "You going to finish that?"

Lennox watched as she dug into the food. "Do you always eat this much?"

"Sometimes," she said. "I do like my groceries." And she plowed into a big dish of veggies. As she ate, she looked up at him and said, "Now we can get the boxes from the storage room, and we can finish packing up. What are we expecting to happen from here on in?"

"Rob," Lennox said. "We still need Rob."

"He obviously still has a lot of anger for you."

"I messed up his life."

"No," she said, "*he* messed up his own life. You just made him pay for it."

"Means the same thing to Rob," Lennox said.

She shrugged at that. "So what do we do to bring in Rob?"

"Not sure," Lennox said. "But I don't suspect we'll have to wait long to find out." He got up and piled the empty cartons in the to-go bag and asked, "Where's the outdoor garbage?"

"Down the hallway," she said. "A big bin drops down to the Dumpster in the basement."

"Good," he said. "I'll take this load out, so we don't have to worry about it later. And I'll swing down below and grab the cardboard boxes."

She nodded.

And he stood, he packed up everything that he could for the garbage, then stepped outside, checked that the hallway was empty, and walked toward the chute. He dumped the trash and then opened the stairwell and ran down to the basement floor. He'd already been in her apartment building and had checked out this level earlier and hadn't found anything of any value. Only a whole roomful of locked up chain-link-style lockers. So no walls to hide behind but plenty of junk to do the job.

That meant a ton of places where somebody could hide, but it wouldn't have been the most comfortable of spots, so Rob would have to choose his poison. Plus it didn't make for easy access, unless Rob left one of the storage units unlocked. Still, that would give away his hiding spot pretty easily.

So Rob rented an apartment here as a foil, just to have a hiding spot in his—or someone else's—storage locker? That could work. That could explain where he disappeared to when the cops were after him, when Lennox had trailed him out his own apartment's patio doors.

Lennox walked to the unit that was hers, used the combination lock, and quickly opened it. He wondered at a woman who kept packing boxes. Grabbing up one large bundle, he moved it out and quickly locked up. Nothing else was in here, just the packing boxes. He shook his head and muttered, "She really wasn't planning on staying."

"Maybe not," a man said from the shadows, "but I could have persuaded her to."

Lennox froze. He turned to see Rob, standing in front of him, with a handgun drawn. "Wow," he said. "This is a little repetitive."

"Hardly," Rob said. "I'm surprised you're still alive."

"Why? Because of your buddy?"

Rob shrugged. "Much better to have a very dedicated and motivated killer coming after you," he said. "Chances are you and I would be equal, but that guy looked like he might even have us beat," Rob said with a laugh.

Lennox thought about Stefano. "He's active military.

Just not our country."

"Of course not," Rob said. "Not even sure what country he is. I think his sister was Norwegian."

"But you didn't care, did you?"

He shrugged. "Nope, I was just looking for a good time. Needed to work off a little lust."

"And how is it that you think a good time is beating up that poor girl as badly as you did?"

Rob grinned widely, a wild look in his eyes.

"But that didn't stop you, did it? And it doesn't matter how young she was either," Lennox said. "You still beat her up and raped her."

"I like rough sex," Rob said. "I'm looking forward to playing with Helena."

"So all that talk about wanting Helena for yourself, … what's that about?"

"Well, I do want her for myself," he said, "but I was just trying to throw you off your stride."

"By telling lies and false tales?"

"Sure, why not?" he said. "Besides, it's not that far off," he said. "I've been fascinated with her ever since I saw her the first time. Unfortunately, that night that I met her, she was already in a tight clench with you. Hence the need to work off some lust."

"So you were interested then?"

"Absolutely," he said. "She's dynamite. But she's also definitely yours, and that made me really angry. Because, if I'd just met her earlier, she wouldn't have given a shit about you."

"She doesn't like rough sex," Lennox said. "So that wouldn't work with her." The fact that he was even talking about Helena with this guy made Lennox furious.

"She's gorgeous, and why the hell should you have her?" Rob snapped. "And then, after what you did to me," he continued, "I couldn't think of anything else. I just wanted to make sure she was mine, that you knew it, and that you died knowing it. And I'm the one who'll be banging her forever, not to mention having the occasional punch up," he sneered.

"Over my dead body," Lennox said.

"Exactly," Rob said, with a big smile. "I wouldn't have it any other way."

"Asshole," Lennox said. His gun was in his waistband tucked in the back. But it would be that much harder to get to, considering Rob already pointed his gun on him. Lennox needed a diversion. "Don't you ever have any remorse about how you hurt that poor girl?"

"She's just a woman," Rob said. "I've had lots of them too. That one, in Thailand though, I don't know why, but I just needed to tear her up a bit. Helena needs to get to know me, and she'll adapt to my ways soon enough."

"Helena and I have known each other since we were kids," Lennox said quietly. "She's been my sister's best friend forever."

And that stopped Rob in his tracks. "Really?"

"Yes," he said, "really."

"Oh, well, it doesn't matter," he said. "If you're not around, she'll turn to me."

"She knows what you've done," Lennox said. "She knows that you raped and beat up that girl and turned her brother to try and kill me."

"Well, yeah, but I didn't do it on my own," he said. "His brother was in the same jail."

"And why is that?"

"Because they were over there together at the same time. And his brother was doing drugs. Got picked up and tossed into jail. His sister was raped because the druggie younger brother was supposed to be sharing the same suite with her and wasn't there to protect her, and the older brother was off at a meeting or something. He wasn't there to protect either of them. So the younger brother turned on the charm and the guilt to make older brother believe that it was you who had hurt her. And that, if the older brother didn't finally get in the act and defend the two of them, then their lives were all completely ruined because of *you*, Lennox."

"How could you even do that to some guy? He's out there, fighting for his country." Lennox saw yet another parallel between Stefano and himself. "Doing the right thing. Here he's got a shitty brother who was supposed to be protecting his younger sister, a sister who got beaten up and raped by an asshole, and then you prime up that guy, and you turn him in my direction."

"Right?" Rob said, laughing. "It's perfect."

"Not perfect," another man said from behind Rob.

Rob froze and backed up flat against the storage units, so he could face the new threat. And there was the kidnapper, Stefano. Lennox quickly pulled the gun from the back of his waistband and pointed it at Rob. "Now what will you do, Rob?" he asked. "There's two of us now."

Rob glared at Stefano and asked him, "What's your problem? Lennox is the one who beat up your sister."

"No," Stefano said, his voice heavy. "I spoke with my brother."

"Oh, that lying little weasel," Rob cried out nervously. "You know he's nothing but a drug pusher, right?"

"I know," Stefano said. "And I kept thinking that maybe

he would get better. He'd been teaching English and doing well, then started to slide. That's why my sister was there visiting him. We knew he was struggling again, and we thought having her there would help."

"And yet," Rob said, "she got badly hurt there too because of Lennox here." Rob motioned his gun in Lennox's direction.

But Stefano shook his head. "No," he said. "I talked to Lennox, and then I talked to her. I already realized that it wasn't Lennox when I initially met him in the apartment here. But I had to go back and talk to my brother to make sure."

"How could you know it wasn't him?" Rob said. "He was there. I saw him." And this time, Rob's voice was getting out of control and echoed throughout the locker room.

Lennox knew Gavin would have noticed how long he'd been gone by now too.

"Because I shot him. *You*," Stefano said. "We raced through the streets, and you ended up torching the small shed we were in, and it went up in flames, *then I shot you*."

Rob shook his head. "Dude, I don't know what you're talking about. It wasn't me. It was Lennox."

"Even though I was badly burned, I know that I hit you with my shot," he said. "I suffered for the burns and for the bullet hole in my cheek," he said. "That's also why we stayed in Thailand for as long as we were, so I could get treated. My brother was then too scared to say anything because he was afraid you would come back after him."

"And again I think you're misguided," Rob said with a light laugh. "That was Lennox, remember? It's all Lennox."

"My brother made it very clear. He overdosed and was saved and was in the hospital recently, since he got out of jail. He's been a much different person."

"When did this happen?" Rob said in a derisive tone. "Your brother is nothing but a drunken user. A junkie."

"Yes, to all of that," he said, "but now he is going home, and we will work to make his recovery happen. This was just a few days ago. After you resurrected this mess. That's why he had an overdose. Because he realized what he'd done."

"He hadn't done anything," Rob said.

"Yes, he did. He directed me to the wrong man. On purpose. And for what? For money? For drugs? Drugs that he then took and overdosed on. He'll turn over a new leaf," Stefano announced, his accent thick, guttural.

"No," Rob said. "He's nothing but a useless man."

"No," Stefano said. "He has time. He is young. He can make a better life."

"Then I should have killed him," Rob snarled.

"Yes," Stefano said, "you should have. And you should have killed me."

"I can do that now," Rob said.

But Stefano immediately cocked his weapon and said, "I don't think so." Instead of killing Rob, he shot once, and Rob's knee exploded, and he went down screaming.

Immediately Lennox turned his gun on Stefano. "He's down," Lennox said. "In our country, we don't shoot men who are down."

"I know," Stefano snarled. "You're weak too." But he held his gun on Lennox as he walked closer to Rob. Then he crouched in front of Rob and said, "I want you to take that gun of yours, and I want you to put it against your own head," he said.

Rob was crying as he shook his head. "You're nuts! You're crazy!"

"No," Stefano said. "I'm not. But now I see clearly. And I know that you are as bad as my brother said. And that you are the one who raped my sister."

"You could fucking ask her."

"I did," Stefano said slowly. "And she confirmed what I already knew. It was not Lennox."

"How the hell could she know that?" Rob asked, moaning, his hand on his knee.

"Because you are not shaped like him."

Lennox realized his massive upper chest in this instance was as good a descriptor as his height and his hair and eye color. Because it confirmed the moment of truth that they all needed here. Lennox walked to Rob and gently took his handgun from him. Lennox reached down and lifted Rob's T-shirt. "Do you see?"

Stefano looked at the scar on Rob's side, from when he shot him, nodded slowly, and said, "Yes, I see." He punched Rob hard with his fist. Stefano stood, looked down at Lennox, and said, "Now what?"

"I'm not sure," Lennox said honestly. "I need to know you're not coming after me again."

"No," he said. "I'm not."

"And Rob?"

"He needs to die," Stefano said calmly.

"Well, he does," Lennox said. "But, if you do that, then it's murder, and that's a whole different story."

"You will protect him even now? After what he's done against you?"

"It's not that as much as our level of honor involved in this," he said quietly. "Rob is a mess. He needs to go to jail for the rest of his life," he said, "but I still need answers."

"What answers could you need?" Rob muttered as he

came around. "There's nothing else to tell you. I hated your fucking guts, and I wanted this guy to kill you. As a plus I would take Helena as mine. And I would beat her up and bash the shit out of her whenever I wanted to. Just for the fun of knowing that you couldn't stop me."

"I get that," Lennox said, as he stared down at Rob. "Which means you'll always be a threat to her."

He laughed and laughed again. "What will you do? Honorable Lennox won't shoot a man who's down," he said. "It's not who you are."

"Maybe this is a good time to make an exception," Lennox said, but he was torn. "How did you keep track of her all this time?"

"Besides Stefano's intel? John," he said. "And Sasha. Individually. I paid them both."

"They were *both* involved?" Lennox had been afraid of that and already had the Mavericks running the financials on those two. Hearing this would hurt both Helena and Carolina, but Lennox would put in a good word to have both of them thrown in some Polish prison, to keep the Red Cross from getting any fallout because of their greed.

"Yes. And you should have heard them rant and rave at me separately when they found themselves kidnapped by this guy."

"Wow," Lennox said. "The Red Cross will really have a fun time cleaning up the rest of their staff, won't they?"

"I thought Sasha and John would both quit after this anyway because they figured they would get found out eventually."

"Yes," Lennox said. "I'll pay them a visit too."

"Of course you will," Rob said. "You might as well just shoot me," he said. "It'll be easier that way."

"No," Lennox said. "I'm not doing the job."

Stefano squatted beside Rob and held out his gun. "You can do the job yourself. None of us want you around anymore."

Rob glared at him, snatched the handgun from Stefano's hand.

Immediately Lennox held his gun to Rob's head.

"I'm not shooting him," Rob said. "But I'll be damned if I go back to a fucking jail again." And he shoved the gun on his jaw and pulled the trigger.

Silence.

Stefano stood, looked down at the body, and said, "It's the best way."

"Only raises another mess of questions," Lennox said, "because of that handgun. *Your* handgun."

"I will leave it behind," he said. He had gloves on, and he held them up and said, "They won't trace it to me."

"Then you better leave," Lennox said quietly, but a hard look was in his eye. "And make sure I don't see your ass ever again," he said, "or it's mine."

Stefano gave him a ghost of a smile. "Enjoy the years with your woman," he said. "And, if you ever see any more assholes like this guy ..."

"I'll do the same thing I did last time," Lennox said. "I'll report him to the authorities and will make sure he gets punished for what he did."

Stefano nodded. "It's much better for everyone that Rob's gone." And, with that, Stefano melted into the shadows and disappeared.

EPILOGUE

"**A**RE YOU SURE I can't look now?" Helena complained good-naturedly, her eyes shut.

"No," Gavin said. "You don't get to look at anything right now."

"That's not fair," she said. Gavin had her in the passenger side of his Jeep. They were heading to Lennox's, and Lennox and Carolina were expecting them.

"And we would have been here a long time ago," Gavin said, "but you're the one who wanted to stop and get flowers."

"Of course I did!" she said, as her arms tightened around the big bouquet. "It's my first visit to Lennox's house."

"Hardly a visit," he said. "You're moving in."

"I am," she said, a blissful smile on her face.

Lennox was, indeed, a lucky man, Gavin thought. He didn't know how the hell these two had finally gotten past their differences, but they had, and that's what counted. And now here Gavin was, taking her to Lennox's house, while she took her first step into their future. Gavin pulled up to the front, parked, and said, "Now I'm coming around to your side."

"Okay, okay," but she hopped out impatiently and waited for him to grab her arm. As they got to the sidewalk, he said, "Now you can open your eyes."

She looked up to see the stone-and-cedar Tudor house in front of them for her very first time, one that Gavin had seen many times. "Oh, my goodness," she said, "it's gorgeous."

The door opened, and Lennox stepped out. She cried out, handed off the flowers to Gavin right before she raced forward. Lennox opened his arms, and she dashed into them. Lennox picked her up and swung her around in his arms.

Gavin stood back and smiled up at them. "You two look perfect together," he declared.

"Good," Lennox said. "It's taken Carolina and me a couple days to get everything ready."

Gavin nodded. His phone went off just then. "Hang on. I'll be there in a minute."

"Don't bother," Lennox said. "I can tell you all about it."

He looked at his phone and back at his buddy and asked, "What is it?"

"The next job," Lennox said. "I've got your orders here. I was going to hand them to you before the call came through, but you guys were late."

Gavin laughed. "Am I going alone?"

"No," Lennox said, "you're going with a friend. You just don't know which one."

"And you?"

"I'm running ground crew," Lennox said with a grin. "I get to stay here with my beautiful Helena."

"Okay, that'll be pretty sucky on my part but perfect for you. Do I get to come inside for a bit before I head out?"

"Sorry, bud."

Just then a military vehicle pulled up to the front of the house.

Lennox held out a brown envelope to Gavin and then pointed. "That's your ride."

"What about my gear?"

"It's all waiting for you." Lennox turned Helena around and said, "Say goodbye to Gavin."

She lifted a hand, confusion on her face.

Gavin smiled and said, "I'll be back."

"We'll wait for you," she said.

He shook his head. "Don't bother. I won't be back for days yet. Have a good one." And he hopped into the truck and headed off. He had the brown envelope from Lennox, but that's all he had. He looked at the driver and asked, "What are your orders?"

"I'm taking you to the dock," he said. "A destroyer's waiting for you."

"Any other details?"

"None," he said.

"Fine, let's go." Gavin was headed somewhere; he just didn't know where yet. And maybe that was okay too.

This concludes Book 10 of The Mavericks: Lennox.

Read about Gavin: The Mavericks, Book 11

The Mavericks: Gavin (Book #11)

What happens when the very men—trained to make the hard decisions—come up against the rules and regulations that hold them back from doing what needs to be done? They either stay and work within the constraints given to them or they walk away. Only now, for a select few, they have another option:

The Mavericks. A covert black ops team that steps up and break all the rules ... but gets the job done.

Welcome to a new military romance series by *USA Today* best-selling author Dale Mayer. A series where you meet new friends and just might get to meet old ones too in this raw and compelling look at the men who keep us safe every day from the darkness where they operate—and live—in the shadows ... until someone special helps them step into the light.

When four members of one family-owned corporation are kidnapped off the streets in Honolulu, Gavin's intel says this is a corporate espionage case ... but is it?

There's not much to like about this case. Too many people are involved, ... including an old friend of Gavin's. But, as Gavin digs deeper into the motives of the suspect pool, events get uglier, and bodies start to fall.

Rosalina has no idea how she ended up in this nightmare, but all she cares about is her ailing parents who have been separated from her and her sister. Even when she and her sister are freed, Rosalina finds no sign of their mother or father. Trying to rescue them means deciphering friend from foe ...

It comes down to the wire as this close family corporation falls apart, revealing the core of darkness inside, ... and leaves Gavin and Rosalina struggling to stay safe as enemies work to take out them both.

Find book 11 here!

To find out more visit Dale Mayer's website.

https://geni.us/DMGavinUniversal

Author's Note

Thank you for reading The Mavericks, Books 9–10! If you enjoyed the book, please take a moment and leave a short review.

Dear reader,

I love to hear from readers, and you can contact me at my website: www.dalemayer.com or at my Facebook author page. To be informed of new releases and special offers, sign up for my newsletter or follow me on BookBub. And if you are interested in joining Dale Mayer's Reader Group, here is the Facebook sign up page.
http://geni.us/DaleMayerFBGroup

Cheers,
Dale Mayer

About the Author

Dale Mayer is a *USA Today* best-selling author, best known for her SEALs military romances, her Psychic Visions series, and her Lovely Lethal Garden cozy series. Her contemporary romances are raw and full of passion and emotion (Broken But … Mending, Hathaway House series). Her thrillers will keep you guessing (Kate Morgan, By Death series), and her romantic comedies will keep you giggling (*It's a Dog's Life*, a stand-alone novella; and the Broken Protocols series, starring Charming Marvin, the cat).

Dale honors the stories that come to her—and some of them are crazy, break all the rules and cross multiple genres!

To go with her fiction, she also writes nonfiction in many different fields, with books available on résumé writing, companion gardening, and the US mortgage system. All her books are available in print and ebook format.

Connect with Dale Mayer Online

Dale's Website – www.dalemayer.com

Twitter – @DaleMayer

Facebook Page – geni.us/DaleMayerFBFanPage

Facebook Group – geni.us/DaleMayerFBGroup

BookBub – geni.us/DaleMayerBookbub

Instagram – geni.us/DaleMayerInstagram

Goodreads – geni.us/DaleMayerGoodreads

Newsletter – geni.us/DaleNews

Also by Dale Mayer

Published Adult Books:

Hathaway House
Aaron, Book 1
Brock, Book 2
Cole, Book 3
Denton, Book 4
Elliot, Book 5
Finn, Book 6
Gregory, Book 7
Heath, Book 8
Iain, Book 9
Jaden, Book 10
Keith, Book 11
Lance, Book 12
Melissa, Book 13
Nash, Book 14
Owen, Book 15
Hathaway House, Books 1–3
Hathaway House, Books 4–6
Hathaway House, Books 7–9

The K9 Files
Ethan, Book 1
Pierce, Book 2
Zane, Book 3

Lovely Lethal Gardens, Books 3–4
Lovely Lethal Gardens, Books 5–6
Lovely Lethal Gardens, Books 7–8
Lovely Lethal Gardens, Books 9–10

Psychic Vision Series
Tuesday's Child
Hide 'n Go Seek
Maddy's Floor
Garden of Sorrow
Knock Knock…
Rare Find
Eyes to the Soul
Now You See Her
Shattered
Into the Abyss
Seeds of Malice
Eye of the Falcon
Itsy-Bitsy Spider
Unmasked
Deep Beneath
From the Ashes
Stroke of Death
Ice Maiden
Psychic Visions Books 1–3
Psychic Visions Books 4–6
Psychic Visions Books 7–9

By Death Series
Touched by Death
Haunted by Death
Chilled by Death
By Death Books 1–3

Broken Protocols – Romantic Comedy Series
Cat's Meow
Cat's Pajamas
Cat's Cradle
Cat's Claus
Broken Protocols 1-4

Broken and... Mending
Skin
Scars
Scales (of Justice)
Broken but... Mending 1-3

Glory
Genesis
Tori
Celeste
Glory Trilogy

Biker Blues
Morgan: Biker Blues, Volume 1
Cash: Biker Blues, Volume 2

SEALs of Honor
Mason: SEALs of Honor, Book 1
Hawk: SEALs of Honor, Book 2
Dane: SEALs of Honor, Book 3
Swede: SEALs of Honor, Book 4
Shadow: SEALs of Honor, Book 5
Cooper: SEALs of Honor, Book 6
Markus: SEALs of Honor, Book 7
Evan: SEALs of Honor, Book 8
Mason's Wish: SEALs of Honor, Book 9

Heroes for Hire

Logan's Light: Heroes for Hire, Book 6
Harrison's Heart: Heroes for Hire, Book 7
Saul's Sweetheart: Heroes for Hire, Book 8
Dakota's Delight: Heroes for Hire, Book 9
Michael's Mercy (Part of Sleeper SEAL Series)
Tyson's Treasure: Heroes for Hire, Book 10
Jace's Jewel: Heroes for Hire, Book 11
Rory's Rose: Heroes for Hire, Book 12
Brandon's Bliss: Heroes for Hire, Book 13
Liam's Lily: Heroes for Hire, Book 14
North's Nikki: Heroes for Hire, Book 15
Anders's Angel: Heroes for Hire, Book 16
Reyes's Raina: Heroes for Hire, Book 17
Dezi's Diamond: Heroes for Hire, Book 18
Vince's Vixen: Heroes for Hire, Book 19
Ice's Icing: Heroes for Hire, Book 20
Johan's Joy: Heroes for Hire, Book 21
Galen's Gemma: Heroes for Hire, Book 22
Zack's Zest: Heroes for Hire, Book 23
Bonaparte's Belle: Heroes for Hire, Book 24
Heroes for Hire, Books 1–3
Heroes for Hire, Books 4–6
Heroes for Hire, Books 7–9
Heroes for Hire, Books 10–12
Heroes for Hire, Books 13–15

SEALs of Steel
Badger: SEALs of Steel, Book 1
Erick: SEALs of Steel, Book 2
Cade: SEALs of Steel, Book 3
Talon: SEALs of Steel, Book 4
Laszlo: SEALs of Steel, Book 5

Geir: SEALs of Steel, Book 6
Jager: SEALs of Steel, Book 7
The Final Reveal: SEALs of Steel, Book 8
SEALs of Steel, Books 1–4
SEALs of Steel, Books 5–8
SEALs of Steel, Books 1–8

The Mavericks

Kerrick, Book 1

Griffin, Book 2

Jax, Book 3

Beau, Book 4

Asher, Book 5

Ryker, Book 6

Miles, Book 7

Nico, Book 8

Keane, Book 9

Lennox, Book 10

Gavin, Book 11

Shane, Book 12

The Mavericks, Books 1–2

The Mavericks, Books 3–4

The Mavericks, Books 5–6

The Mavericks, Books 7–8

The Mavericks, Books 9–10

The Mavericks, Books 11–12

Bullard's Battle Series

Ryland's Reach, Book 1

Cain's Cross, Book 2

Eton's Escape, Book 3

Garret's Gambit, Book 4

Kano's Keep, Book 5

Fallon's Flaw, Book 6
Quinn's Quest, Book 7
Bullard's Beauty, Book 8

Collections
Dare to Be You...
Dare to Love...
Dare to be Strong...
RomanceX3

Standalone Novellas
It's a Dog's Life
Riana's Revenge
Second Chances

Published Young Adult Books:

Family Blood Ties Series
Vampire in Denial
Vampire in Distress
Vampire in Design
Vampire in Deceit
Vampire in Defiance
Vampire in Conflict
Vampire in Chaos
Vampire in Crisis
Vampire in Control
Vampire in Charge
Family Blood Ties Set 1–3
Family Blood Ties Set 1–5
Family Blood Ties Set 4–6
Family Blood Ties Set 7–9
Sian's Solution, A Family Blood Ties Series Prequel

Novelette

Design series
Dangerous Designs
Deadly Designs
Darkest Designs
Design Series Trilogy

Standalone
In Cassie's Corner
Gem Stone (a Gemma Stone Mystery)
Time Thieves

Published Non-Fiction Books:

Career Essentials
Career Essentials: The Résumé
Career Essentials: The Cover Letter
Career Essentials: The Interview
Career Essentials: 3 in 1